THE
HARD

PIE
HARD

Kirsten
Weiss

KENSINGTON BOOKS
www.kensingtonbooks.com

KENSINGTON BOOKS are published by

Kensington Publishing Corp.
119 West 40th Street
New York, NY 10018

All Kensington titles, imprints, and distributed lines are available at special quantity discounts for bulk purchases for sales promotion, premiums, fund-raising, educational, or institutional use.

Special book excerpts or customized printings can also be created to fit specific needs. For details, write or phone the office of the Kensington Sales Manager: Attn.: Sales Department. Kensington Publishing Corp., 119 West 40th Street, New York, NY 10018. Phone: 1-800-221-2647.

Kensington and the K logo Reg. U.S. Pat. & TM Off.

First Printing: March 2019
ISBN-13: 978-1-4967-0898-4
ISBN-10: 1-4967-0898-9

ISBN-13: 978-1-4967-0901-1 (ebook)
ISBN-10: 1-4967-0901-2 (ebook)

10 9 8 7 6 5 4 3 2 1

Printed in the United States of America

To my aunts

CHAPTER 1

It began with a rumble in the dark. Objects clattered on the nearby bookshelf. Silverware and window blinds rattled. Cupboard doors bumped against their frames.

My alarm clock shimmied across the end table. Four a.m.

Never my best at that hour, I sat upright on my futon, my bare feet on the laminate floor, and held my breath. Was this as bad as the shaking was going to get in my tiny house, or would the quake worsen?

Light flared, dazzling, and I staggered to my feet.

Ribbons of light streamed through the front blinds. I turned my head, shielding my face. The glare shifted downward. Something crashed, shattered.

I couldn't breathe, couldn't think. I seemed to split, to become both the watcher and the watched. I saw the clock plummet to the floor and break into two pieces. I saw the bookcase shadow lengthen. I saw myself hunched and cowering, my shoulder-length hair tousled like a mad woman's. Not liking the image, I forced myself to straighten.

It was happening again. It was—

Bam! Bam! Bam!

I shrieked. Careening backwards, I crashed into the book-case that walled off my bedroom from the rest of the tiny home.

"Yurt delivery!" a man bellowed.

What delivery? Heart rabbiting, I grabbed my kimono from the coat hook on the bookcase. I shrugged into the ki-mono, hurried to the door, and threw it open.

Backlit by the headlights of a semi stood a middle-aged man wearing jeans and a plaid shirt rolled to his elbows.

A truck. It had only been a truck. A big truck, with more effect on my tiny house, up on blocks, than it should have. But why was a semi on my lawn?

Baffled, I stared at his sun-roughened face. I'm five-foot-five and stood two steps higher than him in my tiny house, but our eyes were on the same level.

He consulted his clipboard. "You Charlene McCree?" His semi's headlights cut the fog. They illuminated my pink Pie Town van and the picnic table, glittering with dew.

"No. What?" I scraped one hand through my long, brown hair. It figured Charlene was behind whatever was going on. "Yurt?"

Two men clambered from the passenger side of the truck and walked to the rear of the trailer.

"Then who are you?" he demanded.

"I'm Val—what's this about? It's four in the morning! Who are you?" I shivered, yanking my kimono belt tighter. It was August in sunny California, but San Nicholas had its own weather patterns, and the flowered robe was thin.

"It's about the yurt delivery." He frowned, studying his clipboard. "I swear this was the same place as last year."

"Same place as what?" I flipped on the indoor light.

Two more headlights swung up the drive. A yellow Jeep scraped past the Eucalyptus trees that lined the dirt and gravel road. It screeched to a halt beside the picnic table. My elderly piecrust maker flung open her door and stepped out.

Charlene blinked, her blue eyes widening. Her curling loops of marshmallow-fluff hair stirred in the breeze. Then she strode to my doorstep. "Forgot you were coming today," she said.

"You Charlene McCree?" He thrust the clipboard at her.

"The one and only. You need me to sign?" She reached into the pocket of her green knit, tunic-style jacket. Charlene looked remarkably put together for the hour, not a white hair out of place. She was even wearing lipstick, a bright slash of salmon.

"At the Xes," the man said.

"Charlene, what's going on?" I asked.

She squinted at the board. "I can't read this out here. I'll sign inside."

Annoyed, I stepped aside, and she climbed into my tiny home-sweet-shipping-container. Since she was also my landlord, she had certain privileges.

I struggled for patience. "Charlene, what's going on?" I repeated.

"Yurt delivery for the goddess circle," she said. "Sorry I forgot to tell you about it, Val."

"Goddess circle?" I bleated. "What does that have to do with a yurt? And it's four a.m.!"

"Four-oh-six," she said. "You'd better get cracking if you want to get to Pie Town by five."

"What goddess circle?" I asked.

"They come here every year." She drew a pair of reading glasses from her pocket and set them on her nose. "I forgot to mention it to you. It's only for the week."

"What's for the week?"

"The circle." She sat at the tiny table between my kitchen and "living" area and signed the papers.

"This one of those tiny homes?" The delivery man stood in the open doorway and scanned the miniature kitchen, the fold-up table, and built-in desk.

"Yes," I said and turned to Charlene. "But why is he delivering the yurt here?" My lips flattened. "At four in the morning!"

She sighed with exaggerated patience. "Because, this is where they have the circle."

"Here? In my yard? At four?" I blew out my breath and tried for some Zen. Charlene was more than my employee/landlady. We were friends. It wasn't her fault my rude awakening had sent me into a freaky panic spiral. Charlene's zaniness was a part of her charm—when I didn't want to throttle her.

"I don't know why you're so obsessed with the time." She peered over her glasses at me. "And I couldn't cancel. The goddess gals booked it before you moved in. But I am sorry I forgot to tell you."

I gaped. Charlene had apologized twice this morning. She *never* apologized. "But—"

"You'd better get dressed."

Confounded, I stumbled to my sleeping area and grabbed a *Pies Before Guys* t-shirt and pair of worn jeans from the closet.

Hidden behind my bookcase partition, I shuffled into the clothes. What the Hades was a goddess circle? It was probably totally normal for freewheeling Northern California, and I didn't think Charlene would plant a pagan cult on my lawn, but . . .

I'd find out soon enough. Plus, I was embarrassed by my overreaction to the truck's arrival—first thinking it was an earthquake and then thinking . . . I didn't know what I'd been thinking, only that I'd been in the throes of a full-blown anxiety attack.

In my defense, it *had* been four a.m., a confusing time under the best of circumstances.

The rumbling from the truck engine stopped, engulfing my tiny house in blessed silence.

I brushed my hair into a bun and dashed on some light makeup. Hopping into my comfy tennis shoes, I edged around the bookcase.

Charlene stood, arms akimbo, in front of the closed front door and frowned. "You're wearing that?"

I looked down at my t-shirt, jeans, and tennies. "I always wear this."

"You can't wear a *Pies Before Guys* shirt to work."

"Why not?" Pie Town was my bakery, and traditionally, the owner got to set the rules. Besides, we were selling the *Pies Before Guys* tees, so wearing it was free advertising.

"Because it doesn't say Pie Town."

"It does." I pointed to my left breast. "Right here, like I've told you over and over again."

"That's too small to see," she said.

I covered my breast defensively. "They're not too small."

"Not your boobs, the logo! I don't know why you made it so tiny. Don't you have any earrings?"

"Why would I need earrings to bake pies?"

"And there's a stain on that shirt."

"There is?" I stretched the bottom hem forward and examined the shirt. It looked fine to me.

She brushed past and rummaged through my tiny closet. "You must have something besides t-shirts."

"Tank tops."

"Wear this." She tossed a pink Pie Town t-shirt to me, and I caught it one handed. "I'll wait outside."

I gave up looking for the stain and changed my shirt. Since it was chilly outside, I slipped into a Pie Town hoodie too. I grabbed a banana for breakfast and joined Charlene beside the picnic table.

Three men set out long, curving red poles near the cliff.

My face screwed up. If Charlene had forgotten the yurt delivery, why had she appeared on my doorstep at this hour?

"Since when do you care about how I look?" I tugged my hood, which had gotten folded beneath the back of my collar.

"A lady should take care of her appearance," she said.

My cheeks warmed with realization. Was Gordon Carmichael back in San Nicholas? The detective and I'd had a series of dating misfires. Then he'd been sent to Wyoming for some Homeland Security training. Was he going to surprise me at the restaurant? Maybe I *should* wear earrings.

"You're the owner of Pie Town. If you don't care about how you look, why should your employees?" She opened the door to her yellow Jeep. "I'll meet you there."

Something was definitely up. Resigned to whatever romcom Charlene had planned for Gordon and me, I climbed into my Pie Town van. It was nearly as old as I was, but it was the exact color of our pie boxes and had been love at first sight.

I followed her taillights down the narrow track to the main road. We wound through the hills, cobalt in the pre-dawn light, and sped onto Highway One, deserted at this early hour. A few minutes later, we cruised into San Nicholas.

Main Street's iron street lamps were dark, and my van swept through tendrils of delightfully creepy ground fog. I loved San Nicholas at this hour, when the beach town was hushed and the morning full of possibility.

In the brick alleyway behind Pie Town, I frowned. An unfamiliar white van sat in my spot. Charlene's Jeep was parked in hers, which meant I had to circle the block. Clearly, the rocky start to my morning had been a bad omen. I only hoped a stolen parking spot would be the least of my worries.

Scowling, I drove around the brick building and found a spot on a nearby street.

I strode down the alley to Pie Town's rear, metal door.

Charlene clambered from the Jeep and arched her back, stretching. "You ready?"

I thumbed through my keys. "Ready for what?"

"Another day making the best pies on the Northern California coast!"

I yawned and fitted the key to the lock. "Golly gee, yes!" As much as I appreciated Charlene's enthusiasm, it was five in the morning. Yawning, I pushed open the door to my industrial kitchen.

A silhouette shifted in the darkened room.

I gasped, rearing backward, and a hand grasped my arm.

CHAPTER 2

I shrieked. "Agh!"
A second woman's scream echoed inside the kitchen.

A light flared, and I threw up my free hand to shield my face.

The hand released me, and the kitchen's overhead fluorescents flickered to life.

Three people stood in my kitchen—a woman and two men.

The woman, with a headset strapped over her mid-length silver hair, reeled backwards and bounced against the work island. She brandished a boom mic. It swung low over my head, and I ducked.

"Good gad." She shook her head, and her cat-shaped earrings danced. An olive-green messenger bag was slung over her photographer's vest. Her mouth set in a pained smile.

My hands unclenched. "What are you doing in my kitchen?!" I scanned it for signs of damage. Door to the flour-work room: closed. Utensils: neat in their ceramic crocks and simple wooden shelves built into the wall. Metal cupboard doors: shut. "Who are you?"

Behind her, a man with graying hair, wearing a khaki photographer's vest, aimed a video camera at me. A mic and a light protruded from the camera. Beneath his vest, his striped, knit shirt strained across his gut.

A second man, of the tall-dark-and-handsome variety, stepped forward beside the industrial oven. He smiled, his teeth blazing white against his goatee. "Valentine Harris, congratulations," he said in a plummy British accent.

I stared, frozen. The man was Nigel Prashad, consultant to reality TV bakeries, and every baker's dream. "You . . . you . . ."

"Yes," he said. "I am an actual British person." And his blue golf shirt and brown slacks had the razor-sharp creases to prove it.

Charlene sighed. "Isn't he wonderful?"

"What are you doing here?" I gulped. "With cameras?"

"Only one camera." The gray-haired man kept his eye glued to the viewfinder.

"Can't blame you for being gobsmacked," Nigel said. "It's not every day you meet someone from the telly, but we asked your partner to keep our little secret." He rocked on his loafers and beamed, as if he'd offered me a particularly delightful Christmas treat.

My brow creased. *Partner? What partner?*

"It's *Pie Hard*," Charlene said hastily. "The TV series. They're going to feature us on the show!" She danced on her toes, giddy.

"What? That's . . . What?" Frantic, I looked about the packed kitchen for something my morning brain could grasp.

A thin brunette woman with blond highlights leaned against the metal counter. She examined a loose button on her chef's jacket. Ilsa Fueder! *The* Ilsa Fueder, famous French pastry chef and reality TV star! In my kitchen! "Ilsa Fueder," I whispered.

Nigel smoothed his shirt down, revealing the contours of his washboard abs. "My apologies, I should have introduced myself. I'm Nigel Prashad." He winked.

OMG. This really was *Pie Hard*. The reality show brought their pastry chef/business consultant team into failing bakeries and used tough love to whip them into shape. Nevertheless . . .

I pressed a hand to my mouth, heat flaming my cheeks. Why did they think my bakery was in trouble?

Nigel clapped my shoulder. "That's right! You've won a free consultation with Ilsa and me to save your struggling pie shop. And from what your partner described, it sounds like we didn't come a moment too soon. Ilsa? Would you like to add anything?"

The French chef glanced around my kitchen. "Don't like." She flipped her wrist, as if brushing aside the cobwebs of a nightmare.

What was there not to like? I turned to Charlene. "Struggling?" I choked out. "*Partner*? There's been a mistake."

Charlene smiled brightly. "No mistake. They're really here."

If my septuagenarian pie crust maker had brought them here, they'd been lured under false pretenses. "Charlene—"

"We need a minute," Charlene said to the crew. "The delightful surprise is too much for her at this hour." Grasping my arm, she steered me to the flour-work room. She dragged me inside and slammed the door shut.

A long, butcher-block table stretched down the center of the room. Along one wall, a giant metal mixer and other pastry-making contraptions lined a metal countertop.

I crossed my arms. "Are you crazy? We're not a failing business. They're going to learn the truth, and then we'll look like idiots. On TV! Why didn't you talk to me about this?"

The air conditioner rumbled to life. The flour-work room was temperature controlled to keep the dough exactly right.

"I had to keep it secret," she said, "or they wouldn't go ahead. They wanted to film your thrilled reaction."

"Do I look thrilled?"

"We'll be on TV!"

"And when did we become partners? Business partners, I mean," I hastily amended. Charlene and I were partners in a sort of armchair detective club we'd inherited, the Baker Street Bakers. Unfortunately, Charlene didn't have the armchair crime-solver mentality. We always seemed to take a more active role, which usually led to all sorts of uncomfortable situations. For me.

She winced. "They wouldn't do the show unless one of the owners invited them. So I couldn't tell them I worked for you."

"First a goddess circle and now this? How could you keep this from me?"

"It wasn't *first* a goddess circle, then *Pie Hard*. It was *because* of *Pie Hard* I forgot the circle." She clasped her gnarled hands together. "Nigel Prashad and Ilsa Fueder in Pie Town! Can you believe it? He's so sexy."

"He's half your age."

"I'm young enough to be his older sister."

I shoved Charlene's youthful delusions aside. "That's not the point! Why did you tell them Pie Town was in trouble?"

She stepped away from me, pressing her lips together and giving me a knowing look.

"We're not in trouble," I said stoutly, but my insides quivered. I had the bad habit of biting off more than I could chew; hiring new staff before Pie Town was quite ready, buying a new van for deliveries . . . "We're not," I said with less conviction.

"Can you look me in the eyes and tell me we'll be open next year?"

"Well, no, but only because nothing is certain. We could get hit by a meteor."

She placed a hand on my shoulder. "Let me tell you a story, about a young woman who came to San Nicholas with nothing but pluck and a dream of glory."

"I didn't come here with dreams of glory."

"I'm talking about me."

"Oh," I said, shifting my weight. "Sorry."

"And do you know what my dream was?"

"Glorious?"

"I dreamed of doing more with my life. Of doing something exceptional."

By my book, Charlene's life had already been exceptional. She'd even been in the roller derby. But I knew all about unfulfilled dreams.

"This is an opportunity for national exposure." She rubbed her hands together and cackled. "Marla will never be able to top this."

"Seriously? This is about one-upping your arch nemesis?" I'd hoped Charlene and her frenemy, Marla, had buried their geriatric rivalry. Marla had spent a lifetime one-upping Charlene. They'd grown up in the same town. Competed over the same men. And my piecrust maker wasn't the forgive-and-forget sort.

"Mostly this is about Pie Town," she said.

"But Pie Town isn't a turnaround situation. They'll figure it out."

She lifted a brow. "Are you really saying everything is hunky-dory?"

"Well, no, but—"

"You need help. Take it."

I struggled with my injured ego. Pie Town wasn't even a year old, and the first year of a bakery's operations was always rocky. So what if I had expanded too quickly? So what if the budget was tight?

"Nigel and Ilsa are specialists," she said. "The show will

give you free advertising, and you might learn something. And Marla's expanding her YouTube channel."

I relented. Who was I kidding? I could use the help and Pie Town the exposure. "All right. We'll do it. But are there any more surprises I should know about?"

Her blue eyes widened with innocence. "What else could there be?"

Famous last words. I blew out my breath and stepped from the flour-work room.

The cameraman edged backward, focusing on me.

I glanced up at the boom mic and smiled. "Welcome to Pie Town!"

"Cut!" With a gasp of relief, the silver-haired woman lowered the boom mic and set it on the work island. She rubbed her neck. "Now where the hell's Armstrong?"

Nigel smoothed his thick, blue-black hair and grimaced. "No idea. The man's a shambles." He looped his arm over the woman's shoulders. "Perhaps introductions are in order. This is Regina Katz, the apple of my pie."

Regina shrugged him off, but she was smiling. "Save the punning for the show. That's a good one by the way." She turned to frown at the cameraman. "And playing sound tech isn't normally my job."

The cameraman shrugged. "It's not my job either, honey."

Her gaze flicked to the ceiling. "I told you not to call me that."

Regina fumbled a wireless microphone, and then clipped it to the collar of my t-shirt. Roughly, she turned me around and clipped something to the back of my jeans, then tugged my tee over it. "Say something," she said.

"Er," I said, "I'm Val Harris, but I guess you already know that. What—?"

The producer touched her headset and nodded. "Coming in loud and clear. We're good."

"So, what do you want me to do?" I asked Nigel. "How long will this take?"

"Three days, tops, and do what you'd normally do," he said, his brown eyes earnest. "You've got a fabulous story here. Pie Town didn't collapse after your customer died from food poisoning earlier this summer. That speaks volumes for your resilience."

My jaw tightened. "Joe didn't die from food poisoning. It was murder." Even though Joe's murder had had nothing to do with Pie Town, I still felt awful about it. "You won't mention that on the show, will you?"

"Absobloodylootely." Nigel grinned.

"Please don't dredge that up," I said. "We had nothing to do with his poisoning."

"But it hurt your business, right?"

"It did until the police cleared us."

"Exactly why we need to talk about it," he said. "It's critical backstory. So, we'll start today by observing. Carry on as you would normally. You won't even notice us."

Ilsa smiled unpleasantly and examined a speck of dust on her sleeve. "But we will notice you," she said in a thick, French accent.

The producer cleared her throat. "First," Regina said, "we'll need you to sign the waiver allowing us to use your image. Actually, we'll need everyone who works here to sign. Don't worry, if any staff or customers object, we can blur their faces."

"Good." I didn't like the idea of bugging guests to sign waivers, but some of them might like being on TV.

Regina dropped her messenger bag on the butcher-block work island. She dug inside it and handed me a computer pad and a stylus. "Sign here," she pointed, "and here."

I paused, stylus over the screen. "I'd really rather you not mention that man who was poisoned."

"Sure," Regina said. "Whatever."

"Maybe I should read this first," I said

"Go for it," the producer said, her silver cat earrings bob-bing. "But it's boilerplate."

"I've already read it," Charlene said. "Don't worry. You won't be signing away your first born." She two-stepped into the flour-work room.

At least I'd make someone happy.

"Fine." Shaking my head, I signed. I started on the prep work—zesting lemons, cracking eggs, chopping fruit. One day, I'd have a separate prep team to do this for me. For now, I was bootstrapping and did most of the work myself. It was exhausting, but I loved baking, I loved pies, and I loved having my own place.

"Where's the AC?" Regina barked.

I looked up from the metal counter, where I'd just set a bowl of lemon filling beneath a ginormous mixer. "The air conditioner?" I asked.

"Assistant cameraman," Regina said, "and where is he?"

Ilsa raised an eyebrow. "Where do you think he is?" She made a drinking gesture.

The producer swore.

"I don't know why you let him get away with it," Ilsa drawled in her French accent. "It is not good for us and not good for him."

"That's none of your business." Regina stabbed a finger toward the lounging French chef. "And I don't pay you to lean on counters and look bored."

Expression impassive, Ilsa straightened off the counter. She peered into my lemon mixture, and her nostrils flared. "Don't like."

My lips puckered. I turned on the mixer, and its roar filled the kitchen.

The producer blew out her breath. "There are too many people in here. I've got to make some calls. Steve, keep filming." She banged through the swinging kitchen door.

"You heard her," Nigel shouted cheerfully. "Everyone get to work!" He walked into the dining area.

I switched on the huge, industrial oven with its rotating racks.

Yawning, Petronella, my assistant manager, clomped into the kitchen in her black motorcycle boots. Quickly, I explained.

She shrugged, impassive, and snapped a net over her spiky black hair. "Cool."

Work stumbled onward.

The French chef went to stand beside my antique pie safe—a gorgeous, faded-blue cupboard. She stared down her delicate nose and muttered in French. My French was rusty, but I'm pretty sure she was repeating, over and over, "Don't like."

Forcing myself to ignore the pastry chef, I immersed myself in the rhythm of chopping, peeling, and mixing. The kitchen brightened, the sun rose and its beams streamed through the skylights and glittered off the metal counters.

My assistant manager, Petronella, and I filled piecrusts. She slid them into the oven on a long-handled, wooden paddle.

A deliveryman knocked on the door. He walked in without waiting for an answer, loading carts of fruit, meat, and veggies onto the counter.

I signed for them, and returned to Petronella. Beneath her Pie Town apron, she wore motorcycle boots and tight, black jeans. Her ebony hair stood up in angry spikes.

The cameraman moved around the work table.

"How are your classes going?" I asked, feeling awkward under the camera's blank-eyed scrutiny. Petronella was studying to be an undertaker. A part of me hoped her classes would take a long time. I hated the thought of losing her.

"I need to interview a psychologist or psychiatrist about the mourning process. Know any?"

I wracked my brains and came up empty. "Sorry, no. I'll ask around."

The cameraman glided about the kitchen, dodging us. Ilsa did nothing more than lean against a metal counter and glower. Gradually, my neck muscles unknotted.

And then it was six a.m., opening time. I carried the coffee urn to the counter and set out the day-old hand pies, which we sold at a discount.

The producer and Nigel sat in a corner booth, their heads close, speaking softly. They glanced at me and continued their conversation.

Anxious, I tugged at my apron. I unlocked the glass front door, turned the sign to OPEN, and hurried through the Dutch door by the register.

The front bell jingled.

I glanced over my shoulder, expecting one of our elderly regulars—but it was a stranger—a man in his forties, with dark, pomaded hair, wearing a pressed tweed suit.

I realized I was staring and tore my gaze away. There was something familiar about the stranger. Was he connected to the show?

The producer spoke earnestly to her star consultant, but Nigel looked my way. His thick brows furrowed.

I busied myself by turning on the cash register, even though we wouldn't use it for another hour or two.

The stranger ambled to the counter and sat on one of the pink Naugahyde stools.

"We're self-serve until seven a.m." I nodded to the coffee urn and the basket beside it. A sign was taped to the basket: COFFEE, ONE DOLLAR. DAY-OLD HAND PIES, ONE DOLLAR.

"How quaintly trusting." He winked. "I'm Frank."

Huh. My father's name had been Frank.

I never trusted a Frank.

"Val." I pointed to the tag on my apron.

"Val. I love that name."

I clasped a stack of menus to my chest. "Thanks. What brings you to Pie Town?"

"I'm an early riser," he said.

Studying him, I set a tray of white mugs on the counter. "For the coffee." Something about this guy set my alarm bells clanging. But what? And did it matter? Even if this guy did plan on skipping out on the bill, my regulars would be here soon. They'd enforce the honor system on my behalf.

The front bell jangled.

Instead of one of my regulars, another stranger—a young Eurasian man—slouched into Pie Town. Black slacks. Black boots. Black turtleneck. A shock of raven-colored hair fell over one blue eye. I rubbed my thumb across the edges of the paper menus stacked by the register. The guy was either a ninja or a beat poet.

"She's self-serve," Frank said. "Put your money in the basket."

The youth wandered to the counter and poured himself a cup of coffee. He dropped two bills into the straw basket.

"Okay," I said, backing towards the kitchen door. "Well. Bye."

This had to be a set up. Tourists rarely came to Pie Town before eleven a.m. At this hour, tourists were either in bed— or they assumed Pie Town was not a breakfast joint. Had *Pie Hard* brought in fake customers to trip us up?

Someone grabbed my arm.

I gasped, whirling.

Charlene snapped a picture with her phone, and I rubbed my eyes. "Charlene!"

She looked at the photo she'd taken and cackled. "That's a good one. I'm going to Tweet the entire show. Take that, Marla!"

I rubbed my arm where she'd pinched me. "You startled me."

"Why were you in the dining area so long?" Her snowy brows lowered. "You're not trying to talk Regina into letting you out of *Pie Hard*, are you?" she whispered.

"No. I'm committed." Or I should be committed . . . to an asylum. "I signed the form and everything."

"Then what's wrong?"

"Nothing," I said. "It's only . . . there are two strangers here."

"At this hour?" She extended her phone around the corner and watched the men on her screen. "That is weird."

My stomach churned. "You don't think *Pie Hard* brought them in to review us or do something underhanded, do you? Because they seem kind of familiar, though I'd swear I've never seen them before."

The bell over the door rang, and we peered into the dining area. Tally Wally and Graham, two of our elderly regulars, ambled to the counter.

I relaxed fractionally, and we retreated into the hallway.

"The show's never brought in ringers before." Charlene brightened. "Maybe those two weirdos have been following you?"

"They're not weirdos. And why would they follow me? I'm a baker."

"They could be assassins. Maybe the older guy is the ninja's handler."

"He's not—"

"Ooh! Or maybe they're competing assassins. I mean, I know they're not really. But they could be," she said wistfully. "And they're definitely strange."

The best thing about Charlene's cray-cray? It made me face up to my own bouts of insanity. I was freaking out over nada. "Okay. Well. I'm going to get back to work in the kitchen."

Absently, she patted my arm. "Sure, you go ahead. I'm going to have a word with Graham and Wally. They're ex-military." She wandered behind the counter and bent her head toward them.

What did those two being vets have to do with anything? I shook myself. The workings of Charlene's mind were best left unexamined.

The older men leaned across the counter, and Charlene surreptitiously snapped a photo of Regina and Nigel.

I hurried through the kitchen door and bounced off the cameraman's rounded gut.

"Whoops," he said, his camera jerking upward.

Ilsa's eyes narrowed. "I thought you were a baker. Why are you dallying in the dining area?"

"I got caught up . . ." Why was I making excuses? "Sure. You all right, Steve?"

Behind the giant camera, Steve grinned. "No worries. We got some good shots of your kitchen team."

"Great. Thanks." I got to work filling piecrusts.

Charlene strolled into the kitchen. Giving me a significant look, she walked into the flour-work room.

I followed, closed the door behind me, and shivered. This room got a little too cold for comfort. Charlene's tennis shoes left tracks in the flour sprinkled around the long, butcher-block table.

"It's all taken care of," she said. "Wally and Graham will keep an eye on the assassins."

"They're not—" Ugh, why bother? "Okay, fine." Graham and Tally Wally wouldn't do anything crazy. With Charlene in the flour-work room, neither would she.

I returned to the kitchen and put Charlene and the strangers out of my mind. The morning whizzed on. Pies into the oven. Pies out of the oven. Pies into the customers. Pies out the door.

At eleven, I migrated to the register. Our regular group of gamers slouched into the dining area and assembled in their favorite corner booth.

Ilsa emerged from the kitchen.

Red-headed Ray MacTaggart's brown eyes bulged. The gamers' ringleader, he sent his eight-sided dice spinning onto the checkerboard floor.

Ilsa walked around the front of the counter and examined the pies behind their glass cases. The corners of her mouth turned down. Shaking her head, she returned inside the kitchen.

My chest tightened. What was wrong with our displays?

"Psst!"

I looked down the counter.

On their pink barstools, Graham and Tally Wally stared straight ahead. They sipped coffee in synchronized movements.

I walked to them. "Hi, guys. Can I get you anything?"

"Charlene was right," Graham said without moving his lips. He was a rotund, balding man, with a penchant for cabbie's hats. "Something's up."

"Well, there *is* a TV crew in Pie Town."

Tally Wally rubbed his drink roughened nose. "Not the crew, the ninja and Professor Patches."

"Professor . . ." I glanced to the other end of the counter, where the man from the morning sat. So he was back. Or had he ever left? "It's a good nickname." He did look like a college professor, right down to the patches on the elbows of his tweed blazer.

"The only times they've moved have been to go to the restroom," Graham muttered. "It ain't right."

"Yeah." I studied the two elderly men. "Have you been sitting here all morning?"

Graham sipped his coffee. "It's a mission."

"Beggars can't be choosers," Wally agreed.

I edged away. "Okay. Well. Thanks." What had Charlene started?

"Order up!" Petronella, called.

I spun to the kitchen window and grabbed the tray of breakfast pies.

Now, I don't usually bus food to tables, but these were extraordinary circumstances and the gamers were my best customers. Besides, Ray still hadn't picked the dice off the checkerboard floor. They were a slip-and-fall hazard.

I slid the breakfast pies (served all day!) onto the Formica table.

The gamers edged their books and dice aside.

I bent to pick up the dice and extended them to Ray.

Staring at the kitchen window, he didn't notice. "That's Ilsa Fueder," Ray said in a strangled tone, his freckles pale.

"I know," I said. "It's *Pie Hard*. They're giving us a consult." I bit my lower lip. "I hope they're not too brutal."

"The carnage is the best part of the show." His broad face filled with longing. "Ilsa Fueder. How long will they be here?"

"Only for a few days," I said. "Three tops."

Ilsa walked past the kitchen window and nibbled on a hand pie, her expression sour.

I rubbed my hands in my apron. What did she have against hand pies?

Ray's gaze tracked her movements. "I think she looked at me."

"*Pie Hard*?" Zack, a narrow, bespectacled gamer with an uneven beard asked. "Like *Die Hard*?"

"Yeah," Ray said. "Haven't you seen it?"

"I've seen *Die Hard*," Zack said, "the greatest Christmas movie ever made. But nothing about pies."

"Christmas movie?" Henrietta, Ray's maybe-girlfriend (I was uncertain of their status), raised a brow. She wore an oversized Army-green t-shirt and cargo pants. Henrietta shook her tousled head. "*Die Hard*'s not a Christmas movie." She tugged down the front of her usual oversized Army-green t-shirt.

"Are you kidding me?" Zack asked. "Of course it is. What do you think?" he asked me.

Nuh-uh. I knew better than to wade into that controversy. "Sorry, gotta go." I hurried to the register and stopped short by the Dutch door. Uh oh. Had Ilsa been eating a day-old hand pie? Was that why her nose had wrinkled like she'd tasted something foul? Not that the day-olds were foul—they were just a day old. She should know what it was—the day-olds were labeled clearly. The show had never been about being fair, though. It was about drama.

Through the kitchen window, Charlene gave me a thumbs up and grinned.

I smiled weakly.

I was probably overreacting. Everyone who watched the show knew Ilsa was tough on everyone. We ran a clean bakery, and I might even get some good advice.

I smiled with more confidence. After all, how bad could it be?

CHAPTER 3

The crew was as good as their word, observing our work and trying to stay out of our way. I was still aiming for think-positive mode when I drove home that evening—but I couldn't shake the sense of disaster hovering in the wings.

My back to the tangerine and raspberry streaked sunset, I turned east toward home. I was exhausted, and the weather had turned balmy. All I wanted to do now was relax in my yard.

I'd forgotten about the goddess circle.

Women in gauzy clothing drifted about my lawn. One group danced in a circle around a drummer. A catering van sat in my van's usual parking spot. A team of uniformed caterers bustled around the picnic table. They loaded it with large bowls and foil-wrapped containers.

A yurt stood near the cliff. Torches lit the fabric entrance. Two portable toilets were tucked discreetly in a stand of eucalyptus trees.

My stomach plunged, and I slowed the van. So much for kicking back in my lawn chair. How long did Charlene say they were staying? A week? I groaned. But Charlene had done me a solid getting *Pie Hard* to do an episode in my shop. I could live with goddesses for a week.

Forcing a smile, I parked near the corner of my deep blue tiny house/shipping container and stepped onto the loose soil. A drum boomed, and I repressed a wince.

The caterers glanced at me as I walked past the table and reached to unlock my door. I turned the key. The door was already unlocked.

I frowned, puzzled. In the morning's excitement, had I forgotten to lock it? Even if I had, people had been here all day. There should be nothing to worry about. I stepped inside.

Nothing appeared disturbed. My kitchenette's linoleum counters held a neat stack of unopened junk mail and nothing more. To one side of the kitchen, the wooden chairs sat pushed beneath the table in the square dining nook. I leaned sideways so I could see past the bookshelf. My futon was made, the closet doors shut.

Behind the kitchen, a toilet flushed, and I started. Water whooshed in my bathroom sink.

A zaftig redhead in a long, sunset-colored Moroccan-style gown stepped from my bathroom. She extended her hand. "Hi! You must be Val!" A coin scarf around her hips jingled.

"Ah . . ." Blindly, I shook her hand. There was something maternal about her freckled presence, and I guessed she was in her fifties. This, combined with her broad smile, made me want to like her, but she was an intruder, and I let go of her quickly.

"I'm Maureen," she said. "Are you okay?"

I took a deep breath, counted to three. "Um, what are you doing in my house?"

"Charlene said you wouldn't mind. We have two portable toilets, but your trailer has all the running water. Will she be by tonight? I've got a check for her."

Panic rose in my throat. My tiny house was a designated bathroom? "How many women are in your group?"

"Only fifteen."

I ran quick feminine bathroom-usage calculations. "Oh, my God." *Charlene!*

She winked. "Oh, my Goddess, please!" Her brow furrowed. "Wait, you didn't know?"

"No!"

"Oh, no. Charlene told me she'd forgotten to tell you about the morning yurt delivery. I didn't realize she didn't tell you about the water issue either."

Cleansing breaths, cleansing breaths. I could manage this for a week. "That's all right," I said, determined not to be a drama queen.

"Thank you. We don't want to inconvenience you any more than we have to."

The drumming speeded, its pace frenetic. There was a whoop and an answering call. My muscles clenched.

"Since you mention it," I said, "I have to get to work early in the morning. That means I need to go to sleep at a reasonable hour."

She squeezed my arm. "I understand completely. No drumming after nine p.m., and we'll move into the yurt then so you won't hear us. But why don't you join us for dinner? We have plenty of food. In fact, you're welcome to join in the dance circle. It's such a lovely evening, we might even go skyclad."

"Skyclad . . ."

"Naked."

"Right." Riiight. There was no way I was exposing my pasty white body to strangers. I might live near the beach, but I spent most of my time indoors, baking. "Thanks, but I'll probably turn in early. It's been a long day." Note to self: keep the blinds shut.

Her broad face creased with sympathy. "Charlene called

today and told me about your TV show surprise. I imagine it was rather unsettling on top of the four a.m. yurt delivery."

"It threw me," I admitted. "Since my house is on blocks, that big delivery truck shook it so much that it felt like an earthquake. And the headlights shining through my windows were like UF . . ." I motioned to the front, sliding glass doors and shuddered at the memory.

She canted her head. "Were like UF?"

My cell phone rang. Glad for the excuse to stop talking, I dug it from the pocket of my hoodie and saw it was Gamer Ray. "Sorry," I said. "I need to take this."

"Sure. And please join us for dinner. We'd love to hear more about the baking life." She hustled outside, shutting my front door gently behind her.

"Hi, Ray," I said. "What's up?"

He gulped. "You have to help me." His words were low, quick, and urgent.

I straightened. "What's wrong?" Ray had basically saved my life a month or so back and was still limping from his heroics. He also ate more pies than anyone I knew, and I was a big believer in gratitude. I owed him.

"I'm at the Belinda Hotel. The trail beneath the cliffs."

"What's happened?"

"She's dead."

I swayed and my pulse revved. "Dead? Who's dead? Not Charlene?"

The line went dead.

Nausea swam up my throat, and I braced my hand on the small dining table for balance. Not Charlene? I pressed the redial button.

Someone banged on the front door. I flung it open.

Charlene looked up at me from the base of the metal steps.

I sagged against the doorframe. "You're alive!"

"Why wouldn't I be?" She rubbed her wrinkled chin.

Her white cat, Frederick, lay draped around her neck. She claimed the cat was deaf and narcoleptic. I was convinced he was just milking her for free rides.

"I think I might have forgotten to discuss the bathroom situation with you," she said.

"No time." Frantic, I hurried down the front steps, turned to lock the door, and remembered there was no point. "Ray's in trouble."

"Ray?" Her white brows rocketed skyward. "What's happened to Ray?"

"I'll explain on the way. Come on." I hustled her and Frederick into my pink van, and we roared down the hill.

"What's happened to Ray?" she repeated.

"He said he saw someone die." I told her about the call and handed her my cell phone. "Try calling him back. We got cut off."

"Cut off?" she asked, dialing.

My heel bounced on the van floor. "Or he hung up. I couldn't tell." I whizzed past a stand of Eucalyptus trees and around a tight curve. The van's tires squealed. "But he sounded pretty upset."

"Ray witnessed a murder? He could be in serious trouble! If the killer knows he was seen—"

"He didn't say it was murder." I gripped the wheel more tightly. "It could have been anything. Maybe he was mistaken about the whole thing."

"Ray's not stupid." She passed the phone to me. "And he's not answering his phone either. I don't like this."

We turned south on the One and promptly got stuck behind a slow-moving garlic truck. I wrinkled my nose at the smell, my hands clenching and unclenching on the wheel. "Come on, come on," I muttered. This section of the highway was one lane and prone to jam ups.

"Honk at him!" Charlene said.

"We're almost there."

Reaching across me, she pressed her hand on the horn. Charlene leaned out her open window, Frederick's snowy fur whipping in the breeze. "Get moving or get over!"

The truck didn't increase its pace, and it didn't get over either. Finally, we reached the turn-off for the luxury hotel, built of gray wood and stone on the ocean cliff. Emerald lawn rolled toward the setting sun, the sky a livid bruise.

Pulse racing, I parked at the back of the lot. Police cars, blue lights strobing, sat in front of the massive hotel.

"I thought you said he was on the cliffside trail," Charlene said.

"That's what he said." I unbuckled my seatbelt. "I'm guessing this was as close as the police cars could get."

"The trailhead's that way." Charlene stepped from the van and pointed toward a gabled outbuilding, nestled in the rolling hills of the golf course.

We jogged to the paved trail. Thick rope linked low wooden posts, making a fence along the ocean cliffs. The trail quickly sloped downward, the cliffs purpling as the darkness deepened. A cluster of California poppies drooped, their orange petals closed for the night.

From the darkness beneath us, voices rose over the steady crush of waves.

"I should have brought a flashlight," I muttered.

We descended the trail and rounded a bend.

"No need," Charlene said. "Look."

People clustered on the trail ahead. A standing light had been set up, and lights from people's phones bobbed.

A broad figure with sloped shoulders parted from the group and limped toward us.

"Ray!" I hurried to him. "Are you all right? What happened?"

Even in the dim light, his freckles stood in stark relief

against his pale skin. He shook his head. "I was walking the trail, you know, for, um, exercise, and I heard a woman shouting on the cliff up there." He pointed. "And then . . ." He swallowed. "She just came flying off."

"Wait," Charlene said—her voice frosted with disbelief. "You were exercising?"

I glared at her.

"Humph," Charlene said.

"You're sure the woman was shouting, *before* she went over the cliff? That means she wasn't alone on that cliff. It's suspicious, Val." She raised her phone and snapped a picture of the crowd.

"Maybe she was shouting to someone at a distance," I said.

"I don't think so," Ray said, "she sounded angry, but . . ."

"But what?" I asked.

He looked away and didn't answer.

Charlene shot me a look. "But you didn't see anyone up on the cliff with her?"

"I looked up when I heard the shouting, and then . . ." He swallowed and looked sick. "She took a long time to fall." His jaw clenched. "It isn't right. I tried to help her, but she was dead."

Charlene hugged him. "Don't beat yourself up. You couldn't have done anything more."

"She was so alive at the taping this morning," he said, mournful.

"Not Ilsa!" I rubbed my arms. The French baker had spent most of the day sneering at us, but what a terrible way to die. I imagined her foot slipping, a terrified grab for safety, then the fall.

"What?" His brown eyes widened. "No, it was that older woman on the crew. You know, with the cat earrings?"

"Old? Regina was only in her fifties." Charlene's expression tightened.

He shot her a sideways glance. "Her name was Regina?"

"The woman with the cat earrings was the producer," I said. This was awful. "Regina Katz."

"She was pushed." His Adam's apple bobbed. "I saw it happen."

"You saw someone push her?" I asked, horrified.

"No, but the trajectory of her fall . . . I'm studying to be an engineer. She was pushed. I know it."

A wave crashed, abnormally loud. Suddenly cold, I pulled my hoodie over my head.

"You need to talk to the police," I said.

"And then we need to talk to her husband," Charlene said.

"Her husband?" I asked. "We're not investigating." I didn't want Charlene to get carried away with her idea.

"Condolences," Charlene said.

"But he doesn't know us," I protested. Charlene just wanted to investigate another murder, and that would so not be a good idea.

"Of course he does," Charlene said.

I blinked.

"He's the cameraman," Charlene said.

"She was married to the cameraman?" I asked. That explained why he'd called her *honey*.

"Nepotism," Charlene said darkly. "So?"

"I don't suppose it would hurt to talk to the crew," I said, reluctant. "But anything we learn goes straight to the police."

She nodded. "Great. Let's get closer."

Feet dragging, I followed the two to the cluster of onlookers.

"I ran to help her," Ray told Charlene, "but she was . . ." His Adam's apple bobbed. "So I called 911, and then I called Val."

"Let me through," a man shouted. "She's my wife!" The cameraman pushed through the crowd.

A beefy policeman I recognized stopped Steve and said something in a low voice.

The cameraman crumpled, his broad hands covered his face. His shoulders quaked.

Ilsa, the highlights in her hair luminous beneath the artificial lights, placed a hand on his upper back.

He turned to the pastry chef and buried his head on her shoulder.

Her knees buckled, but she straightened. Her expression was unreadable.

Charlene stepped toward them, but I touched her arm. "Let's wait a bit," I said, not wanting to intrude. In spite of Charlene's delusions and Ray's misplaced faith, we weren't murder investigators. However, my heart ached for Ray. What an awful thing to witness—to feel so helpless.

The skin between my shoulders prickled. I glanced behind me, up the trail.

The stranger from Pie Town, Frank, stood with his hands in the pockets of his tweed jacket and watched the action. Something in his man-about-town slouch reminded me of the golden-age actor, David Niven—when he was playing a villain. My dark thoughts were probably because of the atmosphere—the tragic whisper of the ocean, the fluttering police tape, the deepening night.

Behind and slightly above him, the slim young ninja crouched at the base of the cliff. The Eurasian man tossed his head, his dark hair falling over one eye.

Uneasy, I turned to Charlene. "Hey, those guys from this morning are here."

"What guys?" she asked.

"Professor Patches and the ninja."

"Sounds like a boy band," she said. "Where?"

I pointed to the top of the cliff, but the younger man had vanished. "He disappeared."

"Maybe he's a ghost ninja," she said, wry.

"Are those a thing?" Ray asked.

"Sure." She glanced at me, and I thought I caught the shadow of a wink.

Charlene was distracting Ray. Good.

"Anyone can become a ghost," she said.

Leaving them to argue the afterlife, I pondered the day. Something had felt off from the beginning. Had my subconscious somehow seen this coming? Two customers, who'd shown up at Pie Town the same morning as the TV crew, were on the scene of Regina Katz's death. It probably didn't mean anything. This was a big hotel in a small town. Lots of people stayed here, and lots of people who didn't stay here walked its trails. The coincidence didn't sit well, and I gnawed my bottom lip.

"This is worse than getting hit by a car," Ray said, weaving slightly.

I winced. The car accident had sort of been my fault. "Have you given your statement to the police?" I asked, changing the subject.

"No," a familiar voice growled behind me. "He hasn't."

I flinched and turned, excitement and anxiety jangling my stomach.

San Nicholas's lead detective, Gordon Carmichael, a.k.a. Grumpy Cop, stared down at me.

CHAPTER 4

"Hi, Gordon." Even though I was twenty feet from a crime scene, I couldn't help smiling. Then I thought of Ray and Regina and sobered.

Gordon Carmichael was San Nicholas's lead detective. Actually, he was our only detective. Since we weren't a high-crime area, he was stuck sorting out surfer disputes and parking violations more often than murders. That's not a criticism. He came from the big city and had plenty of experience with tough investigations. He was also sexy as all get out—a rangy six-foot-two-inches of muscled goodness with blazing green eyes.

The tall, metal lamp near the body went out, and a gasp rose from the crowd.

I blinked as my eyes adjusted to the sudden darkness. The moon hadn't yet risen, and stars glittered over the ocean.

"I didn't know you were back from your training workshop," I said. We'd almost had an entire first date a month ago, but it had been interrupted by his police work. After that, he went to Homeland Security training in Wyoming.

He sent me a few postcards, so I wasn't taking his disappearance personally (much). I wasn't sure where we stood
now.

"I got back today," he said. "What are you two doing here?
Got your P.I. licenses yet?" he asked pointedly.

"Er, no," I said. Gordon was supportive of our investiga-
tive efforts, but only if we went legit and got P.I. licenses,
which would take years. What pie shop owner has time for
that?

"Then what are you doing here?" he asked.

"Moral support." Charlene stroked the cat around her
neck. Frederick's right ear twitched. "Poor Ray's never seen
someone murdered before."

He lifted a single dark brow. "Who said it was murder?"

"Shouting on the cliff followed by a woman falling to her
death?" Charlene asked. "We spent the day with Regina
Katz, and she wasn't the sort to yell about nothing."

Regina had been quick to shout at Ilsa, and to shout about
the missing assistant cameraman.

Gordon's green eyes pierced into me. "You spent the day
with Ms. Katz?"

"She's a producer for a reality show called *Pie Hard*," I
explained. "They're doing a segment on Pie Town." A
breeze ruffled the tall sea grasses, and I shivered.

"The show with that British pretty boy and the French
chef?" He sucked in his breath. "You mean you're going to
be on *Pie Hard*?"

"Not anymore," I said, "not with the producer dead."
Hold the mustard, Gordon knew the show? "And I wouldn't
exactly call Nigel a pretty boy." He was handsome, in a
British swashbuckling sort of way.

"Steve!" Nigel hurried down the trail. Ignoring us, the
Brit beelined for Ilsa and the distraught cameraman.

"Those are the two stars," I said, motioning toward them. "Nigel Prashad and—"

"Ilsa Fueder." The detective nodded. "Amazing what she can do with fondant."

I blinked. He'd had occasion to cook for me, and he was a great chef. But fondant?

"I know," Ray said. "Can you believe they're here, in San Nicholas?"

Gordon smoothed out his smile. "All right. Ray, come with me. No more talking to these two or anyone else until we're done. Hear me?"

Ray nodded. "Yeah. Right. Sure."

"And you two cowboys—girls—women . . ." Gordon shook his head. "You two loose cannons stay out of this case. I'll be interviewing you tomorrow."

I yelped. "Interviewing? Why interviewing?"

"You spent the day with Ms. Katz, and everyone knows that show." He grimaced. "They're not easy on bakeries."

I jammed my hands into the pockets of my black Pie Town hoodie. "I don't think there's much they can complain about at Pie Town."

"It's reality TV," he said. "They don't go into businesses where there aren't problems."

"We're not perfect, but I wouldn't say we have . . ." I trailed off, considering something else he'd said. "Hold on, you don't think we're suspects? We weren't anywhere near the hotel when she fell. And we had no reason to push Regina off a cliff—"

"There's no evidence she was pushed," he said. "It's only an interview."

"But you implied—"

"We'll talk tomorrow."

"But—"

"Tomorrow." He steered Ray away.

"You know what this means," Charlene said darkly.

The white cat, Frederick, raised his head from her shoulder and stared at me—his blue eyes unblinking.

"Gordon thinks the death is suspicious."

"You're in trouble," she sing-songed. "You just walked into his new crime scene."

"Me? Me alone? All by myself?" Two other people had been by my side. Ugh! Once again, life was not going as planned. Seriously, he couldn't consider me a suspect. The show had just begun, and there were no conflicts . . . I frowned. Regina had shouted about a missing AC. Whoever the missing AC was, he'd never turned up. Regina had been sharp with her French chef Ilsa as well.

"Well, this is unexpected," a man said from behind me.

I started.

My mystery customer from this morning, natty in his tweed blazer, ambled up beside us.

"As unexpected as seeing you twice in one day," I said, warily. The man's voice sent a quiver of recognition through me. "Frank, isn't it?" Where had I seen this guy before he'd walked into my pie shop?

He bowed. "Correct, Valentine."

Huh. Most people thought Val stood for Valerie.

"What are you doing here?" Charlene asked.

"I'm staying at the hotel." He smoothed a lock of his brown hair. "I'd booked a spot at a little inn down the road, but they had some room problems and kindly offered to put me up here."

"How do you know Regina Katz?" Charlene demanded.

A ridge of fur rose along Frederick's back. The cat growled.

His blue eyes widened. "I didn't."

"Then what are you doing here?" she asked.

"I came to see what all the commotion was about." He

winked at me, the lines around his eyes deepening. "It's good to keep a weather eye when cops are around. I saw you talking to one of them. Are you two friends?"

"No." My cheeks burned. "I mean, yes. Sort of."

"I smell a romance." He smiled.

Charlene's eyes narrowed. "All I smell is rotting seaweed."

The dark-haired young man appeared on the trail, mid-way up the cliff. He stopped short, turned and vanished around the bend.

I licked my lips. Had he been watching us, or observing the action around poor Regina Katz's body? Was I going crazy, or had there been something familiar about the younger man too?

Frank cleared his throat. "The better question is: why are you two lovely ladies at this fine establishment? I know you're not staying at this hotel. It may be the luxury you deserve, but you're not travelers, like me."

"Do you travel for business?" I asked.

"It's my curse," he said.

"What sort of business?" Charlene asked.

"Life coach." He turned to me. "I don't suppose you need much coaching with *Pie Hard* making a show about your shop. It's quite impressive, by the way." His eyes glittered. "Your parents must be proud."

My throat closed. My mother was dead, and my father had abandoned us when I was little. I didn't—couldn't—respond. The loss of my mother still stung. I'd stopped caring about my father, since he didn't care about me, obviously. He hadn't even come to my mother's funeral. In fairness, I hadn't informed him of her death. I hadn't known where to find him.

When I didn't say anything more, Frank tipped an imaginary hat to us and ambled up the cliff trail.

"Should we wait for Ray?" I asked Charlene.

"He's a big boy. We've seen what he wanted us to, and now your detective's got him. Let's go." She leaned around and snapped a photo of the crime scene.

"Tell me that isn't for Twitter."

"It's for our investigation," she said loftily. "And Twitter."

We returned to my van, and I started toward home. I had a bad feeling more trouble was on the way. "Charlene, what Gordon said about *Pie Hard* being rough on bakeries?"

"It's only for ratings."

My headlights illuminated a scrubby hillside.

"But it's true," I said. "Our budget is a little tight. We can't give them any other reasons for criticism." My hands tightened on the wheel.

"It doesn't matter now," she said bitterly. "Regina's dead. The show's done. Or at least our segment is."

She was right. I was worrying over nothing. So why was my stomach twisting like dough in a mixer?

We drove up the narrow dirt road to my tiny house, and I slowed to a stop beside my converted trailer.

Drumming filled the night air. The goddess gals (fully clothed, thankfully) danced around a fire in front of the yurt. The picnic table had already been cleared, and my stomach rumbled its disappointment.

Charlene departed, and I retreated inside. I drew the blinds and changed into my comfort PJs. If someone killed Regina, it must have been someone on her crew. Not that I was investigating or anything, but since she was a stranger in town, it was the only thing that made sense. I stared into my refrigerator and pondered its contents. They did not send a thrill up my spine.

Someone knocked on the door.

Straightening from my miniature refrigerator, I took three steps and opened the door.

The redheaded goddess peered inside and held up a paper plate in offering. "I saved some dinner for you."

"Thanks! You didn't have to do that." I was grateful she had. I took the plate, filled with stuffed grape leaves, hummus, pita bread, and salads. My mouth watered.

"I did have to bring you something, after I discovered how you were awakened this morning."

"The yurt delivery wasn't your fault. Sorry if I was a little grumpy."

"You weren't." Her broad face creased, and she tilted her head. "Are you all right? Your auras are off. I'm seeing some stress."

I motioned her inside, and we sat at the fold-down table. "A woman I knew slightly was killed tonight. She fell over a cliff by the ocean."

She clapped a beringed hand to her mouth. "How awful!"

"Please tell everyone in your group not to get too close to the cliff." I nodded toward the windows and the cliff beyond. "The ground is crumbly near the edge."

"I will." She hesitated. "I hope I'm not prying, but . . . I get the feeling there's something from this morning that's still bothering you."

I smothered my annoyance. She was only trying to be nice. It wasn't her fault I was worrying over nothing. "It's been a crazy day. The yurt surprise, then the *Pie Hard* surprise, and now this death."

"Are you sure that's all?"

"I'm a small business owner. We learn to roll with the punches."

She smiled. "Yes, we do. Well, I'd better return to the group. Enjoy the food."

I walked her to the front door and closed it behind her.

Exhaustion hammered me, but I devoured the food. I dropped the paper plate in the garbage and walked into the cramped bathroom.

Looking in the mirror, I felt a sense of disconnect. I swayed and stepped back too quickly, bumping into the folding door.

I blinked, and it was just me—face a little pale, hair a little rumpled. However, for a moment, the mirror reflected a stranger's eyes.

CHAPTER 5

No camera crew lay in wait in the alley behind Pie Town the next morning. I unlocked the rear door, relief and disappointment tangled in my stomach. When I flipped on the kitchen lights and focused on prep work, my Zen returned. Baking was my meditation.

Charlene arrived, then my young assistant pie maker and aspiring poet, Abril. Abril and I fell into our usual work rhythm, broken only by pie shop gossip.

Gray morning light drifted through the skylights and glinted off the metal counters.

At intervals, Charlene stuck her head from the flour-work room and looked around the kitchen. Disappointment etched across her worn face, she retreated.

My chin dipped guiltily. Why should I feel guilty? It wasn't my fault *Pie Hard* was finished.

I stood at the butcher-block work island and crimped crusts, passing them to Abril.

Heat from the industrial oven warmed the kitchen, and a trickle of sweat slithered beneath my Pie Town t-shirt. The scent of sweet and savory pies thickened the air.

Abril filled the crusts with the fruit mixtures we'd prepared. Her long, black hair lay coiled beneath a net and paper hat. "I was wondering . . ."

"What?" I prompted.

"Could my friends and I use Pie Town for a poetry slam? After closing, I mean. We'll clean up afterward. You won't even know we were here."

"Sure. When do you want to use it?"

"Not until this fall. We were thinking September. I could even sell pies. Or we could leave out the day-olds and coffee and let people pay on the honor system, like we do in the mornings."

"Sounds like fun," I said, warming. Charlene might be disappointed, but at least I could help Abril, even if her poetry did tend to stray into the erotic.

She glanced toward the closed door of the flour-work room. Beside it, a giant sliding metal cupboard door stood half-open, exposing kitchen utensils. "Charlene seemed down."

My shoe squeaked on the rubber fatigue mat. "She thought we'd be on TV, and now we're not." I was relieved. Last night, as I wrestled with insomnia, I reviewed some past episodes of the show. They were brutal on the bakery owners. Ilsa was haughty and overzealous, and Nigel had a way of making the hapless bakers think everything would be okay . . . right before he slipped the knife between their ribs.

Abril's brown eyes widened. "TV?"

"Sorry." I latticed a strawberry-rhubarb pie. "You weren't here yesterday, so you wouldn't know. A reality TV show—*Pie Hard*—turned up yesterday, but it looks like the whole thing is off."

She pressed a hand to the chest of her apron, leaving a floury print. "I can't be on television." Her voice trembled.

I was afraid Abril's shyness might be a problem. She didn't even like working the counter. She preferred to stay behind the scenes in the kitchen. "If you don't sign the release," I said, "they'll blur your face out. Or they would have. I guess it doesn't matter now. The producer's dead, and—"

"Dead?!"

I explained.

"Poor Ray." Her face creased. "What a terrible thing to witness." Using a long, wooden paddle, she slid pies onto a rotating oven rack.

I glanced at the clock over the window to the dining area and wiped my hands in my apron. "Time to open."

"I'll do it." The coffee urn was half her size, but she grabbed it and staggered through the swinging door.

Charlene emerged from the flour-work room. Whipping off her apron, she sank onto a chair near the door. Her shoulders caved inward, and she crossed her arms over her green, knit tunic. "Man plans, and God laughs. I really thought the *Pie Hard* team would show today. Marla will never let me live this down."

"You didn't tell her you'd be on the show, did you?" I asked.

"She might have seen some of my Tweets," she admitted.

The swinging door crashed open, and Ray charged into the kitchen. His steampunk t-shirt cradled the swell of his belly. "We've got to do something." His rust-colored hair stuck up in odd places.

Charlene rose from her chair. "You can't come in here! The kitchen is staff only!"

He adjusted the backpack over his shoulder. "I tried to tell them about the angle of her descent and the trajectory of her fall, but they didn't listen. They were too busy asking me weird questions about whether I was up on the cliff. It's like they think I did it or something. The chief acted like this wasn't even a murder."

"But you heard shouting," Charlene said.

"I didn't hear *what* she was shouting," he said. "And I didn't hear anyone shouting back."

"In fairness," I said, "we don't know for sure it was murder."

Charlene glared at me. "She was shouting!"

"The three of us need to investigate," Ray said.

I blinked. "The three of us?"

"You and Charlene have solved murders before," he said. And I'm a witness. I can help."

Charlene laid a gnarled hand on his shoulder. "No can do, son. Val and I are called the Baker Street *Bakers*. You're no baker."

"I've got skills. I'm an engineer." He dug into his backpack and extracted a notepad and pen. "Well, I will be soon. I pay attention to details." He flipped open the pad, and sketched a quick diagram: a cliff, a stick figure falling, an arrow. "See? The trajectory was totally wrong for an accidental fall. Plus, I'm organized."

He had us there. Organization was definitely not my strong suit. If it had been, I might not have been so quick to hire a dishwasher before I actually had the funds to pay him. "We can't investigate," I said, "because it's a police matter. When it comes to the Baker Street Bakers, our strength is that we're local. We know the people in San Nicholas."

"Well, *I* do," Charlene said. "You haven't even been living here a year, Missy."

I ignored her. "The point is, we don't know this TV crew. They're from Hollywood—strangers."

"And one of them killed that producer," Charlene said, ominously. "Ray's right. If Chief Shaw's declared this an accident, it's up to us to find that poor woman justice."

"And I'll bet there's a ton of info about the crew online," he said.

Abril pushed open the swinging door. "Val?" she asked, face pale.

"Just a second, Abril." I crossed my arms over my apron. "Guys, this is a police investigation."

"I'm telling you," Ray said, "there's no investigation."

"Maybe the police are right," I said. "Detective Carmichael's no slouch. If he's going along with the chief—"

Charlene sneered. "He doesn't have much choice. He answers to Chief Shaw, and he wants to keep his job."

Abril cleared her throat. "Val?"

"That's not fair," I said hotly. "You know that Gordon's investigated after Shaw's told him to drop cases. He cares about more than a paycheck."

"I dunno," Ray said. "He didn't argue much with Shaw."

"But he did argue," I said, "right?"

"There's a TV crew in Pie Town," Abril shouted.

We turned to stare.

Color swept her dusky cheeks. "In the restaurant," she said, in a more subdued voice.

Charlene and I looked at each other. We rushed past Abril, bumping shoulders as we passed through the swinging door.

The British consultant, Nigel, sat at the counter beside Tally Wally. Nigel, sleek in a sharply pressed, button-up, blue shirt and jeans, leaned closer, his smile vulpine. "A murder? Poisoning? And you still eat here?" His white teeth glittered. His blue-black hair shimmered beneath the overhead lights.

Wally, rumpled in his brown plaid jacket, slurped from his mug. "The coffee's cheap."

The gray-haired cameraman, Steve, moved in closer. Wires stuck from the pockets of his photographer's vest.

Behind Cameraman Steve stood another man. He also wore a photographer's vest, but over a blue and white Hawaiian shirt. Broken veins tracked across his reddened nose. Stringy, faded-orange hair stuck out in places around his headset.

I wrung my hands in my apron. "No one was murdered in Pie Town." I hurried behind the counter to the men. "And he wasn't poisoned by anything he ate here. It was all in the news."

The red-nosed man shuffled behind me. "Mic. Collar." His beer gut hung over saggy and stained khaki slacks.

"That's also why I still eat here." Tally Wally plunked his mug on the Formica counter. "The food's safe enough, I guess."

Charlene's blue eyes widened. "You *guess*?"

"Besides," he continued, "I've been coming here since before it was a pie shop. Miss the scrambled eggs. They used to put bacon and sour cream on."

"What do you think of the food now?" Nigel asked.

I relaxed. Tally Wally was attached to that stool every morning like a barnacle. He wouldn't give me a bad review.

"The day-old hand pies could be a bit fresher."

My jaw dropped. "Wally, they're day-olds. That's why I sell them for half off. And you love a bargain!"

Charlene shook her finger at him. "Traitor!"

"Hold still." The red-nosed man clipped a small mic to the collar of my Pie Town tee.

Wally shrugged his lanky form. "I'm just saying. A senior discount wouldn't hurt." He winked at Charlene. "Not that one would apply to a young thing like you."

Mollified, Charlene fluffed her ivory hair.

"A discount?" Where was this coming from? "But the day-olds are already half off." Gordon was right. This show was not going to shine a positive light on Pie Town.

"But what about a senior discount on the fresh pies?" Nigel asked me.

"I had not considered a senior discount," I said stiffly. Actually, it wasn't a bad idea. I just wasn't thrilled about having it jammed down my throat on cable TV.

"And this coffee . . ." Wally raised his mug. "It's not as good as that specialty stuff, is it?"

Charlene planted her hands on her hips. "We're a pie shop, not a gourmet coffee shop."

Nigel smoothed his goatee. "But there's nothing stopping you from buying better quality grounds."

"What is *Pie Hard* doing here?" I asked, desperate to change the subject. "I thought after Regina's d . . ." I darted a glance at her husband, the cameraman, and lowered my voice. "I'm surprised the show's going forward."

Nigel frowned. "It's a brutal business, and I'm afraid there's no time for mourning. We have a new producer."

"Already?" I asked. "Who?"

"I don't know," Nigel said, "I haven't met him yet. But we got the word to continue filming, so here we are. By the way, this is our AC and sound tech, Luther."

The red-nosed man bobbed his head and tossed back his lank, orangey hair.

I turned to the cameraman. "Steve, please accept my condolences on your loss."

Steve nodded. The camera was still on his shoulder.

Luther snorted.

The cameraman lowered his camera and whirled on him. "What's your problem?"

Luther raised his hands in a warding gesture. "Nothing."

"You'd have been out of a job years ago if it hadn't been for Regina." The cameraman's nostrils flared.

"Children, children," Nigel said. "We've got work to do, and I know Regina would have wanted us to finish. She was that kind of person. Steve, Luther, shake on it."

"Forget it." Luther rubbed his reddened nose.

Charlene coughed. "Where's Ilsa?"

"She's not here, so you're off the hook today young lady." Nigel waggled a finger at her.

"Off the hook for what?" Charlene raised her nose. "My piecrusts are the best on the Northern California coast. I'm not afraid of Ilsa."

He grinned. "Perhaps you should be." He moved to the urn and poured himself a cup of coffee. "Where are the saucers?"

"Here." I grabbed one from beneath the counter and handed it to him.

The bell over the door jangled, and Wally's "Professor Patches" walked in wearing the same tweed jacket. His brown slacks were pressed within an inch of their life, and his shoes gleamed. "Excellent, you got the message and are all here."

Nigel's expression shifted, and he smoothed his goatee. He rose from the bar stool. "Message?"

Frank bounced on his toes. "I'm your new producer."

Nigel's mug rattled against its saucer. Hastily, he set it on a nearby table.

Steve clunked his camera on the counter. His skin flushed, a red wash rising from his neck to the top of his head. "You?" he choked out.

"When I learned of poor Regina's demise," Frank said, "I contacted the executive producer."

"I thought Regina was the producer," I blurted.

"She was the line producer," Frank said. "But she answers—answered—to the executive producer. We're old friends. At any rate, he convinced me to carry on for this shoot in her place."

Cell phones buzzed in people's pockets. The crew members drew theirs out and studied them, frowning.

"That'll be confirmation I'm taking over," Frank said. "You are lucky I am here and able to step in so fast."

"Yeah." Steve's eyes narrowed. "Lucky."

"But who *are* you?" I asked. He obviously had some connection to the crew, but Regina had acted like he was a stranger.

"Yeah," Steve said. "This is a little unusual, even for reality TV."

"I know of him," Nigel said quickly. "We had lunch once—with him and the executive producer."

Frank rubbed his hands together. "What matters is I'm the line producer now. Where's Ilsa?"

No one spoke.

Finally, Luther pocketed his phone and said, "I don't think she got word we were shooting this morning."

The new producer smiled. "Luther, isn't it? You're the assistant cameraman?"

"Yeah. That and other things."

"Well, maybe you can round her up."

"Anything to get outta here." He shambled toward the glass front door.

"I need him for shooting," the cameraman objected.

"He just makes sure you don't bump into things when you're shooting, right?" Frank asked. "I can help out with that."

Steve stiffened. "He also deals with the sound and carries my spare equipment."

Frank nodded. "I think I can manage that in the interim. Luther?"

In the doorway, the assistant cameraman turned, his expression bored.

Frank tapped his head. "Maybe I should take the audio equipment off your hands for now."

Luther removed his headset and gave it to the new producer, then slouched out the glass front door.

"That was a mistake," the cameraman said, grudging.

"Why?" Frank asked. "I can manage the sound, and he'll be back as soon as he finds Ilsa."

"That's what you think," Steve said.

The new producer cocked an elegant brow. "Oh?"

"He's off to the nearest bar," Steve said. "The guy's a drunk."

Frank looked a question at Nigel.

The consultant nodded reluctantly. "He's probably right.

It's not Luther's fault. It's an addiction. Regina knew how to handle him."

"I've dealt with plenty of addicts in my time," Frank said lightly. "Don't worry about it. I got this."

Steve nodded. "Okay. I guess as long as you can help out, we'll get the shooting done."

Nigel's jaw clenched and he looked toward the kitchen.

"Nigel," the producer said, "please continue."

"Wait," I said. "We can't just go on." I had to nip this in the bud. Sure, we had some budget problems—what small business didn't every now and then? It was obvious how they planned to spin this episode. The show would paint Pie Town as a disaster zone . . . until Nigel and Ilsa showed up to set us straight.

All eyes turned to me.

The clock above the counter ticked loudly.

I shifted, self-conscious. So, they'd hate me. I had to shut this down.

Charlene pinched my arm. "Don't do it," she whispered, her lips unmoving. "We need this show."

"Not if they're going to make us look like idiots," I hissed.

"When has that stopped you before?" she asked. "And you owe Ray."

I swallowed. If the show was cancelled, our odds of finding out what had happened to Regina dropped to zero. In spite of my murder-investigation misgivings, I really did want to find out what happened to her. Maybe that was ego on my part, but Charlene and I had helped in the past. As we'd infiltrated the show already, so to speak, we had a better chance of getting the inside scoop on the murder suspects.

Ray peered through the window from the kitchen, his freckled face plaintive.

Oh, brother. I did owe him for saving my life. Shaw had

screwed up two murder cases in the past—murder cases that Charlene and I had ultimately solved. It wouldn't hurt to nose around a bit, would it?

"We can't go on . . ." I fumbled. "Until we've talked through what happened last night. It's been traumatic for everyone."

"She's right." The cameraman's round shoulders slumped. "I told myself working would keep me from thinking about her, but Regina was my wife. She's all I can think about. And seeing someone else in her place . . ." He drew a shuddering breath and set his camera on the counter. "I still can't believe she fell. Did anyone see anything?"

Nigel braced his hands on the counter behind him. "I heard the commotion, saw the lights, and like a good lemming went to see what was happening. I never dreamed it was Regina. She was a terrific producer, and a terrific lady. I can't imagine the show without her." He glanced at Frank. "No offense."

The new producer pulled a chair from a nearby two-top and sat, crossing his arms and legs. "None taken. Clearing the air is an excellent idea."

"So you and Ilsa were at the hotel when Regina fell?" I asked Nigel.

"We all were," Nigel said.

"Together?" I asked.

"No, of course not," Nigel said. "The crew split up as soon as we arrived at the hotel, after we finished up with you."

"Then you don't really know if the entire crew was at the hotel," I said.

"This sounds a bit like an interrogation," Nigel's dark eyes flashed. "What does it matter where we were?"

Frank rubbed his professorial chin.

"Therapy," Charlene said. "You know, when a disaster happens, everyone wants to talk about where they were. What they experienced. So where were you?"

"In my room," Nigel said. "Like I said, I looked out the window, saw the crowd gathering by the cliff, and I went to see what was going on. I thought they'd spotted a whale."

"And you?" I asked the cameraman. "Did you and Regina go straight back to your room after you finished shooting at Pie Town?"

"No," he said. "We walked along Main Street, checking out the shops. Then we went back to the hotel."

"And were you together the whole time?" I asked.

"Regina and I went downstairs together for an early meal," he said.

"And then?" Charlene prompted.

"I went for an after-dinner walk." Steve jammed his hands into the pockets of his photographers vest. "I thought I'd get some nice sunset shots. Usually, Regina comes with me, but she said she wanted to explore alone." His voice cracked. "If I'd been with her, maybe she wouldn't have . . ." He jerked his hands free and buried his face in them.

"You don't think she went over the cliff intentionally?" I asked, aghast.

His graying head jerked up. "No! Of course not."

"Could she have been meeting someone?" I asked. "Did she get any phone calls?"

"No, she was alone," Steve said. "It was an accident. It had to be," he muttered. "She wouldn't . . ." He shook himself. "Where's the bathroom?"

Charlene pointed.

Leaving his camera on the Formica counter, he strode off in that direction.

"Funny that you and Charlene showed up at the hotel," Nigel said, "especially since you didn't seem too happy to have us in your shop. Did you want to talk Regina into going easy on you?"

"No," I said, "of course not."

"Then why?" His voice hardened. "Because your appearance was quite timely."

"The hotel has a good bar," Charlene said.

"And a friend visiting the hotel called us and told us about the accident."

Charlene elbowed me in the stomach, but I didn't see the harm in telling him the truth. Did he honestly believe our presence there was suspicious? It didn't matter if he did. I had a dozen goddess gals to vouch I'd left with Charlene. I totally wasn't a suspect.

Frank clapped his hands and rose from the chair. "All right team, back to work. This isn't a true-crime show, and Regina wasn't murdered. Her death was a tragic accident."

An accident was the most likely explanation, but I had the sick feeling that there was more to it—that it was murder.

CHAPTER 6

Nigel walked across the checkerboard floor and smoothed the front of his blue, button-up shirt. "All right, Val. Word is you've expanded too quickly. Let's take a look at those books."

"Later." I pointed to Frank and Charlene. "You two. In my office."

Nigel blinked. "But—"

"It's okay," Frank said. "Let me handle this." Nigel's swarthy face contorted.

The producer and Charlene followed me into my office.

I leaned one hip against the dented, metal desk. Though Pie Town looked charmingly retro (and pink), I'd spared all expense on my office. It was more Spartan than King Leonidas, with its ancient desktop computer and metal bookcases overflowing with napkin boxes and paper towels.

Charlene shut the office door, sending a veteran's charity calendar fluttering to the dingy linoleum.

"Look," I said. "Pie Town's not perfect, but it's important to us."

Frank nodded, his expression intent.

"We'll be thrilled with any advice that will help improve Pie Town's products, services, or finances," I said. "If I have to look like an idiot on national—"

"Cable," Charlene corrected.

"Cable TV," I continued, "so be it. But this is my livelihood. If you're here to do a hit piece for laughs, real people are going to get hurt, namely everyone who works in Pie Town."

"Valentine, I can assure you that this will not be a hit piece." He walked behind my desk and made himself at home in the swivel chair. "I genuinely want to help you succeed."

"Do Nigel and Ilsa?" And where *was* Ilsa? The French pastry chef still hadn't appeared. I bent and pressed my fingertips into the metal desk. "I've seen the way they've treated other bakeries."

"Well, I'm the producer now." He put his feet on my desk, brushing the keyboard with his polished heel. "You have my word that we'll run a fair show."

"How exactly did you become the new producer?" I asked. "Because it seems a little random."

His gaze flicked to Charlene. "Maybe we should discuss this privately."

"Fat chance." Charlene folded her arms. "I know all about casting couches, I'm not leaving Val alone with the likes of you."

His dark brows rose. "The likes of me? Why, Charlene. You don't even know me."

"Exactly." She sniffed. "I don't know you, and there's nothing you can say to her that you can't say in front of me."

His mouth pursed. "Because you two are business *partners*."

"That's right." She raised her chin.

Dammit. Somehow, he'd learned the truth. I studied the tile ceiling.

He steepled his fingers on his flat stomach. "Charlene, I know about your little deception."

She sputtered. "What deception?"

"You're not really a business partner," he asked, "are you?"

"I have no idea what you're talking about," she said.

"Don't try to scam a scammer." He grinned. "I checked Pie Town's business records, and you're not listed on them."

"It's a new thing," she said.

"It's all right, Charlene," I said. "No, she's not a partner. Does this mean you'll have to shut down the show?" In spite of my debt to Ray, right now that didn't seem like such a bad thing.

He heaved a sigh, and my chair squeaked beneath him. "Of course not. I don't think we'll need to expose Charlene's little fib to the world. Nigel and Ilsa don't need to know."

"That's surprisingly generous," I said, suspicious.

"Not at all," he said. "As I've already told you, we'll play fair. I know you were surprised by the show turning up on your doorstep yesterday, Valentine—"

I jerked the hem of my apron into place. "I prefer Val."

"Of course, Val. You're trying to make the best of a challenging situation, and so am I." He lowered his chin, his gaze boring into mine.

I shifted, uneasy. "Well. Thanks. But if things start to go south, I'm pulling the plug."

He winced. "I'm afraid you can't do that. You signed a contract. If it were up to me, I'd let you off the hook. But the production company is bigger than I am, and their lawyers can be unyielding."

I muttered a curse.

"It won't be so bad," he said. "Trust me. Now, Valen . . . Val. We really do need to speak alone."

"Why?" Charlene asked.

"It's a private matter."

"On a reality TV show?" She snatched the fallen calendar off the floor and tossed it on the desk. "He's got no good reason to get you alone, Val. I'm staying put."

"I assure you," he said, "I have no ill designs on your friend."

"I'm not leaving." She leaned against the door, and her jaw jutted forward.

"Is this about Regina's death?" I asked.

His brows shot skyward. "Her death? What would I know about that?"

"You did get her job," I said. "You must have some knowledge of the crew."

He grinned. "Yes, and they're thoroughly untrustworthy. But you don't have to worry about them. Like I said, we'll play fair. And no, that wasn't why I wanted to chat with you." He glanced at my piecrust maker. "This really is a private matter."

"It's okay," I said, impatient. "Charlene and I are friends. I can't imagine anything that couldn't be said in front of her."

"Really? You can't imagine . . . anything?" he asked, his expression plaintive.

An overhead fluorescent flickered.

"About Pie Town or the show?" Charlene asked. "No." Her nostrils flared. "But this isn't about Pie Town, is it?"

He rubbed the back of his neck. "I really didn't want to tell you this way."

My stomach knotted. "Tell me what?"

"Are you certain you don't recognize me?" he asked me.

"You do seem familiar." Studying his features, I frowned, last night's sense of disconnect returning. I wasn't looking into a stranger's eyes. Who was he? The atmosphere in the office thickened.

He stood. "I suppose you were too young to remember."

My sense of dread deepened. "Remember what?"

"And if I told you my last name was Harris?"

I swayed, bracing one hand on the cool, metal desk to steady myself. My last name. The sense I'd seen him before. It wasn't possible.

"Frank Harris?" Charlene asked. "You're not . . ." Her gaze ping-ponged between the two of us. "Oh my God. You are."

No. No, no, no. "What exactly are you telling me?" I croaked.

He walked around the desk. "What I'm telling you is that I'm your father."

My father. I stared at the man who'd abandoned me when I was too little to remember him. The man who'd left my mother to fend for herself. And it *was* him. The truth branded me, bone deep.

I turned on my heel and yanked open the door.

Charlene leapt aside.

Breathing hard, I strode down the short hallway and through the swinging door into the kitchen.

Beside the dishwasher, Ray and Abril looked up from their huddle with Gordon Carmichael.

I didn't even wonder why the detective was in my kitchen. But what was Ray still doing there? It didn't matter. I just walked into the alley, slammed the metal door behind me, and slumped against the building's cool brick wall.

The door opened, and Gordon walked out. He shut it gently behind him. "Val? What's going on?"

"I just met . . ." Shaken, I drew a shuddering breath. "That man says he's my father." *My father.* To hide my confusion, I stared at the oily pavement.

"Your father?"

"He's the new producer." Straightening off the wall, I paced the narrow alley.

"But I thought you didn't know your father."

"I didn't!" I stopped and tried to calm myself.

"Tell me what happened."

I drew a deep breath. "He showed up in Pie Town yesterday, and now he's taken Regina's job. I guess that makes him a murder suspect." Given my bad luck, he probably was the killer. "I can't believe this."

"Are you sure he's your father?"

"He says he is."

I exhaled slowly. I didn't know how to explain the strange feeling of familiarity I'd had from the very beginning. "I don't know why he'd lie."

"And you just found out?"

I nodded.

Gently, he placed a broad hand on the small of my back, and warmth flowed from his touch. "Why don't you start from the beginning?"

I did. Though I hadn't seen him much in the past month, it was easy to talk to him. I told him the whole sorry story, starting with Frank's sudden, inexplicable disappearance.

Except that it wasn't inexplicable. My mother had never called the cops. She knew he was alive, and that her marriage was over. Had they ever gotten a divorce?

I should have known these things, but my mother never wanted to talk about Frank. The pain that scrawled across her face always stopped me from asking questions.

Now he was in my pie shop.

"And you believe him," Gordon said.

I paced between the dumpsters. "He's strangely convincing. And there's something familiar about him. The first time I saw him, I felt a connection, but I couldn't figure out what it was. What I can't believe is that he'd show up like this. It's been over twenty years! What does he want?"

There was a hesitation in his emerald gaze. "Did you ask him?"

"I had to leave before I punched him. Could he be

lying?" I asked, but I didn't believe it. Frank was my father. I just *knew*.

"Do you have any photos of him?"

"My mom threw them away when I was little." She even cut him out of my baby pictures, which in hindsight seemed a little extreme. "That's weird, isn't it?"

A seagull landed on the Pie Town dumpster and cocked its head.

"Maybe not. Do you want me to do some checking on him?"

"Is that legal?"

"If he's taken Regina's job, that makes him a person of interest in a suspicious death. I'd be investigating him anyway."

I couldn't talk about Frank anymore. Otherwise, I might start bawling. I changed the subject. "Suspicious death? I thought Regina's fall had been ruled an accident."

His jaw tightened. "It's too soon to rule anything out.

"Is that why you were talking to Ray?"

"He's a witness," Gordon said blandly.

"The chief wants to close the case though, doesn't he?"

"Forget Chief Shaw."

"Okay, then let's talk about something else, because I can't talk about Frank Harris anymore." I pulled back my shoulders. "Are you here to take my statement?"

"I'd planned on following up with the *Pie Hard* crew first. Do you want me to take your statement?"

"There isn't much to say. Ray called us. Charlene and I came to the hotel. The police were there by the time we arrived."

"Why did Ray call you?" he asked, his tone flat.

I hedged. "We've become friends since he got hit by that car."

"So it's nothing to do with the Baker Street Bakers."

"Ray thought someone had pushed Regina, and he was pretty shaken up."

"And that's all?"

"What else could there be?"

He gave me a hard look.

Liar! "Anyway," I said, as my mouth went dry, "the crew showed up in Pie Town yesterday. This has been kind of a whirlwind."

"I'm sure the temptation to stick your nose into this is overwhelming. But you're not a PI, so stay out of it."

"But Frank—"

"Nuh-uh. You're not using him as an excuse to investigate."

"Right." *Wrong.* The man who sired me was entangled in Regina's murder, somehow. It had to be a murder. Gordon wouldn't be bucking Shaw if he didn't think there was something suspicious about her death. Even if I wasn't going to investigate the murder, I'd for sure be investigating Frank Harris.

"Tell me about the crew," he said.

"There's a cameraman, Steve Katz. He's Regina's husband. His assistant, Luther, didn't show up for work yesterday. Ilsa implied he was off on a binge and that it was a regular thing. Regina got annoyed when Ilsa questioned why she didn't fire him."

"Is he here today?" he asked.

"He was, but he left to find Ilsa. He doubles as the sound man, but Frank said he'd take over for today. I guess you know about Nigel."

"How did you get yourself into this?" Gordon rolled his eyes. "Wait, let me guess. Charlene?"

I nodded. "It wasn't a bad idea. We'll get exposure and free consulting."

"Are you going to be able to work today?" he asked.

Pull it together, Val. I drew back my shoulders. "I'm self-employed. I don't take days off, especially when there's a TV crew in my pie shop." Not even when my long-lost maybe-father was the crew's producer. I smiled, queasy. "Thanks for listening, but I can do this."

He squeezed my shoulder, and warmth flooded my veins. "I know you can."

I didn't know. Not at all.

CHAPTER 7

Frank left me alone while I finished the baking and shifted to the counter area to deal with the lunchtime rush. I still didn't know what to say to my possible father. A lot of bitterness tangled into my feelings for the man.

Steve filmed me and the crew. Expression dull, he randomly wandered between my office, where Nigel reviewed my accounts, to the kitchen and into the dining area.

"Order up," Abril shouted from the kitchen and shoved a plastic tray through the window.

I checked the number on the ticket and glanced around the pie shop. When people ordered, they got a numbered, tented table card so we could find them. Finding anyone was tough at lunchtime, when people packed the booths. Ray's crew of gamers were in their usual corner spot. Charlene's rival, Marla, sat wedged between two truckers at the counter. The elderly woman sipped coffee, the diamonds on her fingers twinkling.

Forty-two, number, forty-two.

I sucked in my breath, my eyes narrowed. The "ninja"

from yesterday sat at a square, pink table near the center of the room and had forty-two. His number was up.

Grabbing the tray, I pushed open the Dutch door with my hip and strode toward my ebony-clad quarry. At his table, I smiled and deposited the chicken curry pot pie and salad. "Twice in two days. It's nice to have you back." Nice and suspicious, since he'd been watching the death scene from the cliffs yesterday. San Nicholas might be a small town, but this was bending coincidence too far.

He grunted. "Sure."

"By the way, I'm the owner, Val."

A single blue eye gazed at me through a shock of black hair. "Doran." He was older than I'd first thought. At a distance, his black leather jacket, teen-angst hairstyle, and too-cool-for-school attitude had fooled me. Close-up, the fine lines around his eyes put him in his mid-to-late twenties.

"Nice to meet you, Doran. Is there anything else I can get you?" It was an offer I rarely made. People ordered at the counter, and we had a soda machine and coffee urn so they could fill their own drinks.

"No." He bent to his food and started eating.

And *Namaste* to you too. Thwarted, I returned behind the counter. I forced myself to walk to Frank, who was sipping coffee on one of the pink barstools.

Smile hopeful, he braced one tweed-clad elbow on the counter. "Hi, Val. I wasn't sure you were speaking to me."

I ignored the cameraman who'd swiveled to focus on us. "Hey," I said, all business. "Did the guy at the center table sign one of those waiver forms?"

Marla, at the end of the counter, waved to us. "Waiver? I haven't signed one, and I don't mind being filmed." The older woman fluffed her sleek, platinum-blond hair. "I don't mind at all." She stroked the front of her gold blouse.

Charlene's head popped through the kitchen window, and she glared. "No waiver, no filming."

"It's all right," Frank said. "I'll get her a waiver." He beamed at Marla. "How could we not film someone with such obvious star power?"

Charlene made a disgusted noise and jerked from the window, banging her head. A stream of curses floated from the kitchen.

"About that guy in black," I said.

Frank glanced over his shoulder. "The kid who needs a haircut? No, he said he'd rather be a blur. Don't worry—we won't include any customers who don't want to be included."

"Thanks," I said, foiled again. Those waiver forms had all sorts of interesting information, like full names and addresses.

He glanced at the cameraman. "Val, we really should talk."

"Later." Or never. I bustled to the register, where a line was forming.

Charlene, her shift finished, banged from the kitchen.

Marla rose and moved toward the empty barstool beside Frank.

My piecrust maker beat her to it, turning to Frank and putting her back to Marla.

Head lowered, I watched them. Charlene's face was drawn with suspicion. Frank's was pleasantly bland. The odds were low the man would lie about being my father. I wasn't a wealthy heiress. It wasn't coincidental—he and the TV crew arriving on my doorstep at the same time, was it?

The day passed, customers ebbing and flowing like the tide. Neither Charlene nor Frank budged from their spots at the counter. Marla eventually got up and left, slamming the glass door.

I should have worried about the Marla/Charlene situation. But it was summer in a beach town, and customers kept me too busy. Even when the crowds dwindled, I had tables to clean and orders to take.

Finally, around six, I approached Frank. "Your camera crew is gone, so I'm going to assume they won't be filming me closing the shop. Maybe we should talk."

He broke into a smile. "Wonderful."

"Do you want me to stay?" Charlene asked.

"Thanks," I said, grateful. With all of her quirks, Charlene was a good friend. "But I should probably do this on my own."

Frank rose and laid out some bills on the counter. "Why don't you come to my hotel when you're finished here? Say, eight p.m. in the bar?"

"I'll be there."

He sauntered out.

I turned to Charlene. "What do you think?"

"I'm not sure." She bit her bottom lip. "I haven't been sitting here for my health, you know. Frederick is going to be furious when I get home. I never leave him alone this long."

"I thought you were sitting there to keep Marla from the limelight."

She harrumphed. "If she talks to Frank, next thing you know, *she'll* be the producer. But I've been feeling our new producer out, and he knows a lot about you."

"What did you learn?" I asked, anxious.

"He said he'd been following your life from afar. He knows you graduated with an English degree. He knows when you opened Pie Town. He even knows your engagement busted up with that realtor."

I untied my apron. "Great. My very own stalker."

"I think it's sad. Him, I mean."

I whipped off the apron, tugging it over my head. "Oh, boo hoo. He's sad? He walked out on his wife and child."

Charlene gazed into her coffee cup. "I'm only saying, I'd imagine it's sad for a parent to be on the outside, looking in." She twisted her gold watch, an anniversary gift from her husband.

Regretting my words, I scrubbed my hand over my face. Charlene was estranged from her only daughter. I didn't know the details—she made it clear she didn't want to talk about them. I knew things had gotten bad after her husband's death. I imagined her now, searching the Internet for news of her faraway daughter. "He could have gotten that information recently and online," I said evenly. "It's not proof he's who he says he is."

"Maybe. He does look like you though."

I nodded. "The eyes."

She blew out her breath. "You realize he's a suspect?"

"Yes," I said unhappily. "He benefited by taking Regina's job. Was it a coincidence that he knew *Pie Hard's* executive producer? And that they'd turned up here on the same day? I really do need to talk to him." The thought terrified me. My emotions were at a rolling boil, anger, raw vulnerability, and confusion bubbling together. I couldn't think about that now. "There's something off about this whole show. Nigel's reviewing my accounts, and the cameraman was shooting I don't know what. But they didn't really *do* anything today."

"That's because Ilsa never showed and the assistant camera guy, Luther, never returned. A big part of the show is the baking, and Ilsa is always on the scene for that."

"And now Frank's in charge," I said, uneasy.

"*Pie Hard* is a real show, you know," Charlene said. "We have to assume they know what they're doing."

"I guess," I said, unconvinced.

Standing, she reached across the counter and patted my hand. "You can do this. If you need to talk after you meet with Frank, call." Charlene rose from the barstool.

I followed her to the front door. "If I learn anything from him about Regina's death, I'll let you know right away."

"That wasn't what I meant," she said, "but it'll do." She left. The bell jingled in her wake.

I locked the glass door behind her and flipped the sign to CLOSED.

We clean up throughout the day, so the final mop and wash was no big deal. My only stressor in the closing process was the cash count. I'm an English major, not a mathematician, and sometimes I had to count it out three or four times to get the numbers right. Luckily, I didn't have TV cameras or Nigel watching over my shoulder as I totaled up tonight. I checked the cash count against my records, and locked the money in the small safe.

By 7:45 p.m., I was cruising down Highway One toward the TV crew's luxury hotel. Wind whipped through the open window, tangling the hair I'd loosed from its bun.

I pulled into the wide parking lot. Lights from the gabled hotel glowed cheerfully. Sunset darkened to a purpling ribbon on the horizon.

How could they afford the Belinda? The hotel seemed extravagant for a cable TV show. Did the crew get a discount?

A chill breeze blew off the ocean. I grabbed a black Pie Town hoodie from the passenger seat and pulled it over my head. Looping my purse over one shoulder, I strode across the lot.

The hotel lobby had hardwood floors and high ceilings. White wainscoting accented sand-colored walls. Maybe someday, if Pie Town was super successful, I could sleep in a place like this—but that day was far off.

Figuring the bar couldn't be too hard to find, I meandered deeper into the hotel. Finally, I had to stop and check a map on the wall. There were actually two bars—a wine bar of dark, polished wood, and an airy "anything goes" bar overlooking the ocean. Frank was in neither, and I felt a measure of relief.

Annoyance followed hard on relief's heels. Where was he?

I returned to the wine bar, in case he'd shown up while I'd been in the other. He hadn't. Following the sounds of laughter and clinking glasses, I walked back to the second bar and fumed.

I stared out of the large, square windows at the darkening ocean. Why was I surprised that he was late? I had twenty-plus years of evidence proving the guy was unreliable. This was just more proof that Frank was who he said he was, my feckless father.

My fists clenched. And I was wasting time.

Turning from the windows, I stormed to the reception desk. I should have asked Frank for his cell phone number. If he wasn't in a bar, he was probably in his room. Maybe the desk could call for me.

Nearing the high, white-paneled desk, I slowed, recognizing the dark-haired woman on the phone behind it. Blueberry pie was her game, with the occasional spinach and goat cheese quiche thrown in.

She looked up and smiled, raising one finger to let me know she'd be right with me. Her bun gleamed beneath the ceiling's inset lights. She hung up. "Hi, Val. What are you doing here?"

"Um, I'm here to meet someone from *Pie Hard*. You know, the TV show? They're featuring Pie Town."

Her brown eyes widened. "I wondered if that might be

about you! I knew they were staying here, and there aren't many bakeries in town. How's it going?"

"You probably heard about Regina Katz."

She winced. "Everyone heard. Her poor husband." She shook her head. "He's a wreck."

"Oh?"

"One of the maids must have forgotten to replace his wastepaper basket when she was cleaning the room this morning. He was very upset. *Very*. Of course, he wasn't really upset about a silly basket. But grief makes everything more emotional."

"He came to work today," I said, "but I honestly don't know how he got through it."

"Poor man. Hotel management's talking about putting up new fencing near the cliffs, but it seems too little too late." She leaned forward, her cream-colored blazer pressed against the desk. "And I'm not sure it will help. If someone's determined, a low fence won't stop them."

"You sound like you think it was suicide?"

"I can't imagine what else it would be. The trail is clearly marked and enclosed by a fence. Ms. Katz would have had to climb over it to get anywhere near that cliff, which is well lit."

I adjusted the purse over my shoulder. "But the fence is only a foot or so high. It's easy to step over. People do jump it, don't they?"

"There is a dirt trail on the other side of the fence, closer to the cliff," she admitted. "But it's still not close enough for an accidental fall." She sighed. "Who are you trying to reach?"

"Um . . ." My insides squirmed. "Frank Harris."

"Harris? That's your last name, isn't it?"

"Yeah. I guess it's pretty common."

"I can't give out room numbers, but I can call the room for you."

"Please."

The clerk called, phone pressed to her ear, head canted. She shook her head and hung up. "No answer."

"Oh. Well, thanks. I'll check the bars again."

"Or you could try building three-b."

"Three-b?" I asked.

"The *Pie Hard* crew is renting it as their workspace. I just walked past there, and the lights were on."

"Thanks, I'll do that."

She handed me a map printed on elegant paper and circled an outbuilding. "It's located on the north side of the hotel. Follow the path from this door here." She pointed on the hotel map. "It'll take you through the golf course and right to the front door."

I thanked her again, walked through the hotel and out one of the side doors. Solar lights illuminated the stone paths. I navigated the trails through the rolling lawn to a low, gray, wood and stone building.

The curtains were drawn across the floor-to-ceiling windows. Light streamed through gaps in the fabric.

I found a white-painted door and knocked. "Hello?"

No one answered.

I hesitated, then tried the latch and walked inside.

The gray-carpeted room was L-shaped. A long table loaded with computer equipment ran down the center of one leg of the L. Chairs lined one side of the table.

The room smelled like gasoline, and my nose wrinkled. Good luck getting that deposit back. What had the *Pie Hard* crew been doing in here?

A door clicked shut.

I spun around, but the door I'd come through was closing, slowly. There must be a second door in the room.

"Hello?" I walked past the long table and peered around the corner. This section of the room was empty as well. The curtains were shut and the exit door at the far end was closed.

Walking to that door, I pushed the handle down.

Locked.

This was weird, because I was on the inside. I should be able to open it, right?

I rattled the door, but it was stuck.

Uneasy, I wiped my palm on my jeans. I wasn't locked inside. The room had two doors, and I knew the front was unlocked.

A boom roared behind me, and then a rushing sound.

I staggered.

Acrid, black smoke billowed around the corner of the room.

Pulse thundering in my ears, I raced toward the smoke. The computer table was ablaze, flames licking the ceiling. Tongues of fire raced along the carpet and up the curtains. Coughing, I ran to the first door and pushed the handle down.

It didn't budge.

An alarm rang, deafening.

Panicked, I threw my full weight on the lever, banged on the door, screamed. Smoke seared my throat. I drew shallow, pained gasps.

I doubled over and looked for a way out. Out, out, I had to get out. Forcing myself closer to the flaming table, I grabbed a chair. I hurled it at the curtained, floor-to-ceiling window.

The chair ricocheted off, banging me in the shoulder. I cried out in pain and exasperation.

The smoke was unbearable, scorching my eyes and throat.

I dropped to my knees. Weakly, I kicked at the window. What the bloody blue blazes was it made of? Why wasn't it breaking? I fumbled with the cell phone in the pocket of my Pie Town hoodie.

"911, what is your emergency?"

"Fire," I rasped over the clang of the alarm. "I'm at the hotel in building b . . ." I couldn't remember the name, couldn't think, couldn't breathe. The room telescoped away from me. My vision blurred and went dark.

CHAPTER 8

Cold water dripped down my face. I sputtered, surging upright, cold talons of fear tearing at my chest.

Hard and painful, something else gripped me too—a man. Strong arms dragged me backwards. Fresh air tickled my nostrils, and I sucked in a breath of clean, ocean air. I opened my eyes to the horizon, deepening to shades of cobalt.

"I'm okay," I rasped and struggled to get my feet onto the path beneath me.

The iron grip released, and I turned to my rescuer.

Frank. Water dampened the shoulders of his tweed suit jacket, plastered his dark hair to his head. His eyebrows looked singed.

"You," I whispered, throat raw.

"You're safe now, but let's put more distance between us and the fire." He nodded toward the burning building. Black smoke poured from its slowly closing front door.

He grasped my arm. Together, we staggered farther from the building and collapsed on the cool grass.

I pressed my palm to my chest, rolled to my knees, and tried to vomit the smoke from my lungs.

"Here's your purse." He dropped it on the lawn beside me.

He'd thought to grab my purse? Laughter bubbled up in my throat, and I pressed my hands to my mouth to stifle it before he accused me of hysteria. "Thanks," I choked out.

Frank coughed and sat up on his elbows. "You're welcome."

A firetruck rolled across the golf course. Its headlights bobbed as it sailed up and down the neat rolling hills.

My Pie Town hoodie, t-shirt, and jeans were soaked. The fire sprinklers inside must have kicked in, finally. I shivered. What had taken them so long?

The firetruck groaned to a halt. Men in thick, canvas jackets and yellow hats piled out and swarmed past us.

"Anyone in there?" a grizzled fireman asked Frank.

My maybe-father glanced at me. Blue and red lights flashed weirdly, making strange shadows.

I shook my head, coughed. "No."

Losing interest, the fireman rejoined his crew. An ambulance stopped nearby. Men in blue leapt from the vehicle and hurried to us.

Frank leaned closer. "Deny everything," he said in a low voice.

"There's nothing to deny," I said, indignant. "I didn't do anything wrong."

He patted my shoulder. "Stick to that story."

"It's not a story."

"Sure it isn't."

Paramedics swooped down on us, and he snapped his jaw shut.

One paramedic maneuvered me to the back of the open truck. Sitting me on a bumper, he shined a flashlight into my eyes, looked down my throat, and took my pulse.

Police officers trotted across the lawn. I strained my eyes in the growing darkness, looking for one in particular.

Gordon, in his blue suit jacket, strode purposefully across the rolling lawn. Sighting me, he broke into a run, and my heart lurched, tears pricking my eyes.

"Val!" He wasn't winded when he reached me, perched on the bumper with a blanket over my shoulders. His gaze bounced from me to the smoke seeping from the open doors of the outbuilding. Firemen carrying hoses over their shoulders lumbered inside.

"You were in there?" the detective asked. "What happened?"

"That's what I'd like to know." A short, bulky woman in the hotel's sand-colored blazer strode toward us on five-inch heels. In spite of them, she wasn't much over five feet tall. Her tanned face was lined, the tips of her pixie-cut hair frosted. It flashed in the glare of the emergency lights. "I'm the manager. What did you do?"

"I didn't do anything." I coughed, and the blanket slipped from my shoulders. Making a grab for it, I readjusted. "I went inside and didn't see anyone, and then the fire started and—"

"Fires don't just start," the hotel manager snapped.

"I smelled gasoline," I said. "I think someone was inside with me, and—"

"What were you doing with gasoline in there?" she asked shrilly. "It isn't allowed."

"Ma'am," Gordon said, "if you wouldn't mind waiting over there." He nodded toward the firetruck. "I'd like to finish taking this lady's statement."

"She was inside the building when the fire started," the manager said. "It's obvious what happened."

Hands in his trouser pockets, Frank strolled to join our group. "It's obvious your hotel is liable for criminal acts committed on the premises."

Gordon's green eyes narrowed. "Sir—"

"We are not liable if an arsonist nearly sets herself on fire," the manager snapped.

"Except she didn't." Frank said. "Someone had wedged the doors shut from the outside, locking her in. The same someone I saw leaving the building moments before the fire started."

My blood turned to ice. I hadn't set the fire, and I figured someone had locked me inside. But there's knowing, and then there's *knowing*.

"You saw someone?" Gordon asked.

"That's impossible," the woman said. "Those doors don't lock that way."

Gordon signaled to two uniformed officers, and they strode toward us.

"When I arrived," Frank said, "I found rubber doorstops wedged into both exterior doors. They're the same kind your hotel maids use. Valentine couldn't open those doors from the inside—not blocked by those doorstops. And she couldn't have put the doorstops there and then let herself in. My daughter could have been killed due to your negligence."

The woman drew herself up. "It isn't my fault if—"

"Ma'am," Gordon interrupted and nodded to a tall, African-American cop. "Please go with Officer Billings. He'll take your statement."

She pressed her lips together and followed Billings away.

"You said you saw someone leaving the building?" Gordon asked Frank.

"A man, I think," Frank said. "The light was getting dim, and I was far away. I'm sorry; I can't tell you more than that."

"Did you get a sense of his build?" the detective asked.

"No," Frank said. "I can't even swear it was a man, I'm afraid."

"And what were you doing outside?"

"Looking for Valen—Val. We were supposed to meet in the bar, but I was a bit late and saw her through the window." He motioned toward the four-story, gabled hotel. "She was walking toward the building the crew's been using for editing. I figured she was looking for me, so I followed."

"Kent," Gordon said to the second officer, "please take this gentleman's statement and find out how we can contact him later."

"Are you sure you're all right?" Frank asked me.

"The paramedics said I'll be fine. And thanks," I said grudgingly. He'd probably saved my life, but that didn't absolve him of over twenty years of neglect.

"This way, sir," Officer Kent said.

The two men walked away from us.

"What happened?" Gordon asked.

Tugging the blanket closer, I told him. "I must have passed out for a minute," I finished. "It couldn't have been long. Then Frank was dragging me from the building, and the firetrucks were on their way."

"What's going on?" Steve Katz huffed toward us and fumbled with a high pocket in his photographer's vest. He stumbled to a halt and stared, eyes wide, his gaze bouncing from me to the building. "No, no, no! This isn't happening!"

"I'm sorry." I coughed. "But everything on that big table was on fire, and then the sprinklers came on—"

He whirled on me. "You! You did this to get out of your contract! I told Regina we shouldn't have gotten your partner to keep the show a surprise."

"N-no—"

"Then what the hell are you doing here?" He stepped closer, and Gordon put a restraining hand on his chest.

"Sir—"

"She did this! She didn't like the idea of us being in Pie Town from the beginning, and now she's got her way."

"Back off," Gordon said, his voice hard.

Steve stumbled backward. "Don't touch me! I'll sue!"

Chief Shaw, tall, narrow, and elegant in an expensive gray suit, strolled toward us. "Now what's all this?" he asked jovially.

"This woman." The photographer pointed a shaking hand at me. "She tried to get out of the show, and Regina wouldn't let her. Now Regina's dead. And when that didn't stop *Pie Hard*, she set our equipment on fire. She's set this whole thing up."

"Arson doesn't seem like Miss Harris," the chief said. "What do you have to say for yourself, young lady?"

"She inhaled a lot of smoke," Gordon said. "The paramedics have told her not to strain her voice."

I shot him a startled look. They hadn't said that.

"But before they did, she gave me a statement," the detective continued. "Ms. Harris had an appointment to meet with the show's new producer. When she couldn't find him in the hotel bar, she came here, where she was told the crew was working. The building appeared empty, but someone set the place on fire and trapped her inside. Her movements can be confirmed by the hotel reception."

"Hm." Shaw rubbed his narrow jaw. "It does seem as if someone has it out for your show, Mr . . . ?"

"Katz," the photographer said. "Steve Katz."

"Regina Katz's husband," Gordon said.

"My condolences on your loss," the chief said. "Perhaps we should speak in private." He led the cameraman away, and my shoulders relaxed.

Gordon was frowning.

"What's wrong?" I asked.

He shook himself. "Nothing." His brow wrinkled. "It does seem like someone wants to put *Pie Hard* out of business."

"Not me."

He lifted one eyebrow.

"Sorry," I said. "I guess I'm a little sensitive on the topic. I wouldn't mind if they stopped filming in Pie Town, but not this way."

"Why?" he asked. "What happened today during filming?"

"Not much after you left. They stayed out of our way and just filmed." I expected the other anvil to drop the next day, when Nigel talked to me about my finances. I swallowed, dreading that moment. Would it even come? Would this be the end of the *Pie Hard* filming? I didn't see how they could continue. "One strange thing," I said. "Ilsa Fueder never showed up for work today. Someone—I can't remember whom—implied she hadn't gotten word that filming would go ahead. But you'd think that would make her late, not absent all day."

"I'll talk to her. Why did you really come to the hotel tonight?"

I stared at him. "I really came to the hotel to talk to Frank. The man says he's my father, but under the circumstances, it's hard to believe."

Gordon nodded. "Of all the pie shops in all the world, he had to walk into yours."

"And now he's the new *Pie Hard* producer? How does that even happen? Frank's lying about something." I folded my arms. "Possibly about everything."

"Do you have any proof?"

"Twenty-plus years of history," I said. Bitterness coated my tongue. "A leopard doesn't change his spots." I should know, since I never seemed to learn life's hard lessons.

What was I thinking—going into that building like some movie damsel in distress? It wasn't the first time I'd taken one too many chances, gotten myself into trouble. In fairness, usually Charlene led me right into trouble's path.

As if summoned by a fickle genie, my piecrust maker hurried around the corner of the paramedic truck. She steadied Frederick, who was sprawled over the collar of her long, green, knit jacket. "So it's true!"

Gordon's lips pressed together. "Have you been listening to the police scanner again, Charlene?"

"That would be illegal," she said. "How could you even think such a thing?"

Frederick yawned in agreement.

"News of the fire is all over the Internet," she said. "And with the *Pie Hard* crew staying at the hotel, I had a feeling Val would be in the thick of things."

"And why is that?" Chief Shaw asked from behind her, and she jumped.

"Chief Shaw." She nodded. "Nice to see the SNPD is taking this fire seriously."

He looked down his long nose at her. "And why did you think Val would be involved?"

"Not involved, exactly." She shot me a wary look. "But I knew she was coming here to meet the producer."

"Why exactly *were* you meeting him?" the chief asked.

The blood siphoned from my face, the words sticking in my throat. It was one thing for Charlene and Gordon to know about my maybe-father. Telling the rest of the world was a different story.

"He asked Val to meet him at the hotel," Gordon said. "Charlene can verify that."

She nodded. "Yep. He asked her right in front of me."

"And again," Chief Shaw said, "I ask why?"

"He says he's my father," I rasped. Blue and red lights flashed across their faces, and my stomach lurched.

"He says? You mean you don't know your own . . ." A line of color washed across the chief's cheeks. "I take it you two are estranged."

"Yes," I said.

"That complicates things," Shaw said.

"It does for Val." Charlene jammed her hands on her hips

and squinted up at him. "I don't see what it has to do with the fire."

"Don't you?" the chief asked. "And what exactly are you doing here, Mrs. McCree?"

"I heard there was a fire at the Belinda Hotel. Naturally, I came to make sure Val and the rest of the crew were all right."

"Naturally." He crossed his arms and stared down at me. "Is there anything else you'd like to add, Ms. Harris?"

I rubbed my throat. Maybe saying nothing was a good idea after all. "No," I whispered. "I think I've told Detective Carmichael everything."

The chief sighed heavily. "I was afraid it would come to this."

I stiffened. "Come to what?"

"Come to Val nearly getting barbequed in a hotel room?" Charlene asked.

"Mr. Katz says you never really wanted Pie Town to be a part of this cooking show," the chief said. "Is it true, Ms. Harris?"

"Well," I said, "not exactly, and *Pie Hard's* more a baking than cooking show, but—"

Gordon cleared his throat in warning.

"But this show will be terrific publicity for Pie Town and San Nicholas," Charlene said.

Shaw shook his head. "Murder and arson not so much."

"So Regina Katz *was* murdered," Charlene said. "Ray was right. It wasn't an accident. I knew it!"

"Ray?" Shaw asked.

"He was the man who found the body," Gordon said.

"Right," the chief said. "The young man who happens to be a good friend of Pie Town and Ms. Harris."

Charlene's snowy brows drew downward. "What are you saying?"

The chief blew out his breath. "Valentine Harris, you'll need to come to the station for questioning."

I swallowed my panic. To the station for questioning? The chief couldn't possibly think . . .

It didn't matter. It was only a few questions, Gordon would figure things out. I could trust him.

Gordon stepped forward. "Sir, I'll—"

"You'll do nothing, Carmichael," the chief said. "You've lost your objectivity, and we're going to have a little talk about your performance with Mr. Katz. As of now, you're off the case."

CHAPTER 9

Exhausted and stinking of smoke, I stumbled from the station into fog and darkness. Even Chief Shaw admitted I had a cast-iron alibi for Regina Katz's death. He kept picking at my connection to Frank and the crew, why I was in that building, how the fire had started.

I gripped my purse, slung it over my shoulder, and scanned the fogbound street for Charlene's Jeep. She'd be eager for an update, and I needed a ride. My van was still at the hotel.

A tall, muscular silhouette separated from a light pole.

I took a quick step backward, stumbling.

"Val?" Gordon asked.

Relaxing, I trotted down the brick steps. "You're here. I thought . . ." I thought he was off the case, and guilt gnawed my gut. I could guess how much that bothered him.

"I'm off duty." Amber light from the street lamp made crags of his face.

"Not permanently?!"

"No," he said, "but Katz claimed I pushed him, and—"

"You didn't! I was right there."

"It's all right."

"Are you in trouble?"

"Let me give you a lift home," he said, his voice flat.

My heart sank. He didn't want to talk about it, but he was here, and that had to mean something. "Thanks," I said. "My van's parked at the hotel. Can you take me there?"

"Sure."

I followed him to his sedan, got inside and sneaked a peek of myself in the side mirror. I looked like a frumpy dumpty. My hair was matted, and my clothes were dingy with smoke. Embarrassed, I looked in my purse for a hair band.

He started the car. "How did it go with Shaw?"

I found a band, which was sticky for reasons I didn't want to investigate. "He couldn't get around my alibi for Regina's death." I looped the band around my loose hair.

Gordon's mouth quirked. "No, half a dozen goddess gals plus Charlene are hard to argue with. It's a good thing they were at your house when Regina fell off that cliff. What's the story with the goddesses anyway?" He pulled from the curb.

"I'm not sure. I think it's mainly a getaway for them, and my bluff is a good spot for dancing around the fire."

"Mm hm."

"Or so they say." I hadn't tried any clifftop cavorting my-self.

We drove in silence for a time, and then he asked, "Why do you think someone locked you in that room tonight?" He turned onto Highway One. Traffic was light at this hour. We zipped past fog-shrouded Eucalyptus trees and a British pub with a red call box outside.

"I have no idea. I must have been in the wrong place at the wrong time."

"You weren't investigating, were you?"

I looked away, out the window. "No. I was really there to meet Frank." I wasn't sure I wanted to have the big "are you my daddy" talk. So I'd invented a secondary motive for meeting with him—to find out what he knew about the *Pie Hard* crew. I only hoped he was a witness and not a suspect. My father might be a jerk, but I didn't want him to be a murderer. I gnawed my bottom lip.

"What's wrong?"

"Frank."

"I haven't had a chance to get anything on his background. It looks like I'll have plenty of time now," he said darkly.

I winced. "Are you really off the case?"

"It's no big deal."

"Yes, it is." It was my fault. No wonder our love life had been DOA. I was a career killer for police detectives.

"The chief had to pull me off due to our relationship."

"What relationship?" I asked, exasperated. "We don't have a relationship." We'd never even completed a real date. Police business always interrupted our time together, and then Gordon went to that training in Wyoming.

His expression became a careful blank. "That's not how the chief sees it."

An awkward quiet fell. Maybe I was too insistent about us not having a relationship, but I couldn't take back my words. I'd *wanted* to have a relationship with Gordon. I didn't know how to tell him that either.

The silence stayed locked in place as we turned into the hotel parking lot and coasted to a stop behind my pink van. Lights from the Belinda gleamed, a golden fairyland at night. But this fairytale was dark, with a plot that included murder and arson.

I cleared my throat. It still burned, even hours after the fire. "Gordon—"

"I'll wait to make sure everything's okay."

"Earlier, when I said we didn't have a relationship, I just meant we never really even finished that first date."

"I know."

Now was the perfect time for him to correct that deficiency and ask me out.

Except he didn't.

I stretched my mouth into a smile. "Okay. Well, thanks for the ride." Suddenly anxious to escape his unsettling presence, I stepped from the sedan. Feeling his eyes on me, I hurried to my van, got inside, and turned the ignition. It wheezed, sputtered, and died.

Frowning, I tried again.

The van coughed and gave a final wheeze.

Gordon emerged from his sedan and came to stand beside my door.

I rolled down the window. "It's not starting."

He leaned inside. "Any idea what's wrong?"

I glanced at the dashboard. "No, I . . ."

"What?"

I tapped the fuel gauge. "I'm out of gas. But I swear I . . ."

His brow arched.

My hands tensed in my lap. "I shouldn't be out of gas," I babbled. "I had an eighth of a tank when I drove here."

"An eighth?"

"Well, yeah. Approximately."

"Approximately?"

Tingling swept my cheeks, and I rubbed the back of my neck. Had I screwed up? I'd never run out of gas before, but I'd been discombobulated by Frank's arrival and *Pie Hard* and murder.

Gordon walked to the gas tank and opened the lid, unscrewed the top. He sniffed and studied it for a long moment.

"What?" I asked. "What's wrong?

He shook his head. "Nothing. There's a station not far from here. I've got a gas can in the trunk. I'll buy you a gallon. Stay here and lock the doors."

"Wait." I dug through my purse for my wallet, trying to

make out the bills in the darkness. I flourished a fiver. "Here . . ."

I looked around.

His car was gone.

I pulled my hood further over my head and slouched low in the seat. What was wrong with me?

A phantom of fog swirled past my window.

Paranoid, I rolled it up and locked the doors. Then I flipped on the overhead lights and twisted in my seat to check the rear of the van. No one lurked beside the metal pie racks.

I readjusted myself and stared blankly through the windshield. Maybe I should be upfront and ask him out? On the other hand, would asking him exacerbate the blow of the chief removing him from the case? He was San Nicholas's only homicide detective. This was the second time that Chief Shaw had yanked a case so he could "solve" it himself.

Would Shaw try to do it himself again? Or would he bring in another investigator?

Why was Gordon staring at my gas tank? Did he expect to find some blockage? Because even I knew that didn't make sense. Or . . .

I sucked in my breath.

The tank did not have a lock. Someone must have siphoned my gas. San Nicholas never had a problem with gas thieves. I certainly didn't expect that sort of thing in the parking lot of a fancy hotel like the Belinda, but . . .

I'd smelled gasoline in that room before it went up in flames. Had the gasoline come from my own van? The thought sent a shiver up my spine. *Had* I been targeted?

A gust of wind buffeted the van, swirled the fog, and made eerie specters of the mist. My scalp prickled.

Okay, question one. Assuming the arsonist had siphoned my gas, was it a coincidence he'd taken it from my van? I didn't think so. Which meant . . . Had I been followed? I didn't see anyone following me, but I wasn't looking for a tail either.

Someone banged on my door, and I shrieked. I jumped in my seat and slammed my knee into the wheel. A blinding light shone in my face.

"What are you doing here?" a man's voice snarled.

Because I know better than to roll down a window for a stranger, I cracked it and raised my face toward the opening. "I'm waiting for a friend. He's a cop," I added, shielding my eyes with one hand.

He lowered his flashlight and chuckled.

I blinked. Graham, wearing a green security jacket that stretched across his belly, stood grinning beside my door.

I laughed shakily and rolled the window down all the way. "What are you doing here?"

"I work here." He adjusted his flat, taxi-driver's cap.

"I thought you were retired."

"I am. Just thought I'd keep my hand in, pick up some extra spending money."

"Is Wally here?" I asked.

"In a manner of speaking. He followed that ninja kid and wound up in the hotel bar. I think he's settled in there for the night."

"Oh, no." I didn't like the thought of these two playing detective. That made me a ginormous hypocrite as I was doing exactly the same thing. "You don't have to follow anyone for me."

"It beats cribbage. Wally cheats."

Gordon's sedan glided into the empty spot on my passenger side. He emerged carrying a red, plastic gas can and walked around the front of my van. "Hi, Graham. Everything all right?"

"Some idiots set three-b on fire," he said, "but I wasn't on guard duty at the time, so it's not my problem."

Rats. That meant he wouldn't have noticed anyone siphoning gas from my van.

Gordon poured gas into my tank.

"Don't tell me you ran dry?" Graham asked.

"It looks that way," I said, vague.

He tsked. "You're lucky it happened here and not on a deserted roadside. You girls need to be more careful."

I lowered my chin. "We girls?"

"You and Charlene."

Charlene would be thrilled to hear she still landed in the "girl" category. "Right." We chatted some more, and the older man ambled off, leaving the detective and me alone.

I slid from the van. "Gordon . . ."

He flipped shut the lid to my tank. "All done."

"I'm really sorry about you getting pulled from the case."

"It's not your fault."

It didn't sound like he believed it.

I drove home through sable hills—my headlights making little headway in the thickening fog. To cheer myself up, I flipped on the radio and settled on a jazzy song that had me bopping in my seat, until I actually listened to the lyrics and realized it was "Upside Down." That seemed depressingly appropriate, and I twisted the dial to off.

I turned up the narrow track toward my house and winced as branches whacked the side of my van. Was someone targeting me specifically, or had I just gotten caught in the *Pie Hard* black hole of doom? More importantly, would Gordon forgive me for getting him booted from the case?

Charlene's yellow Jeep was parked beside my tiny house. A white Ford Escort sat beside it. The goddesses weren't around. The ladies were probably sleeping in the yurt, and Charlene was probably hanging out in my kitchen. The Escort must belong to one of them.

I stepped outside and hurried to my glorified shipping container. It was nearly midnight, and though the fog wasn't as thick at my hillside perch, the stars were invisible. I climbed the two short steps and opened the door.

"Hey," a man's voice said.

I gasped, clutching my chest.

Ray sat hunched like a circus bear at my small table. His red hair was rumpled, his round, freckled face pale. His brown windbreaker was unzipped over his band t-shirt and saggy jeans.

"What are you doing here?" I asked.

He yawned. "Charlene told me what happened. I wanted to make sure you are okay."

Because yawns are contagious, I yawned too. "Where is she?"

"In the yurt." His nostrils widened, and he grimaced as if stifling a yawn.

"She told me to stay in here because of the ladies," he continued.

I gritted my teeth. *Don't yawn. Don't yawn.* We'd be doing this all night if we weren't careful. "Oh, no. They weren't naked, were they?" If he interrupted one of their skyclad ceremonies, I didn't know who would be more traumatized.

His broad brow creased. "Naked?"

"Never mind," I said hurriedly.

The door banged open, and Charlene climbed in. Her nose wrinkled. "Phew! You stink."

"Thanks," I said, and stomped around the bookcase to my sleeping area. I rummaged through the closet for my PJs.

"We need to talk this over while it's still fresh in your mind," Charlene said.

"Nothing's fresh in my mind," I said. Cotton PJs in hand, I returned to the dining nook and leaned against the kitchen counter. In a converted shipping container, you never have far to walk.

"Right." Ray crossed his arms, his windbreaker rustling. "Why didn't you tell me about the fire? You should have called. I was at the hotel earlier. I could have protected you."

"Why were you there?" I asked.

His gaze shifted to the sliding glass doors. "Investigating. Why didn't you call?"

"It all happened kind of fast," I said, "and then I went to the police station."

His broad face furrowed. "If you'd told me you were going to the hotel, I could have helped."

"I wasn't going there to investigate," I said.

"Then what were you doing there?" he asked.

"It was personal," I mumbled.

"You may as well tell him," Charlene said. "The cops know. Everyone else will soon enough."

Unwelcome heat stole up my cheeks. "Frank—their new producer—he says he's my father."

His coppery brows drew downward. "He says? You mean . . ." His face cleared. "Oh."

"I went to the hotel to have it out with him." Mostly. Before Charlene could call me on the fib, I told him everything that happened.

Ray pulled a sheaf of loose paper from the backpack near his feet and started scribbling. "What time did you arrive at the hotel?"

I glanced at Charlene for confirmation.

"You left Pie Town around a quarter to eight," she said.

"A little before that, I think," I said. "I was in the bar at eight p.m." Unlike Frank, *I'd* been on time.

Charlene sat at the table across from him and tried to peek at his notes.

"How long do you think you waited for Frank in the bars?" he asked.

"Twenty minutes." I have a rule—if someone's more than twenty minutes late, I leave. "Then I went to talk to the receptionist. That took maybe another five minutes or so, and then I walked to the building—"

"Another five minutes?"

"Probably."

"So, we're talking thirty minutes between the time you arrived and walked into that outbuilding." He held up his timeline for us to admire. Ruler straight lines, color coding, handwriting that would make an architect proud. Damn, he was good.

"There is one weird thing," I said. "When I finally got back to the hotel, my gas tank was empty. I swear I had gas in it when I arrived."

"If the arsonist followed you," Charlene said, "he would have had enough time to siphon gas from your van and splash it around that room."

"That would explain my suddenly empty tank," I said. "Maybe the arsonist didn't want to leave a paper trail by visiting a gas station. Locking me inside that building couldn't have been premeditated," I said, trying to convince myself. "There's no way he could have known I'd end up there, because I didn't know I would until the last minute."

"So the goal must have been to burn that room," Charlene said. "You walking inside must have been a bonus."

"But why?" Ray asked. "Why destroy the *Pie Hard* equipment?"

"And how did he or she set the fire with you inside?" Charlene asked, accusing. "Didn't you notice anything?"

"I smelled gas," I said. "The fire must have been ready to go before I walked into that room. And I remember hearing a door close after I walked inside. I assumed someone came in, but the arsonist must have been leaving. Then he must have slipped out the other door while I came in the front and barricaded that door. Maybe he rigged some sort of fuse to go after he left."

"But why?" Ray repeated. "Why you? Why gasoline from *your* van? To frame you? How could the cops trace the gas to you? And why destroy that equipment at all?" He glanced around. "Have you got a white board?"

"Why would she have a white board?" Charlene asked.

He shook his head. "It's okay. I'll bring one tomorrow."

Charlene looked a question at me.

I shrugged.

"Look," Ray said. "I can't be a part of the Baker Street Bakers unless you let me know when and where you're investigating."

Charlene sucked in her breath. "Now, we agreed to help you, but the Baker Street Bakers are bakers only. And you're a student engineer."

He brandished his time chart. "But I'm useful."

"He has a point," I admitted. I didn't like that he'd been at the Belinda Hotel investigating without us knowing. Bringing him onto the team was a way to keep him safe.

Charlene glared at me, and I shrugged.

"And I can bake," he said. "Next time, I'll bring my famous double-fudge brownies. Ooh! Or maybe lemon bars. And you can't help me if we don't work together." From his backpack, he pulled out a rolled sheet of yellowed paper. He flattened it on the small table. "I've drawn a map of the hotel—"

"Why do the edges look burnt?" Charlene asked.

His face pinked, his freckles darkening. "I used one of our gaming maps. They're standard grid sheets," he added hastily, "even if they do have art around the edges."

She squinted at a sticker on the square marking the out-building. "Is that a wizard?"

"It's Val," he said. "I didn't have any female character stickers."

I grinned. "I'm a wizard."

"Only because you've got a pointy head," Charlene said.

"Now we need to figure out where everyone was when Regina was killed and the fire set," Ray said. "It's a simple process of elimination."

Charlene snorted. "Simple until everyone lies to you. Murder is a serious business, young man. It's no place for an amateur. Son, this is as far as you go."

"What happens if Val gets arrested?" Ray asked. "Then you'll need a partner to help clear her name."

I did not like that prospect. "He did help us figure out the timeline for tonight's arson." We would have gotten there, but he made it happen sooner rather than later. Ray was efficient. "Maybe we could use his engineering perspective."

"I could draft a chart of motives," Ray said.

"There are only three motives," Charlene said. "Love, greed, and revenge. That doesn't make much of a chart."

"Yeah," he said, "but I can create a table with each person's specific motive."

"We've never done tables before," I said. "Charlene, maybe you can help him." If she was busy managing Ray, I would be free to manage Frank.

Charlene blew out her breath. "Fine. Welcome to the Baker Street Bakers. But since you're not a professional baker, you're only an associate member."

He sprang to his feet, knocking over his chair. "You won't regret this. I'll tell Henrietta."

Charlene's eyes widened. "Wait. What?"

He stuffed his papers into his backpack. Limp gone, he hurried to the door and hopped from the trailer.

"Your girlfriend's not a baker either," Charlene shouted after him. "Henrietta can't investigate!"

"We're just friends!" He hollered over his shoulder and squeezed into the Escort.

"He's not going to invite Henrietta onto the team," she said. "Is he?"

The Escort made an ugly grinding sound and inched down the hill.

"We'll give them Internet research to do," I said. "They'll be fine."

"You thought you'd be fine interrogating your father at a luxury hotel."

"It's Internet research. They'll be totally safe." I shifted against the counter. Someone on the *Pie Hard* crew was a killer. I had to keep Ray off their radar. I only hoped I could.

CHAPTER 10

M y van's headlights lit the brick alley. The sky above was a deep, cobalt blue, hinting at the coming sunrise. Through gritty eyes, I slowed, scanning the shadows beyond the dumpsters.

In spite of my smoke-roughened throat and general exhaustion, my heart was light. We had a big wholesale order due this afternoon, and the weather report had predicted a warm, sunny Saturday. Between the order and the beachgoers, Pie Town would be busy.

Two people emerged from the shadows. One carried a spotlight.

I slammed on the brakes and rocked forward. The van screeched to a halt beside our dumpster.

I rolled down the window. "Seriously?"

"Good morning, Valentine." Frank tugged down the cuffs of his tweed jacket and grinned rakishly. "The morning hour is when the baking magic happens, and I understand we don't have any usable shots after last night's fire."

I leaned my head out the window.

The assistant cameraman, Luther, blew into his hands,

and jammed them into the pockets of his bulky, black jacket. A breeze ruffled his pumpkin hair.

Ilsa leaned against the brick wall and scowled. She flicked cigarette ash off the sleeve of her white baker's jacket. "Don't like." The Frenchwoman waved her hand in a banishing motion.

A camera aimed at me, its light blistered my retinas. I assumed the cameraman, Steve, was behind it.

I sputtered. "But . . . how—?"

"How do we go on after our little disaster last night?" Frank smoothed his hand over his slicked, brown hair. "Let's just say I can be tenacious."

"More importantly," Ilsa said in her thick accent, "we have been asked not to leave town."

"Let me guess," I said. "Don't like?"

Frank shrugged. "Since Regina's production company is stuck paying our hotel bills, we may as well work."

"Regina's company?" I asked. "I thought she was just the field or line producer."

"She was," Frank said, "but she very cleverly formed an L.L.C. for tax purposes."

The pastry chef jerked away from the brick wall, her blond highlights dull in the dim light. "Are you going to let us in? Or must we stand out here and freeze while you chitchat?"

It wasn't *that* cold, but she had a point. I hopped from the van and unlocked the alley door to the kitchen while Luther hooked a mic to my Pie Town tee. He smelled of stale beer.

"Say something," the sound engineer said to me.

"Something."

"You're five-by-five." A breeze ruffled the red and orange Hawaiian shirt sticking out from the bottom of Luther's jacket.

"What?"

Luther's ruddy face pinched. "That means loud and clear."

"Oh. Got it." I walked inside and flipped on the lights.

The fluorescents glinted off metal counters, the massive pie oven, and the butcher-block work island. Canisters of dry ingredients and utensils lined the shelves.

"Why hasn't your crust expert arrived yet?" Ilsa asked.

I glanced at the wall clock above the window to the diner. "She should be here any minute."

The pastry chef clucked her tongue. "Late."

"Where's Nigel?" I asked Frank.

Luther shucked off of his jacket. At least one of the buttons on his Hawaiian shirt had gone into the wrong hole, creating a hillock of fabric. "Anywhere I can put this while I work?"

I pointed to the wall hooks behind the swinging kitchen door.

He hung his jacket and patted the pockets of his photographer's vest, as if searching for something.

"And to answer your question," Frank said, "Nigel didn't need to be here for these shots. He's busy at the hotel preparing some business ideas for Pie Town. You're going to love what he's got planned."

That sounded ominous. "What has he got planned?" Worried, I pulled down our thick, three-ring recipe binder from a shelf and opened it on the counter.

Frank waved away the question. "Never mind Nigel. This morning is about Ilsa and your pie team."

"Who are not here?" Ilsa tapped her wristwatch. "Does your staff make a practice of arriving late?"

The alley door slammed open, and Charlene bustled in. She unsnapped her violet knit jacket. Beneath it she wore a green knit tunic, matching leggings, and tennis shoes.

"At last," Ilsa said. "The queen arrives." She turned and strode into the flour-work room.

"I guess that's me then," Charlene said cheerfully, unhooking the gold watch around her wrist and dropping it in her jacket pocket. "Tah." With Luther and the cameraman at her heels, she followed Ilsa inside the flour-work room and banged the door shut.

I pulled out plastic-sheathed recipes for strawberry-parfait pie, lemon-blueberry cream pie, and an almond toffee pie. "Maybe I should just go with them," I said to Frank.

"Would you normally supervise Charlene?" he asked.

"No, she'd boil me in cooking oil, but—"

"They'll be fine. Charlene's a grown woman."

With the baseline personality of a fourteen-year-old. "But—"

The alley door opened, and Abril hurried into the kitchen. Catching sight of Frank, she stopped short. "Oh!" A deep flush crept up her face. Her long black hair was coiled beneath a hairnet. Like me, she wore a pink Pie Town t-shirt with our logo: *Turn Your Frown Upside Down at Pie Town!*

Frank cocked his head. "And you must be . . . ?"

Abril stood frozen, lips parted.

"This is Abril," I said, "poet and pie maker. But I'm not sure she wants to be on TV."

Abril shook her head frantically.

Frank bowed. "Then you needn't be, dear lady. We'll blur your face in any shots. Will that be acceptable?"

She nodded, her brown-eyed gaze darting around the kitchen.

"The crew wants to get some shots of us baking later," I said. "Right now, they're in the flour-work room with Charlene. And today's specials are on the counter." I nodded to the recipe pages I'd removed.

She walked to the industrial refrigerator, pulled ingredients out and set them on the table to prep.

Frank leaned toward my ear. "Doesn't talk much, does she?" he asked in a low voice. "I'll just make myself some coffee." Without waiting for a response, he plugged in the coffee urn, inserted a fresh filter, and dumped in the coffee grounds.

I tried to disguise my annoyance. I didn't like people who didn't work for me messing with my equipment. At least he knew how to make himself useful.

Snapping on my work gloves, I got busy chopping onions and veggies for our breakfast pies.

Frank drifted into the diner. When I peeked through the window, he was sitting on a barstool reading the morning paper.

Abril and I organized ingredients for our fruit pies, slicing and dicing fruit, as busy as two Saturday morning bakers could be. We assembled the ingredients in giant, metal bowls.

Luther emerged from the flour-work room and shivered. "Brrr. It's freezing in there."

"I should have warned you," I said. "It's temperature controlled to keep the butter properly chilled."

"No kidding." He went to stand beside our giant oven and tilted his head back, holding his hands, palms out, by the narrow door. "Ah, this is good. Mind if I stand here?"

"Fine by me." More than fine, since I'd been meaning to talk to him about Regina. I glanced at Abril, but she had her back turned to us both. "It's difficult to believe someone would set your equipment on fire."

Luther's expression hardened. "Is it? People are jerks. A lot of that equipment was my own. It's insured, but the insurance company will never give me the full replacement value."

"Who could have wanted to wreck your equipment?" I glanced again at Abril, who purposefully ignored us. "After what happened to Regina, I'm starting to wonder if someone has a grudge against the show."

Bacon popped and sizzled on the stove.

"Well, there's you." He grinned. "I don't know why anybody signs up for this torture. But I guess the dream of fame trumps looking like a moron on cable TV."

"A moron?" I shook myself. We'd look fine. More importantly, I was no arsonist. "Luther, I did not—"

"Yeah, yeah." He waved his hand, dismissive. "Frank told us the real reason you were at the hotel."

My stomach plunged. Had Frank told people he was my father? We hadn't even had a chance to talk! "He did?"

"Hey, like I said, I get why you might be having second thoughts. So. Do you trust him?"

My face heated. "I don't—I'm not . . ." If Frank had shared my dysfunctional family history with the crew, would the story be part of this wretched show?

He leaned closer, his alcohol fumes overcoming the scent of frying bacon. "Hey," he said, "relax. Frank told us about the show plans in the team meeting. That we're going to play it straight. There'll be no weird editing to make you look dumber than you are, though opening up a bakery has got to be one of the stupidest ideas ever. Bakeries hardly ever make it past their first year."

The show! Luther was talking about the show. "Oh," I said, relief mingling with disquiet. The bakery business *was* rough—we operated on razor-thin margins. I couldn't think about all the reasons I might fail. "To be honest, I'm more concerned about the murder and the fire than how Pie Town looks on TV. How is your crew dealing with everything?"

"They ain't my crew."

"I know. I mean—"

"There's one thing you should know about reality TV crews." His fleshy lips twisted. "They're ruthless."

And Luther wasn't? "But you all traveled together. You must have known Regina well."

His shoulders sagged. "Yeah. Regina was an okay lady. She didn't deserve any of this."

"Any of this? Did something else happen to her?"

His mouth tightened, and he shrugged.

"After everything that's happened," I said, "I can't believe Steve came to work today."

"Why not? He was here yesterday. Besides, Steve has Ilsa to console him."

Abril's shoulders twitched.

"You mean . . . Regina's husband and Ilsa?" I asked, stunned. If this was true, they both had motive to want his wife dead. "They're a thing?"

"Don't like." Ilsa's voice rang through the workroom door.

"Don't like *it*! It!" Charlene shouted. "Use the damn pronoun!"

"You shout about pronouns, when this piecrust is an abomination?" Ilsa asked.

Abril turned, acorn-colored eyes widening, and looked to the workroom door.

Luther smirked. "Here it comes."

"Here what comes?" I asked. "You said there wouldn't be any tricks."

"I said no funny editing. If Ilsa or your partner blow a gasket, that's another story."

"You're not even *French*!" Charlene shouted through the closed door. "Your name is German."

"I was born in Alsace!"

Peeling off my gloves, I speed-walked to the flour-work door and jerked it open. "How are the crusts coming?" A blast of chilled air flowed into the bakery, and I shivered.

Charlene folded her arms over her apron and glared at Ilsa. "My crusts are perfect."

"A perfect disaster." Ilsa sniffed.

"What do you know?" Charlene said. "The French didn't even invent pies. It's an American dish."

"Pies date back to medieval Europe!"

"Not American pies."

"I know pastry, and this . . ." She grabbed a ball of dough

and dropped it with a thud on the long table. ". . . is dense as granite."

"Her crusts are famous," I said, indignant on Charlene's behalf. "We're known for our crusts."

"I am sure you are," Ilsa said. "The Hindenburg is also famous. The Titanic is famous. Krakatoa is—"

"Now you just stop right there." Charlene shook her finger at the pastry chef.

"I have seen enough." Ilsa turned on me. "You. Show me your work."

"S—sure," I stammered, eager to separate Ilsa and Charlene. I loaded rounds of dough onto a lined tray. "We were just about to start filling crusts."

"Don't like." She whisked her hand in front of my face. "I will see you create from the beginning with the cutting and chopping and mixing."

"But we've already done the prep work," I said.

"Don't like. Do it again."

My neck stiffened. "Sorry, I don't have time. We've got a big order due this afternoon. We're filling crusts with what we've got." I pushed open the door with my hip and set the crusts on the counter beside the flattening machine.

Cameraman Steve and Ilsa followed.

Charlene slammed the door shut behind us. "And good riddance." Her voice echoed from the flour-work room.

Ilsa leaned against the metal counter and crossed her arms.

Ignoring the chef's sniffs, tuts, and growls, I flattened the dough, lined the tins.

Luther raised his head, sniffing the air. "Do I smell coffee?" He drifted toward the swinging kitchen door.

"You're supposed to be assisting me," Steve snapped.

"Shout when you need help." Luther vanished through the door to the diner.

Abril and I returned to our usual rhythm of crimping and

filling. Abril's hands shook every time Ilsa harrumphed. Her slim shoulders tensed with each roll of Ilsa's eyes.

Charlene emerged from the workroom and sat on her blue chair by the wall. She watched us, her gaze narrowed.

Abril folded the eggs, cheese, and hash brown mixture into a crust for a breakfast pie.

Ilsa sighed heavily and shook her head.

"I can't do this." Abril raised her hands and stepped away from the counter. "I can't be on TV."

"But your face will be blurred," Charlene said.

"It doesn't matter," Abril said. "I can't do it."

"It's all right," I said. "You don't have to."

Charlene rose and walked to her. "Oh, yes you do."

Abril shook her head. "But—"

"Let me tell you a little story," Charlene said. "A story about a pie maker who got jilted at the altar."

I hadn't been at the altar! Grinding my teeth, I glanced at the cameraman. "Charlene, I don't think this is the time."

"As I'm sure you've guessed," Charlene said, "I'm talking about Val."

"Charlene!" I forced a smile and turned to Steve.

He zoomed closer.

"And did Val give up after being publicly humiliated?" Charlene asked. "Her dream wedding in tatters? Her fiancée taking up with a yoga instructor? No. And when someone dropped dead after eating one of her breakfast pies—"

"Abril," I said quickly, "could you help with something in my office?"

She gave a quick smile of relief. "Yes, please." Abril followed me into my barren office, and I shut the door.

"I know they're going to blur my face on the show," she whispered, "but it's still . . . Everything I do is wrong."

"No, it isn't. You're doing fine. Ilsa doesn't like anybody. That's the way she works. But I've watched some of her shows, and she does usually come up with good suggestions. She's difficult, but we can both learn from her."

"Maybe." She plucked at her bottom lip. "But she makes me nervous."

"You've got nothing to feel nervous about. You're only baking the way I've asked you to, so any criticisms she has of your techniques is on me."

"But what about Charlene?"

I tugged at my hair. "I know! I wish she'd quit bringing up all my failures on TV, but there's no way to stop her." Plus, she was my landlord, which gave her added leverage.

Her dark brows swooped downward. "I meant, everyone loves her crusts, and Ilsa said they were a disaster."

"Oh. Right. Don't worry; we're not ditching her piecrust recipe." Charlene would revolt, and so would half my customers. "Are you going to be all right?"

Abril raised her chin. "I am a blur." She blinked. "That's a poem. I need to write that down." She pulled a purple notepad and pen from her apron pocket and hurried from my office.

Instead of returning to the kitchen, I walked to the dining area. I turned the sign in the diner window to OPEN and unlocked the door.

Abril emerged from the kitchen and set out the day-old hand pies with their half-off sign and a basket for payment.

A stream of retirees trickled in and poured themselves coffee from the urn.

Marla wandered in behind the retirees, and my eyes narrowed. Every strand of her bottle-blond hair was in place, as if she'd just come from the beauty parlor. Which was, of course, impossible at this hour. She was definitely trying to get in on the reality show action, and Charlene would not be pleased.

I greeted everyone, spending more time chatting than I

normally would to avoid Ilsa. When I couldn't put it off any longer, I returned to the kitchen.

In the corner by the pie safe, Frank spoke in a low voice to Ilsa. Her face pinched, but she nodded. I don't know what he said to her, but for the rest of the morning, she watched silently as we worked.

At nine, the bell over the door jingled, and I glanced through the window into the diner.

Ray, in his comic book t-shirt, limped to the register. Henrietta ambled beside him in her usual shapeless, Army green.

I hurried through the swinging door to the register. "Hi, guys. What can I get for you?"

"*Pie Hard's* back?" he asked. "Is Ilsa Fueder here?"

Unfortunately. "Yeah, she's in the kitchen."

"Do you think she'd give me an autograph?" He flushed. "I know it shouldn't matter, after . . ." He looked down the counter. "But I'll kick myself later if I don't ask."

Henrietta crossed her arms and looked in the opposite direction.

Frank swiveled on his barstool. "Are you two friends of Valentine's?"

"They are," I said.

"Ray saved Val from getting run over by a car," Henrietta's lips pinched as if that wasn't a good thing.

I frowned. Henrietta's round face was grim. Even her sandy hair looked angry. Was she upset that Ray was detecting? Maybe she could get him to give it up.

"In that case," Frank said, "I'll speak to Ilsa and get you an autograph."

Ray's broad face broke into a grin. "Thanks! And I'll have one of those mini breakfast pies with bacon," he said to me. "Henrietta?"

Marla waved at Frank from her table in the center of the restaurant. "Yoo-hoo! I'm ready to sign that waiver."

"Of course." Frank joined her at the table

"I'll have the spinach and goat cheese mini." Henrietta turned on her sensible shoes and strode to the corner booth.

Shooting me an apologetic look, Ray paid. I stuck the ticket in the wheel and spun it to face the kitchen.

Abril grabbed it, nodded, and a moment later set a tray on the window with both mini pies and a side of greens.

I carried the pies to the corner booth. "Here you go. So, Ray—"

He cut his gaze to Henrietta and gave a tiny shake of his head. He hadn't brought her into the Baker Street Bakers.

"Anything else?" I asked.

"No, thanks." Henrietta laid her hand atop Ray's and gazed at me through lowered eyelids.

Ray blushed.

So much for "We're just friends." These two were an item. Henrietta seemed unhappy with me for some reason.

"Besides, Ray, you should be cutting back," she said. "You need to save to get your car fixed."

"What's wrong with your car?" I asked.

"It's making weird noises, but it still runs fine."

"For now," Henrietta said.

"It did sound odd the other night," I said.

She whipped toward him. "Other night?"

Ray flushed.

Crumb. What had I done? "Okay, you know where to find me," I said quickly and retreated to the kitchen.

My assistant manager, Petronella, arrived and took over for me in the kitchen while I worked the register. The breakfast rush was light—mainly retirees who met here for pie and gossip. The real rush would come at lunchtime, when the beachgoers got hungry.

The cameraman migrated into the restaurant and filmed the diners. Frank roamed the checkerboard floor getting permissions and interviewing happy customers.

The bell over the front door jangled. Chief Shaw strode into Pie Town, two beefy, uniformed cops beside him in a policeman sandwich. They bee lined for Ray and Henrietta in the corner booth.

The cameraman swiveled toward the police.

"Ray MacTaggart?" Shaw asked.

"Um, yeah?" Ray said.

"I figured you'd be planted here," Shaw said. "I'd like you to come to the station with us."

Henrietta gasped, paling.

I slid from behind the counter. What did my best customer have to do with the police?

Frowning, Ray slid from the booth and hitched up his jeans. "Sure, but why?"

"Because you were at the scene of two capital crimes—murder and attempted murder by arson. And that doesn't look good, son."

CHAPTER 11

"Another Pie Town murderer!" Marla sagged in her chair, her wrinkled hand to her platinum-blond head.

"Ray's not a murderer," Henrietta shouted.

"Now, now, it's only a few questions," Chief Shaw said, and his entourage led Ray from Pie Town.

Henrietta slithered from the booth. Her olive-green cargo pants squeaked on the pink vinyl. "Val, you have to do something!" She rushed to the counter.

"I feel faint," Marla said.

"He's only being questioned," I rasped and rubbed my neck. My throat was still raw from the fire. "He wasn't arrested." But taking him to the station meant things were serious.

Henrietta clawed a hand through her sandy hair. "But he's being questioned because of you. He told me you three were investigating that woman's death. That's why he was at the hotel that night. That's why they're blaming him for the crimes."

"Is that why you're upset with me?" I asked.

"Shame," Marla intoned. "But I'm sure it isn't all Val's fault. Charlene no doubt dragged her into it."

At the counter, Frank, Luther, and Tally Wally swiveled their bar stools to face me.

Wally rubbed his ruddy nose. "Val, did you get young Ray involved in a murder?"

"He got me involved." It sounded whiney, and I stuffed my hands in my apron pockets. "Henrietta, I'm sorry this happened, but honestly, it was Ray who called me. I didn't drag him into anything."

Cameraman Steve edged closer, lens aimed toward me. It shook slightly.

This was awful. Steve's wife had been murdered, and we were discussing it like it was no big thing. What must he think?

Frank put his hand on the camera and gently forced it down. He shook his head and said something in a low voice to the cameraman.

Steve's salt-and-pepper brows lowered. Mouth tight, he hurried through the Dutch door, past the register, and into the kitchen.

Luther arched a brow and blew on his coffee.

"Ray never would have tried to be a detective if you hadn't gotten him hit by that car." But Henrietta's angry expression wavered.

"I didn't mean to," I said. Had I somehow encouraged Ray? Because it felt like the opposite. "It was a strange concatenation of events."

"Charlene's cat is here?" Tally Wally spun his lean form on the barstool to face the door. "I don't trust that animal."

"No," I said, "concatenation means *series*—"

"Then why don't you say *series*?" He swiveled back toward me.

"I will next time," I said, weary. But I really liked that word.

At the counter, Luther bit into a hand pie and angled his head toward us. A glob of cherry filling dripped like blood down his chin.

"The point is," Henrietta said, "Ray's a part of your crazy team now. I didn't think you left team members in the lurch."

"We don't," I said, fighting for calm. I liked Henrietta. It bothered me that she thought I was the enemy. "I can't help him in the police station, but we will figure this out. Ray has no motive. They'll release him soon."

Marla harrumphed and blew into her coffee mug.

Frank shook his head.

I drew Henrietta away from the counter and whispered, "It had to be someone from the *Pie Hard* crew."

"Who?" she asked.

"I don't know. Yet. And if it makes you feel any better," I said more loudly, "Shaw considers me as much a suspect as he does Ray."

Marla snorted.

"It doesn't," Henrietta said. "I'm going to the police station." She turned and strode out the door.

Smiling sympathetically, Frank refilled his coffee from the urn. "She must care a great deal for that young man. Don't worry. She'll figure out this isn't your fault."

Irrational, childhood indignation boiled in my chest. Frank hadn't earned the right to comfort me. "Can we talk?" I jerked my chin toward my office.

"Sure."

Luther's gaze burned a hole in my back as I walked to my office and held the door for my father. I followed him inside and shut it.

He leaned against my battered metal desk. "How can I help?"

"You can't. I don't know you. Frank, it's been twenty-five years."

He blew out his breath, his shoulders slumping beneath

his tweed jacket. "I suppose that's fair. You have no reason to trust me after all this time."

So why did I want to trust him? I braced my back against the door and crossed my arms against the desire. "How can I even believe you're my father?"

He whistled. "So that's how it is."

Silence stretched and strained between us. My ribs felt broken, and squeezed my breath from my lungs.

"How much did your mother explain to you?" he finally asked.

"She didn't." Talking about Frank hurt her too much. I stared hard at the dusty shelves lining the wall.

He winced. "If it makes a difference, I didn't want to leave."

"It doesn't. And don't try to tell me Mom drove you away."

"No, she didn't." His lips pursed. "I was reckless when I was younger."

I edged sideways, nudging the wall calendar on the door. "What does that mean?"

"Your mother and I agreed it would be best for you and for her if I left."

"Mom . . . agreed?" I asked, incredulous. My mother had been devastated by his desertion. There was no way this could be true.

"I gambled and got involved with some bad people. But I don't gamble anymore," he said, quickly, shifting against my desk.

Could there have been more to the story then she'd told me? It was possible, because she'd never said much. When he left, I was too young for that sort of heart-to-heart. Later, when I understood he wasn't returning, I stopped asking. I thought I stopped caring, but the twist in my gut revealed the lie.

"That's when she moved to L.A.," he said.

"To Orange County," I corrected. "And where did you go?"

"Vegas." He stretched out his legs.

I raised a brow. "So you could quit gambling?"

His smile was rueful, and he clasped his hands together. "It wasn't easy, and I fell off the wagon more than once."

"And now?"

"Now I work with other gamblers to help them with their addiction."

"As a life coach," I said, my voice flat, disbelieving.

"My clients don't need any more shame. *Life coach* is a kinder title than addiction counselor."

"A life coach who just happens to worm his way into *Pie Hard* as a producer when the first one dies."

"That was a bit of luck."

"Not for Regina."

He shook his head. "No, of course not. That was terrible. But it was for me. It gives us a chance to work together, don't you see?"

"But how did you pull it off?"

He leaned forward, conspiratorial. "The executive producer was a client of mine."

My arms dropped to my sides. "What brought you here in the first place?"

"I wish I could say you did. The truth is, a client brought me to San Nicholas. I can't tell you who. That's confidential. When I learned I was going to San Nicholas, I immediately thought of you." He dug into the inside pocket of his blazer and pulled out a leather wallet. "I may not have been in your life, Val, but I've kept up with you. Your mother sent a card every Christmas." He opened the wallet and pulled out a photo, extended it to me.

Unwillingly, I stepped forward and took it. An ache ripped through my chest. It was a photo of me with Santa. I was thirteen—a bit too old for Santa's lap—but Mom insisted on one every year.

It was really real. Frank was my father. There was no other way he could have had this picture. I thought the Santa photos had been our private joke. It turned out she'd been sharing it with someone else.

"You and Santa, every Christmas." He handed me another photo, and another, until my twenty-first Christmas.

Mom had been diagnosed with breast cancer then. The photo shoot embarrassed my twenty-one-year-old self, but I couldn't deny her.

"When the pictures stopped coming, I knew she was gone." He stared at the dingy linoleum floor.

"Yeah." My voice cracked, and I blinked rapidly. I was not going to cry in front of this man. "And did you ever send anything to her? Like child support?" I already knew the answer. He'd been in touch with her, and he'd known where to reach her. He just never bothered.

"I tried," he said, "but she didn't want any. She sent my money right back."

My lungs compressed. "What?"

"After a while, I stopped trying."

"That doesn't make any sense." I paced the small office. He couldn't be telling the truth. My mother had struggled when I was growing up. We always had a roof over our heads, but we moved around a lot in search of greener pastures and cheaper rents. At first, I was too young to understand why I had to switch schools every two years or wear unfashionable hand-me-downs. Later, I learned to bargain shop like a pro.

"Your mother was a proud woman," he said.

I gnawed my lower lip. That, at least, was true.

"Taking my money was the last thing she wanted," he said.

"Hm." Absently, I rubbed my arms. Could I risk believing him?

"I knew you might not want to see me," he said, "but I

couldn't resist looking in on you here. I'm proud of what you've accomplished with Pie Town. I know it couldn't have been easy."

It hadn't been. It still wasn't, and I winced at what I knew Nigel would find in my financial statements.

I straightened off the door. Business might be tight, but Pie Town wasn't going under. It was typical of new businesses to have challenges at the start. I had nothing to be ashamed of. I'd rather think of Pie Town problems than my father. "Thank you for telling me this."

"I'm only sorry I couldn't tell you sooner."

"*Couldn't*?" I asked.

His gaze darted away from me—to the tile ceiling, the ramshackle bookshelf, the closet door. "Didn't. I was away for so long; I didn't know how to find my way back. And then your mother was gone, and it was too late." He levered himself off the metal desk. "I know this is a lot to take in. And I understand that you aren't ready to play the role of daughter, and that you may never be. But I would like the chance to get to know you, if you're willing."

Someone banged on the door.

I twitched, startled, and opened it.

Charlene stormed inside. "Mademoiselle *Don't Like* is going to be the next to die, because I'm going to wring her neck."

I rubbed my forehead. "Ilsa?" I'd forgotten all about the French chef. I was supposed to be demonstrating my pie latticing technique. "I left her alone with Abril. Is she okay?"

"Abril is latticing strawberry-rhubarb pies like a champion. That French witch told Abril her work is passable but unimaginative."

"It's pie lattice," I said. "How much imagination does it take?"

"Tell that so-called pastry chef!"

Frank smiled. "I'll talk to Ilsa. She has high standards,

but her skills can only work in your favor. Trust the process."
He left the office, vanishing around the corner.

I moved toward the door.

"Trust the process?" Charlene asked, halting my progress.
"What happened? Did you learn anything more about your
you-know-what?"

"I think he really is my dad." I handed her the photos.
"He had these. My mother sent them to him."

She flipped through the pictures and handed them back,
her expression pained. "All right. So he's legit. How did that
get him to being the *Pie Hard* producer?"

"A strange concatenation of events."

"A strange what?"

I sighed. "Dumb luck. Frank really does know the executive producer. And I think he wanted to help me in his own,
strange way. Come on. Let's rescue Abril."

When we returned to the kitchen, Abril was calmly sliding pies into our rotating oven while Cameraman Steve
filmed.

Abril smiled. "Good, you're back. They wanted to film
you instead of me, since I'm only a blur."

I looked around the kitchen for the Frenchwoman.
"Where's Ilsa?"

The cameraman jerked his head toward the rear door.
"Alley. Smoke break."

"I hear Ilsa was a little rough," I said, glancing at Charlene.

Abril hung the giant, wooden paddle on its hook and
wiped her hands on her apron. "She had some interesting
ideas about making the crusts more decorative. She said she'd
show me tomorrow. You were right. When you get to know
her, Ilsa's actually pretty nice."

Charlene sniffed.

The alley door opened, and Frank and Ilsa strolled inside,
laughing. She smiled at him. "I will go shopping now." She

turned to Abril. "Tomorrow, you will be amazed at what you can do!" She bustled through the swinging door to the diner.

"Ilsa's leaving?" I asked. "Does that mean filming is over?"

"You must be wondering at our schedule," Frank said. "The fact is, since the police have told us not to leave town, we're taking things a little more slowly than usual. But that just means this will be a great show. Did you know that *Pie Hard* rarely comes to pie shops?"

"Imagine," Charlene said dryly.

"I've spoken with Nigel," Frank continued, "and he's working up some great ideas to improve your bottom line. Ilsa's got some tricks up her sleeve too. I think you'll be happy with the results."

"So, no more filming today?" I asked, hopeful.

"We'll keep Steve and Luther here. They'll stay out of your way and get more shots of the baking. At lunch, I'll interview more of the diners to get their take on the food. Nigel gave me a list of questions." He fumbled in the pockets of his tweed blazer. "Meanwhile, I've got an errand of my own to run. Steve, you good without me?"

The cameraman nodded, somber.

"Great. I'll be back in time for lunch." Frank hurried from the kitchen.

"Don't mind me." Steve brushed a dusting of flour off his photographer's vest.

In the dining area, someone dinged the counter bell.

"I'll get it." Abril whisked through the swinging door.

"That pie oven is a great visual," the cameraman said. "I've never seen one that big. I'd like to get some shots of you removing pies."

"I'm behind on my crust count." Charlene stalked into the flour-work room and slammed the door. The utensils and pans hanging on the nearby wall rattled.

I glanced into the oven. "You'll have to wait a few minutes. None of the pies are ready for extraction yet."

"Ready for extraction. Good one." The cameraman shot me a pained smile. "And I'm sorry I accused you of sabotaging the show. I wasn't thinking straight. I haven't been thinking straight since . . ." He coughed and looked to the alleyway door.

"It's all right. I understand." I paused, my voice softening. "I can't imagine how difficult this must be for you."

He shook his head. "I want to work. If I wasn't working, I'd be sitting in my hotel room drinking. Regina wouldn't want that."

"I'm sorry I didn't get a chance to know your wife better." I had to figure out a way to ask him about Ilsa. Ray was being questioned by the police, and someone on the crew had locked me inside a burning room. But the thought of sticking my nose into such a private matter made my stomach writhe.

"Regina was an amazing woman," he said. "Nothing got her down."

"She must have been, to keep Ilsa on the show after everything."

Steve lowered the camera. "Ilsa?"

Ruthless. I would be ruthless. I gritted my teeth. "I heard about the affair."

"That's over," he said, looking everywhere but at me. He dug into the pockets of his khaki vest. "It's been over for a year now. And yes, if you're wondering, Regina did know, and she forgave us both. Ask Ilsa if you don't believe me."

I blew out my breath. That had gone easier than expected. "I believe you. Do the police know?"

He shuddered. "I hope not. If the police find out, it will only muddy the waters. Ilsa had nothing to do with Regina's death. I'm telling you, we were over and done. The police should be looking at . . ." He clamped his mouth shut. "Never mind."

"Looking at whom?" I asked. "If you know something, you should probably tell the police."

"It's nothing."

"Are you sure?"

"Yes. It's even older news than Ilsa and I."

"The police are considering this a murder investigation. Someone burned your equipment and nearly killed me. If you know something, tell them. The sooner the police sort this out, the safer everyone will be."

"I'm sure they know about Luther by now."

"Luther?"

As if summoned, the sound tech ambled through the swinging door. The bottom buttons on his Hawaiian shirt gaped, exposing his hairy stomach. "How's it going in here?"

"Fantastic," Steve said to him, "since you don't have to be involved."

"Why not?" I asked.

Luther tapped his headset. "No sound necessary for the background shots. Hey, Frank called. He wants us to join Ilsa's shopping expedition."

Annoyance creased Steve's brow, but he nodded. "You know the location?"

"I wouldn't be much good if I didn't." Without waiting for a response, Luther exited the kitchen, the door swinging behind him.

"See you later," Steve said. He paused by the door. "And let's just say this wouldn't be Luther's first time playing with fire." He disappeared through the door.

My brows furrowed. What was *that* supposed to mean?

I peeked into the industrial oven. Grabbing the paddle off the wall, I whisked pies from the oven and slid them onto the tiered cooling racks.

Abril and Petronella walked into the kitchen. "Is he gone for good?" Abril asked.

"He's gone for now," I said. "Is that why you wanted to work the counter? To avoid him?"

"I'm sorry," Abril said. "I know no one will see my face, but it feels strange to have a camera aimed in my direction."

"I think it's cool," Petronella said. "We're gonna be infamous."

"Thank you both for hanging in there," I said. "This is definitely above and beyond the call of duty."

"I like working here," Abril said. "I want Pie Town to do well, and if that means a reality TV show . . ." She exhaled heavily. "I'll do it."

The counter bell dinged. "I'll get that." I hustled into the dining room. It was too early for the lunch rush, and only half the seats were filled. Marla still sat like a barnacle at the center table and sipped coffee.

Gordon stood at the register, his handsome face serious.

In spite of everything, I smiled. I might not know exactly where we stood, but there was just something about his firm ruggedness that was irresistible.

"Is your father here?" he asked.

"Frank?" I was suddenly too hot, though the overhead fans were spinning and the air conditioners humming. "No. He stepped out but said he'd be back for lunch."

Gordon nodded. "We need to talk."

CHAPTER 12

Forks clinked on plates, coffee mugs rattled, the sounds of a regular day at the pie shop. But inside me, everything had stilled. "About the murder? Are you back on the case?" I asked. *Please tell me you're back on the case.* I pressed one hand atop the counter and leaned toward the detective.

"No." A muscle pulsed in Gordon's jaw, but he looked crisp in his blue suit. The badge clipped to his belt glinted at the opening of his sports jacket. A bulge at his other hip gave away his holstered weapon.

"This is awful." I reached to claw my hands through my hair, and then remembered I was wearing a chignon and a net. So I settled for wringing my Pie Town apron. This would be the second time Gordon had lost a case to Chief Shaw, because of me.

The diners along the counter watched us covertly.

"I suppose you haven't heard anything about Ray then," I said in a lower voice.

"I heard he was brought in for questioning."

"It's nuts. Ray has no reason to hurt the *Pie Hard* crew. He's no crazed stalker." Though I wondered if he'd given the police his "walking for exercise" excuse the night he'd found Regina's body. If he had, and they didn't believe it—

"That isn't why I came to talk to you. Have you spoken to your . . . ?" He trailed off. "Can we speak in private?"

Stomach tight, I opened the Dutch door and nodded to the short hallway leading to the kitchen, the bathrooms, my office.

He followed me into the hall, and we paused outside the office door.

"Have I talked to my father?" I asked.

He nodded.

"Yes," I said. "It looks like he really is my dad." I wasn't sure how I felt about that, and I gnawed my bottom lip. There was a lot of anger still festering, but a part of me had always wanted us to connect. "The worst of it is, I'm starting to feel sorry for him."

"You are?" He bent his head to me, his gaze probing.

"I guess he and my mother broke up after he got himself into trouble gambling. Frank says he and my mom both agreed it would be best. But I can't be sure if he's telling the truth. My mother never spoke much about him, and I couldn't bring myself to ask."

"I don't know what to say. I can't imagine what it would feel like to be abandoned by a parent. But I do know that you've been amazing about it all."

"Have I?" I laughed bitterly. "I'm still not ready to forgive Frank, even if what he said is true. I've spent too many years despising him." I sighed. "But I was a kid. Of course I didn't have the whole story. I only saw the aftermath. Maybe I haven't been fair." The adult, intelligent thing to do would be to forgive. Seeing Frank in person—as a person—lightened some of the anger, but I wasn't there yet.

"Hm." He stared at his polished shoes.

"Thanks for letting me vent." He might not be my boyfriend, but he was a good person. And I still hadn't given up hope. "You said you wanted to talk to me about something?"

"What?" He looked up. "Oh. It's not important. Look, I should go." But he didn't move.

Our gazes locked, and my heart jolted. His green eyes seemed to darken.

I swayed toward him.

"See you." He turned on his heel and walked into the diner.

I pressed my palms to my cheeks. *Ugh!* I'd misread that situation. What else had I misunderstood?

Okay, be practical. He might not be my boyfriend, but he was a source. "Wait!" I scurried after him and stopped behind the cash register. "What about Ray?"

"I'll see what I can find out," he said over his shoulder and walked out the glass front door.

Chagrined, I watched the door close slowly in his wake. He'd sent postcards! Was he interested in me or not? In any case, I wasn't going to chase after him.

Charlene pushed the kitchen door ajar with her shoulder and fiddled with the latch on her gold watch. "What did Carmichael want?"

"I'm not sure," I said.

"So, he just came to see you? I told you he liked you."

I cleared my throat. "I don't think so." His asking after my father had been more than the casual inquiry of a friend. But Gordon had said he was off the case, so it couldn't be related to that. Could it? I shook myself.

She smiled. "I remember when my husband and I first met. He took his sweet time too. But it was worth it." She blinked rapidly and rubbed the corner of one eye.

Heart squeezing, I glanced away, giving her a moment. "What are you still doing here?"

"I stayed to see if I can—" She went rigid. "Marla!"

Blandly, Marla looked up from her coffee. "Yes, Charlene?"

"I knew it!" Charlene thundered through the Dutch doors like a big-rig with a killer clown at the wheel. She slammed her hand on Marla's table. The salt and pepper shakers rattled. "I should have known you'd horn in on *Pie Hard*."

"What did you expect when you were humble-bragging all over the Internet?" Marla fluffed her hair, exposing the diamonds winking on her earlobes. "We both know who's more photogenic. I have so much experience on camera."

"On your own stupid web show. That doesn't count! Now, scat!"

She sipped her coffee. "But that cameraman might come back."

I glanced at Frank, who was sipping coffee at the counter. "I don't think there'll be any more filming today," I said.

"Good," Marla said. "I have my own show to shoot. So many interesting news items today. Ta!" She strolled from the restaurant.

"She's going to blog or vlog or whatever about Ray being taken to the station," I fretted.

"It's only a webcast," Charlene said.

"And the Internet is forever. This is not good."

"It's Marla. I'm outta here. Frederick is peeved I've been spending so much time away."

Charlene's cat, Frederick, spent most of his life comatose. I doubted he noticed her absence, but I nodded.

Charlene left. Customers swept in. Customers swept out, and the end of the day found me sweeping up beneath Frank's watchful gaze.

"Maybe I should see you home." Frank straightened the lapels of his tweed jacket. "I don't like that someone locked you in that burning room."

I pushed a mop around the checkerboard floor. "I didn't like it either, but it was most likely a case of wrong time, wrong place."

He cocked his sleek, dark head. Bits of gray flecked his sideburns. "How do you figure that?"

"Because I don't know anyone on the crew. No one has any reason to hurt me."

"Your business must be worth something. Have you got a will?"

"No." I plunged the mop into a bucket filled with sudsy water and wrung it out.

"I guess that makes me your sole heir—once your estate makes its way through the courts. I've heard that's a long and arduous process. You should get a trust."

I resumed mopping, squatting to get beneath the tables in the booths. Was that why he'd come? To check my net worth? "Are you saying you're a suspect in my attempted murder?" I asked tightly.

He grinned. "No. As amazing as your pie shop is, I don't want it. I've seen the hours you work. Those five a.m. mornings! Ugh. Don't you have someone to do the cleaning for you?"

"Did Nigel tell you about my finances?"

He winced. "Broad outlines."

"Then you have your answer." Someday, I hoped I'd be able to afford more staff. Today was not that day.

He brightened. "He did say your numbers were normal for a business this age, though you might have expanded a mite too quickly. Why did you buy the pie van when you only had one wholesaling client?"

"My car died, and I needed new transport." I grunted and scrubbed at a difficult stain. A chunk of hair fell into my eyes, and I didn't bother brushing it away. "Since I had to spend the money anyway, I figured I may as well think forward and get a van. I got it on the cheap."

"I should hope so. It's ancient."

A flush of heat rolled through me. "But if Nigel's implying I need more wholesaling clients, he's right. I'm just not sure how to get them."

Frank thumped his chest with one hand. "That's why we're here. We'll have Pie Town shipshape in no time."

I leaned on the mop. "But why are *you* here, Frank? Really."

"I've told you, I stayed to make sure you get home safely."

My question had been a bit more existential, but I let it go. "I'm not going home right away." My cell phone rang in my apron pocket. I dug it out. "Hello?"

"Val? It's Ray."

My shoulders slumped with relief. "They let you go. What happened?"

"The same questions over and over again. I'm kind of wiped. Can we do the Baker Street Baker thing tomorrow?"

For a moment I blanked. Did we have something planned? Then I figured he was speaking generally. "No problem. I'll see you then." We said our goodbyes and hung up.

Frank raised an elegant brow. "Have you got a date? That young detective, perhaps?"

I grimaced. I was so not going to talk about my lame love life with him. "No, I'm planning on tracking down your sound guy, Luther."

"He's not mine. I'm temporary help, remember? Why do you want to talk to him?"

"He said something interesting to me today, and I want to follow up on it."

"Interesting how?"

"Interesting regarding Regina's death," I hedged.

"Ah." He studied his empty coffee mug. "I wondered if you'd poke your nose into that."

My face tightened. "Meaning?"

"I read the newspaper articles, Val. I know about the murder earlier this year in your shop—everyone does. It's natural for you to take an interest, especially since your friend was arrested—"

"Taken in for questioning."

He raised his hands in a warding gesture. "Of course. But the point is, someone tried to hurt you last night. If that isn't a warning to back off, I don't know what is."

"Warning noted and ignored."

He snorted. "And where do you expect to find our assistant cameraman?"

"The cheapest bar in town."

Frank laughed. "You've pegged the man to a *t*. Why don't I come with you? I could use a drink, and I can be persuasive."

"Sure." I planned to invite Charlene, but I didn't think Frank was telling me the whole truth about his presence in San Nicholas. Maybe a drink would loosen his tongue. In vino veritas, and all that jazz. Besides, if things went sideways, Charlene could always follow up with Luther.

I finished cleaning and grabbed my purse from the office.

Frank lounged by the front door and swung his key ring around his index finger. "I'll drive."

"Why don't you follow me?" I didn't want to be dependent on Frank for a ride.

"As long as I don't have to get in your van—"

"What's wrong with my van?"

He shot me a pained look.

"The pink matches our pie boxes," I said, defensive.

"It's not the color that's off-putting, it's the age. That van's older than I am."

I doubted that. "Fine. We're headed to the British pub. It's on Highway One, on the way to your hotel. Do you know it?"

"How could anyone miss it? It's got a double-decker bus parked outside."

I watched him step into a silver Tesla, and for a moment I

regretted my urge for independence. Coaching addicts must pay well. Then I walked around the corner and into the alley. The sun was low on the horizon, and the alley deep with chill shade. Suppressing a shiver, I stepped into my van.

I pulled onto Main Street, and Frank slid from his spot.

Traffic on the highway was thick, but mostly in the other direction—beachgoers returned home from their Saturday in the sun, windows down, surfboards strapped to the tops of their cars.

Five minutes later, I pulled into the pub's gravel driveway. A red callbox stood outside the pub—a two-story, yellow building with a peaked roof. A crimson double-decker bus parked to one side of the pub.

Frank joined me outside the open front door. Music, laughter, and warmth streamed from inside.

Frank bowed with a flourish. "After you, my lady."

I walked inside. Round, metal platters dotted the ceiling. Framed photos and soccer jerseys and maps of Great Britain filled the dark wooden walls.

I scanned the long bar but didn't see Luther slouched over one of the stools.

Frank and I wandered through the restaurant. We finally found Luther on the rear, outdoor patio. He sat alone in a green plastic chair in the farthest corner from the fire pit.

Zipping my Pie Town hoodie to my collarbone, I walked to the matching plastic table.

Luther sat with his back to a makeshift fence of empty, metal beer barrels.

"Hi, Luther," I said. "May we join you?"

"Yes, you may," he said in the slow, distinct speech of someone who's had too much to drink.

We pulled up plastic chairs and sat.

"Can I buy you a cup of coffee?" I asked hopefully. I wanted the truth from Luther but not to become his enabler.

"Beer," he said, and I sighed. "The waitress knows what I've got."

Frank rubbed his hands together. "What's good here, Val?" He flagged down a young, blond waitress in shorts and a tight, white t-shirt.

"I recommend the fish and chips. Or the burgers." It was hard to go wrong with burgers, and the pub packed them between pretzel buns loaded with cheese and other toppings.

We placed our orders, and the waitress disappeared into the throng.

"I hear you had a good day with Ilsa," Frank said.

Luther meditated on that. "Steve got some decent shots," he finally said.

"Did she find what she needed?" Frank asked.

Luther shrugged. "Dunno. Ask her."

"Has the insurance come through on the equipment you lost?" I asked, knowing it hadn't. No insurance company worked that quickly, especially when arson was involved. I didn't know how else to ease into the subject. Steve hinted that Luther had been involved in a fire before, but how do you accuse someone of arson without really accusing them, especially when you didn't really know what you were accusing them of?

"Nah," Luther drawled. "They'll take their time. What do they care who suffers? They're the man." He pointed at Frank. "And now you're the man."

Frank's brows lifted.

"Was Regina the man?" I asked.

His broad face crumpled. "Regina . . . Regina. Regina was all heart."

"She could be tough though," I said. "I saw it in Pie Town."

Luther stared at the beer barrel wall. "Yeah, well. Some people don't respond to carrots. They need sticks."

"People like Ilsa?" I asked.

The waitress returned with our drinks, and we fell silent. I fiddled with my beer mat, impatient for her to leave.

She centered Frank's Bloody Mary on the mat. Set my beer on the mat. Edged my water away from my elbow. Clunked Luther's beer on the table, frowned, and flounced away.

"Ilsa?" I prompted.

"Ilsa's Ilsa." The sound man pointed his wavering finger at me. "And don't you forget it."

"Who else did Regina need to get tough with?" I took a sip of the beer and put it down, centering it carefully on the paper mat.

"Regina sure didn't take any guff from Nigel. She had his number. Oh, yeah."

"His number?" I asked.

"Not the poster boy everyone thinks," Luther whispered.

"Who is? We all have moments we're not proud of." Frank met my gaze.

I looked away and sipped my water.

"I'm sure even you've had a few, Luther," he continued.

"A few?" He snorted into his beer. "Try a lifetime. Never should have married that . . ." He belched and swore colorfully. "Never trust a woman. They'll ruin you."

"Even Regina?" I asked.

His eyes glazed. "Regina was different. Good woman. Classy."

"I can't imagine how difficult her death must be for Steve," I said. "Is he okay working?"

"Says he is," Luther said. "Hard to tell."

I turned the mug on the beer mat. "Steve told me he and Ilsa were long over," I said casually.

Frank raised his brows.

"I guess," Luther said.

"Steve also told me you've had some experience with fires," I said.

Luther's mug crashed to the brick, and I started in my chair. Clearly, I'd hit a nerve.

A seagull squawked and flapped into the air. It resettled on the wall of barrels.

The assistant cameraman cupped his hands in front of his mouth. "Man down."

"I'll get you another." I turned in my seat, looking for a waitress.

Ilsa stood behind me in her pastry chef whites, a determined expression on her face.

"Ilsa!" Frank rose and drew a plastic chair from a nearby table. "Join us."

She adjusted it and sat. "I will," she said in her French accent. The baker folded her arms over her chest. "Why are you interrogating Luther? I don't like."

"Interrogating?" I asked. "The last few days have been—"

"You are snooping," she said. "Leave Luther alone. It is not fair, when he is in this condition."

I flushed. I *had* offered him coffee.

"If you want to know something," she said, "ask me."

"Ask you?" I said.

"Me."

"Okay." I straightened in the plastic chair. "You've missed a filming day. Where were you?"

She shrugged. "I didn't think we were filming, so I went to the beach."

"Steve said you and he ended things a year ago," I said, hoping to catch her off guard.

She nodded. "Yes. And?"

I blinked. She seemed unfazed I knew about the affair. "Did Regina know?" I asked.

"He told her about us and begged for forgiveness for

his . . ." Ilsa's mouth compressed. "How do you say . . . ? Slip? She asked him to break it off, and he did."

I stared. "And everyone was able to continue working together?"

One corner of her mouth slipped upward. "You Americans are so puritanical. But Regina was a woman of the world. She understood her role in our affair and took responsibility."

"That was big of her," I muttered.

Doran, in all black, wandered into the patio. He scanned it as if looking for a seat.

My breath caught. Both he and Frank had turned up in Pie Town the day of Regina's murder. And now Doran was here. True, this was a small town, and dining options limited. But even in a place like San Nicholas, running into him over and over seemed weird. What was he doing here?

His gaze met mine and shifted away. Doran tossed his head, a raven's wing of hair falling across his eyes. He turned and strode inside the pub.

"What's wrong?" Frank touched my arm.

"What?" I asked. "Nothing. I was just thinking about what Ilsa said. What role did Regina play in her husband's cheating?"

Ilsa looked away. "I misspoke. English is not my first language."

She seemed to speak it pretty well when she wanted to. "It sounds like Regina had a generous heart." The producer seemed to have forgiven both Ilsa and her husband, and she hadn't seemed like a pushover. I gnawed my bottom lip. Did I really think forgiveness was weak? Was that why I was holding a grudge against my father?

"Yes," Ilsa said.

I glanced up, startled. Ilsa hadn't read my mind, she was responding to the last thing I'd said.

She looked at her hands atop the plastic table. They were covered with purple and reddish burn marks.

I glanced at my own scars—testimony to working in a kitchen.

"Her heart was big," Ilsa said. "Bigger than anyone imagined. Steve was right to do as she wished. Our affair was short and stupid and meaningless. His relationship with Regina was real."

Maybe Ilsa was a more generous person than I'd first thought too. Then again, it was easy to be magnanimous when your rival was dead.

CHAPTER 13

Frank insisted on following me to my tiny house on the bluff. Even though I still felt awkward with him, I was glad to have him behind me on the lonely drive home. He parked his Tesla beside my van, stepped out and surveyed the milling women, the yurt, and the tiki torches.

"It's a long story," I said.

He barked a laugh. "It would have to be."

A waning moon rode low above the obsidian ocean. The night air raised gooseflesh on my skin, and I rubbed my arms.

"I'll let you get inside and warm up," he said. "We'll be doing a solid day of filming tomorrow, so be ready."

"Great!" Great, great, great. I felt the same about the show as I did about Frank—torn. I'd committed to *Pie Hard*. I wasn't quite ready to do that for Frank.

He watched me climb the two steps into my tiny house, and then he got into the sports car and drove down the narrow road.

Hurriedly, I shut the door, opened my laptop in the dining

nook, and searched for info on the *Pie Hard* crew. Being TV personalities, they weren't hard to find. There were almost too many articles—gossip about on-set and off-set frictions. Ilsa vs. Nigel. The crew vs. Ilsa. But there were no big reveals—it was all petty stuff about who had the bigger trailer or was the more demanding diva.

I frowned. The "diva" label didn't seem fair to either Nigel or Ilsa, though the pastry chef could be razor-tongued.

Something small and clawed scampered across my roof, and I glanced up. "Squirrels," I muttered. At least I hoped it was a squirrel and not a rat.

Giving up on the cast, I focused my search on Regina and her husband, Steve. The two had worked together for decades, but their careers had taken off with the advent of reality TV. One of their early shows, *Movie Myths*, analyzed movie stunts and determined whether they were realistic or not. The only scandal from that show was when shrapnel hit a stuntman after a boat explosion. The injury wasn't serious.

I cocked my head. They filmed *Movie Myths* not far from here—up the coast. I was surprised they'd gotten the permits. California was nothing if not ecologically correct, and blowing up a boat would have made a major mess.

Thirty minutes later, I learned Luther had joined the Steve and Regina team on their next reality project—one of those home improvement shows that achieved impossible home makeovers over the course of a weekend.

Yawning, I walked into my tiny kitchen and fetched a mug from the cupboard.

Someone banged on my door.

The mug slipped from my hand and bounced off my fingertips. I caught it just inches from the laminate floor and exhaled slowly.

Bored with waiting, Charlene stepped inside and planted her fists on her slim hips.

Her white cat, Frederick, draped over her shoulder like a stole. His purr made the shipping container vibrate.

"Good," she said. "You're back. I was starting to worry."

"Tea?"

"Why not?"

I filled another mug with water and set both in the microwave. "Frank and I went to the British pub. Ilsa and Luther were there. Want anything?"

She shook her head, her loose, white curls dancing. "Ilsa and Luther? Now there's an unlikely couple."

"I don't think they're together. Not that way, I mean." I filled her in on what I'd learned, which amounted to "not much:" an unsubstantiated hint that Luther had experience with fires, and that Ray was free.

Another knock, softer this time—Charlene reached behind her and opened the door.

Hair done up in a loose bun, Maureen stood at the base of the steps. She wore a red and black caftan with a coin bra over it—like a steampunk belly dancer. A coin belt jingled about her broad hips. The red-headed goddess handed Charlene a couple of photos. "These are the pictures I was telling you about."

The microwave dinged.

Charlene jammed the photos into the pocket of her green, knit jacket. "Thanks!" She slammed the door shut.

I winced. "Charlene! You almost hit her in the face."

"She's fine." Charlene busied herself pooling Frederick on the table. "You were saying about the pub?"

"I'd finished. What are those pictures she gave you?"

"What, these?" She blinked and patted her pocket. "Nothing. Goddess stuff. You wouldn't be interested."

What was she hiding? "What's in the photos?"

"Nothing to do with the case," she said, bracing her elbows on my kitchen counter. "Just some personal business. So how are you and Frank getting on?"

"Fine, I guess. It's still weird. I want to do the right thing, but it's so hard to forgive. I almost wish he were a bad guy. Then I could despise him and not feel so bad about it."

"On the bright side, he still could be a killer. He was gone from your life for a long time. Who knows what he's been up to?"

"That's not a bright side, and you're changing the subject. You're hiding those pictures. What's the deal?"

She turned to my tiny dining table and stroked Frederick's white fur. "I don't know what you're talking about."

"Charlene . . ."

"Oh, all right." She faced me and braced her hands on her hips. "They're photos of aliens in a tree."

I blinked. "What do you mean *in a tree*?"

"You know, in the actual wood."

"Do you mean, petrified aliens?" Was that a thing?

She looked at me sideways. "I don't know about petrified, but don't worry; the photos aren't from around here. They're from Australia."

I stiffened. "Why would I be worried?"

She angled her chin down. "Everyone knows you've got alienophobia."

"Everyone?" I laughed shortly, unsmiling.

On the table, Frederick's ears twitched.

My wacky phobia wasn't something I advertised. The only reason Charlene knew about it was that she once dragged me on a UFO hunt. My phobia was only a mild case. It wasn't like I had a panic attack every time a raccoon waltzed across my rooftop—which was a good thing, because these woods were raccoon central. And was *alienophobia* truly a word?

"I might have told Maureen not to show you the photo," Charlene admitted. "And then she might have asked why. You can't lie to one of those goddess types. They just *know*."

"You told—" I shook my head. " I think I can look at a picture of wood without freaking out." It was just a photo. So what if my pulse was speeding? If my breathing had quickened, I could chalk that up to Charlene's blood-pressure-raising ramblings.

Her blue eyes widened innocently. "Oh? So, you want to see it? You're sure?"

I busied myself making the tea. "What is it? An odd pattern in the wood grain?"

"You have to look at it to know."

I shrugged. "Never mind." I didn't need to prove myself. "There's no point."

"Are you sure?" she asked.

I cleared my throat. "Anyway, Frank seems to be making a real effort to connect."

Her brow furrowed. "He ought to."

"But I can't stop thinking that this reconnection is conveniently timed with a murder we happen to be investigating."

She crossed her arms over her chest. "You think he's got something to hide?"

"Don't you?"

She slumped into a chair beside the fold-out table. "Yeah. I do. I'm sorry, Val. I want this to work out for you. He's your father. But—"

"But you don't believe it's an accident he's crawled back into my life now. Neither do I." So why was disappointment curdling in my gut? I'd known what kind of guy he was for twenty-five years.

"We'll figure this out," she said, her tone soothing.

I swallowed my angst. "There's something else. That guy, Doran, showed up at the pub."

"The ninja with the hair that's always falling in his eye?" she asked.

"That's the one." I sat across from her and set her mug beside Frederick. I turned mine in my hands. "He's not from around here, but he keeps turning up."

"So he *has* been following you. Isn't it weird when something you joke about winds up being true?" She snapped her fingers. "Oh! What if Frank's here to protect you from the ninja?"

A headache sprouted behind my eyeballs. "He's not a ninja!"

Frederick raised his head and shot me an irritated look.

I forced my grip on the mug to relax and took deep breaths. "Sorry. You know that already. I'm a little tense."

She patted my arm. "Who wouldn't be under the circumstances? You're under a lot of pressure, what with the Pie Town finances, and Carmichael avoiding you, and the camera putting on ten pounds."

"Gordon's not avoiding me." Was he?

She jabbed a finger at me. "Ah, ha! You *are* worried about finances."

"The budget's a little tight, that's all. The finances are fine. But I do think it's strange that this ninja—" My gaze flicked to the white-painted ceiling. *Don't encourage her.* "This guy keeps showing up. Especially after Regina's death and the fire."

"I'll ask Ray to see what he can dig up about this ninja online. He looked like a Millennial, so he's probably all over the Internet. The younger generation can be so narcissistic."

I smothered a laugh. So sayeth the woman who'd lured a reality TV show to San Nicholas.

She took a sip of tea and made a face. "Tastes healthy."

Frederick's stomach rumbled.

"I'd better get home and feed the cat." Lovingly, she

picked him off the table and draped him over her shoulder. "Will you be okay here alone?"

"I doubt I'm in any danger with a yurt full of goddess worshipers on my doorstep."

"Then I'll see you in the morning." Yawning, Charlene ambled from the tiny home. The door banged shut behind her.

Even though it wasn't that late, I changed into my pie-patterned PJs and settled down on my futon to think. My brain tank was on empty. When I should have been pondering the murder, all I could think about was my father.

Someone rapped lightly on my door.

"It's open." Rising to my feet, I stepped to the other side of the bookcase that acted as a wall for my bedroom.

Maureen stuck her head inside, the bells hemming her black caftan sleeves tinkling. "We're about to start the dancing. Do you want to join us? It's lots of fun."

"Thanks for the invite, but I've already changed into my pajamas."

"Don't let that stop you. I'm wearing a coin bra." She shimmied, and the coins tinkled over her caftan.

I smiled. "How could I compete with the costumes?"

"We're cooperative, not competitive. But if you don't feel up to it, there's no pressure. Can I ask you something though?"

I plucked my laptop off the table and folded it shut. "Sure."

She stepped inside my tiny house. "You thought the yurt delivery truck was a UFO, didn't you?"

I stared, thunderstruck. I hadn't even admitted that to Charlene. "How did you . . . ?"

"I'm a psychiatrist. You'd be surprised how many people come to me with abduction experiences."

Abductions? "I've never been abducted," I said, my voice rising. "I just watched *X-Files* when I was too young."

"In any case, you have nothing to feel embarrassed about—many people share your phobia."

Outside, someone began drumming. Another drummer joined in, the beats playing off each other.

I coughed. "I'm not embarrassed, just impressed you connected the dots." I scrambled for a change of subject. "Can I ask you a question?"

"Certainly."

"My assistant manager is studying to be an undertaker. She needs to interview a psychiatrist about the mourning process. Would you have time to talk to her?"

She pulled a business card from the bell sleeve of her embroidered caftan. "Give her my number." She glanced around my tiny home—kitchen, work/dining area, bookshelf blocking the bedroom. "Look, if you want to talk about it while I'm here, I won't charge you. But there's much cheaper therapy to be had. There's nothing better to get you out of a bad mood than dancing, especially in your pajamas."

I forced a smile. "Thanks, but I'm beat."

"If you change your mind, come on out." She backed from the trailer and shut the door behind her.

I returned to my futon and picked up the tea cooling on the end table. Through the glass doors, the women danced and whirled, veils flying in a colorful blaze, and for a moment, I regretted not joining in.

Mug in hand, I walked outside and waved at the Goddess Gals. The air was crisp with salt and eucalyptus, and I inhaled, feeling the pound of the drumbeat reverberate through my bones.

In the corner of my gaze, something shifted. I whipped my head toward the motion.

A tall shadow, eerily elongated, moved through the eucalyptus trees.

Heart thumping, I glanced toward the Goddess Gals. One

of them could have gone into the woods to hug a tree, but why now, when the party was in full swing?

The shadow vanished into the thicket.

A breeze lifted my loose hair, pebbling my flesh.

I'd swear the wind carried a whisper of laughter.

CHAPTER 14

Unable to sleep, I arrived at Pie Town an hour earlier than usual and parked in the narrow alley. Stars glittered in the ribbon of sky between the brick buildings. Light streamed from Pie Town's kitchen window, making golden trapezoids along the garbage bins.

I clutched the steering wheel in a vise-grip.

I'd turned that light off.

I knew I'd turned it off. Last night Frank followed me from room to room, complaining, while I double-checked that the lights were off and locks bolted.

My breath made a noisy trail in the frigid van.

Someone was in Pie Town.

I shook myself. It was probably Charlene. I usually beat her to work, but she had her own key.

I slipped from the van and crept to the door. *It's only Charlene.* I tested the knob.

Locked.

Trying not to make a sound, I unlocked the door and sidled inside. Crates of fresh raspberries sat stacked on a metal counter. A delivery man must have arrived early, and

Charlene had accepted the supplies. My shoulders slumped. So, not a robber. I'd been paranoid.

Three pies sat atop the pie safe, where the staff put day-olds they were taking home. A clunk emerged through the closed door of the flour-work room.

Just because you're paranoid, doesn't mean you shouldn't be careful, and I shot the deadbolt on the metal alley door. Dropping my purse on the metal countertop by the sink, I walked to the flour-work door, opened it.

Charlene, a jacket over her apron, her hands coated with flour, glanced up from the long, floured table. "You're letting the cold air out." A delicate, black net encased her fluffy white hair. I provided disposable hairnets, but she insisted on bringing her own. And also that black was sexier.

I stepped inside and gently shut the heavy, metal door. "What are you doing here so early?" I asked in a low voice.

"Couldn't sleep." She dumped a bowl of chopped butter into a giant mixing bowl mounded with flour. "You?"

"Same."

Into the bowl, she drizzled a brownish liquid from a bottle hand-labeled *SECRET INGREDIENT*. "This way, we can get a jump on work before filming starts."

"Yeah." I made no move to leave. "I want to believe Frank," I said, plaintive, "but I can't. I've spent my life thinking he's a lying rat. His appearance here now is just so . . . coincidental."

"Maybe he's a secret agent," Charlene said. "That would be exciting. It would also explain his mysterious appearance here right before a murder. He's trying to stop that ninja. Or there could be another agent on the *Pie Hard* crew. Maybe KGB?"

"They're called the FSB now." I was starting to get the hang of Charlene's conspiracies. I didn't think she believed them, but they were more fun than facing the truth.

Her face fell, and she gave a quick shake of her head.

"The secret agent theory won't fly. Any secret government agency worth its salt would have created a false Internet history for Frank if that was the case."

"Right."

"Or . . . Frank is presenting himself as himself, so he *wouldn't* have a false history. He couldn't be your father if he was pretending to be someone else. What irony. Only his real identity can get him close to the KGB agent."

I tried to unknot Charlene's logic, gave up. "I don't think the KG—FSB theory works either. Why would a foreign agent infiltrate the *Pie Hard* crew?" I asked. "To steal your secret recipe for the Russians?"

"I'll bet it's that kraut pastry chef—"

"Ilsa's from France."

"Her first and last name are German. That's just the sort of mistake the Russians would make. Ilsa could be the spy." She edged closer to me and glanced around the flour-work room. "I think she figured out my secret ingredient," she whispered.

Anyone with a working nose could figure out her secret ingredient was apple cider vinegar. "Assassins, ninjas, spies . . . are there any illegal professions we've forgotten?"

"Mafia?"

"That's about as likely as a UFO abduction." I laid my hand on the kitchen door, cold beneath my palm.

"I don't think I've heard you joke about aliens before." She emerged from behind the table. "Maybe having those goddesses around has been good for you. You might even loosen up, take a chance, try new things." She leaned toward me and clasped her hands under her chin.

"I'm not going to Area 51 with you, Charlene."

She sniffed and dropped her hands to her sides. "You can be such a stick in the mud."

"I'm not totally risk-averse. I did open a pie shop."

"And what have you done for yourself lately?"

I bit the inside of my cheek. Maybe I should have gone dancing with the goddesses last night.

"Take 'em off," she said.

"What?"

"Your shoes. Take them off."

"Why?"

"Sheesh," she said. "You act like I invited you to walk across hot coals with Tony Robbins."

She once had. "I just don't see the point."

"Don't you trust me?"

"Is that the point? And there's flour all over the floor. I'm not taking off my shoes."

"Take. Them. Off."

"Fine." Leaning against the door, I pulled off one tennis shoe, then the other. "Happy?"

"Socks too."

I tugged off my socks and shoved them inside the empty shoes.

"Now walk around," she said.

I walked around the long table, the flour cool and soft between my toes. "Now what? Am I supposed to have some sort of Zen revelation?"

She grinned. "I just wanted to see if I could make you do it. You're such a sucker."

I rolled my eyes. "I'll let you get back to the crusts." Grabbing my sneakers, I opened the door and strode into the kitchen.

A slim figure in black, face covered by a ski mask, froze beside my antique pie safe.

Fear screwed me to the rubber floor mat.

We stared at each other for a long moment.

Then the moment broke, and my nostrils flared. "Stop!"

He whipped around. Grabbing a day-old pie from the top of the safe, he hurled it at me like a discus thrower.

I shrieked and ducked as the pie whizzed over my head.

It splattered against a cupboard.

I threw one shoe, the other. Both sailed past his left shoulder.

Charlene raced from the flour-work room and hurled a spatula. "Take that, Russkie scum!"

It pinged harmlessly off the burglar's chest.

"Damn." She raced inside the flour-work room.

He dashed for the alley door. Not noticing I'd bolted it, he struggled with the handle. He swore and ran back toward the pie safe and the swinging kitchen door to the dining area.

"Oh, no you don't." I wasn't going to let this jerk get away. I'd had enough of being smoked out and scared. I grabbed a skillet off its wall hook and flung it. The pan zipped over the black-clad intruder's head. Even though I couldn't see him through the ski mask, I'd swear, he grinned.

The pan ricocheted off the ginormous pie oven and hit him low on the back of the head.

He grunted and staggered into the pie safe. He fired two more day-old pies at me, discus-style.

I dropped into a crouch.

The pies hit the cupboards. They smacked wetly to the floor.

Clearly, he hadn't spent his youth watching *Three Stooges* movies, or he'd know the proper way to throw a pie. I peeked over the work island.

He grabbed a crate of berries and hurled it in my direction. The wooden crate skimmed low, skipped across the butcher-block work island, and hit the counter behind me. Raspberries exploded from the crate, scattering across the black floor mats.

"You bastard!" Raspberries weren't cheap! I grabbed a sauce pot and chucked it across the work island, but not quickly enough.

He ducked. The pot banged against the wall and clattered to the floor.

He grabbed a glass measuring cup from a nearby counter and pitched it at my head. The measuring cup slowed, hanging in the air. I could count every rotation. Then I remembered to stop the special effects fascination and start moving. I dropped low. The measuring cup shattered against the wall, and I shrieked. Something stung my cheek.

Charlene barreled from the flour-work room and brandished a rolling pin. She flung it like a throwing star. It skimmed in front of his nose.

The intruder jerked backwards, slipped, fell. He vanished behind a work table and as quickly sprang to his feet.

I reached for another skillet, and discovered there weren't any. A thick Vogue magazine lay on the counter near Charlene.

"Magazine!" I shouted.

"Yeah!" She tossed it to me.

I threw it, The magazine fluttered, rustling like a bird over the work island. It struck his head and fell harmlessly to the floor.

"You picked the wrong damn kitchen!" Charlene hollered.

He staggered to the alley door and struggled with the lock.

I wasn't going to let him get away. I raced across the kitchen. My feet hit a slippery patch and flew from beneath me. I fell, catching a metal counter on the way down with my armpit. Pain jolted through my chest. My feet skidded, cartoonish, on a patch of un-matted floor.

The burglar unbolted the door and flung himself into the alley.

"Run! Run. you coward!" Charlene shouted.

I straightened, triumph surging through my veins. "That's right!" I wasn't going to get pushed around or burned out again. I whooped, turning to Charlene. "Yippee-pie-ay, mother—"

Something hit me in the face. My vision darkened, and I staggered. I gasped, spluttering.

A pie fell at my feet.

I wiped my hand across my eyes, and it came away cherry. "Why'd you do that?" I gaped at Charlene.

Her lips quivered. "Whoops. I might have gotten overly excited."

"You threw a pie at me!"

"Friendly fire. It happens."

"You did that on purpose." Something dropped to my shoulder, and I brushed a chunk of crust and cherry filling to the floor.

"Heat of battle. We should call the police."

"I will." The mat was unpleasantly slick, and I kept one hand on the counter for balance.

"Why are you walking that way? Are you hurt?" Her jaw sagged. "Your feet! You're cut!"

I looked down. My feet were stained crimson. "The raspberries," I said. "Why was that crate even open?"

"I might have put some in my yogurt for breakfast," Charlene admitted, grabbing a broom from one corner. "But it was only a few. And the delivery came early. You're lucky I was here to accept it."

Keeping the phone three inches from my sticky ear, I called the police and reported the intruder. While I wiped my face with a dish towel, the dispatcher promised to send someone right away. I hung up and brushed raspberry clots from my feet. The berry stain wouldn't come off as easily.

"Fire," Charlene said.

My throat tightened. I dropped the towel into the sink. "Where?"

"No, we need to check to make sure there's no fire. The last time you walked in on someone, the building was booby-trapped. What if someone—?"

"Charlene, go outside and wait." I hurried through the swinging door into the restaurant.

Ignoring my request, Charlene followed. No gas dripped from the pink booths. No sticks of dynamite topped the Formica tables.

I sped to my office and opened the door. "Nooooo," I howled.

The books and boxes that had been on the metal bookshelves were now on the floor. Straws in paper wrappings littered the linoleum. Drawers hung open from my desk. The closet door was open wide, revealing a tumble of overturned supply boxes and my small safe, which was thankfully closed.

At least my old computer was still in one piece. It was also on. I knew I should have password protected it.

Cursing, I sat at my desk and stared at the screen. None of the files were open, so I'd no idea what the intruder had seen. Why had he been snooping on my computer?

Someone pounded on the alley door, and we jumped.

"The police." I hurried into the kitchen and opened the door.

Jake, one of our regular delivery men, huffed inside carrying crates of fresh veggies. He brushed past me and thunked the crates on an open counter. The deliveryman lifted a clipboard from the top of the crates and extended it to me. "Here you . . ." His gaze traveled the kitchen. The crimson smears on the floor, the remains of pies spattering walls and tables, the scattered pans and cutlery. ". . . go."

"Thanks." I took the clipboard and hastily signed.

"Everything all right in here?" he asked, his biceps flexing.

"Fine," I chirped.

"Okay." He backed through the kitchen door and into the alley.

Charlene sniffed. "You think he'd never seen a pie fight before."

I shut the alley door, and there was another knock.

Startled, I yanked it open.

Glowering, Gordon stood in the doorway.

I cringed. "Oooh." I must have shut it in his face. "Sorry."

"What happened?" Beneath his suit jacket, his shirt collar was open, exposing a V of hair and a sliver of muscular chest.

"What are you doing here?" Charlene asked. "You don't work the early a.m."

"No, but the dispatcher knows to call me whenever there's a pie-related incident."

"A one-man Pie Town task force, eh?" Charlene asked.

One corner of his mouth quirked. "Something like that. I heard there was a break in?" His gaze traversed the wrecked kitchen.

Talking over each other, Charlene and I told him what happened. He took notes in a miniature leather-bound book.

He arched a brow. "And so you thought you'd throw pies at him?"

"Her," Charlene said.

"He started it," I said.

"I thought you weren't able to identify the intruder," he said to me.

"*She* was tall and slim," Charlene said. "It had to be Ilsa."

"It could have been a man or woman," I said. "And I didn't throw any pies. That would be wasteful." That hadn't stopped Charlene.

"It was self-defense," Charlene said, typing on her phone with her thumbs. "I grabbed whatever was handy."

"Are you tweeting this?" I asked, exasperated.

"Someone may know something," she said.

"Right," Gordon said. "Anything else that might help us I.D. him or her?"

Charlene drew back her shoulders and raised her chin. "Val hit him in the head with a skillet."

"Ouch." Gordon scribbled a note. "That'll leave a mark."

"It only grazed the back of his head," I said. "And it wasn't cast iron. It barely fazed him."

Two uniformed policemen arrived and peered in through the alleyway door. Gordon nodded to them. "B-and-E. Anything missing?" he asked me.

"Not that I could tell," Charlene said.

He shut his notebook and met my gaze. "All right. We'll print your office and the doors. I noticed some scratches on the rear lock."

My eyes widened. "The deadbolt."

"What about the deadbolt?" he asked.

"I bolted it after I came in, and he struggled with it when he was leaving. He must have been inside the whole time. I locked him in with us!"

"I'll dust the deadbolt for prints."

"I did notice he was wearing gloves," I said.

"We'll take the prints anyway," he said. "Maybe he removed them at some point. It's not easy typing with gloves on. And Val?" He leaned closer, his green eyes darkening.

My heart beat faster. "Yes?"

Slowly, he reached for me, and brushed a lock of hair over my shoulder. "You've got cherry pie in your hair."

CHAPTER 15

Cameraman in tow, Ilsa strode into the wrecked kitchen. Her blue eyes widened, her grip tightening on the paper grocery bag in her arms.

Raspberries lay scattered over the black-matted floor. Fragments of pie splattered the walls.

She sucked in her breath, expelling a torrent of French. "How do you expect to work in this disaster zone?" Ilsa smoothed the front of her white chef's jacket. "This is a health code violation!"

Steve adjusted the camera on his shoulder, rustling the fabric of his brown windbreaker. He grinned and pressed a button. Its tiny red light switched on. We were rolling.

Gordon looked up from his notepad. "What are you two doing here?"

"Ah." Ilsa smiled seductively at Gordon. "Like."

My mouth pinched. Gordon had that effect on a lot of women.

"I see the authorities have taken an interest." She nodded to the police officer printing the door to the dining area. "It is about time." She edged past an overturned crate of rasp-berries.

The cameraman, Steve, tracked her moves.

"The more important question," she said, "is why are the police here—and not the health inspectors? Those piecrusts may be a culinary crime—"

"My crusts are perfect," Charlene snarled.

"—but I did not think the police would be involved." Ilsa set her bag on a metal counter and leaned closer to Gordon.

"There was a break-in." I straightened Charlene's over-turned chair with a thump. "And you know we don't leave the kitchen like this. You saw it the other day."

Lugging a black bag, Frank walked into the kitchen and stopped dead, scanning the wreckage. "Holy mackerel." He dropped the bag and ran his hand over his slicked-back hair. "What happened here?"

Was it my imagination that Gordon stiffened? The detec-tive folded his notebook shut and slipped it into the inside pocket of his navy blazer. "I'll leave the officers to finish up. Do you need help putting this place back together?"

"No," I said. "It isn't as bad as it looks."

"All right. I need to go." He brushed a kiss across my cheek.

Startled, I stared at him as he left and the heavy alley door swung shut.

I touched my fingers to the spot, still tingling from the contact. It was only a friendly kiss on the cheek, but he'd never done that before—at least not while on the job.

"Earth to Val." Charlene snapped her fingers in front of my nose. "We've got to get busy if we're going to be ready for opening."

"Were you robbed?" Frank straightened the lapels of his tweed jacket

"I need the tripod," the cameraman said.

"Sure, sure," Frank said. "Val?"

"It doesn't look like anything was taken," I said, "but we surprised an intruder. Charlene and I drove him off."

"With a pie fight? I'm sorry we missed that," he muttered.

I shot Frank a sharp look.

He had the grace to look abashed and unzipped the black bag at his feet. "I guess I've gotten more interested in production work than I thought I would. On the bright side, he mustn't have been a very serious burglar—to be chased off by two women with pies." He handed Steve the tripod. "Val, can we chat for a moment?"

Charlene threw up her hands. "Who's going to clean this place? You know I can't do any heavy lifting." She stomped into the flour-work room and slammed the door.

I edged around the central work island and picked up my shoes, lying near the blue pie safe. "What's up, Frank?"

"Do I want to know why you're barefoot?" His brow creased with concern. "What's that on your feet? Blood?"

"Raspberries." I grimaced. I wondered if I could get replacement berries in time. "What's up?"

Steve clipped the video camera onto the tripod, and sat it on a corner of the counter.

"I've talked it over with the crew," he said, "and we plan to finish filming today."

Disappointment surged in my chest. Why did I care if he left? The show was nothing but trouble, and I knew Frank wouldn't stick around. He never had. "Is Chief Shaw letting you leave town?" My feet were dry, the raspberry stains set like a tattoo, and I tugged on my socks.

He crossed his arms over his tweed jacket and leaned one hip against the counter. "No, but we don't know when we'll be released, so we need to be ready to go when it happens. Apparently, my production schedule has been lollygagging."

I smiled at the word and wriggled my feet into my tennis shoes. "I admit that a part of me is glad it will be over."

"Will you?" he asked, expression intent.

"I mean . . ." I floundered. I didn't want to hurt his feelings, but I wasn't ready to bury the proverbial hatchet or have a tearful family reunion on camera. "Ilsa was right," I said, gruff. "We can't start work in the kitchen until we get this mess cleaned up."

"Oh," he said, "don't worry, the crew will help."

"That is not my job," Ilsa said.

"If you want to finish filming today," he said, "it is. Then we can all take a break and enjoy a vacation at the hotel until the police tell us we can go."

Her lips pursed. After a moment, she nodded. "I would like a holiday. Come, Steve."

The cameraman's jaw clenched, but he made a final adjustment to the camera on the tripod and got to work, righting overturned boxes and dumping raspberries into one of the sinks.

"Err," Frank said, "I need to go check something." He scuttled from the kitchen.

"How predictable." Her voice was icy. Ilsa peeled back a black fatigue mat and set it against a counter. Raspberries scuttled across the bare patch of linoleum.

I filled a bucket with soapy water. "Oh? Do you know him well?"

"It does not take long to understand a man like that," she said.

Steve grunted. "Producers."

Like Steve's wife had been? I pressed my mouth shut.

We had the kitchen ship-shape just as Abril walked through the alley door.

Steve unclipped the camera from the tripod and set it on his shoulder.

Abril paused, took a half step back, then lifted her chin and walked inside. She grabbed her apron off a hook by the door. "What are we doing today?"

"Today," Ilsa said, "I am going to teach you how to style a piecrust." She glanced toward the closed flour-work room door.

"Style a crust? How French," I joked.

Ilsa stared impassively down her long nose.

"Because French fashion . . . I'll get Charlene," I said.

"Since your piecrust maker does not line the tins or prepare the pies," she said, "I do not think she needs to be included."

Also, Charlene would flip her lid if she heard we were "styling" her crusts. She griped whenever I added little cutout stars to the tops of our blueberry pies. Charlene was a piecrust purist—a stance I respected. Usually. Some pies, like key lime, really do taste better with graham cracker crusts.

Luther, his Hawaiian shirt untucked beneath his photographer's vest, sidled into the kitchen. Silently, he clipped a mic to my t-shirt.

My eyes watered from the alcohol fumes wafting off his skin. How long had he and Ilsa stayed at the pub last night? Ilsa, crisp in her baker's whites, didn't seem worse for wear.

"But have no fear," Ilsa continued, "I will be teaching Miss Charlene how to make a chocolate piecrust."

Charlene would rather slam her hands in the industrial oven than change her crust recipe. I cleared my throat. "It's *Mrs*. And I'm not sure that's necessary."

"You mean . . . like a cookie crust?" Abril asked.

"No," Ilsa said. "We'll be adding cocoa to her existing dough mixture. But that is neither here nor there."

"Say something," Luther said to me. He pressed his hand against the headphones over his ears.

"Is this okay?" I asked.

"Yeah," he said. "You're good. Abril?"

She cleared her throat, and he winced, adjusted her mic.

"Try again," he said.

"The rain in Spain stays mainly in the plain," she said.

He gave her two thumbs up, and then slouched toward the swinging door to the dining area.

"You're supposed to be the AC too," Steve shouted after him. "Assistant to the cameraman!"

Luther made a rude gesture and continued from the kitchen.

Steve swore. "He's drunk. Again."

"Leave him alone," Ilsa said.

The cameraman reddened but fell silent.

Ilsa and I discussed today's specials—almond toffee, lemon-blueberry cream, and a whiskey pulled-pork shepherd's pie. The latter would be my lunch today. Have I mentioned I love my job?

"No," Ilsa said. "None will work for this exercise." She snapped her fingers. "The strawberry-rhubarb."

We didn't have any ready, but there was no time like the present. Abril and I got busy mixing the ingredients, and we filled the bottom half of a dozen pie tins.

Ilsa pulled plastic cookie cutters from her bag. She laid them in neat rows atop the butcher-block work island.

Abril returned with a tray lined with balls of dough on wax paper.

While Steve filmed, Ilsa demonstrated techniques for braiding pie dough. "You can lay this across the top of a pie as part of the lattice, like so." She demonstrated over a pie tin mounded with strawberry rhubarb. "Or, you can make a longer braid and run it around the edge."

"It seems to take a lot of time," I said cautiously. Time was a luxury some bakers didn't have.

Ilsa tossed her blond-streaked hair. "That is only because

I was demonstrating. See?" She whipped a braid together in seconds flat. "It is a matter of practice. You try."

Glancing nervously at each other, Abril and I braided thin strips of dough. I grinned. Mine looked okay. Not bad on the first try.

Ilsa sneered at my braid. "Don't like. Again."

I sighed and did it again. Again. And . . . again. Eventually, I got the hang of it.

"Now," Ilsa said, "flowers and leaves." She ran a ball of dough through the flattening machine twice, and then laid it on the lightly floured surface. Dipping the plastic cookie cutters into the flour, she shook them, and a soft snowfall drifted to the board. "We use these plastic cutters because they leave an impression in the top of the dough." She cut a series of serrated leaves from the dough and pointed to the etched veins of the leaves. Ilsa cut more leaves and flowers, arranging them across the pie in an elaborate lattice, braid and floral design.

I had to admit, it looked better than anything I created.

"You now," she said.

Cutting the leaves and flowers was easy as pie. Laying them out in a manner acceptable to Ilsa was more challenging.

Abril got there before I did. Smiling, she extended the pie she was working to Ilsa. "Like this?"

Ilsa nodded, grudging. "Good."

"There's something hedonistic in this frenzy of foliage," Abril said. "The crusts twine around each other as if in an embrace."

We stared at her.

Okay. Awkward. I cleared my throat. "Abril's a poet."

"What kind of poetry?" Ilsa arched a pale brow. "Erotic?"

"And her crust is a lot more elegant than mine," I said quickly. "I don't think I have an artistic eye."

"No," the pastry chef agreed. "You do not."

I tugged on the hem of my Pie Town tee. Now Ilsa was just being mean.

"Once you know the pattern," Abril said, "it's easy."

"You should sketch your designs on paper first," Ilsa said, "so you have templates to follow." She glowered at me. "Especially you."

"And we need to get back to our regular work, or we won't have enough product for today." I wiped my hands on a towel hanging from a wall peg. The show might be good P.R., but I still had a business to run. I wish they would have saved the filming for a Monday—when we were closed.

"Don't you understand?" Ilsa asked. "*This* is the level you must aspire to if you wish to become a premier pie shop. You complain business is bad? Then be better!"

Abril shot me an anxious look but said nothing.

My smile stretched tighter. "There's always room for improvement." Nigel must have told her what he'd found in the Pie Town accounts. I wished she hadn't mentioned it in front of Abril. When the show aired, the world would know our little problems. "And your piecrust looks gorgeous. Yours too, Abril."

"But the pie is not baked," Ilsa said. "You do not yet know how it will look. Now brush those crusts with egg whites. I will finish the rest, and you can work on your . . ." Her mouth twisted. "Breakfast pies."

We did. Ilsa even pitched in, and we got our baking schedule back on track.

I was starting to warm to her. When her pies came out of the oven, they were stunning—golden brown and overflowing with rose and peony blossoms. I wouldn't go wedding-cake on every piecrust, but we could pick a few specials to decorate. These crusts would look fantabulous around the holidays.

"I'll take care of the dining area." Abril left the kitchen to set up the coffee urn and prep for our early morning customers.

"Thanks for teaching us this," I said to Ilsa. "The crusts definitely make these pies look special."

She sniffed. "You doubted?"

Steve moved in for a close-up.

"It's nothing personal." I dried my hands in my apron and tried to ignore the camera. "Pie Town means everything to me. My mother and I dreamed of opening this for years."

"Where is your mother? Why is she not here?"

My vision blurred. *No waterworks. Not on TV.* The loss still hit me at random and uncontrollable moments. I blinked rapidly. "She passed away. But I wish she could have seen Pie Town. That's only one reason why I need it to work, and I'm glad you're here. But the fire at the hotel has put me on edge."

"And now this morning's break-in," she said. "It seems someone is out to get you. Perhaps the fire was aimed at you and not *Pie Hard*."

"But the problems began with Regina's murder," I said. "Has the crew learned anything new about her death?"

She turned and stared down her elegant nose at me. "I do not think this is the time or place to discuss such matters."

I hoped that meant she was willing to talk later. "When would be the right time or place?"

"Never." She looked sidelong at me through thick lashes. "Or perhaps there is some information you would like to share with me? You seem quite close to the handsome detective."

"He's not investigating Regina's death."

"So you do not deny being involved with him romantically?"

I opened the industrial oven for no reason, releasing a blast of pie-scented heat. Squirming inside, I peered at the pies, gliding past on the rotating racks. "I can neither confirm nor deny," I said blithely.

"But he questioned me about Regina," the pastry chef

said. "Why is he off the case now?" Her blue eyes narrowed. "Because the police suspect you, and as your boyfriend—?"

"No!" Okay, sort of, but I wasn't going to admit that. Especially not with Steve filming our conversation. "I had nothing to do with Regina's death or that fire."

"So you say it is coincidence someone broke into Pie Town?" She canted her head. "Or *did* someone? People will do all sorts of things to create drama on TV."

"You think I faked the break-in?" I blinked, more surprised than outraged. "Charlene saw the whole thing."

"Exactly. Your partner." She straightened her shoulders. "And speaking of whom, now into the breach I go. Wait to make the pecan pies until I return. And be sure to roast half the pecans, and only half. That is the secret to a flavorful pie." She snapped her fingers. "Steve? Come." She strode to the door of the flour-work room, knocked once, and walked inside.

The cameraman trailed after her.

I wavered. Should I follow and play peacemaker? I knew how Charlene would react to the suggestion of adding cocoa to her precious piecrusts.

Abril, face ashen, hurried into the kitchen, the door swinging behind her. "Val, you need to come quick." Wisps of ebony hair had escaped near her delicate ears.

"What's wrong?"

"It's Luther. He collapsed."

CHAPTER 16

I raced through the swinging kitchen door and into the dining area. On the other side of the counter, Tally Wally and Frank tugged a greenish Luther to his feet. A morning coffee klatch of retirees stared, forks and mugs raised halfway to their mouths.

"What happened?" I stopped short, one hand on the Dutch door.

"A little under the weather." Luther scratched his belly where his Hawaiian shirt and saggy pants did not meet.

"Don't worry." Tally Wally heaved Luther into a chair beside an empty table. "It's nothing he ate."

Luther rubbed his eyes. "The floor. It's swimming."

Frank caught my eye. "Don't worry, Val. We'll take care of this."

"How?" I asked. "Does he need a doctor?"

"He needs rest," Frank said. "I'll call a cab to take him back to the hotel. I don't think he'll be much use today."

"You're no Regina," Luther said accusingly. "You don't take care of me."

Frank braced his hands on his hips. "Is holding the AC's hand supposed to be part of the job?"

The front bell jingled.

Nigel, looking perfect in a plain, white button-up shirt and khakis, strode through the front door. He carried a leather portfolio beneath one muscular arm. "Cheerio, everyone. I am ready for my close-up." He winked, his brown eyes twinkling.

"Have you got a car outside?" Frank asked. "Luther needs to return to the hotel."

Nigel made a quick U-turn. A minute later, he leaned through the front door. "Luther's chariot awaits."

Together, the men poured Luther into the double-parked car.

I followed, watching anxiously. The summer air still had that early morning smell, and dew glistened on the impatiens hanging from the iron lamp posts. Across the street, a woman swept the sidewalk in front of her art gallery. From the gym next door, barbells clanged faintly.

Frank handed money to the driver and shut the car door. "Sorry about that, Val. This has been a difficult shoot for everyone."

Luther's problems seemed long-term, but I nodded.

"My coffee's getting cold." Tally Wally limped into Pie Town, and the rest of us trooped after him.

"I'll just set up in your office then," Nigel said, "shall I?" Without waiting for an answer, he strode through the counter's Dutch door and turned toward my office.

Nigel saw the dark underbelly of my finances. I'd been exposed, so there wasn't much point in getting huffy about him taking over my private office. I sighed and stared through the windows at the departing car. One benefit of owning your own business is a sense of control, but I saw now that it was just an illusion.

"Quite a morning you've had," Frank said. "First a break-in, now Luther."

"I've seen worse," I said, my words clipped.

He eyed me speculatively. "I'll bet you have. We'll wait for Charlene and Ilsa to finish so you and your *partner* can meet with Nigel together. Besides, Ilsa has our only camera-man."

"Great." Smile taut, I turned on my heel and walked into the kitchen. A part of me dreaded hearing what Nigel was going to tell me. I could stand having my ego taken down a peg or two if he had solid ideas for boosting business.

I didn't hear any battle cries echoing from the flour-work room, so I kept busy doing what I'd normally do—baking up a storm.

Curious, I slid trays of pecans into our smaller oven. I'd never heard of roasting only half the pecans for the pies, but I was willing to try nearly anything once.

Soon, my mood improved. Baking always lifted my spir-its. There's a certain satisfaction in making something tangi-ble—especially something people rave about. A big order was due today for one of our best customers, the Bar X—a western-themed event space down the coast. If Nigel could tell me how to land more clients like the Bar X, it would all be worth it.

Abril and I filled piecrusts and slid them into the indus-trial oven. She removed the finished pies with long, wooden paddles and placed them on cooling racks. The kitchen filled with sweet and savory scents.

My assistant manager, Petronella, clomped through the alleyway door in her motorcycle boots. Her spiky, licorice-colored hair gleamed, loaded with product.

"Hey," I said. "One of the women in the goddess group at my house is a psychiatrist. She said she'd let you interview her if you still need someone."

"I'm saved," Petronella said. "What's her number?"

I found my purse on the hook by the flour-work room and dug around until I found her card. "Here," I said, pleased to help.

"You're a lifesaver. Thanks." She stuffed the card in her back pocket, looped an apron over her head, and pushed through the swinging door into the dining area. She worked the counter, flitting between the register and customers in spite of her clunky boots.

Sundays, in general, were busy—locals stopped by for breakfast and brunch. Later, beachgoers flooded in for lunch and they picked up pies for takeaway in the afternoon. Sundays were good days. The trifecta of murder, my father, and Nigel's upcoming critique of my finances threatened my happy-baking bubble.

I mixed the pecan-bourbon mixture in one of the giant mixing bowls, and then added the half-and-half, roasted-to-raw, pecan mix.

Charlene and Ilsa emerged from the flour-work room. My crust specialist wore a thoughtful look on her face. Ilsa's blue eyes glittered with triumph. Neither appeared worse for wear.

The cameraman followed behind them, and took up a position beside the dishwasher.

"How did it go?" I asked.

"The proof's in the pudding." Charlene slammed a tray of nearly-black rounds of dough onto the counter.

"You did not fill the pecan pies yet?" Ilsa asked.

"No, and the bourbon pecan filling's ready to go." I nodded to a giant, clear-plastic pitcher filled with pecan pie goo.

Her eyes narrowed. "And you only roasted half the pecans?"

"Yep. Just like you said."

"Excellent," Ilsa said. "Use these crusts."

Obediently, I ran the near-black crusts through the dough

flattener and lined a dozen pie tins. Ilsa layered semi-sweet chocolate chips over the bottom. I poured the bourbon pecan filling into the crusts, and Abril slid them into the industrial oven.

Nigel edged into the kitchen. Grinning, he leaned against the industrial dishwasher beside the cameraman.

"The cocoa crusts can, of course, be used with a variety of pies," Ilsa said. "But as your piecrust *specialist* can attest, it's a simple matter of adding cocoa to your existing dough recipe."

"Ilsa and I have come up with some other great ideas," Nigel said, smoothing his goatee. "But while we let those pies bake, why don't you and Charlene come with me for a chat in your office?"

I couldn't avoid the bad news any longer, and my stomach lurched.

"Val handles the finances," Charlene said, untying her apron. "You don't need me."

"I don't mind," I said. "Besides, we're partners, right?" I wanted her moral support.

We followed Nigel, and Cameraman Steve followed the three of us into my office. Nigel arranged two chairs from the dining area for Charlene and me. The chairs lined up at an angle beside an easel covered in a black cloth. A lamp on a metal pole spotlighted the chairs.

He motioned us to our seats, and I winced against the bright light.

Nigel went to stand beside the easel, and we waited while Steve locked his camera into a tripod.

Steve looked up. "Okay. Go."

Nigel nodded, expression solemn, and turned to us. "I've reviewed your accounts," he said. "It seems like you may have expanded your operations prematurely, but what's done is done. What you need now is more consistent and predictable daily orders. You've also quite cleverly set up your business to minimize customer service—with the self-serve coffee, for example. You've been able to keep labor costs low this way, and this is something you should continue."

Chest tightening, I nodded. This was nothing I didn't already know. What worried me was what came next.

"What you need," he said, "is to expand your wholesaling business. And to attract more customers, you need a niche."

"Aren't pies our niche?" I asked and shifted on the pink chair.

"Yes," he said, "but this is Silicon Valley, and people expect more."

Charlene snorted.

"What's wrong, Charlene?" He rose, facing the camera, and raised a brow. "Don't you *crust* me?"

She rolled her eyes. "You need to add more excitement and intrigue to your menu." He strode to the easel.

"To pies?" Charlene's brows rocketed skyward. "What do you want us to do? Add a hidden surprise?"

"No." He whisked the cloth from the easel and revealed a placard with pastel drawings of bell jars banded with colors. In a neat row beneath them had been drawn similarly colored shot glasses. "Pie in a jar, and samples in a shot glass."

"Pies," I said, skeptical. "In a jar." Pie belonged either in a tin or someone's mouth—not a jar.

The office door opened, and Ilsa walked inside carrying a tray of four-ounce Ball jars filled with layers of pie. Beside them were shot glasses filled to the rim with pie filling. She set them on the dented desk.

"They are beautiful," she said. "They are unique. And, they are smaller than your five-inch mini pies."

My mouth watered. Holy Hannah, they looked good. I might need to rethink my pie philosophy.

Charlene sucked in her cheeks. "So are our hand pies, and hand pies are traditional. Do you know we have a recipe from the California Gold Rush?"

"But hand pies are mostly dough," Ilsa said.

"That's what makes them good," Charlene said.

"These jars have crust at the bottom but are mostly filling," the pastry chef said. "It's a different experience, more of a snack. Of course, these are all crumb crusts."

Charlene stiffened on her chair.

"It would be different," I said, darting a glance at my friend. "I can see how the jars would bring in a hipper crowd. But I'm not sure how it would boost our wholesaling."

"Trust me," Nigel said, "it will. Hotels, restaurants, and other businesses will want these, because their customers will want them. You can also promote them as party favors for special events."

I rubbed my chin. The Ball jars did have an old-west feel. Would the owner of the Bar X go for it?

"But that isn't all." He removed the placard, revealing an image of a pie tin filled with slices of different kinds of pies. "A sampler pie tin."

The cameraman moved closer to me, zooming in.

I leaned forward, intrigued. A sampler tin. Why hadn't I thought of that? "And we'd charge the regular price for a full tin?"

"Exactly. That way, everyone in the family or business can get exactly the slice of pie they want. And a sampler like this is different, unique."

I nodded, excitement rising in my belly.

"But wait, there's more." He dropped that placard and revealed another labeled *PIE SUBSCRIPTIONS* in elegant blue script.

"Are you talking about a pie of the month club?" I asked, fascinated. "Like the wineries have?"

Charlene sneered. "For pie? Ridiculous. Who orders pie in advance?"

"You can call it what you like," he said. "But describing it like one of the California wine clubs is something people will understand." He removed the placard, revealing another beneath: *THREE-MONTH SUBSCRIPTION -2 SAVORY, 1 SWEET*. He whipped that away, unveiling a second: *SIX-MONTH SUBSCRIPTION -3 SAVORY, 3 SWEET*. "Customers sign up for subscriptions. They choose whether they'd like the pies delivered on the first Tuesday or Friday of the month. Then they select whether they want vegetarian or meat-filled savory pies."

"Giving us a more steady income." Ooh, I liked this idea. A lot. Especially since the only start-up cost for the program would be the time it took for me to announce it on my website.

"Of course," he said, "you could also offer an annual subscription."

I nodded, enthusiastic. This was really cool.

"This is really cracked," Charlene said.

I shot her a warning look.

"Finally," he said, "you need to do a better job getting the word out about Pie Town. Review your budget. I saw you don't do much advertising. I worked the numbers, and unfortunately, I don't think you'll be able to change that in the near future. But I have a solution." With a flourish, he removed the subscription placard. The poster board beneath read: *PIE MAKING CLASSES*.

"Classes sound like a lot of work," I said, cautious.

"Exactly!" Charlene folded her arms and leaned back in her chair.

"It's about providing an experience. You'll need a minimum of six participants, and a maximum of twelve. That's all you can really fit into your kitchen. Promote the classes on your website and at your counter to corporations and private parties. Invite a local reporter to attend to get some press." He lifted two yellow folders off my desk and handed them to Charlene and me. "Here are some sample promotional materials. Charge a hundred dollars per person."

I flipped through the pages of sample ads, complete with pie graphics and Pie Town's smiley face logo.

Charlene sputtered. "A hundred dollars? To learn to make pie?"

I gave her the side-eye. Inviting *Pie Hard* here had been her idea. Why was she bucking Nigel's suggestions?

"To learn to make *a* pie," he corrected. "The student makes one pie, takes it home with them, and they're done. But what they're paying for is the group experience, the entertainment, not the pie itself. All you'll need to do is provide the ingredients, drinks, and snacks. You make money off the class, and the corporation promotes Pie Town to all its employees."

"We could try it." I could run classes in the evenings.

"You're already nearing burn-out," Charlene said. "How are you going to take on this extra work?"

"I can't imagine we'd have many students to start with," I said, my excitement growing. This could work. "So it would just be an extra evening or two a month. And it doesn't have to be me leading the class. Petronella or Abril might be interested. I'd need to add the class info to the website, but that's not hard."

"So? Will you two commit to these changes?" Nigel handed us two new blue folders with the *Pie Hard* logo. "Since you're partners, it's critical you're on the same page."

I thumbed through it. It contained a simple, three-page plan of action and new, projected financial statements. I sucked in my breath. The numbers at the bottom gradually shifted from red to black, showing a profit. I glanced up at him. "These numbers. How—?"

He sat against the desk and clasped his hands. "Things are going to work out for Pie Town, Val, and Charlene. You've got good instincts, even if you do tend to leap before you look. You should both be chuffed."

"Eh?" Charlene asked.

"Proud," he translated.

"Thanks." Embarrassing as it was, tears pricked my eyes. I'd put everything I had into this business. I left my home in Southern California. I invested my mother's life insurance policy. I even slept in my office the first few months of operations because I couldn't afford my own place. Pie Town had become more than a business. It was home. Nigel's validation both relieved and touched me.

"You've got an advantage over traditional bakeries, because people can sit and eat," he continued. "You've created an experience with your fifties-style diner. And an experience is exactly what people want these days. Now, I'm asking you to expand that experience, to give your customers more options. Will you commit?"

"I'll commit," I said, forgetting that Charlene and I were supposed to be partners. "I love these ideas. They're inexpensive, creative, and doable."

Charlene snorted.

"Charlene?" he asked. "This won't work unless the two of you are on board."

She glared at me.

I gave her a look. Apparently, she'd forgotten she *wasn't* my business partner.

She exhaled heavily. "Fine. Whatever. We'll try."

"Don't try," he and Ilsa said in unison. They smiled at each other. "Do."

He turned to the cameraman. "What do you think? Did we get it?"

Steve lowered the camera from his shoulder. "We got it, and we are done with this beast." He stepped backward and bumped into the closed door. The veteran's calendar fluttered to the dingy linoleum.

"Wait." I stood and retrieved the calendar. "Done? You mean done for good?"

"Yep," Nigel said. "Steve and Luther will return in six weeks to video how the implementation is working out. However, may I say—it has been a pleasure working with an actual pie shop. Most of our shows are about generic bakeries, donut shops, or cupcake places. You've got a nice little business here. Best of luck to you both."

"Thanks!" That was it? We'd survived the show, and it hadn't been awful. Then, insecurity reared its gnarly head. "But, are you sure my finances—"

"Are typical of a start-up," he said. "You two have been operating less than a year, Val. Keep the faith. Just . . . no more sudden expansions. All right?"

"Right." I grinned with relief.

"We're not quite done," Ilsa said. "We need some shots of you taking the black-bottom pecan pies from the oven and then customers tasting them."

"Right," I said. "I'll meet you in the kitchen. And I have something for both of you as well."

The crew bundled up their things and left Charlene and me in my office.

I hugged her. "Charlene, this was awesome with a side of awesomesauce. They gave us great advice, and we'll get publicity out of the show. Thank you for forcing me to do this."

Her nose wrinkled. "Pie in a jar? Pie in a shot glass? Pie Town is about nostalgia, the classics."

"But we should provide samples," I said. "So why not put them in shot glasses? And if we use an old-fashioned Ball jar, it's still got nostalgia value."

"I can't believe you're going along with these nutty ideas."

"You were the one who brought *Pie Hard* here."

Her lips pinched. "I only wanted to be on TV. I didn't want everything to change!"

"You still make the best piecrust in northern California," I said.

"Humph. Do you really expect me to make chocolate crust? It's just wrong."

"Chocolate is never wrong," I said solemnly and nudged her shoulder. "Come on. Let's see how that bourbon pecan pie tastes with the black crust."

We migrated to the kitchen.

Abril stood in front of the open oven. Swiftly, she slid a wooden paddle in and lifted out a black-as-sin bourbon-pecan pie. It smelled heavenly, but we had to wait for the molten filling to cool before we could taste it. Finally, I cut the pie, lifting a wedge free. I slid a fork into the tip and took a bite.

The breathy-sweet bourbon-pecan was even better with the touch of chocolate. I closed my eyes. And the pecans tasted out-of-this-galaxy good. Ilsa's half-and-half trick worked. "Wow."

"And now," Ilsa said, "let's see what your customers think."

We cut super-thin slices of the pie and together we trooped into the restaurant. It was nearing lunchtime, and the pink booths and tables were nearly full.

While Steve filmed, we distributed samples of the bourbon-pecan pie.

Nigel and Ilsa chatted with customers and signed autographs.

I presented the entire crew with black Pie Town hoodies. Steve filmed the gift giving, only taking a break to accept his own hoodie.

I found Ray and his sandy-haired girlfriend, Henrietta, in their usual corner booth with three other gamers. Half-eaten sample plates of bourbon-pecan sat on the paper mats in front of them.

Henrietta wore her usual, shapeless cargo pants and an over-sized, Pie Town, *Pies Before Guys* t-shirt. I hoped that meant she'd forgiven me for letting Ray on the Baker Street Bakers team.

"Ilsa's talking to people," Ray said breathlessly. "Oh, God. She's coming over here!" He shrank in the booth, his black t-shirt rumpling.

Henrietta took a bite of the pie and paused, the fork hovering beside her mouth. "This is good, Val. Really good." She smiled, and I knew we were friends again.

Beaming, Ilsa stopped beside their booth. "What do you think?"

"I think I've just been converted to pecan pie," Henrietta said.

Ray took another bite and moaned. "I'm in love."

Henrietta's eyes narrowed.

I wasn't sure if he was talking about the pie or Ilsa. I remembered he wanted an autograph.

"Would you mind signing some menus for this group?" I asked the pastry chef and pulled a fistful of narrow, paper menus from my apron pocket.

"Who shall I sign them to?"

"Ray," he croaked.

Bending over the table, she signed a menu and passed it to him.

Starry-eyed, he stared at the autograph.

"And my name is Henrietta," his girlfriend said.

Ilsa signed a menu for Henrietta and the other gamers and migrated to another table.

"I can't believe I met her," Ray said. "And I have proof!"

"That isn't why we came," Henrietta said.

I glanced at the other gamers. "You mean you're not here for your regular gaming?"

Henrietta shook her head, her loose hair floating about her ears. Glancing around the packed restaurant, she leaned closer. "Ray found something. We've got motive."

CHAPTER 17

"Motive?" I glanced anxiously around the packed restaurant. The cameraman focused on Nigel, who chatted with Marla at her central two-top. Smiling benignly, Frank sat at the counter. He watched Ilsa sign autographs for a sunburnt family of five. Drying beach towels hung over the backs of their chairs. I didn't think the crew members could hear Ray and Henrietta, but I didn't want to take any chances.

"Let's talk in my office," I said and motioned to Charlene, who sidled into Marla's shot.

The four of us trooped into my office, still decorated with the easel and Nigel's drawings, and I shut the door.

"This had better be good." Charlene leaned against my metal desk and crossed her arms over her green knit tunic. "You're ruining my TV moment."

"Ray and Henrietta say they've found something. And half the show's been about you."

"And yet Marla's managed to shove in." She growled.

Ray dug a computer tablet from his backpack and opened it to reveal a complicated-looking diagram. "Okay, so I did online searches for everyone on the crew and created dossiers from what I found."

Charlene snatched the tablet from him and frowned. "Where are they?"

He came to her side and touched the screen. "There's Ilsa's."

Charlene whistled. "Her last kitchen burned down?" She shot me a significant look.

"In Vegas," he said. "But that's not the most interesting part of the story. Before the fire, Ilsa had filed a sexual harassment complaint against the owner. Then after the place burned, she left."

"What if she set the fire?" Henrietta gestured in a wide motion and knocked a box of straws from the metal bookcase. Paper-wrapped straws rolled across the linoleum, and I sighed. I'd just put those back.

"Whoops." She knelt to retrieve them. "Maybe she set the fire at the hotel too."

I helped her stuff straws into the box. "Was there anything to suggest arson?" Did Ilsa lock me in the burning room? I swayed, suddenly dizzy, and braced one hand on the floor. I'd come to like Ilsa, or at least respect her. It just proved how poor my judgment was.

"No," Ray admitted. "All the newspaper articles said it was an accident. But they could have been wrong. The fire burned down half the restaurant."

I shuddered. We didn't do much frying, so a kitchen fire wasn't quite as likely in Pie Town. Along with alien abduction, fire was one of my worst nightmares—even more so after the hotel incident.

"And there's more," he said. "There's something weird about that new producer, Frank Harris."

"Oh?" I said, dread puddling in my stomach.

"The weird thing is," he continued, "I can't find him on the Internet anywhere."

"Not everybody lives their life online," Charlene said. "Some of us still put photos in albums and use the phone to call people."

Charlene wasn't one of those people. Straightening, I smiled wryly and set the box of straws the metal shelf.

"I know," he said, "but there should be *something*. He's a ghost. It's like he doesn't exist."

"TV producer isn't his normal job," I said, defensive for no good reason. "He's really a coach, working with people with addiction. He only took this position because Regina died."

"How does someone go from coach to producer?" Henrietta asked.

"He knew someone." I sat against the ancient, gray steel desk.

"That might explain why he's here," Ray said, "but it doesn't explain why he's not online."

"What do you mean?" Charlene asked.

"That's the other thing I discovered," he said.

Something crashed in the kitchen outside the door. My shoulders hunched. I pressed my palms into the cool metal desk, forcing myself not to rush from the office. Whatever happened, Abril and Petronella could handle it.

"It's only a rumor," Henrietta said.

"Nigel's rumored to have a gambling problem," he said.

"Nigel? British Nigel?" I asked. The consultant seemed so . . . together.

"It's a rumor," Henrietta said, "that's all."

"But if your producer works with addicts," Ray said, "maybe he's really here to wrangle Nigel."

"That would explain how Frank knew the show's executive producer," I said, remembering Nigel's odd reaction when he'd first spotted Frank in Pie Town.

"But why doesn't this Frank dude have a website?" Ray asked.

"He's from a different generation," I said. "And maybe he wants to keep his work private."

"So private clients can't find him?" Ray's broad face tightened with disbelief.

"The engi-nerd has got a point," Charlene said. "What coach doesn't have a website? Even you-know-who has a website." You-know-who was her arch-nemesis, Marla Van Helsing.

I gnawed my bottom lip. "I'm sure there's a reasonable explanation."

"There's only one way to find out," Charlene said. "He's your father. Ask him." She winced.

I buried my face in my hand and repressed a curse. *Charlene!*

Henrietta's eyes widened. "The new producer's your father?"

Ray looked away guiltily. So he hadn't told her.

I blew out my breath. "It looks that way. I haven't seen him since I was a little kid."

Henrietta touched my arm. "I'm sorry. That's got to be rough."

I smiled, grateful. "Did you find anything else?" I asked briskly.

"Not really," he mumbled and retrieved his computer tablet from Charlene. "I'll email everything to you."

"Thanks," I said. "Ray, this is good intel."

"Sure."

"We'd better get back out there." I strode from the office and held the door for everyone.

At the kitchen door, Charlene touched my arm, halting my progress. She waited until Ray and Henrietta brushed past us in the dimly lit hall before speaking. "I'm sorry, Val," she said in a low voice. "I didn't mean to spill the beans about your father. It just came out."

"It's okay." I rubbed the back of my neck. "I shouldn't be so sensitive."

"I know I razz you about being jilted at the altar—"

"I wasn't."

"—and your weird UFO phobia—"

I folded my arms. "Oh, come on."

"—and about not being able to seal the deal with Carmichael . . ."

My eyes narrowed.

"But I wouldn't tease you about family. You're a good person," she said in a low voice. "And you were an innocent child. It wasn't your fault your father left."

My shoulders dropped. "I don't know why I've been keeping it secret. I don't have anything to be ashamed about."

"No," she said, "you don't."

So why did I feel so awful?

"At least him being my father gives us an in on questioning suspects," I said. "Like you said, all I have to do is ask him why he doesn't show up online."

But when I walked into the dining area, my father was gone.

I stood nervously at the entrance to the hotel's wine bar and scanned for Frank. He didn't sit in one of the high, leather chairs at the bar. He didn't stand in front of the wall of wine bottles, perusing the selection. A couple of women in high heels and short, sparkly dresses sat giggling together at one corner of the u-shaped wooden bar. A waiter in a red vest removed a bottle from the wall rack behind the bar.

Someone squeezed my elbow and I jumped.

"Val, good of you to come." Frank looked dapper in a navy, double-breasted blazer and slacks. He brushed a kiss across my cheek, and I stiffened. "I'm glad you called."

I toyed with the leather purse strap on my shoulder. "Well, now that the show's over, who knows when we'll see each other again?" The thought squeezed the air from my lungs. I guess I wasn't as indifferent to Frank as I liked to think.

"Why not tomorrow?"

"Tomorrow?"

"The show's over, but your chief of police hasn't given us permission to leave. I thought I'd stop by Pie Town for lunch."

"Tomorrow Pie Town is closed," I said.

"We'll make something work." He nodded to the bar. "Can I buy you a drink?"

I smoothed my shirt. "Um, sure."

We walked to the bar, and he pulled a high chair out for me.

"How did you enjoy doing the show?" he asked.

"Aside from the murder?"

"Aside from that."

The bartender, young, handsome, and dark-eyed, approached us at the bar. He scanned us appraisingly, then handed us wine menus in thick, leather binders. Unspeaking, he returned to the two women at the other end of the bar.

"Nigel had some interesting suggestions." I'd already started writing new web copy for his ideas. "And Ilsa showed us a few new tricks with the piecrusts. In fact, the day went smoothly." Suspiciously smoothly for a reality TV show that thrived on drama and disaster. Frank promised he wouldn't do any fancy editing to make us look bad. But could I trust a man with decades of untrustworthiness under his belt?

"*Pie Hard* has a track record of taking bakeries to the next level." He flipped open the binder and perused the menu. "This is on me, by the way."

I checked my menu and swallowed hard at the prices. "I take it your coaching business is doing well?"

"Well enough that I'll be returning to it once the police

tell us we can go. But I hope we can keep in better touch. In the past, I haven't been much of a father to you, but we're both different people now."

"Both? You talk as if I was responsible for you leaving," I said. My voice was high and thin.

He looked away. "No, of course not. I didn't mean it that way."

My nails bit into my palms. *Sensitive much?*

The waiter drifted to our side of the bar. "Can I get you anything?"

Ashamed by my outburst, I stared hard at the menu.

Frank ordered and turned to me. "Val?"

"I'll take the Paso Robles Zinfandel." It was one of the cheaper wines on the menu, but old habits die hard.

The waiter nodded, collected the menus, and left.

Change the subject to something that won't make me freak out. "Has the crew said anything to you about Regina's death?"

He frowned, his expression perplexed. "No. Why would they?"

"The police think it was murder. There must be some talk."

"I'm a newcomer," he said. "No one's confiding in me. And maybe it's best if we both stay out of this. I know you've had some successes solving crimes in the past, but you had some near misses too. There's a point where everyone's luck runs out."

"Are you speaking from experience?" I asked sharply.

He shifted on the tall chair. "You could say that."

I blew out my breath. "Sorry. I don't know how to act around you. I guess I'm still angry, which I know is stupid and unfair, but I can't help it."

"You have every right to be angry."

"And you being reasonable isn't helping." I toyed with a scarlet paper napkin. "Why did you really leave?"

"I told you why. I was dragging your mother and you down with my gambling, and I'd gotten involved with some unsavory characters. Your mother and I both agreed it was best if I left."

"And now you help other gamblers, like Nigel."

His expression turned bland. "Nigel?"

"It's not exactly a secret he has a gambling problem."

"Oh?"

"And he definitely reacted when you walked into Pie Town on the first day of shooting."

"When it comes to addiction," he said, "client confidentiality is critical. If addicts don't trust the people trying to help them, the entire program falls apart. You wouldn't want that, would you?"

My cheeks warmed. "No, of course not."

"I didn't think so. One thing I've learned with this ridiculous show is that you're a good person, Val. I've talked to your staff and customers. They like you. More importantly, they respect you."

I laughed shortly. "I wouldn't go that . . ."

Doran, dressed all in black, slouched into the wine bar and took a chair near the two women. He brushed back his shock of dark hair. It immediately returned to its original position, over one eye.

". . . far," I finished, my breath quickening.

"What's wrong?" Frank asked.

I leaned toward him. "That guy who just walked in," I said in a low voice. "The one dressed in black. Have you noticed him hanging around?"

Frank glanced toward him. "I think we're staying at the same hotel."

In his black jeans and t-shirt, ninja-guy didn't look like the sort who could afford a luxury hotel. These days it was hard to tell a tech millionaire from a skater dude. "He's been hanging around Pie Town too."

"Has he been bothering you?" Frank made to rise from his chair. "I'll talk to him."

"No," I hissed, grabbing the sleeve of his tweed blazer. "He hasn't done anything creepy. There's just something about him." Something familiar and disturbing at the same time.

"You should trust your instincts," Frank said. "If you think something's off, it's off. Let's find out what."

"Wait—"

Rising, he approached Doran.

I crumpled the napkin. What was he doing?

The waiter appeared and slid two glasses filled with ruby liquid onto the bar. Thanking him, I took a hasty swig. *Dammit.*

Frank said something to Doran and the two ladies, and they all stood and shifted left, taking chairs beside ours.

"That's more like it." Frank beamed. "What's the point of going to a bar if you don't meet interesting people? Tiffany, Brittany, Doran, this is my daughter, Val. She owns the local pie shop."

The women giggled.

"What do you do?" Doran asked him. He seemed more vampirically pale than usual, so he wasn't spending much time at the beach.

"Up until five p.m.," Frank said, "I was a TV producer. Who knows what will come next? And you?"

"Graphic artist." Doran's voice trembled slightly, and his jaw clamped shut.

"We work in pharmaceuticals," Tiffany—or maybe it was Brittany—said. She shifted, the sequins on her skin-tight sapphire dress twinkling in the bar's soft lighting. "Pricing."

"What were you doing before this?" Doran asked, never taking his gaze from my father.

"Before?" Frank blinked. "Ah, I see. You're curious about my path to becoming a producer."

"Something like that," Doran said.

"My career path was random and unexpected. I was a speck of whirling dust in a mighty wind. But for all that, I've done fairly well for myself. Graphic designer, eh? You freelance?"

Doran nodded.

"That must keep you on your toes," Frank said and motioned to the waiter.

He glided toward us.

"Another round for my friends," Frank said. "On my room bill."

The waiter nodded and walked to the rear of the bar. He drew a bottle from the racks that lined the wall.

"So what brought you all to San Nicholas?" I asked brightly. Why did Doran look like he wanted to take Frank's head off? Maybe he wasn't interested in me at all. Maybe it was Frank he was after.

"We're attending a conference in South San Francisco," Brittany said, "but we thought it would be more fun to stay by the beach."

"And you?" I asked Doran.

"Vacation."

"How long are you—"

Doran rose. "I have to go." He strode from the bar.

"Not a very friendly fellow, is he?" Frank asked.

"No." I stood. "Thanks for the drink, but I should go too. Baker's hours."

"But, Val—"

"Lunch tomorrow, right?" I hurried after Doran.

He turned a corner in the long, elegant corridor.

I broke into a jog, my footsteps muffled by the thick gray carpet veined with gold. I wasn't sure what I was doing— Doran was probably returning to his hotel room, and I didn't want to tackle him there. I couldn't shake the feeling that he was somehow connected to more than Frank. He was connected to me.

Maybe I should have asked Ray to track Doran online, but I still didn't know his last name. I reached the junction in time to see Doran's lean, black-clad form whip around another corner.

Hurrying forward, I trotted toward the next corner. Ahead, a door shut with a solid thud, and a salt-scented breeze ruffled my hair.

At the bend, the hallway widened. Comfy-looking, gray-blue chairs sat before tall picture windows. They faced the ocean, an ebony pool in the darkness. Outside, spotlights lit a winding path.

Doran was nowhere in sight.

Had the graphic designer gone outside? And did I really want to follow? I rocked in place, wavering.

Yes, I did.

I trotted to the exit door, pushed it open, and walked outside. The night was cool, and I shivered. Waves crashed in a dull, rhythmic thud beneath the nearby cliff. Ground lights along the trail lit the cliff's edge and the low, wood and rope barrier fence

I strode down the looping path through the golf course and toward the vague, charcoal line where sky and ocean met.

Rubbing my arms, I looked around. Where had Doran gone? There were no trees or bushes to lurk behind—just divots of sand traps and soft swells of lawn, yellowish in the glow from the footpath's solar lamps. The new moon was a shadow in the sky. Stars burned hard and glittery as diamonds, making me feel small, vulnerable.

I turned toward the hotel, turned back to the golf course. Had I been mistaken? Maybe he hadn't come outside after all. I definitely heard a heavy door close and felt an outside breeze.

I walked to the top of a grassy rise.

An irregular shadow wavered across the edge of a sand trap.

I halted, my heart jack rabbiting. It wasn't Doran lying in wait. The shadow was too long, like someone stretched out, asleep.

Legs leaden, I walked toward the dark irregularity. It was nothing. Just an odd shadow, or a discarded golf bag, or . . .

I hissed a quick intake of breath.

"Ilsa?"

The chef lay, still and silent, just beneath the lip of the sand trap. Lips parted, expression empty, her eyes stared lifelessly at the rolling lawn.

CHAPTER 18

"Oh," I breathed. "Oh, no." I fell to my knees beside Ilsa's still form and pressed my fingers beneath her jaw. Her skin was warm, but I knew she was dead. Her head canted at an odd angle, her eyes open and unmoving and vacant.

Darting looks around the darkened golf course; I scrabbled in my purse for my phone and dialed. Ilsa hadn't just dropped dead. Someone had killed her. Someone who might be nearby.

"911, what is your emergency?" a female dispatcher asked.

I tried to make myself smaller, less conspicuous. "This is Val Harris. I'm at the Belinda Hotel." My voice shook. "On the golf course. I've found a body."

"Is the person injured?"

"No, she's dead." Kneeling, I couldn't see the hotel or cliff trail. Both were obscured by the rolling lawn.

"I'm dispatching units now. Are you certain she's deceased?"

"Yes." God, yes.

"Are you in a safe place?"

"I think so." Was I? Elbows pressed to my body, I stood and walked to the top of the slope where I could see anyone coming.

The night sky stretched cold and vast overhead. The golf course rippled away from me. On the ridge, I stood out like a pie at a cakewalk. The killer was gone. He had to be, right? Because the killer couldn't be a she. Ilsa, my last female suspect, was dead.

A siren wailed in the distance.

"Ma'am? Ma'am?" the dispatcher prompted.

My thoughts jumbled. "Sorry, what?"

"Can you tell me which hole you're near?"

"Um . . . I'm by a sand trap behind the hotel, between the hotel and the cliffs. I mean, on the west side of the hotel," I babbled. I was no golfer! How was I to know which hole this was?

"All right," she said. "I'll stay on the line until the police units reach you."

I paced beside the body. This wasn't happening. But it was.

After what seemed like hours, but could have been only ten minutes, the dispatcher said, "The first unit is pulling into the hotel parking lot now."

"Thanks," I said, embarrassingly grateful. I'd seen bodies before. In my short life span, I'd stumbled across a startling amount of corpses. Something about Ilsa's death was different. Death never failed to shake me, but Ilsa's form looked diminished somehow, void.

I backed away and stared hard at the ground, searching for evidence. Dry sand doesn't hold footprints. If there was a clue on Ilsa's body, I knew better than to touch it. No discarded bits of jewelry or weapons glinted in the even grass. There was, however, bruising on her neck. Had she been strangled?

A tall, lean figure jogged across the golf course. His flashlight beam swept the grass.

I waved. "Over here!"

"Val?"

"Gordon?" Pocketing my phone, I raced to him.

He grasped my shoulders. "Are you all right?" He wore my favorite fisherman's sweater and jeans, so he'd been off duty when the call had come in.

I nodded, wanting to fling myself at him. Then I did.

His arms, strong and comforting, wrapped around me. "Oh, Val," he rumbled. "Why did it have to be you?"

There was a slight pressure on the top of my head, as if he'd kissed it.

I stepped away. "It's Ilsa. Ilsa Fueder from the show. Gordon, she didn't die naturally."

"Show me."

We hurried to the sand trap.

He knelt and touched his fingers to Ilsa's neck, shook his head, rose. "Why were you here?"

"I was meeting Frank for a drink."

An odd expression crossed his face, and my brain stumbled. What did he know about my father? This wasn't the time to ask.

"Go on," he said.

"The show finished filming today, so I thought this would be our last chance to talk."

"Did you suggest this meeting, or did he?"

My gaze clouded. "I did."

"Are you sure he didn't suggest it somehow?"

I heated. "I called him, and he invited me over. Why?"

"And what happened next?"

Sirens roared closer. Blue and red lights zipped toward us.

"I met him in the wine bar," I said. "A guy who keeps hanging around Pie Town, Doran, showed up, and Frank invited him over for a drink. Doran seemed uncomfortable, and he left in a hurry. So I followed him—"

"Why?" He ripped out the word.

"There's just something strange about the guy. He keeps turning up. He was at the crime scene after Regina was found. He keeps coming to Pie Town. Seeing him at the hotel bar seemed like too much of a coincidence."

"What does he look like?"

I described him.

He took notes and sighed. "And then what?"

"Then I lost him in one of the hallways. I heard a heavy door closing and thought it was the door leading to the golf course, so I went outside. That's when I found Ilsa."

"About what time was this?"

Figures raced from the parking lot and across the lawn.

In two strides, Gordon was at the top of the low hill. He motioned to the newcomers.

I checked my phone and realized I'd never ended my call with the dispatcher. Her voice squawked faintly over the line.

Wincing, I put the phone to my ear. "Sorry. The police are here."

Gordon returned. "You were saying?"

I hung up and checked my calls. "Okay, I called 911 at 8:43 p.m. I found her no more than a minute or two before that."

"GC!" Chief Shaw, flanked by two paramedics, hurried toward us. "Is that you? And not Ms. Harris again?"

"I'm afraid so," Gordon said.

"What have we got?" the chief asked.

"Possible murder victim," Gordon said. "Ilsa Fueder." He pointed toward the sand trap.

The paramedics jogged to the body.

The chief started. "Not the pastry chef!" He grimaced.

"Sorry, GC. It looks like this is my case too. And you, young lady, are going to have to come to the station to answer some questions."

Arms crossed over his fisherman's sweater, Gordon straightened off my van as I emerged from the police station. Tendrils of fog wreathed the iron lamp posts and drifted down the brick steps.

In spite of my exhaustion, I smiled with relief. "Hi."

He opened his arms, and I walked straight into his warm embrace.

We stood there for a long moment. My heart was pounding. "I'm so glad you're back from Wyoming," I said.

"Me too. I've missed you."

I looked up. "Have you? I mean—"

He stopped me with a kiss that seared my veins. When we broke apart, breathing hard, I could still feel its fiery trail on my lips.

I gasped, emotions whirling, legs trembling. "Aren't you worried Shaw will find out?"

"That I was kissing one of his witnesses? I'm off the case, remember? I might as well enjoy it."

"Is that why you were waiting for me?"

"That and I was worried."

Gordon was more than a badass detective. He cared about people. That was why he joined the force, and that was why I found him so irresistible.

"How are you holding up?" he asked.

"Better than Ilsa," I said sadly. The pastry chef could be abrasive, but she knew how to braid a piecrust like nobody's business. She convinced Charlene to try a variant on her sacred piecrust recipe. There was more to Ilsa than met the eye. "The funny, not-funny thing is—I was starting to think Ilsa killed Regina."

He angled his head. "Because of the kitchen fire at the last restaurant she worked at?"

"You knew?"

He grinned. "I have Internet access too. Word is there were conflicts with Ilsa in the Pie Town kitchen."

"Not that you're investigating," I said wryly.

He shrugged. "It's not my case."

Because of me. My chin lowered.

"And that isn't your fault," he said, as if he could hear my thoughts. "I'd like to hear more about this Doran character."

"Usually I'm trying to wheedle information out of you."

A single, elegant brow lifted. "Then I guess you owe me."

"I guess I do. The only thing I learned about Doran is that he's a graphic designer. I don't even know his last name. But I'll tell you everything I can." I glanced over my shoulders at the light streaming through the police station's windows. "Just not here."

"Why don't I follow you back to your place?"

My heart turned over. "Perfect."

I climbed into my pink van and waited for Gordon's sedan to pull up behind me. We caravanned down the empty streets and drove into the scrubby hills.

A shiver of nervicitement ran through me. Gordon was coming back to my place. He'd been there before, but not after a kiss like that.

I maneuvered the van up the dirt drive and let it drift to a halt by the tiny house. Tiki torches flickered in front of the yurt entrance, but no goddess gals were in sight.

He parked beside the picnic table and stepped out, meeting me at the front steps. "What's with the yurt? Wait." He held up his hand. "Do I want to know?"

"A goddess group."

"Oh, I definitely want to know."

I opened the door and ushered him inside my tiny house.

"Tea?" I asked from my elf-sized kitchen.

"Why not?"

Stomach fluttering, I heated water in the microwave and set boxes of tea on the fold-out table. "Charlene lets this group rent the yard every year for their annual retreat. A fact that she forgot to mention in the excitement of her big *Pie Hard* surprise."

"*Pie Hard* was a surprise?"

I handed him a mug. Our fingers brushed against each other and my skin jolted from the contact.

I cleared my throat. "When Charlene contacted the producers, she told them we were business partners. They insisted she keep it a surprise to add to the drama."

He sat at the small table, his knees bumping against its bottom. "And has there been much drama?"

"Charlene didn't like Ilsa criticizing her crusts—you know how she is. But Charlene wouldn't kill over that."

He smiled. "I'd already put Charlene in the 'highly unlikely' category of suspects. And Abril?"

"And Abril?"

I pulled out a chair and sat across from him. "Why? Did Petronella say something?"

"She is my cousin."

"Abril wasn't thrilled about being on TV," I said, "and Ilsa's criticism unnerved her. But in the end, they were getting on okay."

"What else happened?"

"Honestly, the crew were surprisingly mellow. I'm not sure if it was because Frank told them he wanted this to be a positive show, or—"

"Frank said what?"

"He told them he wanted the show to end on a positive note," I said.

"Did he tell you that?"

"Yes, and Luther confirmed it. Why? Do you think he would lie about it?" We were chatting like old friends, but that kiss . . . To hide my confusion, I looked away.

His craggy profile reflected in the darkened window. "Just trying to get clear on the facts."

"Most of the conflict happened behind the scenes—between crew members. Steve wasn't happy about Luther's absences, which apparently were drinking-related. Ilsa defended Luther. Luther was broken up about Regina's death—"

"And the cameraman?"

"Steve seemed upset too," I said, "but he said he wanted to work to keep his mind off things. The only person who seemed to be calm about it all was Nigel."

"And then there's your father. Did he give you a better explanation for why he turned up?"

I opened my mouth, closed it. If Nigel was getting help for a gambling problem, he deserved his anonymity. This was a murder investigation, and Ray turned up rumors of Nigel's gambling.

"What?" Gordon asked.

"Frank told me he's a kind of coach for people with addiction problems. That's what brought him to San Nicholas."

The detective's handsome face darkened. "A coach," he said. "And who is his client?"

I hesitated. Why was I stressing over this?

"Val, if his client is a member of the crew, I have to know."

"You're right. I'm sorry." Of course I could trust Gordon to do the right thing with the information. "Nigel apparently has some gambling problems."

"Nigel? Your father specifically said Nigel was his client?"

"He was kind of vague for confidentiality reasons."

"Confidentiality." Gordon rose and looked through the sliding glass door. He sipped his tea.

"Is something wrong?" I asked. "Whenever I bring up Frank, you seem annoyed."

Swiftly, he turned. "No. I'm working an ugly case right now. A stabbing. They were teenagers, and now two lives are . . ." He rubbed his forehead. "You can't just leave that stuff at the office."

"I'm sorry, I didn't know."

"There's no reason you would. You'll see it in the papers tomorrow. Forget about it. I'm worried about what you've landed in."

A knot formed in my belly. "Do you mean the murders or Frank?"

"Both." He set the mug carefully on the square table. "You haven't seen your father for a long time. A lot of things have happened in both your lives."

"And?"

"And I think you should move slowly."

"I am, but Frank and the crew will be going as soon as the chief tells them they can."

"And that means you have to lay it all on the table while he's in San Nicholas? Aren't you going to see him after he leaves?"

"I don't know, but Frank's here now."

He studied me. "What's wrong?" he asked.

"Ray did some Internet digging on the *Pie Hard* crew. He said Frank wasn't anywhere online, that he was an Internet ghost. I guess a part of me *is* worried I won't see Frank again." He'd disappeared so completely from my childhood. How could I believe he wouldn't disappear again? I turned the mug on the table and studied the ripples in my chamomile tea. "Though I'm not sure why I care."

I looked up and again caught that strange, hard expression on Gordon's face—part anger, part regret.

My brain cleared in a sudden flash, leaving me dizzy. "You know something about him."

"No."

"You do." My grip tightened on the mug. "What aren't you telling me?"

"I don't know anything. I'm a cop. I'm naturally suspicious."

"No," I said. "It's more than that."

"Sure it is. Your father is a suspect in a murder investigation."

It was more than that. I could see it in his eyes. Gordon was lying.

CHAPTER 19

Laughter and cheerful feminine voices woke me at seven a.m. I groaned, pulled the blankets over my head, and turned from the sunlight streaming through the vertical blinds. Monday was my day off. The smell of bacon lured me, nose twitching, from beneath the covers. Throwing a robe over my pie pajamas, I staggered out the front door and into the yard.

"Good morning!" Maureen caroled, her broad face wreathed in a smile. She wore a brick-red, Moroccan-style caftan with gold embroidery at the collar. The hood hung down her back.

A buffet in metal warming trays ran down the center of the table, decorated with banana leaves and ginger flowers. Women in flowing robes wandered the lawn in clusters, noshing and gossiping. A caterer's van parked near the cliff's edge. On the horizon, the ocean was pale blue against the sky.

I yawned and stretched. "Morning. How's yurt living?"

"The yurt is now a contemplation zone from ten at night until seven in the morning. That means no talking."

I grinned. My nights were about to get quieter.

"Help yourself." She nodded toward the table. Was I imagining it, or had its wooden legs sunk deeper into the soft earth beneath the weight of all that food?

I heaped a plate with bacon, eggs, fruit, and a slice of coffee cake.

Maureen watched, frowning.

I hesitated, my hand hovering over cups of OJ. "Am I being greedy?" I asked, self-conscious.

"No, of course not. But your aura looks disturbed. Is everything all right?"

"I suppose you'll hear about it soon enough. Ilsa Fueder, the French pastry chef who was part of the *Pie Hard* crew? She was found dead last night at her hotel."

Maureen gasped. "Not Ilsa! I have all her cookbooks! But she's marvelous. Such a strong force, such vitality. I can't believe she's dead."

Strong force was one way to put it. "She was pretty intense on camera, but she gave us some great ideas for Pie Town." She was passionate about doing baked goods right. Ilsa might have come on strong, but she had my respect.

"I'll have to call my sister. She used to work with Ilsa."

I straightened. "Really? When?"

"This was before Ilsa became big, of course. They worked together in a fancy, European-style restaurant and bakery in Vegas."

"In Vegas?" I asked, excited. Did I have an actual lead? Now that Ilsa was dead, I wasn't sure it mattered, but I pressed on. "Was that the restaurant that had to close because of a fire?"

"It was awful. My sister was out of work for weeks. The restaurant never recovered."

"Is there any chance I can talk to your sister?"

"Annie sleeps late, but if you want to call her later, she's usually off on Mondays." She drew a slim, leather notebook from the pocket of her caftan and scribbled a phone number. "Just tell her you're a friend of mine."

"Thanks."

Maureen ambled into the crowd as Charlene's sunshine-yellow Jeep rumbled up the drive.

I bit into my bacon, which was starting to cool.

Charlene parked beside my shipping container, and she and Ray hopped from the Jeep.

"I got your text." Charlene tugged down the sleeve of her green knit tunic. Beneath her matching leggings, she wore pink and purple striped socks.

Frederick, eyes shut, lounged over her shoulder. An odd sound emerged from his parted mouth. I think it was a snore.

"I didn't get a text," Ray said accusingly. His skin was splotchy, his spine bowed. He shifted his backpack over his rounded shoulder. The movement rumpled his black t-shirt with its cartoon-character front. He hitched up his faded, saggy jeans. "And it was Ilsa!" He blinked rapidly. "I can't believe she's dead. It was like she knew me."

"Sorry." I winced. I'd sent Charlene a text after I'd escaped Shaw's clutches last night, but I'd forgotten Ray. "It was really late when I left the station, and I haven't gotten into the habit yet of sending you updates. But I just got a lead," I said, trying to make up for my lapse. "Maureen's sister worked with Ilsa at that Vegas restaurant. Ray, do you want to call her?"

He jerked his gaze from the table. "But I don't know her."

"You can say you know Maureen," I said, nodding toward her, at the far end of the table.

"But I don't know Maureen," he whispered. "It would be weird. I'm not good at talking to people I don't know. No, you can make the call."

Charlene cleared her throat. "I figured we could use Ray at the hotel today."

"Hotel?" I gave myself a slight shake, nearly upending my paper plate. "Today?" I didn't remember making plans to visit the hotel. Besides, my father would still be there. What if I ran into him?

Maureen wandered up to us, her hip scarf jingling. "Would you two like some breakfast?"

"No thanks," Charlene said, ignoring Ray's obvious interest in the spread. "We've eaten."

"Come inside," I said. "You can tell me about the hotel." I didn't think the goddess gals had anything to do with, well, anything. It just didn't make sense to blab about our investigation in front of strangers.

Ray snagged a piece of bacon and followed me inside my tiny house, which felt even tinier with three people inside. "Um, have a seat." I motioned to the dining nook.

Ray sat and hunched over the table like Papa Bear stuck in Baby Bear's chair. He took a bite of the crispy bacon, then sighed and dropped it on the table. "It's no use. I can't eat. Not with Ilsa dead."

"Val, tell us everything." Charlene arranged Frederick on the table and sat.

Leaning against the kitchen counter, I explained about finding Ilsa's body and my interrogation at the police station. When I finished, my plate was clean. I pulled a footstool to the table, even though it really wasn't meant for more than two people. I pushed the discarded bacon aside with one finger.

Ray stared at his empty hands, limp on the tabletop. "But why Ilsa? She was innocent."

"Obviously, because she knew too much," Charlene said, bumping elbows with me.

"Knew what about who?" he asked.

"Whom," I corrected absently and scooted the wooden footstool closer to the table. "We've only got three murder suspects left: Nigel, Steve, and Luther."

"And Frank," Charlene said. "And that weird ninja kid Doran."

"I don't care what she knew," Ray said, his voice rough. "Ilsa didn't deserve to be murdered."

Frederick yawned, exposing sharp, white teeth and a rough, pink tongue.

"Frank couldn't have done it," I said, uneasy. Even though Ray didn't know Ilsa, her death clearly affected him. "I left him in the wine bar when I went chasing after Doran."

"But you don't know when Ilsa died," Charlene pointed out. "She could have been killed before you arrived."

"We need to learn her time of death," Ray said.

"Oh," Charlene said, "can you hack into the police station's files?"

Ray's jaw set, determined.

"That would be illegal," I said, afraid of his answer. Gordon would never forgive me if we hacked the SNPD. "Ilsa's body was still warm when I found her."

"But what does that mean?" Charlene asked. "Bodies don't drop to room temperature in an instant. It takes time."

"Bodies lose one point five degrees per hour," Ray said promptly, "varying on the corpse's environment."

We stared at him.

"I'm a student engineer," he said. "I remember formulas."

"She was lying out in the open," I said. "Most likely she was killed after dark, when the killer had less chance of being seen. I got to the hotel at eight, around sunset. So it must have happened while I was with Frank." The murderer had taken a terrible chance—killing her on the golf course. "Ilsa's body was hidden from the hotel and cliff trail by the golf course's hills. But people cut across the golf course at night. Killing her there was chancy."

"Or a mark of desperation," Charlene said.

"But this gets us closer to time of death." Ray whipped a

graph pad from his backpack and sketched a black line across it. "The lighting gets dim before the sun is completely down." He made a mark on the line. "But it doesn't get completely dark immediately after sunset." He made another mark, noting the time—*8:05*. "What time did you say you found the body?"

I dumped my paper plate in the garbage bin beneath the sink and returned to my perch on the wooden footstool. "Eight forty. I called 9-1-1 at eight forty-three."

He nodded. "If the killer needed darkness, he had a narrow window—say between eight twenty and eight forty. It won't be exact, but we can time things tonight to learn how long it takes after sunset to get real dark."

"At least we know the killer is a man," Charlene said. "We're all out of female suspects. And since it's our day off, there's no better time for suspect interviews. We need to go to the hotel." She pointed to the glass doors, and the cliff and horizon beyond.

"Good idea, but you can't bring a cat to the Belinda," I said.

On the table, Frederick yawned and stretched his furry white legs.

"That's not a problem," she said. "The goddesses will watch him."

I heaved myself off the footstool. "All right. Let me get dressed."

It didn't take me long to slip into jeans and a tank top. Since you never knew about the weather, I tied a black Pie Town hoodie around my waist. Soon we were bouncing down my dirt driveway in Charlene's Jeep. Herb Alpert and the Tijuana Brass blasted on the CD player. I'd never admit it to Charlene, but I was becoming a fan.

"I don't trust Nigel," Ray said. "The guy with the British accent is always the villain."

"Only in the movies," Charlene argued. "Nigel's no killer. It's got to be Steve. The spouse always does it."

I rested my elbow on the rear window ledge and watched traffic drift past on the One.

Charlene veered right into the hotel driveway and squeezed her Jeep into a compact spot.

Three local news vans sat parked in a far corner of the lot.

"You don't think they're here because of Ilsa?" I asked, rubbing my lower back. Charlene's Jeep had hit every bump on the rutted dirt road from my house.

"I'm sure of it," she said. "Ilsa's got a following, and two deaths on the crew make a big story."

Carefully, I opened the door, trying to avoid scratching the paint on the red Honda beside us. I wriggled from the car, and Ray popped out with a grunt.

A breeze raised goosebumps on my bare shoulders. We made our way through the parking lot, and I untied the light-weight hoodie from my waist and slipped my arms inside. Ray steered me around an island of wildflowers as I tugged it over my head.

The hotel lobby doors swished open. We walked inside the high-ceilinged entry, our feet sinking in the silvery-gray carpet. The reception area smelled like sagebrush and the ocean.

Ray inhaled. "So this is what rich smells like."

"I prefer pie." I pointed to a phone mounted above the wainscoting on a sand-colored wall. "Let's call Nigel, and see if he's here."

A light blinded me. "There she is!"

Squinting, I threw up my hand to shield my face.

"Ms. Harris, what do you know about these tragic deaths?" A female reporter I recognized from a San Francisco station shoved a microphone in my face.

"What?" I stepped backwards and onto Ray's foot.

The cameraman behind her twisted the lens, zooming in.

"First the *Pie Hard* producer and now one of its stars, Ilsa Fueder." Her blond hair was lacquered perfection, her lipstick-red suit sharp as a blade. "And these aren't the first deaths connected to Pie Town. A man was murdered in your bakery earlier this spring."

My spine went rigid. "He wasn't murdered there. He only died there." I scanned the elegant lobby for my moral support.

Charlene and Ray had vanished.

"Sorry, I have to go." I chose a random direction and fled, but I couldn't shake the reporter.

"Why are you here?" She trotted beside me. "To meet with the crew?"

I flipped my hair over my shoulder. "For breakfast. Try the mimosas."

"What have the police told you about the murders?"

Get away, get away, get away. "Nothing. I'm in the dark as much as anyone."

"But you haven't been in the past—"

I darted into an empty conference room, slammed the door shut, and shot the bolt into the ceiling. Chairs sat stacked against two walls.

This was ridiculous. I didn't have anything to hide. Why was I running? I kept moving. There was a door on the opposite side of the room, and I hurried to it. It opened into another conference room, which in turn had a door opening onto the golf course.

I slipped outside and walked around the hotel perimeter until I found another entry. The heavy, glass door opened onto a long hallway with picture windows facing the ocean and a gray carpet threaded with gold.

Wary of stumbling on more reporters, I turned a corner and sidled past hotel rooms.

A door opened behind me. Someone grabbed my arm and yanked me backward.

I yelped like a scalded coyote.

Nigel released me and looked up and down the hall. "Quick. Inside."

Rubbing my arm, I stepped into the gray-and-white room. He shut the door and bolted it.

Towels and children's swimsuits hung from every conceivable surface—from the big-screen TV, across a modern desk chair, over a concrete-colored lamp. A picture window faced the ocean. A beach ball sat near a couch with lime green and mercury-colored cushions.

"This can't be your room," I said.

"Absobloodylutely not." The consultant's accent had migrated from Queen's English to Cockney. He raked a hand through his coal-black hair. One button on his dress shirt was in the wrong loop. "Some of my fans let me hide in here. Are the reporters still in the hotel?"

"I ran into one in the lobby."

His shoulders slumped, and he dropped onto the edge of an unmade bed. "What a shambles." He hadn't shaved that morning, the shadow darkening his cheeks making him rakish.

"I've heard no publicity is bad publicity." And I really hoped it was true.

He gazed at me balefully. "Bollocks. The show's dead without Regina and Ilsa. And I liked Ilsa. Regina too."

"I did too."

He shot me a surprised look.

"You've met Charlene," I said.

He barked a laugh. "I suppose you thrive on challenging personalities."

"Where were you last night between eight and eight-forty?" I walked to the couch. Edging a damp, striped towel aside, I sat.

He arched a piratical brow. "Is that when Ilsa died? If you're trying to suss out my alibi, the police have already asked, and I don't have one. I was in my room, woefully alone," he said, his posh accent creeping back. Nigel smiled, wistful. "A pity you didn't join me."

It was a half-hearted pass, so I ignored it.

"Though I hear you have something going with the rozzer," he continued. Has he told you anything? Do they suspect anyone?"

"He's off the case."

"But he must know something. What have you heard?"

"He can't talk about it. Did you see or notice anything last night? Do you have any idea who might have done this?"

Arms crossed, he fell back on the unmade bed and studied the ceiling. "Ilsa could be a little rough on the crew, but no more than Regina."

"Who is also dead."

"Really," he drawled, "if crews murdered every demanding star and producer, there wouldn't be any of us left. Dealing with egos is part of their job."

"And what's your ego like?"

"I like to think I'm easy going, but I'm sure I've given the crew plenty of aggro. We're like a family, always in each other's pockets, and that makes it easy to get on each other's nerves."

"Yet for all your closeness, no one seems to have any idea who wanted to kill Ilsa and Regina." Or were they covering for someone?

My cell phone rang in the pocket of my Pie Town hoodie. I checked the number. Charlene. "Do you mind?" I asked Nigel. Without waiting for a response, I answered the phone. "Where are you?"

"Ray and I are in the spa. It was the only place we could go where reporters wouldn't follow."

"Why were reporters following you?" How would reporters even know Ray and Charlene were involved in anything?

"I'm a local celebrity," Charlene said. "And they *were* following me. Ray too."

I rolled my eyes. "Fine. I'll meet you there."

There was soft murmuring, as if Charlene had covered the phone with her hand. "Give us an hour or so," she said. "We're getting massages."

"Massages?"

"Paparazzi are stressful!" She hung up.

Irritated, I blew out my breath. I hoped they weren't couples' massages, because that would be an image I'd never get out of my head.

Damn. And now it *was* in my head.

Someone knocked—shave-and-a-haircut.

Nigel walked to the door and peered through the peephole. "Steve." He yanked open the door and the cameraman hurried inside.

Steve cursed. "I didn't think I'd be able to shake them."

"Makes you wonder about those days you were paparazzi," Nigel said dryly. "Turnabout and fair play and all that."

Steve glared. "My wife and Ilsa are dead. I'm not in the mood for your jokes." He was wearing jeans and a baggy college sweatshirt rather than his usual photographer's vest. His gray hair was rumpled.

"But you don't mind taking advantage of my shelter," Nigel said.

Steve's hand trembled. His gray hair was rumpled. "And you didn't mind taking advantage of my wife."

"Taking advantage?" I asked.

"Mind out of the gutter, please," Nigel said to me. "Steve thinks the show was too good for me."

"It was," Steve snapped.

Nigel sketched an ironic bow. "And yet, like a loyal serf,

I offered Steve shelter in my borrowed abode." He flipped a towel off the desk chair and motioned Steve toward it. "I was watching for him when you walked past. Though now I'm wondering why I bothered."

"Because you owe us." The cameraman collapsed in the cushioned chair. A towel slid off its back and into a smooth, brushed-nickel wastebin. "My wife may have been forgiving of your debts, but I'm not."

"What do Nigel's debts have to do with Regina?" I asked.

"She was kind enough to lend me some money during a small financial difficulty," Nigel said.

The cameraman snorted. "Small?"

"And I will pay you back," Nigel said. "Eventually."

"What are you doing here?" Steve asked me.

"She's interrogating the suspects," Nigel said. "I have no alibi. You?"

His jaw clenched. "I was in my room most of the night, like everyone else."

"Not everyone," Nigel said. "Ilsa was apparently wandering the golf course by moonlight."

"There was no moon," I said. "It made the golf course darker." Why was Steve here when he had his own room to hide in? Had he come to have it out with Nigel, or was he really seeking shelter from the reporters? "Did you see Luther at all last night?"

"And by last night," Nigel said helpfully, "she means between eight o'clock and eight forty."

"How could I?" Steve asked. "Like I said, I was in my room." He ran a palm over his gray hair. "You have no idea how much there is to do after a death."

My heart dipped. I knew all too well, but I looked to Nigel.

He shrugged. "What he said."

"Was I imagining things," I said, "or was Ilsa protective of Luther?" She'd seemed defensive of him at the pub, but she'd been critical of his absences. Had she been protecting him, or had she been trying to keep him from telling me something?

"Ilsa isn't—wasn't—the monster people thought she was," Steve said.

"Her personality seemed a little . . . erratic," I said.

"She was the *hard* in *Pie Hard*," Nigel said. "But it was all a TV persona to build conflict within the show."

"Story is about conflict," Steve said. "I don't know how many times I heard Regina say that."

"You worked with Ilsa," Nigel said to me. "You know the truth. She might have been rough on people, but she was a marvelous pastry chef."

"If a bit high strung," the cameraman said.

"That isn't fair," Nigel said.

Steve kicked aside a beach ball. It ricocheted off the entertainment center and bounced off a couch. "Come on, one minute Ilsa was all smiles, and the next she was mad as blazes. Her mood swings were legendary. I think she was bipolar. You could never tell if she was using hyperbole or telling the flat out truth."

That might account for her erratic attitude toward Luther, but she hadn't seemed all that off.

"Has that cop friend of yours said anything?" Steve asked.

"Like I told Nigel, he's off the case."

"He's still a cop. He must hear things."

"What do you need to hear?" Nigel asked. "Only three suspects are still standing—you, me and Luther. And I know I didn't do it."

"Well, I sure as hell didn't," Steve said. "And there are four suspects. You forgot our new producer. Something's not right about that guy. I've put in a call to the execs in L.A. With everything that's happened, they're going to have to give me some answers."

I looked toward the curtained windows, my neck tensing.

Nigel paled. "Why would our temporary producer kill Regina?"

"He stole her job, didn't he?"

"That doesn't seem a likely motive," I said faintly. "I heard it was only a temporary job. And I left him at the bar before I found Ilsa."

"Oh?" Steve jammed his fists on his hips. "How long did it take you to find her? Because I saw Frank wandering the golf course last night before Ilsa was found."

CHAPTER 20

Worried, the second thing I did when I left Nigel and Steve was call Frank. The first thing I did was check to make sure there were no reporters lurking in the hotel hallway.

Phone clamped to my ear, I huddled in a window nook overlooking the golf course and the glittering Pacific.

The call went to voice mail. "You know the drill," Frank said. "Leave a message."

"It's Val. Call me. It's urgent." I hung up and crept to the lobby. It was clear of reporters, and I darted to the high reception desk.

A sleek receptionist looked up from her computer and smiled. "How can I help you?"

"Can you put me through to Luther Armstrong's room?" I glanced behind me.

She pointed me to a phone on the wall. "Just pick up the receiver, and the phone will ring."

"Thanks." I hurried to the phone.

Two reporters with matching cameramen appeared out of nowhere and sidled up to me.

Ignoring them, I tapped my foot, listening to the phone ring.

A camera light flared. Shoulders hunched, I faced the sand-colored wall.

The phone kept ringing. Reluctantly, I hung up.

"Have you met with what's left of the *Pie Hard* crew?" the blond reporter asked as she smoothed the front of her scarlet blazer.

I brushed past her and into the hallway.

"Do you believe someone on the crew is the killer?" a portly male reporter shouted.

"Some are saying an obsessed fan might be to blame. Do you think that could be true?"

I fled down the hall toward the spa. "I don't know anything."

"Some are calling this the Pie Town killer," the female reporter said. "What's your response?"

I stumbled at that. Pie Town killer? Nigel was right. There was such a thing as bad publicity. I broke into a jog.

"What about the hoodie?" the man called.

"On sale for $19.99," I tossed over my shoulder. *My Pie Town hoodie? What was that about?* I pushed through the wooden door to the spa.

A spa employee in a blue golf shirt looked up. She braced her hand on the smoked-glass reception desk and smiled. "Can I help you?"

I glanced over my shoulder at the frosted-glass door. None of the reporters followed me inside. "I'm waiting for two of your guests," I said in a low voice. A fountain trickled on the reception desk. I felt underdressed in my jeans and hoodie. "May I wait here?"

She motioned to one of the slate-colored lounge chairs. Soft-looking white blankets lay neatly folded at their feet.

"Thanks." I sank into it and waited. I played with the

mini sand garden on the end table. I picked up a healthy lifestyle magazine and flipped through the pages. I fiddled with the adjustments on the chair, which fully reclined. Did those two really have to get massages?

Forty-three minutes later, Charlene, skin glowing, emerged in her green tunic and leggings. She paid and sat with a sigh in the lounge chair beside mine.

"Where's Ray?" I snapped.

"Changing, I guess. After what he's been through, he needed some T.L.C. Did you learn anything?"

Ray *was* pretty upset about Ilsa's death, I thought guiltily. I shouldn't be so judge-y about the massage. In whispers, I told her about my meeting with Nigel and Steve. "You don't really think Steve could have seen Frank on the golf course?" I asked. "It was dark."

"There are lights on that course," she said in her outdoor voice. "And since they've been working together, he'd probably recognize his own producer."

The receptionist shot her a look sharp as a katana blade.

"Right," I said quietly, hoping Charlene would take the hint and lower the volume.

She patted my hand. "It may not mean anything," she boomed. "Frank's got no motive we can see to bump off Regina and Ilsa."

"Shhh." The receptionist pressed a finger to her lips and pointed to a sign that read: *QUIET ZONE*.

Ray emerged from the spa and shambled to us. Round face pink, he collapsed onto a chair beside mine. The blanket at his feet slipped to the wooden floor. "Wow. You were right, Mrs. McCree. I do feel better. Thanks."

"Stick with me kid." She patted his knee. "Just not too close. It'll ruin my street cred if people think I'm friends with a nerd. You understand."

"How'd you avoid the press?" he asked me.

I explained about Nigel and Steve. "When I couldn't find Frank or Luther, I ducked in here. For all I know, reporters may still be waiting outside."

"I suppose we can't hide in here forever," Charlene said.

"No." The receptionist glowered. "You can't."

"Come on." I heaved myself off the comfy chair and peeked out the door.

The carpeted hallway was empty.

I motioned to Ray and Charlene, and we crept from the spa.

Charlene drove us from the hotel, dropping Ray at a modern-looking condo on the beach side of the highway.

The two of us drove past the dog park. A familiar-looking sedan parked beside the wire fence—Gordon's. Two golden retrievers romped on the lawn.

"So what's next?" she asked.

"I left a message for Frank to call me," I hedged, tearing my gaze from the dog park. "And we don't know where Luther is. I'll call Maureen's sister, Annie, but we can't do much more until we locate Luther. Plus, I have some errands to run."

"Want company?"

"Oh, you'd be bored," I said quickly. "Just grocery shopping."

"I need to go grocery shopping."

"And then I need to get the van's oil changed."

"You're on your own." She swerved right, onto the road leading into the hills and to my blue-painted, converted shipping container.

She retrieved Frederick from the goddess gals, waved, and zoomed away, *Whipped Cream* blaring from the Jeep's speakers.

I waited five minutes, then got into my pink van and drove down the narrow road. Eucalyptus branches scraped the sides of the old VW, and I gritted my teeth. I really needed to trim those branches.

On the main road, I turned west, toward town and the dog park. When I arrived, Gordon's gray sedan was still parked along the sidewalk. He sat inside, his head bent toward his computer.

I parked on the street and walked to his car window.

He rolled it down. "Hey, Val, what's up?" In his dark sunglasses all I could see was my own wavering reflection.

"I just came from the hotel," I said.

He tossed his computer tablet on the seat and unfolded his tall, muscular form from the car.

My pulse quickened.

"Did you run into the reporters?" His voice, concerned and commanding, sent a ripple of awareness through me. It didn't hurt that he looked darn good in his dress shirt and navy slacks.

"Yeah." I leaned against the sedan. "I think I was a disappointment."

"They're all over this case. For once, I'm glad Shaw is taking point. Did you see the chief on TV this morning?"

"I'm sorry I missed it." I crossed my arms and grinned. I couldn't help smiling around him. "What are you doing at the dog park? I thought the fairy problem had been taken care of."

Before Gordon left for his extended training trip to Wyoming, the SNPD fielded complaints about supernatural lights in the dog park. He'd caught the very human, very embarrassed culprit and let him off with a warning.

He glanced through the open window at the computer tablet. "It was. I'm just catching up on paperwork."

"I ran into Steve and Nigel."

He arched a brow. "Ran into?"

"Okay, I was looking for them, but that's not the point." I

crossed my legs. "Steve told me he saw Frank on the golf course the night Ilsa was killed."

Gordon's expression smoothed. "Did he?"

"I tried calling Frank, but he's not answering," I blundered on. "He's not . . . He's not at the police station, is he?"

"Not the last time I was there, but I'm off the case, remember? Shaw's not keeping me informed." He shifted his weight and looked towards the dogs. A Chihuahua joined the two retrievers, and yapped in steady, high-pitched barks.

My heart cratered. So Gordon did blame me for his removal. "I wish I could make this up to you. It's unfair you're off the case."

He turned toward me, his gaze remote. "You have nothing to apologize for. It's just one of those things."

"I shouldn't worry about Frank—I barely know the man." I dropped my arms. "But for some reason—"

"Val." He pulled off his sunglasses and polished them on a loose bit of his shirt fabric.

I dragged my palms down the thighs of my jeans and waited, dreading what might come.

"There's something I need to tell you," he finally said, meeting my gaze.

"Shaw thinks my father's a suspect, doesn't he? On the positive side, Shaw is nearly always wrong, so that means Frank couldn't have killed anyone."

"Val . . ." He used a tone I'd never heard on him before—hesitant, unsure.

My lungs tightened. "What's wrong?"

"The press has this," he said rapidly, "so I'm not breaking any confidences by telling you. A man was seen on the golf course around the time we think Ilsa was killed. He was wearing a Pie Town hoodie."

I braced my hand against the roof of his sedan and jerked it away, palm burning. So *that* was what the reporter had meant about a Pie Town killer and the hoodie. "I gave the entire crew black Pie Town hoodies," I whispered, horrified.

"I'll make sure the chief knows."

"They're not . . . They're not really calling him the Pie Town Killer, are they?" I shouldn't have cared. Two people were dead. Pie Town couldn't take another hit like it had this spring, when someone had died at my counter. If Pie Town went under . . . I couldn't start a new business. It would be over. I had so many new ideas. Pie in a jar! Pie shots! Pie samplers!

His expressive face grew serious. "I hadn't heard that, but I haven't been watching the news since the chief's conference this morning. We'll figure this out, Val."

"Will we? You're off the case." My laugh was shaky. If I lost Pie Town, would I have to leave San Nicholas? This part of California wasn't on the high-affordability list. It was only because of Charlene's low-rent tiny home that I was able to make ends meet. I shook my head. I couldn't worry about what might happen to Pie Town. There were more pressing concerns. "Were you able to learn any more about Frank?"

"I did," he said and nodded to a green park bench. "Let's sit."

I had to sit down for this? That was never a good sign. "This is bad news, isn't it? Just tell me."

"Frank isn't who he seems to be."

"You mean he's not my father?" Disappointment and relief twined inside my gut.

"He is your father, but he's not exactly an addiction coach."

"Not exactly?" My voice grew shrill. "How not exactly?"

"Your father's an enforcer for the mob."

CHAPTER 21

I stared at Gordon in horrified disbelief. Birds chirped on the electric lines running through the tree branches above. Dogs frolicked in the park. The sun shone merrily on our shoulders. And my world imploded. "What?"

"They call him the Persuader." The line of his mouth tightened.

"What?"

He averted his gaze. "I'm sorry, Val. I've triple checked this. I didn't want to say anything until I was certain. That's why I've been so distant lately. That and the stabbing case. Keeping this from you has been pure hell."

"My father is a mobster?"

"Low level, if that makes you feel any better."

"Why would that make me feel better?" I raked my hands through my hair. This wasn't happening. My father? In the mob? Did that make me part of the "family?" It wasn't possible. "My life is a telenovela! TV shows, ninjas, mobsters. What else? Are you my secret long-lost brother? Do fairies really exist? Maybe Charlene's right about Bigfoot." Oh, God. Did that mean UFOs were real too?

"My parents would be pretty surprised to learn we were brother and sister," he said, wryly.

Breathing heavily, I dropped my chin to my chest. If my father was a criminal, it would explain why my mother had cut contact with Frank so completely. "What exactly do you mean by enforcer?"

"He's a debt collector."

Nausea clenched my throat.

Frank had lied to me. What had I expected? I'd known he was no good from the start, but I'd wanted to believe him. He'd been so charming. Frank didn't look or sound like a goon. "Are you sure? Shouldn't he be . . . I dunno, bigger? Or meaner?"

"Val, your father's the Persuader."

I slumped against the sedan.

"I know how disappointed you must be."

"I shouldn't be. I hardly know the man. There's nothing to be disappointed about." My voice shook.

He pulled me to his broad chest and wrapped his arms around me. "I'm disappointed too. You deserve better."

Tears heated my eyes. Turning my head toward the dog park, I blinked them away. Frank had been in my life for less than a week, and I'd let him get under my skin. After twenty-five years, I should have been smarter. I rested my ear against Gordon's chest and listened to the soothing, steady beat of his heart, inhaled the scent of his woodsy cologne. "Thank you for telling me," I mumbled. "It's better to know." Ignorance truly was bliss, though. I pulled away. "Does the chief know?"

"I had to tell him, though I didn't tell him why I was looking into Frank. Fortunately, he didn't ask."

"This is going to move Frank up the suspect list, won't it?" Was my father a killer? Had those elegant hands broken bones?

He nodded. "Shaw will still need to figure out Frank's motive. Staying at the Belinda, he had means and opportunity. A mobster in the mix raises eyebrows. Has your father given you any hints or sign about what he's really doing here?"

"No." But I was damned sure going to find out.

Not even the Goddess Gals could cheer me up when I returned to my tiny house. Chest aching, I retreated to my sleeping area behind the bookcase and curled up on my futon.

It all made sense now. I thought my mother refused to speak about my dad because he'd hurt her so badly. The truth was far worse.

Sighing, I got Annie's phone number off my kitchen counter. Now that Ilsa was dead, calling her was probably a moot point. I called her anyway.

"Hello?" a sleepy voice asked.

"Hi," I said dully. "This is Val Harris. I'm a friend of your sister, Maureen."

I glanced out the big glass doors. The goddesses sat in a circle in front of the yurt, their arms raised over their head. As one, they let out a whoop.

"Yes?" she asked.

"I own a pie shop, and *Pie Hard* came to film us. Ilsa Fueder died." I went to perch on the futon.

"I heard. It's awful."

"I understand you worked with her in Las Vegas. Were you and Ilsa close?"

She snorted. "High and mighty Ilsa? Are you kidding me?"

"I wanted to ask you about the fire at the restaurant you two worked at. Did anyone ever figure out who set it?"

"I only know it was arson. Rumor had it the owner might have set it himself. But as far as I know, no one was ever arrested."

Tires crunched up the drive, and I checked my watch. Just past eleven, time for the lunchtime catering truck.

Outside, a car door slammed, and I wrinkled my brow. I hadn't heard an engine.

"Could Ilsa have done it?" I asked.

There was a long silence. "She was furious with the owner, and I saw her do some crazy things—throw dishes at people, shout at customers. But I never thought she set that fire."

Someone rapped on my door.

"Well," I said, "thanks. I'm sorry, someone's at my door. I have to go."

"Good luck with *Pie Hard*. They're rough on bakeries."

"So they say." We said our goodbyes and hung up.

"Val?" Frank called. "You in there?"

I hesitated for a moment, wondering if I could play possum. But then I rolled off the futon and walked to the door. I opened it and stood unmoving, blocking the entry.

"Hey!" Natty in a tweed sports jacket and pressed, brown slacks, Frank smiled up at me. "I got your message and thought I'd swing by and see if you were home."

Unable to speak, I didn't budge from the doorway.

He gazed across the lawn at the goddesses, sitting motionless in a meditation circle beside the yurt. "So they're still here. May I come in? I'd love to see your place."

"It's not mine. It's a rental." Grudgingly, I stepped aside. I didn't want him inside my home, but I couldn't inflict him on the Goddess Gals. Being a mobster had to carry all sorts of bad karma. It might wreck their groove.

He climbed the two steps into my container home and took in the kitchen, eating area, desk set into the wall, bookcase. "You won't be renting for long, I'll bet. Soon you'll have a string of Pie Towns across California. Have you ever thought of franchising?"

My lips flattened. "No." He'd probably try to turn them into a money laundering scheme.

He ambled into the kitchen and peered inside a cupboard. "I used to live in a trailer, before I met your mother. It wasn't as nice as this one. Not as big either."

"Was that before you joined the mob?"

He shut the cupboard and turned to me, his arms loose at his sides. "Ah."

My chest ached with disappointment. He wasn't denying it. Pulling out a chair beside my miniscule dining table, I dropped onto it with a thud. "Then it's true."

"There are all sorts of shades of truth."

"No, there aren't. You're either in the mob or you're not."

"You sound just like your mother." He came to sit across from me.

"Did she know what you were before she married you?"

"Before she married me, I worked as a car salesman. Afterward, too. It was a steady job, and I was good at it."

I rolled my eyes. Of course he'd been great selling cars. That explained his hokey charm.

"Some of the guys started a weekly poker game. It seemed innocent enough." He wiped his brow. "But once I got a taste of winning, I wanted more. And then I started losing and couldn't stop. I became a gambling addict. Your mother tried to be patient, but then some collection agents showed up on our doorstep when you were home."

"What kind of collection agents?" I asked. I didn't remember any of this, but of course my mother would have shielded me.

"The wrong kind. Your mother and I agreed that for her sake and yours, it was time for me to leave."

When he put it that way, it almost sounded selfless. I clenched my fists. Dammit, he was persuading me! "That doesn't explain how you came to become a collection agent for the mob. The Persuader, isn't that what you're called?" Nausea swam up my chest and into my throat.

"I'll assume your detective found that out for you."

"Does it matter who found out?" I asked, my voice shrill.

"Of course not, but you don't understand—"

I leaned back in my chair. "I think I've seen enough movies to understand everything. How far do you go to persuade people, Frank? Breaking legs? Threatening families?"

He raised his hands and reared away. "Heavens no! I persuade. How do you think I got out of my own little problem? I was always able to talk the men they sent out of breaking my arm. I can be charming when I put my mind to it. And so the mob sent higher ups, and then more higher ups. Soon they realized it would be best for all concerned if they just made me part of the team. It's so much cleaner to reason people into paying their debts rather than bringing in the heavies. The authorities take a dim view of that sort of thing."

"You're telling me the mob has reformed," I said, mouth slackening. How gullible did he think I was?

"Not exactly." One corner of his mouth tilted upward. "I prefer to think of myself as providing their white glove service. I only work with elite clientele with high income-earning potential that could be impeded by injury."

There was a whoop from outside, and a drum began a slow, steady beat.

"Without the jargon?" I asked.

"I work with actors, dear. They can't earn money to pay up if their legs are broken or their faces bruised. It's only logical I—"

"Wait, actors? You mean you haven't been in Vegas all this time? You've been in Hollywood?" I grew up alone, in not-so-far-away Orange County.

"My employers are in Vegas. My work takes me to various places. Mostly Canada. You'd be surprised how many films are made there these days. That and Iceland. Now that country is amazing."

"And you want me to believe you just *talk* people into paying."

"Talk, cajole, I work with them to figure out ways to pay, get them onto payment plans. I've got a ninety-eight percent success rate, knock wood." He rapped on the fold-out table.

"That's Formica. And the other two percent?"

"Ah, I step away from the situation at that point. Not sure what happens afterward, and don't want to know."

"Oh, my God." How could he rationalize this?

"Val, I help people. I keep them away from the goons and leg breakers, and ensure a peaceful resolution to any contractual disputes."

"You work for the mob!"

"Think of me as the lesser of two evils. I've saved many people from extensive pain and suffering. And I get them into treatment. I've got a ninety-eight percent success rate there too. As I learned the hard way, that debt is never going to get paid if you keep digging the hole deeper with more gambling."

"It's still the mob."

He smiled, rueful. "I see you have your mother's superpower."

"What's that?"

"Resistance to persuasion. It's incredibly attractive. She's the only woman I knew who had it. Well, her and—" He shook his head. "Did she tell you how we met?"

"No."

"I tried to sell her a used VW. A real lemon. She saw right through me. I knew then and there she was the one."

"Whatever," I said. "Why are you really here?"

His blue eyes widened. "I told you. I'm working with Nigel. He owes a lot of money, and his face is his fortune. He's never going to earn an income to repay it all if my colleagues have to get rough with him."

"So you're *persuading* him. Out of the goodness of your heart."

He pressed his broad hands to the gold-flecked tabletop.

"Not entirely. I made my own deal, remember, and I'm well compensated. Ninety-eight percent success! I'll admit, knowing who I represent motivates people to listen. And once they're open to listening, they see a lifeline. I have a chance to set them on the straight and narrow."

It was the biggest cock and bull story I'd heard since Charlene claimed aliens in the dog park were masquerading as fairies. Sap that I am, I wanted to believe he wasn't a bad guy, that even if he was working for the mob, he was actually helping people get out from under them. That he didn't use violence. It shouldn't have mattered one way or the other. The mob was the mob. But he really was persuasive.

"Please," he said. "Do you think for one minute your mother would have married a knee breaker?"

"No," I said slowly. My mother had always been sensible, by the book. I couldn't imagine her getting swept off her feet by a mobster, but how well do we know our parents' younger selves? Maybe she'd learned her lessons the hard way.

He sighed. "You don't trust me."

"It's a lot to swallow."

He spread open his hands. "What can I do to gain your trust?"

My breathing grew loud in my ears. "You can tell me everything you know about the *Pie Hard* crew and these murders."

"I have told you everything."

A cloud covered the sun, darkening the tiny house.

"Why were you on the golf course the night Ilsa was killed?"

"I wasn't."

"You were seen wearing a Pie Town hoodie."

"Then someone made a mistake."

"Then where were you before you met me in the bar?" I asked.

"I was on a phone call. The hotel will have a record of it. That's why I was a tad late meeting you at the bar that night."

"I heard Nigel borrowed money from Regina," I said. "Was that to pay off his more . . . urgent debts?"

His lips twisted. "He had? He'd told me he'd borrowed from a friend, but I didn't know who had been foolish enough to do so. Still, Regina makes sense. She and her husband are wealthy, and I think she had a soft spot for Nigel."

"What do you know about her finances?" In any murder, the spouse is the most likely suspect. Regina's money was now Steve's, no divorce or lawyers needed.

"Just gossip. She and her husband made their money in real estate, and I believe their TV shows have done well. But Regina was the power behind that success. She knew what made good TV. Everyone I've spoken with agrees on that."

"What about Luther?"

He smiled, rueful. "I wish I could help that poor soul with his drinking problem. I believe he mentioned something about going to the beach today. The one with the crab shack?"

"Sam's Crab Shack and Bar?" I knew that beach. "Great. Thanks." I scraped back my chair.

He looked up at me from the table. "You're not going to try to find him alone?"

"It's broad daylight," I said. "What could happen?"

"And now you've just jinxed yourself." He stood. "I'm coming with you."

I forced a smile. "It's okay. You don't have to. I'm sure you're busy." I needed some alone time to process his latest revelations.

"But I want to."

I grabbed my purse off the kitchen counter, and Frank followed me outside. The caterer's teal van had arrived, and their team was setting up the picnic table.

Maureen fluttered to us, her coin belt jingling. "Are you leaving so soon? Won't you stay for lunch?"

"What a delightful prospect," Frank said, taking her plump hand and brushing a kiss across its back.

"No," I said. "We can't. But thanks."

"Surely Luther can wait," Frank said.

"No." I glared.

He sighed and tipped an imaginary hat to Maureen. "Duty calls." He opened the passenger door of the silver Tesla.

I leveled a glare at him.

He smiled in return, his hand on the open car door.

Oh, h-e-double hockey sticks. Maybe bringing along some muscle wasn't such a bad idea. Luther was a big guy. If he'd been drinking, I wasn't sure I could handle him. "Fine. You can come." I lowered myself inside.

Frank got in beside me, and we zipped off. He managed to avoid the branches on the sloped driveway that I always scraped.

Soon, we were flying down the One, the top down and the wind whipping my hair. Frank darted around a big rig and waved jauntily to the driver.

I gripped my seatbelt.

"There's nothing like a convertible on a sunny day at the beach."

"In theory." I clawed my hair into a bun. A piece whipped free and stung me in the eye.

He glanced at me. "Should I raise the top?" Frank shouted.

"We're almost there." I pointed to a turnoff ahead.

"Right." He screeched around the corner, and we bulleted toward the shore. Frank piloted the sports car into a parking lot surrounded by high sea grasses and low dunes. Since it was late Monday morning, the parking lot was only half-full—I guessed by local teens on their summer break.

Frank screeched to a halt in a spot furthest from the beach and surrounded by empty spaces. He winked. "No sense getting this beauty dinged up."

I stepped from the Tesla and headed toward the bar, a low, gray-painted building with weathered, wood sideboards. A crooked deck wove across the sand toward the water. We started toward the door.

"Look there." Frank halted, pointing. A man lay sprawled, the top half of his body on the sand and his feet on the deck. "Is that Luther?"

My stomach rolled. "Oh, no." I veered around the bar and onto the beach.

I raced toward the assistant cameraman. *Not Luther. Let him be alive.*

"Val," Frank called, "wait!"

My shadow fell across Luther's still form.

He opened one eye, and I breathed a sigh of relief.

"Getting some sun?" Frank huffed up behind me.

Luther's Hawaiian shirt gaped, exposing his hairy belly. "Can't a man enjoy the beach without being harassed?" he asked, his words perfectly clipped. For once, maybe he wasn't drunk.

"No rest for the wicked," Frank said.

"What do you two want?" He tossed a handful of sand at Frank's feet.

"Watch it." Frank's brow creased with annoyance.

"I thought the filming was over," Luther said.

I sat cross-legged in the sand beside him. "I'm sorry about Ilsa. I could tell you two cared about each other."

He squeezed his eyes shut and moaned. "If I knew who killed them, I'd kill him myself."

"You know more than the police, I'll bet," I said.

"That's what you say." Luther opened his eyes and stared at a seagull hanging motionless high above us.

"Maybe you can help bring their killer to justice," I said gently. "What's happening with the *Pie Hard* crew? Because it has to be someone on the crew, don't you think?"

He glared at Frank. "Maybe."

"The police are asking all sorts of questions," my father said. "You must admit, you're not the easiest assistant cameraman to work with—"

"AC and sound," Luther corrected.

"Be that as it may," Frank said, "Regina kept you on. Why?"

"I've been pondering that very question." Luther sat up and rubbed his head. Sand trickled from his hair. "I was always on thin ice with her, but she wouldn't let me quit. She insisted I could fight the booze. For a while I believed her, but she was just projecting."

"Projecting?" I asked. "What do you mean?"

"She thought she could fight, cure herself. Hell, maybe she could have. If a miracle could happen to anyone, Regina could make damn sure it happened to her."

"Wait," I said. "Are you saying Regina was ill?"

"Ill?" Luther blinked blearily. "Regina was dying."

CHAPTER 22

"Dying?" Stunned, I stared at Luther, sprawled in the sand.

The waves crashed—a rising drumbeat. A seagull wavered in the sky. It ha-ha-ha'd at us, then landed on the bar's shingle roof.

Luther scratched his sunburnt cheek, and a trickle of sand drifted from his fingers onto his Hawaiian shirt. "There's no cure for what Regina had."

"What did she have?" Frank knelt in the sand beside him. A breeze flapped the bottom of his tweed blazer.

"Lou Gehrig's disease, ALS."

A roar of laughter rose from the outdoor bar, and involuntarily, I turned my head toward the weathered, gray building. I didn't know much about Lou Gehrig's, but I knew it was awful.

"When was she diagnosed?" Frank asked, somber.

"Nine months ago. I only found out because . . ." He looked toward the ocean and blinked rapidly. "She told me if she had to fight ALS, I could damn well fight my drinking problem. We'd agreed I'd go to rehab after we finished shooting this season."

"How much time did she have?" Frank asked.

Luther shrugged. "Three years? Five? Ten? Hell, with Regina, I wouldn't have been surprised if she beat all the doctors' predictions. She was that kind of determined."

Small black birds with long, narrow bills raced along the shoreline. Swerving up and down the sand, they avoided the lap of waves.

"Did anyone else know about her disease?" I asked. If Regina was dying, this put a new perspective on motives.

"Aside from Steve? I don't think so. After we finished the season, they were planning on going to India together, try some special treatment. Stem cells, I think." Luther shook his head. "She'd be in India, and I'd be in rehab. Now none of it's going to happen."

"You can still go to rehab," Frank said. "It sounds like Regina would want you to."

His laugh turned into a cough. "Regina doesn't want anything anymore. Besides, who'd pay for it?"

"Regina was going to pay for your treatment?" I asked.

"Yeah. Don't think Steve was too happy about it, but it was Regina's money."

"Her husband didn't have money of his own?" I asked.

"They came up together. Both of 'em started from nothing, and they were always share and share alike. But Regina was the driving force. She made the big bucks. But if you think Steve killed her for the money, you're wrong. He knew she was dying. All he had to do was wait, see? There's only one person who would have reason to kill her."

My heart sank. Nigel. He was the only one left, assuming Luther was to be believed. "You think Nigel killed Regina?"

"He owed her money. Lots. I'm guessing she was pushing him to repay, and he gave her a shove over the cliff."

Frank rubbed his chin.

"And Ilsa?" I asked.

"She must have seen him throw her off." Luther shot upright and pointed. "That ninja kid."

"You think he looks like a ninja too?" I shook myself. Focus. "What about him?"

"What the hell's he doing here?" He pointed.

Dark head bent, Doran slogged up the beach, his hands in the pockets of his khakis.

Startled, I jumped to my feet and brushed sand from my jeans. "You've seen him before?"

"That kid's been turning up since we got to San Nicholas," the assistant cameraman said. "Who is he?"

"That's what I intend to find out," I said grimly and started forward.

Frank grasped my arm. "Maybe we're seeing threats where there aren't any. The young man is staying at the same hotel we are, and this is a small town. Of course we're seeing him everywhere."

"He's a freelance graphic designer," I said. "How's he staying at such an expensive hotel? And why for so long?"

"Maybe he has a wealthy client here?" Frank said.

Doran crested a dune near the parking lot.

"Let's ask him." I moved to pull away, but Frank's grip tightened.

"It isn't safe, Val," he said. "You can't accost random strangers and demand answers."

"Then come with me."

Doran wove through the cars near the beach's edge. The sun glittered, blinding, off their windshields.

"I'm no detective, Val, and neither are you. Two people have been killed. This is serious."

"It's broad daylight." I shook myself free. "He's not going to try anything in a parking lot." I jogged beside the crooked deck toward the line of seagrass that marked the boundary of the black pavement.

"Val! Wait!"

Ignoring him, I slogged through the sand and arrived, panting, in the lot. Doran was nowhere in sight. I wove past the cars clustered by the sand's edge, past teenagers unloading body boards and hampers and towels, past an elderly woman walking her corgi.

I swore beneath my breath. Doran had vanished. Maybe he'd gone inside the bar?

Frank caught up to me. "I told you this was useless."

"You told me it was dangerous. He could be in the bar."

"He was coming from the beach. Why wouldn't he just use the beach entrance?"

"Well, he's not here," I said, exasperated and wishing I'd tackled Luther with Charlene instead. Nothing ever stopped her from charging into an investigation. That tendency had gotten us both into some sticky situations.

"I'm checking the bar." I strode inside the weathered gray wood building. Fishing nets hung from the ceiling. Picture windows looked out over the beach. The interior was mostly empty, the bulk of the patrons on the deck outside, retirees by the look of them.

Frank rubbed his hands together. "Now that we're here, we may as well have a drink."

"It's a little early," I muttered.

"It's never too early for a Bloody Mary or a mimosa," Frank said. "Want one?"

"No." Dammit, Doran wasn't here. He must have left in a car.

"Maybe the bartender saw something." He ambled to the bar.

Lacking any better ideas, I trailed behind.

A burly, middle-aged bartender with startling blue eyes ambled to us.

"A Bloody Mary for me and a mimosa for the lady," Frank said cheerfully.

The bartender smiled and grabbed a bottle of vodka off the shelf.

"It's only polite," Frank said to me in a low voice. "If we're going to bother him for information, the least we can do is order." He lowered himself onto a barstool.

Frustrated, I sat beside him. This was a waste of time. Unless Doran was skulking in the bathroom, he wasn't here. I was stuck. Frank had already settled in, and he was my ride. I did love mimosas. I also knew the bartender, Tom, slightly. He had two kids under the age of ten, and they both loved cherry pie.

Tom mixed our drinks and set them on the damp bar.

Frank slid a fifty toward the bartender and kept his fingers resting lightly on the bill. "I was wondering—"

I touched the sleeve of Frank's tweed blazer. "Hey Tom. We're looking for someone, maybe you've seen him around. Mid-twenties, a bit younger than me. Always wears black. Nearly black hair that falls over one eye. Tall, thin, but not skinny."

Tom nodded once, his expression sobered. "Yeah. I was planning to tell you about him. What with the kids' ballet practice and ukulele practice and drum practice and surf lessons, I haven't had a chance."

Startled, I straightened on the barstool. "You were? Why?"

"A guy like you described was in here a couple days ago. He was asking about you."

"It might not be the same person," Frank warned, toying with his celery stick but not drinking. He hadn't taken a single sip, which made me feel better about driving with him. "It's not as if we have a photo to show you."

I gripped the bar and leaned closer. "What was he asking, exactly?"

"He started by asking about Pie Town, then about the old guy who was killed there last spring. It's all public info, so I didn't see any harm. I mean, everybody talks about that murder."

"He wasn't killed there," I said heatedly. "He just died there." Poison. It was complicated.

"Everyone knows you weren't to blame. You even got a commendation for trying to save his life."

"Not exactly." It wasn't an official award or anything, just some nice words from the mayor.

Frank nudged me. "I always knew you'd grow up to be a hero. Ever since you were a little girl—"

Tom's pale eyes lighted. "Are you Val's father?"

Frank nodded.

Tom shook his hand. "Nice to meet you, sir."

My jaw clenched. He may have been my biological parent, but he wasn't my father. Fathers stuck around. I took a swig of the mimosa. "But about Doran . . ."

"Doran?" the bartender asked. "Was that his name? Anyway, the questions started to get personal. He said he'd read about you online. That business at the Bar X Ranch, remember?"

How could I forget? It had only been a month or so ago that a killer had threatened a shootout at the Bar X's corral, with me between the gunslingers. "Yeah," I said, terse.

"He wanted to know what kind of person you were."

"What kind of person I am?" I rubbed the base of my neck.

The bartender laughed. "Yeah. I told him to check your online reviews."

"Sounds vague to me." Frank removed the celery stick and took a token sip of his Bloody Mary.

"What else did he ask?" I said.

He wiped a beer mug with a towel. "How you got in-volved in all those murders if you weren't, you know, *in-*

volved. I told him it was bad luck. Don't think he believed me though." He polished the mug more vigorously. "It *was* just dumb luck about all those bodies dropping around you, wasn't it?"

I nodded. Bad luck and some prodding from my partner in crime solving, Charlene. She had a talent for trouble.

"Of course it was," Frank said heartily. "What else could it be? Besides, this is a small town. Everyone knows everyone else's business. It's not that big a stretch that Val would be connected to some crimes. I'm sure other people around here are too."

"Yeah." Tom looked at me sideways. "Well, let me know if you need anything else." He vanished into the kitchen.

"Weird." Suddenly thirsty, I took another gulp of the mimosa. "There *is* something going on with Doran. I thought he was interested in *Pie Hard,* but it seems like he's interested in me." But why?

Frank set his near-full glass down with a clunk. Red droplets splashed the polished wood bar. "He's probably curious about *Pie Hard*, which just happened to be shooting in your pie shop. You know how people get about Hollywood and stars."

I sipped the mimosa. Frank was right about one thing, I could drink these any time of day. "Okay, let's say that's true. *Pie Hard* is cool, but it's not that cool."

"It doesn't need to be a top-rated show to attract a stalker. Nigel and Ilsa are both popular figures."

"Then why kill Regina? She's not in the public eye."

Frank snorted. "You don't read the industry blogs, do you?"

"No, but Ra . . ." I stopped myself. It was one thing to get Ray involved. Telling suspects about his involvement was another story. "We did an online search for people on the show. I didn't see anything about Regina on the industry blogs."

He rolled his eyes. "That's because her name's in code."

He pulled a cell phone from the inside pocket of his blazer and tapped the screen. "Let me see . . . Okay . . . Here it is . . . And cake, cake, cake . . . Ah, there we go." He handed me the phone.

I stared at the screen and a story about a TV show called *Cake Rage*. "This is a fiction site."

He laughed. "That's just a cover. Trust me. The names have been changed, but nothing on this site is fictional."

I read the "story," a short tale about a reality TV show producer named Queeny. She dominated her staff, inserting herself into every facet of their lives and making them crazy. The staff put up with it because the pay was high. "All right, so Queeny is Regina and *Cake Rage* is *Pie Hard*. I get that. But do you think the rest is really true? You can't believe all the Hollywood gossip you hear."

"It doesn't sound too off the mark though, does it?" he asked. "Regina lent money to Nigel. Why? What did she get out of it?"

"The pleasure of helping someone out of a rough spot?"

He raised his Bloody Mary in a mock toast. "She gets power. Gifts always come with a catch, even if the giver doesn't know it."

I drummed my fingers on the bar. "That's cynical."

"And then she gets involved with poor Luther, even setting him up to go into rehab."

"Luther was lucky to have someone who cared." What was wrong with helping people? It didn't hurt me to help Petronella find a psychiatrist to interview or to help Abril hold a poetry slam in Pie Town. Everybody won.

"Regina was a meddler. Little wonder someone bumped her off."

I furrowed my brow. I wasn't a meddler. Was I? "Hell." Of course I was. Only meddlers became amateur criminologists.

We abandoned our drinks and walked from the bar. The

sun beat down on our shoulders, and I tugged off my light-weight hoodie.

The parking lot had grown crowded. Cars clustered near the sand. Sunlight glittered off their windshields.

Frank aimed his key fob at the far-off Tesla. It beeped twice.

"Sir?" a male voice called.

We stopped, turned.

A bare-chested teenager in board shorts trotted toward us, his hand extended. "You dropped this."

Frank's eyes widened. "My wallet?"

We walked toward him, weaving between a pink Jeep and a Honda.

Frank stretched out his hand. "Thank you, young—"

A boom. A blast of heat that rocked me sideways. I stumbled to the pavement.

My ears rang, the roar mingling with the crash of the waves.

Frank grasped my shoulder. "Valentine! Are you all right?"

I rose on shaky legs.

Frank's Tesla was a mass of flames, a black column of smoke billowing toward the ocean.

CHAPTER 23

Waves of heat rippled the parking lot. I stared, mute and disbelieving, at the blazing Tesla. The ringing in my ears faded.

A fender clattered to the nearby pavement.

I yelped, jumping sideways against a blue Honda Civic.

"Whoa," the teenager said, his eyes wide.

"Whoa indeed." Frank rose and brushed a speck of grime off the sleeve of his tweed blazer.

"Someone blew up your car." My voice shook.

"Like, whoa," the teen said.

"Oh," Frank said, "that's not my car. Good thing too. I hate dealing with insurance companies."

"Someone blew up your car," I repeated. "Blew it up. With a bomb."

He patted my shoulder. "You're in shock. Maybe you should sit down. Young man, will you call 911 while I attend to my daughter?"

"Yeah. Cool." The teenager pulled a cell phone from the pocket of his board shorts and made the call.

Frank sat me against the hood of the Civic.

I hugged my arms, my teeth chattering.

He shrugged out of his blazer and draped it over my shoulders. "Here. You're all right. No one was hurt."

"B-b-bomb." Vaguely, I noticed people pouring from the bar behind us to point and stare.

"Yes." He took my hands and turned them over. Examining my palms, he brushed dirt and gravel from the skin. "Cars don't normally explode on their own. Did you know all those movie scenes where the hero shoots a car and it blows up, or the car falls off a cliff and blows up, are completely fake? Some colleagues and I tried to blow up a car by shooting its gas tank, and it just doesn't work. We couldn't get the gas to ignite no matter what angle the bullets hit. Now, if you *did* manage to set the gas tank on fire, it would burn just like that Tesla, but the car wouldn't actually explode." He rubbed his chin. "Of course, that car's an electric. Must be the battery that's burning so hard."

A siren wailed in the distance.

"The police are on their way," the teenager announced.

"Thank you, young man," Frank said. "And thank you for returning my wallet. Not everyone is so honest. If you hadn't delayed us, we might have been close enough to the explosion to have gotten hurt."

Like a mouse mesmerized by a cobra, I stared at the burning car. We might have been inside that car. Someone had wanted us inside that car, and they hadn't cared who else got hurt in the process.

A car bomb. This wasn't Afghanistan. It was San Nicholas! "Who uses car bombs?" I shrieked.

"Yes," Frank said, "it does seem a bit of overkill."

"Overkill!?" I sputtered. "How can you be so calm about this?"

"What's done is done."

"It's a car bomb!"

"Yes, Val," he said patiently. "We get that. But you're alive to shout at me. We've survived."

A squad car screeched to a halt in front of us. Two uniformed officers piled out. Frank motioned to them.

A firetruck wailed into the lot. Men in canvas coats and yellow hats got busy setting up a firehose.

Gordon's sedan parked on the side of the highway. He leapt from the car and ran to me, his expression taut. "Val! What happened? Are you all right?"

I nodded and pointed a quivering finger toward the blazing Tesla. For such a small car, it was really going. "It was a bomb."

He glanced at Frank. "That your car?"

"I was driving it," he hedged. "But no, it belongs to a, er, friend."

A pulse beat in Gordon's jaw. "I'll need the name of that friend."

A news van with a radio dish on the top and a five on the side lurched into the parking lot.

Gordon swore. "Wait here." He strode to the uniformed cops and said something to them.

They nodded and set up a cordon around the car fire.

Gordon returned to us. "Frank. I'd like a word." He jerked his head toward a far corner of the parking lot.

"Certainly, detective." Frank followed him.

I gnawed my bottom lip. If the bomb had been planted while we were here, at the beach, Luther could have done it while we were in the bar. And Doran had also been lurking. Anyone could have followed us here.

The blond reporter scrambled from the van. She gestured with her microphone to the burning car. Her companion aimed his camera at the scene, at the firemen dowsing the flames. Tugging down the front of her red blazer, she looked around.

I slouched lower against the Honda, warm against my bare shoulders, and leaned my head against its door. Maybe someone planted the bomb earlier—last night, this morning before Frank stopped by . . . I shuddered. What if it had gone off at my house or near the Goddess Gals? How many people could have been hurt or even killed?

I could have been killed.

My vision narrowed, blackness closing in. I shook my head, trying to clear it. Frank was right. I was alive. Thinking about what might have been was just sending me into a panic.

The teenager came to sit beside me against the car. "You okay?"

"Yeah," I said. "You?"

"I'm cool."

That established, we sat in companionable silence until Gordon and Frank rejoined us. On the surface, Frank was his usual insouciant self, but there seemed a certain hardness behind his Sinatra eyes.

Gordon's green eyes burned with fury. "Val, I need to take your statement," he said in clipped tones. "Alone."

I followed him to the spot on the pavement where he'd interviewed Frank.

"Tell me everything," he said.

And I did, including my suspicions of Doran.

"Has Frank said anything to you about problems with his associates?" he asked. "Any trouble?"

"He admitted he worked for the mob, though he claims his method of persuasion is one-hundred percent verbal."

Gordon pursed his lips.

"Wait," I said. "Are you saying . . . You think the car bomb was planted by the mob?"

Two more news vans rolled into the beach parking lot. The acrid scent of burning car rolled over me.

"I'm not saying anything. But a car bomb is an extreme measure for your run-of-the-mill murderer."

A wave of heat rolled through me, and I wasn't sure if it was from the car, the summer sun, or my own horror. "But that would mean . . . If the mob was involved in the car bomb, could they be responsible for the two murders? But why? Frank works for them."

Chief Shaw strode toward us. "GC! What have we got?" He stopped short and looked down his long nose at me. "Ah. Ms. Harris. Do I take it this is another pie-related incident?"

The reporters converged on us.

"No. I don't know," I said frantically.

"All right," Shaw said. "GC, take statements. I'll deal with this mob." He walked to the press and raised his arms. "The investigation is ongoing, and we have no comment at this time," he said loudly.

They shouted questions at him.

I turned back to Gordon. "Does this mean you're back on the case?"

"It means I'm taking statements. Any beat cop can do that." He nodded to a patrol cop, speaking to the teenager by the Honda. "Shaw knows about your father's background. You should prepare yourself."

My hands trembled, and I jammed them in the pockets of my jeans. "For what?"

"A mob enforcer takes over a TV show after the on-site producer is murdered. Then another woman is killed. Then a car bomb—a Vegas mob hallmark—explodes at the beach."

Frank's employers are based in Vegas. "But the bomb nearly killed Frank," I argued. "Why would he set a bomb in his own car?"

"I thought it wasn't his car."

"You know what I mean," I said.

"Yeah, and I know something stinks, and the mob's connected. Shaw isn't stupid. Neither are you." He laid a gentle hand on my shoulder, and a shiver rippled through me. "I'm sorry, Val. You didn't ask for any of this." His voice was soothing, compassionate, disconcerting.

My eyes stung. I told myself it was from the smoldering car, but I knew better. "Gordon, I've known for a long time that my father was . . . not a good person. And even though I want to believe what he told me about being a non-violent enforcer is true, it probably isn't. And I'm not proud of it, but I'm still holding a grudge over the last twenty-five years. In spite of all that, I can't see him as a murderer."

He gazed earnestly into my eyes. "Look, I may not be on the case, but I'll keep digging."

My breath hitched. "Thanks," I said, my voice higher and thinner than I liked.

"No matter what we find out about your father, you're a good person. Nothing's changed on that score. No one who knows you will feel any differently."

"GC?" Shaw jerked his chin toward the bar.

Gordon nodded. "Have you called Charlene?" he asked me.

"Should I?" I asked, surprised.

"Your father's not going to be able to drive you home, and I'm not sure I can either."

"Right." Besides, Charlene would want to hear what had happened from me and not from the Channel Five news.

"Keep your head down." Gordon waded through the scrum of reporters to the chief.

I pulled out my phone and called Charlene.

"What?" she asked grumpily.

"Something's happened," I whispered.

"What's wrong? Are you all right?"

The concern in her voice broke the dam inside me, and tears leaked from my eyes. I turned away from the crowds and pressed a hand to my face. "There was a car bomb. No one was hurt, but Frank's car was blown up." I forced my breathing to steady.

"Where are you?"

"In the parking lot of Sam's Crab Shack."

"I'll be there in ten minutes. Are you alone?"

I laughed hollowly. "No, the police and fire are here, and a Huns-invading-Rome-sized horde of reporters."

"How'd they get there so fast? Never mind. Make my ETA five minutes." She hung up.

The reporter and her cameraman broke from the group and trotted to me.

"Ms. Harris," the blond reporter asked, "was your car targeted in the bombing?" She jammed the microphone in front of my chin.

"No," I said, truthfully. The Tesla had been my father's. Sort of.

"Where were you when the bomb went off?"

"In the parking lot." Unnerved, I scanned it now. The fire was out, and firemen poked through the ruin of the Tesla. Nearby Highway One was jammed with rubberneckers. With a sinking heart, I realized Charlene's five-minute estimate was way off. There was no way she'd be able to speed through this traffic. At the parking lot entrance, a uniformed policeman set orange cones, blocking anyone from getting inside.

"So you were nearby when the bombing occurred," the reporter said. "Do you believe this is connected to the *Pie Hard* murders?"

At least they weren't calling it the Pie *Town* murders. "I'm letting the police do the investigating." That was a flat-out lie. I didn't know for sure who the target of the bomb was—me or Frank or both of us. The blast had shaken me like nothing else had, and the only defense I could see was to catch the killer before he struck again.

Unless this really was a mafia hit.

I shivered and tugged Frank's blazer tighter around me. What could I do against the mob?

CHAPTER 24

Monday night, a thick fog settled on the coast. I spent the evening at Charlene's, watching *Stargate* reruns, drinking her root beer and Kahlúa concoction, and mulling over the case. We didn't reach any new conclusions, but she lifted me from my doldrums.

The next morning, I drove to town at my usual ungodly hour, down gloomy streets slick with fog, past darkened Victorians and salt box houses.

Abril waited outside the alley door, her slim shoulders hunched beneath a colorful poncho. She straightened off the brick wall as I parked the van and stepped out.

"I heard about the car bomb yesterday," she said. "Are you all right?"

"No one was hurt," I hedged, because I wasn't all right. A bad night's sleep had taken the edge off my fear, but anxiety still pricked the edges of my awareness.

"But your bones could have been ripped cruelly—"

"Yes, I know." I jammed the key in the lock and opened the heavy door. "We were lucky."

"At least *Pie Hard* is done with us." She followed me inside. "Hopefully they'll take their troubles with them."

If the police would let the crew leave. "Today's specials are on the counter." I nodded toward the recipes in their plastic sheaths laid out beside the sink. "I need to check on something, but I'll be right back to help you." Leaving Abril in the gleaming kitchen, I checked Pie Town's doors, windows, closets, because—paranoid! But I couldn't find any obvious signs of illicit entry. So I returned to the kitchen and got to work.

The alley door slammed open, and my shoulders hunched.

Charlene, in a mustard yellow tunic and leggings, strode into the kitchen.

I relaxed. "Hi!"

She eyed me. "You okay? You seem jumpy."

"What? No. I'm fine."

She nodded. "You will be," she said, gruff. Charlene disappeared into the flour-work room.

Soon Petronella joined us, her motorcycle boots clomping through the kitchen. The normalcy of the morning soothed my shaken nerves, and sweet and savory scents filled the kitchen.

I set out the coffee urn and turned the sign in the window to OPEN.

Tally Wally and his friend Graham took their places at the counter. A bead of sweat trickled down my forehead. Normal, everything was normal.

Thirty minutes later, I peeked out the window to the dining area. Tally Wally and Graham still sat at the counter and sipped coffee, but the room was otherwise empty.

I frowned. A group of retirees was usually here by now, pushing the center tables together for their Tuesday morning coffee klatch.

Shrugging, I got back to baking, one ear cocked to listen for the bell over the door.

It didn't ring.

Okay, Tuesdays were usually slow, so it probably didn't mean anything. But when no one showed up by ten and Tally Wally and Graham were still at the counter, I emerged from the kitchen.

"What are you two still doing here?" I asked the older men.

Graham ran a hand over his balding head. "You want us to go?"

"No, I'm just surprised. You're usually gone by seven."

"We're sticking around to see what happens next." Tally Wally rubbed his drink-reddened nose.

My stomach bottomed. "Next?"

Wally shifted on the pink Naugahyde barstool and glanced at his friend.

"What do you think is going to happen next?" I asked slowly.

"You know," Wally said. "In case any suspicious characters come in carrying any suspicious packages that tick suspiciously."

"You can't keep your eye on everything." Graham folded his arms over his broad stomach.

"Suspicious . . . You mean a bomb?"

"If you see something, say something," Wally said. "That's my motto."

"Did Homeland Security steal it from you?" Graham asked caustically.

I stared around the otherwise empty restaurant. "You don't think people are staying away because of the car bomb yesterday?"

"Word is . . ." Graham leaned over the counter and accidentally knocked his cabbie's hat sideways.

I caught it before it could hit the floor.

"The bomb was planted by the m-o-b," Graham whispered.

"Hard to believe they'd bother with tiny San Nicholas," Wally said.

"I dunno," Graham said. "We used to be a hotbed for mob activity during Prohibition."

"Bootleggers," Wally agreed, nodding.

I opened my mouth to protest, but what could I say? Thanks to Frank, I *was* connected to the mob. "Where did you hear that?" I asked weakly.

Graham pressed a finger to his broad nose. "A little bird told me."

Wally patted my hand. "People'll get over it. Just you wait and see."

I blinked, dazed. This couldn't be happening. Were my regulars afraid to come to Pie Town because of yesterday's car bomb?

Of course they were. Who wanted to be near a bomb magnet? "Right. Sure. Can I get you anything?"

Graham raised his white coffee mug. "As long as the urn is full, I'm good."

"Same here," Wally said.

"Well, ring if you need anything." I stumbled back to the kitchen.

Petronella glanced up from the pie she was filling with blueberries, did a double take. "Something wrong?"

"Stop baking," I said. "It's going to be a slow day."

"Tuesday is always slow." Petronella's face turned a shade paler. "The bomb. You think people are going to stay away. But this is different—"

The bell over the front door rang, and my heart leapt.

"See?" she said. "Customers!"

I glanced through the window to the dining area. The blond reporter and her cameraman strolled inside. Ignoring the ORDER AT REGISTER sign, they settled into a booth.

I muttered a word that was definitely Not Safe for Work. "Press."

Abril shook her head. "I'm not going out there."

"Do you want me to go?" Petronella asked.

"No." I straightened my spine. "I'll take their orders."

I walked into the dining area. Pasting a smile on my face, I handed them menus. "Hi! When you're ready to order, just come to the counter and ring the bell."

The blonde smiled toothily. "Slow day?"

"You know how it is." I shrugged. "Tuesday mornings."

"How are the breakfast pies?" the cameraman, middle-aged and grizzled, asked.

"Do you like bacon?"

He nodded.

"Then I recommend the bacon and browns."

He stared at the menu as if unconvinced. "How big is the mini?"

"Six inches in diameter," I said. "It's a meal and comes with a green salad."

"You don't know my cameraman," the reporter said. "We'll take two. I'll have his salad."

So much for counter ordering. It wasn't as if I had anything better to do. I nodded toward the urn. "Coffee's self-serve." I bustled into the kitchen.

"What do they want?" Abril asked.

"Two mini bacon and browns." I loaded up a tray with plates of salad and warm pies and carted them out to the reporters. Steaming mugs of java sat on the table in front of them.

I slid the plates onto the table. "Here you go. And here's the check. Ring the counter bell if you'd like anything else."

"Is it true your father is a mob boss?" the blonde asked.

The checkerboard floor lurched, and I grabbed the back of the pink booth for balance. "What?" I asked, hoarse. A mob boss? That was worse than enforcer.

The cameraman slid from the booth. "Hey, you don't look so good. Maybe you should sit down."

"I'm fine."

But he drew up a chair, and my legs folded beneath me.

"I see you're not denying it," the reporter said.

"I can't deny what I don't know, and I don't know Frank. He left my mother and me when I was little, and I met him for the first time as an adult last week. I don't know anything about him aside from what he's told me, and he sure didn't tell me that."

"Becks," the cameraman said to her. "Come on."

An odd expression crossed her face. It might have been sympathy. "All right," she said, "I believe you. And the mob thing is unsubstantiated, though that car bomb . . ." She shook her head.

I swallowed. "How did you know Frank was my father?"

She shrugged. "Birth and death certificates are easy." The reporter eyed me. "But I guessed the mob angle was too good to be true. The reunion thing could be a story though." She made a frame with her hands. "Father and daughter reunited by *Pie Hard* murders."

I rose, gripping the chair. "This isn't the way I wanted to meet my father."

"But it's the way it happened." She leaned closer. "He saved your life at the hotel when there was that fire. You two were nearly blown to pieces yesterday. Whatever's going on with the *Pie Hard* crew, you're both involved. Tell me what you know. Making the truth public could save your lives."

I stood. "If I knew the truth, I'd tell the world. But I don't know who's behind these murders or why." I speed-walked into the kitchen and let out a deep breath when I was safely inside.

Abril slid pies from the massive, industrial oven. "These are the last of them. Are you sure you want to stop baking?"

I glanced at the wall clock over the window to the dining room. "Cut the recipes in half for now. I'm going to run out and grab a paper. I'll be right back." Instead of cutting through the dining area, I used the alley door. I didn't want to give the reporter another chance to pepper me with questions.

Beneath gray skies, I walked to a kiosk on Main Street. Avoiding the wad of gum on the handle, I extracted a free local paper. The car bomb was front page news.

I stood beside an iron lamp post, moss flower basket dangling from its hook, and read.

An anonymous source in the lab stated that the bomb had been placed under the driver's seat.

Frank kept the Tesla's top down, so placing a bomb there would have been easy. It was out in broad daylight, and though the parking lot wasn't packed, it wasn't empty either. If the killer placed the bomb there while we were questioning Luther or in the crab shack, he'd taken a risk, but not an impossible one.

I scanned down further. The source could neither confirm nor deny whether the bomb looked like a mob hit.

I groaned. Confirmation didn't matter—the article neatly planted the seed of mob involvement. How had the press caught on to the mob angle so quickly, when it had taken Gordon days to make the connection? Was there a leak in the SNPD? Frank and I sure hadn't said anything.

"Hi, Val," a man's voice boomed from behind me.

"Ugh!" I clutched my chest, crumpling the paper to it, and whirled to face Ray. "Hi." I started breathing again.

A backpack hung over his rounded shoulder. He wore a loose blue pea coat over a t-shirt with a comic book villain on the front. "I heard about the car bomb."

Again, he hadn't heard the news from me. I opened my mouth to apologize.

"It was bad enough losing Ilsa and seeing Regina . . ." He looked across the street at the olive oil shop. Rows of green bottles lined its windows. He cleared his throat. "But you're a real friend. I couldn't take it if you died. So don't."

I blinked, touched. "Okay. I won't. Thanks."

"You okay?"

"Not a scratch."

"I was coming to Pie Town to talk to you," he said, "if it's okay. We need to get this guy and fast."

I grimaced. "I agree. But there are some reporters there I'd rather avoid. Do you mind if we go through the alley entrance?"

"Cool."

He followed me around the corner, into the alley, and inside the kitchen.

Charlene peeked through the window to the dining room and shook her head, growling. "I don't like this. Not one bit. It's quiet in there. *Too* quiet, if you ask me." She turned around. "Oh, hi Ray."

"Yesterday's bombing might have scared people off," I said. "I think we can expect today to be slow. We'll keep baking, just in case we get more reporters, but cut back fifty percent."

Abril twisted her hands in her apron. "You don't think this will last, do you?"

Ray shifted his weight, his face tightened with impatience.

"I don't know. I hope not." *Please, please, please let things get back to normal.*

"Buncha cowards," Charlene said.

"If you two want to go home," I said, "I understand."

Petronella's jaw jutted forward. "I'm not letting some jerk chase me away from Pie Town. This is my job."

Abril bit her bottom lip. "My mother is sick today. It would be better if I could go home to watch my little brother."

Charlene growled, low and menacing.

"That's fine," I said quickly. "Like I said, it looks like it's going to be a slow day."

She nodded and untied her apron.

"Ray, you said you wanted to talk?" I asked.

He set his backpack on a section of counter that was not covered in flour and pulled out a sheaf of wrinkled papers. "I've been making charts."

Charlene rolled her eyes.

"Let's go to my office," I said, "and we can look them over. Petronella, are you okay on your own for a bit?"

She tossed her spiky hair. "I'm the assistant manager. Of course I'm okay alone."

Ray, Charlene, and I trooped into my office, and I shut the door, rustling the calendar on its back.

"What have you got?" I asked.

"I thought we should diagram the suspects and motives." He unrolled a long sheet of poster-sized paper. "Do you have tape?"

"Um, I think so." I rummaged in a desk drawer, found a roll and handed it to him.

He taped the paper to a blank spot of wall beside the bookcase. "Okay, no one has a real alibi for Regina's murder, so let's look at the motives. Nigel owed Regina money." He traced a blue line between a box that read NIGEL and a center box that read REGINA. "He might have killed her so he wouldn't have to repay."

"Except now Steve wants him to pay up," Charlene said.

"But he might not have expected that." Ray drew a line between Regina's square and another. "Then there's Steve. The husband is usually the guilty party, and he was having an affair with Ilsa, so we know there were problems in the marriage."

The office door jerked open. Gordon, in his blue suit, strode inside. He took in Ray, holding the paper against the wall, and Charlene's innocent expression. "Val, have you been investigating without a P.I.'s license again?"

"Um . . . Yes?" I squeaked.

"Good." He sat against my desk. "What have you got?"

"What have . . . ?" Slowly, I shut the drawer and walked

around the desk. "You mean you're not going to arrest us for interfering in an investigation?"

"I'm off the case. Remember?"

"Cool," Ray said. "We can have a real policeman in the Baker Street Bakers."

"You're only an associate member," Charlene barked. "You can't invite new members."

Gordon's mouth quirked. "Just tell me what you've found."

Ray quickly explained the chart.

"There's something I haven't had a chance to tell you," I said to Ray. "I only learned it yesterday, but Regina had Lou Gehrig's disease. If Steve wanted to get rid of her without a divorce, it would have been a lot simpler to just wait it out."

"Maybe he wanted her gone now so he could be with Ilsa?" Ray asked.

"I don't know," I said. "Ilsa said they'd broken it off, and I believed her."

"And if he wanted to be with Ilsa, why kill her?" Charlene asked. "You're a cop, what do you think?"

"I think your thought process is fascinating," Gordon said.

"Then there's the new director, Frank." Ray glanced at me apologetically. "Sorry, Val, but we have to consider him, even if he is your dad."

"No, Ray," Charlene said, her voice soothing. She laid a hand on my shoulder. "Now isn't the time."

I waved my hand, dismissive. "It's okay. All I've been doing is considering him. He got Regina's job, but I don't think it's a motive for murder, since it was only temporary." What if Frank was as evil as the mobsters you see on TV? What if he was killing other people on the show to put pressure on Nigel to pay up? I shuddered.

"Don't go there," Gordon said gently.

"It's not Frank," Charlene said.

"Why not?" Ray asked.

"Because he's Val's father. She's not related to a killer."

"I don't think it works that way," I said, glumly. "But thanks."

"And then there's Luther," Ray said, pointing to an orange square. "I don't know why he'd want Regina dead, but he's got issues."

Gordon rubbed his chin.

"Which doesn't make him a killer," I said.

"Next is Ilsa's murder." Glancing nervously at the detective, Ray unrolled a hand-drawn map of the hotel and taped it to the wall. The paper was yellowing, with scorch marks around the edges. An *X* marked the spot of Regina's body.

Charlene squinted. "Is that a treasure map?"

Gordon coughed into his hand and turned quickly away.

Ray's cheeks reddened. "It's grid paper from a roleplaying game."

"Those don't look like grid squares," Charlene objected. "Those are octagons."

Ray taped it to the wall. "Because players— I mean people—can move in more than four directions. The point is the map is to scale."

"And that *X* mark is awfully fancy," she said. "It looks like a pirate's *X*. How'd you find out where Ilsa's body was found?"

"That's a good question," the detective said.

Uneasy, I shifted my weight. Ray was definitely not the killer, but where had he learned of the murder spot? Not from either of us.

"I checked with the hotel," Ray said.

Why would they give out that information? I shrugged off my suspicion. It was a small town. He probably had a source. And Ray was no killer.

"It looks great," I said quickly. "No one seems to have an alibi for Ilsa's death either. Everyone claims they were in their hotel rooms. Unless you heard something else?" I asked Gordon.

He shook his head.

"The crew's rooms are all on the first floor overlooking the golf course," Ray said. "It would be easy for someone to slip out, kill Ilsa, and slip back into the hotel. But what's the motive?"

"Obviously," Charlene said, "Ilsa knew too much. She was blackmailing the killer and was meeting him on the course for a pay-off. And the killer strangled her. Right Carmichael?"

The detective lifted a shoulder, dropped it. "It's a theory."

"But Ilsa wasn't well liked either," I said. "She fought with Nigel—"

"That was just for show," Ray said, "to make good TV."

"And she snapped at Steve and Luther," I continued. "Though she did seem weirdly protective of Luther when I tried to question him at the British pub." On the other hand, was she merely protective of information he had? Was there something he still hadn't told me? "You're missing a suspect."

Ray cocked his head. "Who?"

"Doran," I said. "He's been around every time something's gone wrong."

"You mean the guy you call the ninja?" Ray asked.

"What's his last name?" Gordon rose and walked to the wall. He studied the pirate map.

"I don't know," I said. "He says he's a freelance graphic designer, but he didn't have his card on him."

"You mean he wouldn't give it to you," Charlene said.

"If he's a freelance designer," Ray said, "he'll have a website. Doran can't be that common a name. I'll find him."

"Let me know when you do," Gordon said.

"Just make sure you keep your investigations to the Internet, Ray," Charlene said. "Bad enough someone tried to blow up Val."

He raised his reddish brows. "Are *you* going to stick to the Internet?"

"I don't need to," I said. "I'm already a target, which means I have nothing left to lose." I looked around the office at my friends, and a cold knot hardened in my stomach. The truth was quite the opposite—I had too much to lose. I suspected the killer knew it too.

CHAPTER 25

Restless, I wiped down the counter. It gleamed dully beneath the overhead lights. I put down my cloth and gazed at Pie Town's empty tables. It was happening all over again—a violent crime, followed by vanishing customers. Could my bakery handle that sort of disaster twice in one year?

The cellphone in my apron pocket rang, and I checked the screen—Gordon. Heart lifting, I answered. "Hi."

"You made the six o'clock news." A dog yipped in the background.

So Pie Town was famous, and not in a good way. I stared out the front windows. Fog had returned with the setting sun. Outside, Main Street was a gray mass. A hunched silhouette passed in front of the blinds. "Are you at the dog park again?" Dog park duty had to be the worst for a real detective. Sure this was a small town, and detectives sort of did everything. I suspected this was Shaw's way of keeping Gordon away from the case.

"Some kids overturned the picnic table. A friend called to let me know you were on TV."

A friend and not a colleague? He'd told his friends about me? In spite of everything, the thought warmed me. "I'm closing up now. Can I swing by the dog park?"

"It's a public park. I can't stop you." He paused, his voice growing husky. "And I wouldn't want to."

Charlene strolled through the front door. To her mustard yellow tunic and leggings, she'd added a quilted brown jacket and Frederick.

"Great," I said. "I'll be there in thirty minutes."

"See you then." He hung up.

Charlene dusted off a dust-free barstool. "See who when?"

"Gordon."

"The plot thickens." She arched a white brow. "Did he call you, or did you call him?"

"Does it matter?"

"Men like to be the ones doing the chasing, even if it is the twenty-first century."

"He joined the Baker Street Bakers," I pointed out.

"Hmph. Not officially. And he didn't contribute much. He did more listening than talking."

"He's a good detective."

She nodded, sat. "I'm glad I caught you. I worried you might close up early, but I should have known better. You've still got that fighting spirit."

"I should have closed early." I shrugged, half-hearted. "We only had eight customers." Even the reporters eventually abandoned their booth and left. I sent the staff home, figuring I could deal with any customers myself. Since there hadn't been any, it hadn't been a problem.

She rumpled her loose curls. "There must be something we've missed."

Frederick raised his head and yawned an agreement.

"I spent the day pouring over Ray's dossiers," I said. "Two things. First, we should have brought an engineer on the team before. I mean—dossiers? Maps to scale? He's amazing."

She snorted. "And the second thing?"

"I didn't find anything."

"How are we supposed to investigate out-of-towners?"

I dropped my towel on the counter. "Those articles about the other TV shows Regina produced . . . They included names of people who worked with her and Steve." I trotted to my office and sat in front of the computer.

Charlene followed, standing behind me and peering over my shoulder.

I typed, pulling up websites. Luther had been a part of Regina's crew for decades. There were other names—sound engineers and executive producers and actors. Unfortunately, there were no phone numbers. I searched the Internet, but couldn't find anything.

"This is a bust," Charlene said. "You know what we need?"

I swiveled to face her. "We need Ray."

On her shoulder, Frederick opened one sleepy blue eye, closed it.

She folded her arms. "I was going to say we need a drink. Just because he has maps and dossiers, doesn't make him a real Baker Street Baker."

"I thought he was an associate member? Whatever he is, he knows his way around computers better than either of us."

"Speak for yourself." She sniffed.

"I'm calling him."

He picked up the phone on the first ring. "What's happened? Has someone been killed?"

"Uh, no, but we need your help. Charlene and I thought we'd try to contact members of Regina's old TV crews. We found some names online, but haven't been able to track down any phone numbers. Do you think you—"

"Great idea. I'll get on it now." He hung up.

"Well?" She leaned one hip against the dented metal desk.

"He said he'd start searching now."

"Did he say when he'd finish?"

"Err, no."

"You're hopeless. But, you'll be happy to know the Goddess Gals are leaving tomorrow. They're having a farewell feast tonight. We're both invited."

"Nice." I untied my apron. "I'll meet you at my place. But first, there's someone I need to talk to."

Her blue eyes narrowed. "Not about the case."

"No. I'm meeting Gordon at the dog park."

She winked. "Don't do anything I wouldn't do."

Since that covered approximately nothing, I nodded and hung my apron on the hook behind the office door.

She followed me into the alley and watched me lock the rear door.

Feeling paranoid, I drove her to her yellow Jeep, parked on Main Street, and watched while she got in and started the car. I followed her a block, then turned toward the dog park.

Gordon's sedan was parked across the street from its chain link fence. Fog swathed the eucalyptus trees, and though I couldn't see any dogs, cheerful barks sounded from the park.

I pulled up behind him, and he stepped from his sedan.

We met in the street.

He pulled me into an embrace, and I inhaled the scent of his woodsy cologne. "Bad day?" he asked, his voice reverberating through me.

I sighed. "Aside from the reporters," I said, my words muffled against this suit jacket, "who didn't order much, Pie Town was dead. I'm not sure if it's the mob thing or the car bomb that scared everyone off." I sniffed, smelling something besides woodsy goodness.

He stepped away and gave me an apologetic look. "Sorry,

I had to go to the dump after our meeting this morning. I did shower, but my shoes . . ." He trailed off.

"What were you doing at the dump?"

"That stabbing case I mentioned. We found the knife." Gordon gazed into my eyes. "But forget about my day. If your business is down, it couldn't have been the mob rumor—that didn't hit the news until this afternoon."

A Prius glided past, its headlights were weak in the deepening fog.

"*Pie Hard* was supposed to help my business. Instead, it may kill it. And Frank . . ." My throat tightened.

His hands slid to my shoulders. "What about your father?"

"He lied to me again. Frank told me he didn't hurt people, and even though it was completely ridiculous, I let it slide, because what else was I going to do? But a reporter told me he was a mob boss."

He lifted a brow. "Mob boss? I don't think so. All signs point to him being a low-level employee. As to not hurting people, Frank's never been brought up on charges."

"That only means he's never been caught," I said, bitter.

"His only real brush with the law was when you were a toddler, and he was still living with you and your mother."

Icy surprise struck my core. I didn't remember anything like that. "What happened?"

"You disappeared. Your parents panicked and called the cops. They found you asleep in an old refrigerator box you used as a toy chest. Case closed."

My hands clenched. "Until Frank joined the mob."

"Unless there's been a recent hostile takeover, your father's not the boss. He works for—" He shook his head. "Never mind who he works for, but he's a worker bee."

"How do you know all this, if Frank doesn't have any police records?"

"I didn't say there were no records, only that he'd never been brought up on charges. Trust me. My intel's solid."

"It doesn't matter." The damp seeped through my hoodie, and I crossed my arms to warm myself. "He works for organized crime. My mother was right not to have anything to do with him."

"Probably," he said, his tone carefully neutral.

"The reporter also said the car bomb looked like the Vegas mob."

"Car bombs were a Vegas mob tactic in the seventies and eighties," he said. "We haven't seen much of that lately. And no, we don't have the forensics from the bomb beneath Frank's car."

"That's not what the paper said."

Gordon's nostrils pinched. "We've got a leak. But even if we did have more, I wouldn't be able to talk to you about it."

Across the street, mist swirled, making phantoms of the fog. "Because I'm a suspect."

"No," he rumbled. "Because I'm off the case."

Off the case *because I was a suspect.* I pinned my arms to my stomach. "Then how do you know you don't have the forensics back yet?"

"Because Shaw's rampaging through the police station shouting about the lack of evidence. Why do you think I'm hiding out at the dog park writing reports?"

"You could write them at Pie Town," I said.

"Shaw's banned me from Pie Town until the murders are cleared."

"What? That's totally unfair. Plus, how he's going to clear the murders when everybody has a motive, and nobody has an alibi?"

He made a noise low in his throat. "We'll make this right."

"I just . . ." My eyes warmed. "I just don't want Frank to be a murderer."

He brushed his broad hand across my cheek. "What he is doesn't change who you are."

"It does if I give him a pass for all the terrible things he's done."

"He's your father," he said, his emerald gaze understanding. "No one would blame you for having mixed feelings."

"We're related, but he didn't raise me. Frank left my mom and me for a life of crime."

"Maybe. There's something odd about the timing . . ." He shook his head. "Keeping him at arms' length is a good idea, but let me do more investigating into his background before you make any decisions."

I nodded, silent. I'd already made my decision. Frank had ruined my childhood, and now he was ruining my business, my livelihood. I wasn't going to let that go.

CHAPTER 26

I stepped from my van and inhaled the Eucalyptus scent of home.

Caterers busied themselves between the picnic table and their teal van. A campfire lit the thick fog swirling on the hillside. Tiki torches flickered in front of the yurt. The goddesses seemed to be doing some sort of twilight yoga near the cliff.

Light streamed from the windows of my converted shipping container, and I stilled. It was probably a goddess using the bathroom. Why were *all* the lights on?

Charlene, her hands in the pockets of her quilted brown jacket, opened my front door and leaned out. "How was Gordon?" she asked. Her mustard-colored leggings blazed in the dim light.

Frederick, his eyes shut tight, burrowed his head against her neck.

I sighed and slammed shut the van door.

The cat's ears twitched.

"Sensible," I said, "as usual."

"I don't think I'd want a police detective who was otherwise."

I walked to my house and climbed the steps, brushing past her. "It wasn't a criticism."

The tiny home was nippy, I guessed from all the goddess gals trooping in and out to use the bathroom. They were low maintenance, but I was glad they were leaving tomorrow.

"But he got me thinking."

"Does your head hurt?"

"Gordon's involved now. He's putting a lot at risk by going behind Shaw's back. Maybe we should cool off a bit."

"And leave things to Shaw? Are you crazy?" She lifted Frederick from her shoulder. Arranging him on the foldout table, she sat in a chair beside him. "It's the car bomb that's rattled you, not Gordon."

"Can you blame me?" I walked to the kitchen and stared into a cupboard. "I can't stop thinking about it." I shut the cabinet door. "Was the car bomb meant for Frank or me? After someone trapped me in that fire, I have to wonder if I was the target. There's no reason for someone to make an attempt on my life unless they thought I was a threat. And the only thing I can threaten anyone with is solving the case." I frowned. *Was* it the only reason?

She rubbed her chin. "Maybe. But everything that's happened has affected both you and Pie Town. Regina's death should have shut down the show, until your fa—Frank stepped in. And then there was that fire that nearly killed you, and then Ilsa, whose body you were conveniently nearby to discover. I'm surprised Shaw hasn't arrested you yet."

I leaned against the sink. "He tried," I said, glumly.

"All right, let's assume Frank was the target. Why kill him?"

"He might have figured something out and tried to put the squeeze on the killer. With his mob connections, I wouldn't put it past him to try to use that to his advantage—rather than tell the police."

She tilted her head. "Blackmail's not really his modus operandi."

My fists clenched. "He's a mobster. I wouldn't put anything past him. They kill people."

"You're afraid he might be the killer?"

"I don't know." Fed-up, I joined her at the table and dropped into a narrow chair. "I don't know anything about him but what he's told me, and I can't trust that."

"You know what Gordon's told you," she said gently. "Do you trust him?"

"Yes, but even he admits he doesn't have the whole story." I smiled. "Gordon did tell me about a time I fell asleep in my toy box. My parents couldn't find me, panicked, and called the police. I can imagine the police report: *Child found in refrigerator carton*." I loved that refrigerator carton.

"Forget memory lane. If Frank was the killer, why plant a bomb in his car?"

"Maybe Frank did it himself to throw suspicion from him?" I said. "I almost wish the bomb was aimed at me. That would imply Frank's innocence. It would also track with locking me inside that burning room."

"But you said the room smelled like gasoline when you walked inside. That room had been prepped to be set ablaze before you got there, and the killer couldn't have known you were going to be there."

I gnawed my lower lip. "No, I don't see how he could have. So why lock me inside? Because I might have stopped his plan? Or because he wanted me dead."

She unsnapped her quilted jacket. "And if he wanted you dead, I ask again, why?"

"If I had died in that fire . . ." I trailed off.

She stroked Frederick's chalk-colored fur. "What?"

"I would have looked guilty, wouldn't I?" I asked. "I wasn't enthusiastic about *Pie Hard* being in my shop, and everyone on the crew knew how I felt." My hands turned clammy. "The hotel manager thought I was an arsonist who'd gotten caught in her own fire."

"So it was done to frame you? Whatever the motive, locking you inside had to have been spur of the moment. Maybe the killer wasn't thinking much at all."

"And there's something else," I said. "Two of our suspects—Luther and Ilsa—have been connected to arson. The fire could have been a way of throwing suspicion on either of them."

"But why break into Pie Town? It must be about you. Maybe someone is threatening you to get at Frank."

"It's possible the burglar was just a burglar," I said.

"You really think the break-in was a coincidence?"

"No."

"Right," she said. "Got any root beer?"

"And Kahlua." I rose and made our drinks. On a foggy night like this, we should have gone for hot chocolate and cinnamon whiskey, but I was out of both.

I handed her the tall glass.

"Cheers, ears!" She raised it in a toast and took a gulp, smacking her lips. "That hits the spot."

Someone knocked on the door, and I opened it.

Maureen stood on the ground at the base of the steps. "Hi. The caterers have finished setting up. I hope you'll both join us for . . ." She looked between the two of us. "Did I interrupt something?"

I gulped my Kahlua and root beer. "No." I was ready for a distraction from murder and my father.

"Then you're welcome to join us." She smiled an invitation.

I shrugged into a thick vest and followed her into my yard. I figured I'd duck in, grab a plate, and go hide in my tiny house. But the goddesses surrounded me, peppering me with questions about pie, which is my favorite topic. Charlene's favorite is anything weird and macabre. She was right at home with their conversations about auras, astrology, and attachments.

Frederick seemed to enjoy himself as much as a comatose cat could. The women cooed over him, cuddling his limp form.

". . . and then we all did soul retrievals," a woman named Marissa was saying. She waved her plump hands enthusiastically. "I discovered that I'd left a piece of myself back at the trauma point, and that was why every time I saw a Stellar Jay my stomach knotted."

Charlene nudged me, and the grape and quinoa salad on my paper plate slipped sideways. "Maybe that's why you're afraid of UFOs," she whispered loudly.

My face grew hot. "Charlene!"

Marissa's brow furrowed. She was in her mid-sixties, with loose, long blond hair and an easy smile. "Is that why you're not well this evening? I can see the tension in your aura."

I grabbed a plastic glass of pomegranate champagne from the picnic table and took a swig. "No. It's . . ." The last thing I wanted to do was talk about Frank. I blew out my breath. "Yes," I lied. "UFOs. Being out in the open at night, the fog, not being able to see what's coming. Little green men could be anywhere."

Marissa set her plate on a nearby rock and squeezed my hand. "You poor thing. Why don't you try a soul retrieval?"

"Yes, Val," Charlene said. "Why don't you?"

"Ah . . ." No. No way. No to the third power.

"It's only light self-hypnosis," the goddess gal said. "You're in control the whole time. It's not like those shows on TV, where people quack like ducks and forget where and who they are. Maureen can explain it better." She motioned to a small cluster of women in flowing caftans, and Maureen wafted over.

"That's okay," I said. "I—"

"Val's interested in learning more about a soul retrieval," Charlene said.

My lips pressed tight. I had not said that.

Maureen turned her round face toward me. "Oh?" She adjusted a clip in her thick red hair, done up in a zaftig bun.

"For her little UFO problem," Charlene said.

Maureen smiled at me. "You are? I'd love to guide you through a retrieval. You've been such a patient hostess. It would be our way of saying thank you."

"Oh," I said, "you don't need to thank—"

"You're welcome," Charlene said. "Let's do this."

Maureen gestured to the yurt. "Why don't we go inside for some privacy? Marissa, will you ask everyone to stay outside until we're through?"

"Sure!" She bustled to a cluster of women.

Charlene collected Frederick, and we followed Maureen to the yurt.

She swept aside the cloth door, and we walked inside.

I gasped. Like my tiny house, the yurt looked a lot bigger on the inside than the outside. Maybe the illusion was due to the high, domed ceiling, or the curve of the wood beams arcing toward the central hole at the top. Giant pillows lay scattered across the layers of colorful carpets strewn along the floor. Sleeping bags had been neatly rolled and stacked in one corner, beside a pile of suitcases.

"What do you want Val to do?" Charlene asked Maureen.

"Find a comfy spot to lie down." She motioned to a Turkish rug and a pile of pillows.

"No, thanks, I'll stand," Charlene said, and pointed to her knees. "These babies don't bend the way they used to."

"I meant Val," she said. "And Charlene, Val might want some privacy."

Charlene gave me an outraged look. "What about Frederick? He wants to see how it ends."

On her shoulder, Frederick wasn't seeing anything but the back of his eyelids.

"It's fine." I found a soft-looking Persian rug and lay on my back, my head on an over-sized throw pillow, my fingers laced atop my stomach.

"Uncross your ankles," Maureen said, draping a blanket over me. "And put your arms at your sides."

Repressing a grumble, I did. I'd done a lot of crazy things in my life—mainly with Charlene—but this had to take the prize.

Maureen led me through a relaxation exercise. "Now," she said. Her voice was soothing. "I'd like you to close your eyes, and imagine you're on a beautiful forest path. It's a warm day, and as you walk down the path, you see a beautiful bubble. You walk closer, and see a door in the bubble. Open the door, and step inside."

Either I was a visualization powerhouse, or Maureen had the gift, because the forest leapt to my mind's eye.

"Inside," she continued, "there's a comfortable lounge chair in front of what looks like a TV screen. Sit down. The TV screen turns on, and you can see everything that's outside. You feel the bubble zoom backwards, back through time, and you see your life passing on the screen." She paused for a long moment. "Now I want you to go back to the first time you felt your fear of being taken."

My breathing quickened.

"You're safe," she murmured. "These are only memories. They can't hurt you."

Duh. So why was my heart racing? A bubble wasn't even scary.

"The first time you felt this way . . ." she prompted.

I always had that fear. I couldn't have been born with it. Something must have happened when I was young. Did I have it in kindergarten? I thought I might, so it must have started sometime before then.

"Are you there?" Maureen asked.

"I'm not sure," I said, my eyes still closed. "It was before kindergarten. Sorry, I just don't remember."

"It's okay," she said. "Trust the process. Know that you're at that point in your life when you first encountered this fear. What do you see?"

I thought of the light pouring through the front window of my tiny home, and my mouth went dry.

"You're safe," she murmured. "This is only a memory."

"Light coming through a window," I blurted. That hadn't happened when I was young. It had happened a few days ago. This wasn't working.

"Light. What sounds do you hear?"

"Men's voices." I frowned. Why did I say that? I hadn't heard men's voices when the yurt builders had arrived. If I had, I wouldn't have panicked, thinking UFOs were on the attack.

"Men's voices. More than one man?"

I imagined the light, feeling my way. There *were* voices. My bedroom door banged open, and a strange man grabbed me from my bed. My stuffed animals tumbled to the thin carpet while my mother screamed, and—

I jolted upright, breathing hard.

"It's all right," Maureen soothed. "You're all right. You're home and in the yurt."

"What did you see?" Charlene asked, leaning closer. "What happened?"

I stared, uncomprehending, my chest heaving. "Charlene, I was taken."

CHAPTER 27

Charlene grabbed a notepad and pen from the pocket of her quilted brown jacket. "Taken?" Frantically, she flipped through the pages. "What did they look like? Tall and gray? What was the spaceship like? Were you probed?"

"Not by aliens, by people." My heart thudded against my chest. The red skeleton of the yurt's roof now seemed a cage. I stumbled to my feet, accidentally kicking one of the over-sized throw pillows.

"You were probed by what looked like people?" Charlene scratched her head with the end of the pen. "Could've been fairies."

"What do you remember?" Maureen asked. "If you're open to sharing."

"Of course she is," Charlene said.

Maureen rolled her eyes. "Good grief, Charlene. We don't know—"

"It's fine," I said quickly. "I think I do want to say it out loud before it slips away." The memory was distant but clear. "It was night. I was in bed. My mother was shouting, and that scared me. And then a man burst through the door and grabbed me from my bed. He took me from the house to a room with cinderblock walls. He gave me ice cream—"

Charlene snapped her gnarled fingers. "So that's why you never eat pie à la mode. You connect ice cream to the trauma."

"No, I love ice cream." I glanced at the circular hole at the top of the yurt, the wooden strips bending toward its apex. "But ice cream changes the texture of the crust."

"That's true," Charlene said. "And the crusts are the best part."

"Anyway," I said, "I was too scared to eat it—"

"That doesn't seem like you," Charlene said, and patted her stomach meaningfully.

"Anyway . . ." My eyes narrowed. "The ice cream didn't have time to melt before my father showed up. He took me home, but . . ."

"But what?" Charlene asked.

Uncertain, I hesitated. "I remember there was a police car out front. Frank asked me to play a game, and we went inside through a window. Instead of putting me to bed, Frank put me in my toy box. Then he shouted, and my mother and a policeman were there."

Charlene's ivory brows lowered. Frederick lifted his head off her shoulder and gazed at me, his arctic eyes serious.

"I'm guessing at some point when you were still young," Maureen said, "you saw a TV show or movie about UFOs. Then you put the lights and experience of being taken together with the stories of alien abduction."

"When did your father leave you and your mother?" Charlene asked.

"I'm not sure. I was so small when all this happened—I think around three? But he must have left shortly afterward. Maybe that's why I'd forgotten it all. I was so young . . ." I stared down at the brightly patterned carpets. Had it really happened? Even now it was hard to believe. I'd heard of false memories, but I didn't think Maureen had been leading me. And the knowledge felt true.

"How do you feel now?" Maureen asked.

"Feel?"

"About UFOs."

I thought about it. "The thought still makes me queasy, but I guess the idea doesn't bother me as much."

She nodded. "That's to be expected. You've taken a big step by uncovering the source of your fear. That fear may fade away on its own, or you may need to do more work." She pulled a business card from the voluminous sleeve of her caftan. "Call me if you'd like to work on this more."

"Thanks."

We stumbled together over a cushion. Weaving slightly, we left the yurt.

Charlene followed me inside my tiny house and shut the door. "Do you know why your father brought you in through the window?"

Frederick was still staring at me. It was unnerving.

"No. Why? Do you?"

"Maybe I have my suspicions, but . . ." She gripped my shoulder. "No. It wouldn't be right for me to guess. Not about your father. When you figure it out, call me."

"What suspicions?" I jerked my vest into place. "If you know something, tell me."

"We'll talk later. Just don't do anything rash." She squeezed. "At least not without me."

"But—"

She turned and left, banging the door behind her.

Irritated, I drew the blinds, kicked off my shoes, and curled up on my futon behind the bookcase.

Gordon found the police report about them finding me in my toy box. I rubbed my temple. Strange that the report had stayed on file so long.

Had the policeman suspected there was more to the

story? There must have been, or my father wouldn't have snuck me inside the house. He hadn't wanted the police to know the truth.

I sat up, my pulse thudding in my ears. It must have been Frank's fault I'd been snatched. Had I been taken to force him to pay his gambling debts? Was that what had ending things between my parents? It would explain why my mother had made him leave.

And then Frank had shown up in my pie shop like nothing was wrong. A slow fuse of anger burned up my spine and into my brain. My mother had been right to kick him to the curb.

Someone knocked softly at my door.

I rose and opened it.

Maureen stood on the ground beneath me. "I didn't feel good about the way we left things. May I come in?"

I stood for a moment, unsure, then stepped away from the door, and she climbed the two steps and came inside. "Would you like some tea?"

"I'd love some."

She sat at the dining nook table while I heated water in the microwave.

"I've got chamomile and cinnamon ginger."

"Cinnamon ginger," she said, tossing her red hair.

I took the same and brought the steaming mugs, spoons, and a plastic bear filled with honey to the table.

She stirred honey into her tea. "It's a lot to take in, isn't it?"

"That loan sharks kidnapped me to get my father to pay his gambling debts? I'll say." I sat down across from her.

Her brown eyes widened. "What?"

"It's the only answer that makes sense," I said bitterly. "Especially when you know my father."

"Maybe you should ask him before jumping to conclusions."

"There's not much point. He's lied to me about everything else."

"Hm." Looking away, she sipped her tea.

"You disagree?"

"I don't know your father," she said.

"Consider yourself lucky," I muttered.

"And I don't know you very well either. But I wonder if avoiding your father is coming from strength or from fear?"

"It's coming from anger." I studied my tea, the movement of the spoon clanking against the sides of the chipped mug.

"Which comes from . . . ?"

I sighed and set the spoon on the table. "Fear." I'd heard Yoda's speech in *Star Wars* too.

"Instead of developing strategies not to be afraid—like avoiding your father—you might consider if you're willing to be afraid and move forward anyway."

I held the mug beneath my nose and inhaled its cinnamon-ginger scent. Contrary to what Charlene might think, I did plenty of things that scared me. Risking everything to open a pie shop. Stumbling around in the dark on one of her Big Foot hunts. Chasing after killers. I was willing to be afraid. Was I willing to take that risk with Frank?

"This is different," I muttered. "I barely know him, and the things I've learned aren't good."

"There are people who aren't healthy to have in our lives. But if you don't really know your father, can you be certain he's one of them?"

I pondered that. "No, I guess not."

"In that case, isn't the real question, can you set healthy boundaries with your father?"

I snorted. "Oh, yeah, boundaries. That's easy."

She smiled over her mug.

She was right. I could storm off and refuse to talk to Frank again. Or, I could ask him for the full story, even if I wasn't quite willing to trust it. Maybe I already had the story. Maybe everything people were saying about him was true.

What if it wasn't? I had a chance to reconnect with my father. If I didn't make the attempt, I might regret it later.

"Thanks for the tea," she said. "I'd better get back to my gals." Rising, she ambled outside.

I sat on the steps and watched the bonfire—listened to the drumming and the laughter. When the women began to dance, I didn't join them—and no one asked me to. I was content to sit and watch as the fog lifted and a waxing moon appeared in the night sky.

CHAPTER 28

"Where were you yesterday?" Petronella held a plate of turkey pot pie at shoulder level and glowered at the elderly man seated at the table. She'd added a purple stripe to her short, black hair, but other than that, she was a study in irritated monochrome. Black jeans. Black t-shirt. White apron.

The white-haired customer quailed in his chair. "I can't eat here every day."

"Yes," she said, "you can."

I hurried from behind the counter. "Petronella's just teasing you, but we're so glad you came in today, Mr. Howe. Would you like more coffee?"

Our Wednesday lunch crowd was lighter than usual, but a vast improvement over yesterday's. The gamers, sans Ray, were in their corner booth. I gnawed my bottom lip. I hoped Ray wasn't out investigating on his own. Or with Henrietta, for that matter.

"I just got a top up." The customer eyed Petronella warily. "But thanks."

I steered my assistant manager into the kitchen. "What was that about?"

Abril opened the door to the industrial oven, and heat blasted out. Pies glided past on rotating racks.

"He's at that table every day," Petronella said, "even if it's only for coffee. He got scared off like all the rest."

"Well, he's back now. Don't *you* scare him off."

She sighed. "I know. I overreacted. I'm sorry. I don't know what got into me."

"You're worried." Abril slid a long, wooden paddle inside the oven and pulled out a raspberry pie. "But customers are returning."

Petronella snorted. "You're an optimist."

"And you're a pessimist," Abril said. "But how can people resist our pies?" She set the raspberry pie on a cooling rack and sniffed it. "These succulent berries, bursting with tart flavor, and a crust that melts on the tongue—"

"Right," I said, interrupting her poetic flow. "We've been through worse, and we're in a much better position than last spring." Plus, this morning I'd introduced one of Nigel's ideas—the sampler pie. On the chalk board on the sidewalk, I'd drawn a colorful picture of a pie tin filled with six different slices. We'd already sold two samplers, which wasn't bad for noon on a Wednesday after a bomb scare. Maybe Abril's optimism was contagious.

"And you're in a better position too with your mortuary courses," I said to Petronella and felt a twinge of regret. I smiled. "You've got bigger things ahead of you." I didn't want her to leave, but that was selfish.

She rubbed the black stubble on the back of her neck. "Yeah, but a wedge-shaped slice of my heart will always be in Pie Town. This was my first managerial position, even if it is only assistant manager. I've learned a lot at this job."

The bell over the front door jingled.

"I'll get that." I walked through the swinging door and paused behind the register.

TV-star handsome, Nigel stood in the center of the checkerboard floor and looked around. His midnight hair was windblown, as if he'd just come from a walk on the beach, and he wore a navy golf shirt and khakis.

He caught my eye, smiled, and took a seat at the counter. "I'm knackered."

I strolled down the counter to him. "Aren't you sick of us yet?"

He scratched his goatee. "I wanted to take a last look at the bakery that beat *Pie Hard*."

"Beat?"

"Murdered."

"You don't mean they're shutting you down?" I asked, dismayed. Charlene would be devastated if she lost her shot at TV celebrity.

He nodded. "I doubt I'll ever get a job like this again. I like the chalkboard outside, by the way."

"It was your idea. You're good at what you do. You'll find something."

He puffed out his cheeks and exhaled slowly. "It won't be the same, not without Ilsa and Regina. On the positive side, Pie Town will be famous."

"Oh?"

"Frank talked to the executive producer in L.A. We have all the footage we need—more than we need, since we got stuck here so long. They're going to promote your show as a tribute to Regina and Ilsa, their last show, and the last *Pie Hard*."

"I imagine you have mixed feelings." I certainly did, guilt and anxiety plus a dark part of my heart leaping at the thought of publicity for Pie Town.

He shrugged elegantly. "That's show business." Nigel

scanned the chalkboard menu on the wall behind me. "And I'd like a mini shepherd's pie."

"Good choice." All of the potpies are comfort food, but there's something extra soulful about the crispy-creamy potato crust on top of a shepherd's pie. "Coffee?"

He nodded.

I handed him an empty mug, then walked into the kitchen and plated a mini shepherd's pie, adding tossed green salad on the side.

I returned to the counter and slid the plate in front of him.

"Quick service," he said.

"Slow day." My smile was quick and taut. I had to trust that business would continue to improve.

"Ah." He poked at the potato crust with his fork, and a ribbon of steam rippled into the air. "I heard about the car bomb. You were lucky. I'm glad you weren't hurt."

"Frank was lucky too."

"I keep forgetting he's a part of our crew," he muttered, not meeting my gaze.

"How long have you known Steve and Regina?" I asked.

"Regina hired me for *Pie Hard* three years ago. I couldn't believe my luck. In the real world, being a consultant to small businesses is a hard slog. Most don't have the money or just don't see the need for advice."

"But you worked with high-end restaurants," I said, "didn't you? I'd think they'd be more used to bringing in consultants."

"Not as much as you'd think." He doodled in the potatoes with his fork. "It was a bit of an adjustment shifting from restaurants to bakeries. I think that's why I was looking forward to your shop—you're both restaurant *and* bakery. Thanks to Regina, things were turning around for me. She even loaned me that money. Then she died." He stabbed the shepherd's pie. "I don't know what comes next."

"It's amazing how close you all became, when the rest of

the crew worked together so long. Was it difficult for you and Ilsa to become part of the team?"

"Regina, Steve and Luther were close, but they never made us feel like outsiders. We all worked closely together, traveled together."

I raised a brow. "Traveling first class must have gotten expensive."

"We didn't at first. It's only been this last year that Regina began upgrading us—out of her own pocket. She said travel was stressful, and the show successful, so we should enjoy the process. I don't think Steve was happy about it though." He prodded the pie with his fork.

"Did the travel upgrades start about nine months ago?" That was around the time she'd been diagnosed with ALS.

He looked up. "I suppose so, yes."

A mug crashed to the floor, and I gave a little jump.

Petronella hurried from behind the register to clean up the mess.

"Did you know Regina had been diagnosed with Lou Gehrig's disease?" I asked him.

He grimaced. "Luther told me last night. I was gutted when I heard. Why didn't she tell me?" he asked, plaintive.

"I'd imagine it's a tough thing to tell people, having to deal with their reactions on top of your own."

"Maybe."

"How long has Luther had an alcohol problem?"

"I didn't notice it until . . ." He frowned.

"About nine months ago?"

He nodded. "But it had been going on for years. Ilsa told me he'd been better at hiding it before."

So the news of the ALS had sunk Luther in despair, and Regina decided to live like she was dying, which she had been.

Marla walked in, pausing in the center of the black-and-white floor for effect. She fluffed her platinum-blond hair and strolled to the register.

"Just a sec," I said to Nigel and went to take her order.

"Is Charlene here?" she asked.

"Sorry, no," I said, insincere. I didn't need those two brawling in the dining area. "What can I get for you?"

She eyed Nigel. "I thought the show was over."

"It is."

"Then why's he here?"

"For the pie?"

"Hm." She toyed with the diamond pendant at her neck. "Since you haven't blown up yet, I'll have a mini chicken pot pie."

"Ha, ha." I clipped her order to the ticket wheel in the kitchen window and spun it toward Abril.

Marla sauntered down the counter and sank onto a barstool beside Nigel.

I returned to him, eating his shepherd's pie.

"This is top shelf." He pointed with his fork at the pie. "I hope we haven't done more damage to your shop than good."

Marla laughed. "Don't worry. There's nothing you can do that Charlene can't make worse."

I shot her a repressive look. "Once Regina and Ilsa's killer is caught, things will return to normal."

Marla tossed her head. "You think that will actually happen? Have you any idea how many murders go unsolved?"

"Nope." We *had* to solve this crime. I couldn't keep wondering if my father might be involved in the murders.

"Me neither," Nigel said, "but I can imagine there are buckets."

"Order up!" Abril called through the window.

I turned, grabbed Marla's pot pie, and set it in front of her.

"Thank you," she said. "You can go now."

Turning my back to Marla, I planted one hip against the counter. "I keep thinking there's something we're missing," I said in a low voice to Nigel, "something that will explain everything."

"Such as?" he asked. "Everyone's a suspect. No one has alibis. That bomb could have been placed on Frank's car at any time, and it was parked at the hotel, where we all spent the night."

Time. It all seemed to come down to time. Regina's had been running out, but the killer couldn't wait or didn't know about her death sentence.

I eyed Nigel. He didn't know about Regina's illness until after her death—or so he claimed. Did that give him a stronger motive?

He reared back on his barstool. "What? You're looking at me strangely. What's wrong? Is there something in my teeth?"

"You're fine," Marla said. "Val's just a little odd."

He grabbed a napkin holder off the table and grinned into the reflection. "Are you certain?"

"I was thinking about the past," I said.

"That some secret lurking deep in her past caused Regina's death?" He set down the metal dispenser.

"I'm not—" I straightened, blinking. Was it that simple?

"And now you look terrified," he said.

"What did I tell you?" Marla jabbed her pot pie with the fork. "Odd."

"I need to find Luther," I said.

Marla snorted. "If he's not here, please do. Go."

"Do you know where he is?" I asked Nigel.

"The hotel bar would be my guess."

"Thanks." I bustled into the kitchen and untied my apron. "Petronella, could you hold down the fort for a few hours?"

"Sure," she said, loading bowls into the industrial dishwasher. "It's not like we're busy."

"Is something wrong?" Abril asked.

"No—"

The alley door banged open and Charlene strode inside, her sky-blue tunic flapping about her thighs. She wore matching leggings.

"Good, you're here," the two of us said simultaneously.

"Why?" Charlene asked.

"We need to talk to Luther."

"I agree," she said. "But we're not going alone. I'm calling for backup."

My heart leapt. "Gordon?"

She made a face. "Are you kidding? He's on duty. We can't bring anyone official. I hate to say it, but we need Ray."

"Why?" Petronella asked. "Did you learn something about the murder?"

"Not learn," I said. "Suspect. And Luther's at the bottom of it."

CHAPTER 29

Jittery, I winced against the glare of sunlight on chrome in the Belinda Hotel parking lot. I had a sick feeling that something was about to happen, that we were too late.

"Give me a hand, will you?" Charlene leaned from the passenger side of the van.

Gripping her elbow, I helped Charlene to the pavement. I could feel the bones in her arm, thin and fragile, and a wave of unwanted sadness swamped me. Even with Frank in the picture, she was the closest thing I had to a parent. I shook off my fears of the future. She wouldn't want me to be morbid, not when we were on the case.

Her cell phone rang, and she excavated it from the pocket of her sky-blue tunic. She frowned at the number and put the phone to her ear. "Ray?" She cocked her head. "What's taking you so long?" She sighed. "Fine. Call us when you get here." She hung up and shook her head. "Car trouble. He'll be delayed."

"If I'd known, we could have picked him up." I strode toward the chic hotel. Wind whipped strands of hair from my ponytail. Popcorn clouds scudded above the gray-painted, gabled building.

"He was on the opposite side of town," she said. "It would have taken too long."

"Fine. Let's just make sure we stay in a public place when we meet Luther."

"The bar's public, and it serves drinks. Luther's probably been there all morning." She made a drinking motion with one hand.

The lobby's sliding doors parted, and we hurried through it and to the dark-paneled wine bar. It was empty—no surprise at this time of day. Abandoning it, we checked the other lounge area—a bar with blue and gold carpets over polished hardwood floors. Large, square windows overlooked the ocean. A telescope stood before the central window, beneath the peaked, white-painted roof. Couples sat on blue sofas and leaned toward each other across small, square tables.

Luther wasn't among them.

"Maybe we should call his room?" I suggested, worried. He was probably at a different bar. I had a bad feeling I couldn't shake.

"Good idea. You do that." Charlene wandered to the telescope and squinted into the eyepiece. She fiddled with the focuser, straightened, peered through the scope again. "Or, we could go down to the cliffs. Look." She pointed through the window. "He's on the trail."

"We said we'd stay public."

"You said we would," she said. "Besides, there are people golfing. The greatest danger we'll face is getting clocked by a stray ball." She trotted into the hall.

"This is a bad idea." I followed her through the thick-carpeted hallways until we found a door to the rolling lawn.

Luther's bulky form disappeared behind a swell of grass.

"Over there," I said, jogging toward the cliff at a pace I hoped Charlene could match.

Dodging a golf cart, I cut across the lawn to the other side of the looping path. It wound around a low, grassy knoll and down to the beach. Below, Luther plodded across a thin stretch of sand and toward the glossy black tide pools. "Luther!" I shouted. The wind whipped my words into the frothing Pacific.

He didn't turn, his shoulders hunched, his brown windbreaker flapping.

Charlene huffed to a halt beside me. "Blast the man. If I walk down that hill, I'm going to have to walk up it again." She bent, rubbing her knees. "My aching joints."

Her phone rang, and she glanced at the screen. "That's Ray. He must be here."

"If not," I said, relieved. "I'm sure he'll get here soon." My scare-anoia was probably groundless, but it felt better having him for backup. "I'll be right back." I jogged down the narrow, dirt trail and called Luther's name.

"You said public," Charlene shouted after me.

Ignoring her, I continued down the steeply sloping trail. "Luther!"

He didn't turn, though it was little surprise he couldn't hear me over the roar of wind and waves. However, I *was* startled when he walked into the slick tide pools. Luther didn't strike me as the starfish-hunting type, and the tide was coming in, dark waves flowing steadily closer.

I reached the beach and jogged to the first cluster of low, slick rocks. Small, gray-green anemones lined the crevices. I slowed to avoid squishing the tiny animals. Or plants. Or whatever they were.

One foot skidded beneath me. I steadied myself and blew out a shaky breath. Or, I could stay right here on the sand. Luther had only one way to go, and that was to return toward me. I didn't need to risk my neck.

He walked further into the tide pools. A wave sloshed over his shoes.

What was that idiot up to?

He plodded onward, shoulders slumped.

My blood turned to ice. "Oh, damn." He wasn't returning to shore. Ever. "Luther!" I screamed.

Careful of the spongy, green anemones dotting the rocks, I picked my way forward. "Luther! Don't!"

There was a faint cry behind me.

I glanced over my shoulder.

Charlene hopped up and down at the top of the cliff, waving her arms.

Confused, I turned toward Luther.

He'd stopped, reaching the end of the tide pools.

I stood thirty feet from him on a peninsula of treacherous rock. Three feet away, on the other side of a pool where a small octopus swam, was what looked like a dry patch of pitted stone.

Taking a breath, I hopped to the stone. I landed and wobbled on my toes, gasping and staring into a jagged pool of crystalline water. A narrow, olive-colored fish darted beneath me.

Regaining my balance, I cupped my hands around my mouth and shouted Luther's name.

He stood as if frozen.

Aside from Steve, Luther seemed closer to Regina than anyone. They shared a battle, though against different diseases. Was that battle about to destroy Luther as well?

A wave splashed nearby, the spray chilling my cheek.

Terrified, I forged onward, creeping across the sharp, slippery rocks. "Luther, come back!"

He glanced over his shoulder. "I killed her! It's my fault! Let me go!" His words were slow, slurred.

I stilled. Had I been wrong?

Jaw tight, I edged forward, feeling my way along the

rocks. "This isn't the way, Luther. Regina was a fighter. She would have wanted you to fight too."

"You don't understand." He moaned, or it could have been the wind. "Too much has happened."

"Then help me understand." I slipped on a piece of seaweed and smashed my knee into a rock. Smothering a yelp of pain, I stood, grimacing. "Regina wanted you to live." She'd wanted everyone to live to the fullest. She was generous—the luxury hotels, helping Nigel with his gambling, cutting Luther slack with his drinking. "She wanted Ilsa to live too. I know you weren't responsible for her death. Ilsa cared about you. She protected you."

"It was my fault," he shouted. "Everything was my fault."

Icy water surged over the rock, wetting my tennis shoes. *Turn around, turn around.* "I don't think you could have protected Ilsa." My voice trembled. "She took a risk, and she died—"

Luther's feet flew from beneath him. His arms flailed, and then he went down. Landing on his back, he lay still.

My breath stopped. I stood rooted to the spot. "Luther!"

Then I was moving again, sidling across the rocks.

A wave swept over Luther's face. He didn't move, didn't sputter.

Two seals bobbed in the waves to the west, their sleek bodies slipping through the ocean.

I gritted my teeth and edged forward. Seals looked cute from a distance, but they could be mean when they felt their territory threatened. "Pay no attention to me, large, sharp-toothed animals," I muttered. "I'm just passing through."

The water rose to my ankles. If I didn't reach him soon, we'd both be pulled out to sea.

I steeled myself. *Just go. Go!*

I darted forward, scrambling and sliding, falling to my hands in places, until I half-fell beside his burly form.

His face was gray, his eyes closed. Luther's orangey hair shifted in the water like seaweed.

I grasped his windbreaker and shook him. "Luther, you have to wake up."

A ribbon of red coiled in the water near his ears. Soon the tide would cover him completely.

Cautiously, I lifted his head and felt beneath it. My numbing fingers detected a lump.

"Wake up!" He was too heavy to drag to safety, but I couldn't leave him. Charlene knew where I was and Ray was on his way. They'd send help. If I could keep his head out of the water, someone would get to us in time. "We'll be okay." I prayed we'd be okay.

Grunting, I levered his body to a seated position. His head flopped forward, and I winced. I'd forgotten my first aid lessons about head injuries, but I'd a pretty good idea I shouldn't be rattling his brain against his skull.

The waves flowed past the top of his hips.

Red streamers of blood drifted across the water, and I tried not to think about the great whites that lurked off the coast. My fingers dug into his sopping windbreaker. "Luther, open your damn eyes."

The seals bobbed closer, interested.

Experimentally, I gripped him beneath his armpits and tugged. He didn't budge. "Help!" I shrieked, my eyes warming with tears of fear and fury. "Help!"

A wave rippled across the rocks, sweeping past my knees. I staggered and clung to Luther for balance.

The seals darted in opposite directions, as if startled.

A dark shaped moved through the water, and I closed my eyes. "Not a shark, not a shark." It was a trick of the light, a swell of seaweed. Nothing to worry about. I opened my eyes, and the dark shape had vanished.

"Sharks are not waiting around for me to stick my toe in the water," I muttered.

"I could have told you that," Frank said behind me.

I yipped and one foot slid sideways. My knee slammed into Luther's back. I straightened, cursing. "What are you—?"

Expression grim, he rolled up the sleeves of his tweed jacket. "Charlene told me what was happening. An ambulance is on its way, but I don't think we've got time to wait, do you? Move aside."

He took my place behind Luther and dragged him toward shore.

"Look out," I said, too late, as Frank stepped into a deeper pool and sank to his hips.

Luther's head slipped beneath the waves.

CHAPTER 30

I jumped, waist deep, into the tidal pool. Heedless of the tiny sea creatures we'd startled, I grabbed for Luther.

But Frank clambered out as quickly as he'd gone in. He had Luther's head and shoulders out of the water before I could help.

"Walk behind me," he said. "You can guide us to shore."

I scrambled from the water and did as he asked. Frank was risking his life for me. I couldn't think about that now. There were too many other things to worry about, like where to step next.

He dragged Luther backward, inch by painful inch.

I directed him around deep pools and slippery patches of thick sea plants. The water slowly receded to our shins.

"Something bothering you?" he huffed.

Seagulls shrieked and wheeled overhead.

"Let's just get Luther to shore. Move a bit to the right."

"Don't tell me you can't talk and walk at the same time?"

"Your other right," I ground out, "and it's not important."

"I thought you meant *your* right," Frank said. "Not *my* right."

"This isn't the time."

"Do you have better things to do?" he asked, panting.

I steered him around a gap in the rocks. "I remember what happened when I was a kid."

He set Luther down and braced the unconscious man's back against his knees. "You remember what, exactly?" Frank mopped his forehead with the back of a tweed sleeve.

"I remember a strange man taking me from my room," I said, talking rapidly. "You came to get me and snuck me past the police cars and in through a window." *Tell me it's a false memory, it didn't happen, it was a dream.*

"Oh." He looked toward the far-off cliffs. "That."

My nails bit into my palms. "Oh that? That's all you have to say? What happened?"

He lowered his head, a muscle pulsing in his jaw. "I didn't think they'd take you, but of course I wasn't thinking at all. All I cared about was the gambling high. It was the lowest moment of my life. That's why now I work to help people like N—"

"Stop it, just stop it!" Disappointment skewered my gut. "I've known you a week and I'm already fed up with your lines."

"I guess I can't blame you."

"And stop trying to be reasonable! Nothing about this is reasonable."

"I don't suppose it is, but we should keep moving." He hefted Luther's bulk and walked backward.

I started to argue, but angrily clamped my mouth shut. *Not the time.*

We moved slowly, slower than the tide that swept around our shins and ankles, trying to suck us under.

I guided Frank around more pits and crevices. "And why didn't you tell the police what had happened?"

"The police would have made it worse. You don't understand what these people are like."

"I suppose that's when mom threw you out," I said, my voice rising.

Frank's grip loosened. He cursed, and Luther sagged to the left.

I leapt forward, but my feet zipped from beneath me. I reached backward to brace myself, and hit the rocks hard.

"Valentine! Are you all right?"

I gasped from the cold and pain. My palm stung. My butt hurt. My pride festered. "I'm fine." Reeling, I reached for Luther's shoulder, but my father got there first.

"It's all right. I've got him. You just watch the rocks for us. And yes, that was when your mother and I agreed it was best I leave."

We edged backwards, and then my foot sank into sodden sand.

Luther jerked, thrashing, and Frank dropped him onto the beach. A waved rolled over him, and Luther's eyes blinked open.

"Nice timing." Frank kicked him lightly. "Now on your feet."

The assistant cameraman groaned. "Why'd you save me?"

"Don't look at me," Frank said. "My daughter seemed to think you were worth saving."

Charlene hallooed, and I looked up the cliff. Blue lights flashing, an ambulance rolled to a stop at its edge.

"He should get checked out," I said, jerking my head toward the cliff. "He hit his head pretty hard."

"But he confessed before the fall," Frank said. "He said he killed Regina."

Frank and I eyed each other.

"Are you going to tell the police," Frank asked, "or shall I?"

I sighed. "I'm sure Chief Shaw will want to hear it from us both."

Luther lolled on the sand. It crusted one side of his face.

"Unless you have something to add?" I asked him. I didn't quite believe his confession. Luther was drunk and suicidal, and in his own way, I thought he'd loved Regina.

He rolled to his side and vomited.

"Ugh." I wrinkled my nose.

"This is why I don't stick my nose in," Frank said. "And I'm not carrying him up that trail."

I looked down at the man, arms wide and collapsed on the beach. "Can you stand?"

"Blagh." Luther shook his head. "I think so."

We helped him rise and hauled him up the path to the top of the cliff. A crowd of golfers and tourists gathered by the ambulance. Two men in blue uniforms hurried forward and took Luther off our hands.

Charlene tossed a blanket over my shoulders. "Are you all right?"

"I'm fine. Thanks." My shoes squished with cold salt water, and my jeans were soaked, but I was sweating after our trek up the cliff.

A uniformed police officer approached us.

Frank intercepted them, and I turned away.

"What's up?" Charlene whispered.

"Luther confessed," I said, "but I don't think it was a real confession. He was drunk and depressed."

"No kidding."

I stiffened.

Doran, dressed in his usual black, lurked on the edges of the crowd and watched us. *Watched*! Luther had nearly been drowned, and he'd been looky-looing instead of helping. I stabbed my finger toward him. "Hey!"

Doran turned and strode away.

Anger flared inside me. I was fed up with being stalked by this jerk. "Hey!" I trotted after him.

He glanced over his shoulder and broke into a run.

What was he up to? I raced after him. "Stop!"

Ninjalike, he jumped into an abandoned golf cart and zoomed toward the hotel.

A man shouted.

Huffing, Charlene grasped the side of a golf cart. At the wheel, a man in plaid pants and a flat cap gaped.

She clambered into the passenger seat. "Follow that golf cart!"

I piled into the back.

Frank raced toward us.

The driver swiveled to look at me. "What—?"

"Well, don't sit there like a bump on a log," Charlene said to the driver. "He's getting away!"

The driver purpled. "Who are you?"

Charlene reached across with her foot and slammed down on the accelerator. The golf cart lurched forward.

Frank leapt, grabbing the grip bar. One foot landed on the bumper.

The cart swerved, but stayed upright.

"Are you crazy?" the driver shrieked.

"Either I drive, or you do," Charlene said.

"I'll do it, I'll do it! Get off my foot!"

Frank coiled sideways and sat heavily beside me. "What's going on?"

"Doran stole that golf cart," I shouted over the roar of the motor.

We zipped around a sand trap.

"Hurry," Charlene urged the driver. "You're losing him."

The driver's broad face reddened. "I can't lose him on a golf course. There's nowhere to go."

"He's putting distance between us," Charlene said.

"That's because we're carrying more weight," the driver snarled.

"Good point." She turned in her seat and tapped Frank's shoulder. "We need to lighten the load."

Frank folded his arms. "I'm not leaving this golf cart."

"You're slowing us down," she said, giving him a useless push.

He rocked against me, and I gasped, grabbing the handle.

The golf course unfurled in front of me, leaving the ambulance, the crowd, the ocean shrinking in the distance. Suddenly, I felt sick. I never could ride backwards.

I twisted, craning my neck to look forward, and swallowed hard. "He's headed for the hotel parking lot."

"Step on it." Charlene swatted Frank from behind. "And you be a better human."

"Ow!"

The golf cart careened over a hillock. The rear wheels went airborne, and I shrieked.

The back end of the cart hit the lawn, flinging me toward the edge of my seat.

Frank grabbed the collar of my hoodie and yanked me against the seat.

"Watch it," Frank and Charlene hollered.

We were getting closer. Doran was only fifty feet ahead of us.

"How am I supposed to drive with you maniacs trying to kill each other?" the driver asked.

Doran's golf cart stopped beside a decorative rock formation. He leapt from the cart and darted around the corner of the hotel, toward the parking lot.

"He's getting away," Charlene said.

The golf cart shuddered to a halt. The driver folded his arms over his chest. "Ride's over."

"Thanks!" I scrambled from the cart and raced to the hotel. Plowing through a garden area of black tanbark and lavender bushes, I rounded the corner of the building. Footsteps and heavy breathing followed behind me.

In front of the hotel, Gordon leaned inside the driver's side of his sedan, the door open, a radio in his hand.

Doran raced past.

Ray, in baggy jeans and a comic book t-shirt walked around his white Escort, parked at the valet stand. Keys dangled from his extended hand.

Doran ran toward the uniformed valet.

"Everything's under control here," Gordon said into the radio as I pounded past.

Ray made to hand the keys to the valet.

Doran snatched them from his hand and jumped, skidding across the hood of the Escort.

"Hey!" Ray shouted.

"That's my stalker." I wheezed. "Stop him!"

Doran whipped inside the Escort and started the car. It lurched forward.

Ray hurled himself onto the Escort's roof.

"Don't!" I screamed. Again, I was too late.

The car putted down the driveway at a lazy crawl. Black exhaust spewed from the tailpipe. Ray gripped both sides of the roof, the side of his face pressed to the white metal.

Charlene stopped beside me. Bent nearly double, she reached up to grasp my shoulder. "Idiot."

"What's Ray thinking?" I asked, horrified.

"Ray's fine," she said, panting. "Car troubles, remember? That car can't do more than five miles an hour."

A siren wailed in the distance.

She pulled her cell phone from her jacket pocket. Squinting, she aimed it at Ray and the car.

At a crawl, the car made a ninety-degree turn. Ray's hips slid sideways, his sneakers dangling off the edge. He inch-wormed back to the center, his jeans squeaking against the metal.

Jaw slack, Gordon came to stand beside us in the shade of the hotel. "What the hell?" He shrugged out of his blue suit jacket.

Ray's body swayed atop the car.

"Attempted car theft," I said, watching the slow-mo action movie unfold. "I think."

"Remind me why I transferred to San Nicholas?" Swearing, Gordon handed me his blazer and jogged to the Escort, now doing an unhurried donut around an island lush with California poppies.

Frank joined us, and we watched Gordon chase the car, meandering around the island.

Ray's curses floated through the air.

"I don't think I've ever seen anything quite like that," Frank said. "Is life in San Nicholas always this . . . eventful?"

"No," Charlene said, "but it's always this weird."

The ambulance drove around the corner of the hotel, its siren shrieking, blue lights flashing. It bumped over the sidewalk and into the parking lot.

Unhurried, the Escort escaped the gravity well of the flower island and puttered into the ambulance's path.

Brakes screeched. The ambulance bumped the side of the Escort.

Ray rolled off at a leisurely pace, vanishing with a thud behind the car.

"Ray!" I ran to the crash site. Henrietta was so going to kill me. Good boyfriends are hard to find. If I'd damaged hers a second time . . .

Gordon yanked Doran from the car and jammed him against the hood. He cuffed his hands behind his back.

I ran to the opposite side of the Escort.

Ray lay on his back and stared into the blue sky, a silly expression on his face.

I dropped to the pavement beside him. "Ray, are you okay?"

"I've always wanted to do that," he said. "Being a Baker Street Baker is the coolest."

The car coughed, sputtered. Another explosion of exhaust shot from its tailpipe.

"He must have hit his head," Charlene said. "I'll get help."

"Tell me you got video," he said to her.

"Duh. Of course I got video," Charlene said.

Grinning like an idiot, he tried to sit up. "Lemme see."

I pressed my hand to his chest and forced him to the macadam. "Don't move. Let the paramedics check you out first."

Charlene handed him the phone, and he settled on the pavement to view his antics on the small screen.

A paramedic, black bag in hand, trotted around the front of the car and knelt beside us. "You're supposed to ride *inside* the car, son."

Ray smiled dreamily.

I shot the paramedic a worried look.

"I can't wait to tell Henrietta," Ray said.

Still a little motion sick, I rose and sloshed around the car to Doran. My jeans were cold, clammy and irritating.

"Why?" I shouted. "Why are you following me?"

Frank strolled to my side. "More importantly, why did you run?"

"I'm not running," Doran said—expression sullen.

Gordon growled. "You stole a car."

"And a golf cart," Charlene chimed in.

Doran gazed skyward and blew out his breath. "I wasn't following you, Val, not at first. I just wanted to figure out how you were connected to *him*." He spat the last word.

"Him, who?" Frank pressed a hand to his chest and his eyes widened. "Him, me? Why?"

Doran glowered. "Because you're my father."

CHAPTER 31

I gaped at Doran, braced against the Escort, his hands cuffed behind his back against the car. "Your father? He's your father? But that means . . ." I trailed off, stunned. Suddenly I could see it, his blue eyes, and his oval-shaped face. I'd seen it in my mirror every morning.

The ambulance siren chirped, and I jumped.

"Give her a minute," Charlene said. "She'll get there."

"I know what it means," I snapped. "I just . . . You're his son? Seriously? You're my—"

"Brother by a different mother." Doran's shoulders caved inward. "Sorry I was freaking you out."

"You were," I said. "You seemed to be everywhere."

"Everywhere *he* was. Tracking his comings and goings. Like I said, it wasn't about you. It's not your fault you're his daughter."

"Did Frank abandon you and your mother too?" I asked.

"Yeah."

Doran and I might have more in common than I'd suspected. "Did he get you kidnapped by loan sharks when you were a kid?"

Gordon's head whipped toward Frank, and his face hardened to granite. "What?"

"It was a long time ago," Frank said hurriedly. "Really, Val, you need to let that go."

"How are we supposed to let it go," Doran said, "when nothing's changed?"

I braced my hands on my hips. "Yeah."

Frank raised his hands and backed away, his gaze darting about the parking lot. "All right, all right. I'm feeling a little ganged up on here."

"*You're* complaining to us about gangs?" Doran tossed his head, flipping his long, black hair out of his eyes for roughly a millisecond. "You're in the mob."

Frank drew away, consternation written across his face. "Let's take a breath. Who's your mother?"

"You don't even—" Doran lunged at him.

Gordon wrestled him against the dust-covered white car. "Okay," the detective said. "That's enough."

"Wait—you're not Takako's son?" Frank asked.

Doran ground his teeth. "How many different women have you been with?"

I swayed. Did I have an even bigger family than I knew? "That's why you've been lurking?" I asked. "Hold on. Doran, were you the one who broke into Pie Town?"

Doran cut a glance at the detective.

"If you were," I said quickly, "I won't press charges."

"Oh, yes you will," Charlene said. "I dented my favorite rolling pin."

"I won't," I said. "And the golf cart wasn't stolen. It was never removed from the hotel's property. I'm sure Ray won't press charges over the car."

Ray popped up from behind the Escort. "What?"

"You got to ride on the car roof," I said. "It was your dream, wasn't it?"

He rubbed his ginger head. "I dunno."

"Trust me," Charlene said. "The video I shot's gonna launch both our Internet careers." She smirked. "Good luck topping this, Marla Van Helsing."

"I was trying to figure out Frank's connection to you," Doran said. "You were obviously important to him—more important than I was—"

"I didn't even know you existed," Frank said.

"Hey." One of the blue-shirted paramedics nodded to the ambulance. "Can we leave now? I want to get our guy checked out at the hospital."

Gordon nodded. "Go."

"I guess I won't press charges either," Ray said, "not against Val's brother."

Gordon made a disgusted noise, but he unlocked the cuffs.

Doran rubbed his wrists. "When I learned Frank was in the mob, I wanted to figure out what game he was playing before I approached him. Or you."

"What did you learn?" I asked.

"I'm not playing a game," Frank said. "Everything I've done has been completely aboveboard."

"You're putting the squeeze on Nigel for the mob," I said.

He rolled his eyes toward the detective. *"Allegedly."*

Frank was impossible! I clawed one hand through my loose hair and handed Gordon his suit jacket. "You must be so glad you're off this case."

"No." He slipped into the jacket. "Though I hear you got a confession from Luther."

"How'd you find out so quickly?" I asked.

"We have these things called radios," Gordon said. "The two officers at the scene took a statement from your father. I expect Chief Shaw will call you in to confirm."

"Then we need to prove who really did do it before that happens," I said.

"We?" Gordon asked. "*You're* not supposed to prove anything. At least not publicly. You're a civilian."

"And since Luther's being arrested," I said, "there's no harm in me throwing a small farewell get-together tonight for the *Pie Hard* crew."

Gordon rubbed his chin. "Am I invited?"

"You're first on my list," I said. "Doran, you'll come, right?"

His expression turned sullen. "No way."

"He'll be there," Gordon growled.

"Great," I said. "Frank, you can get Steve and Nigel to Pie Town tonight after closing, can't you? Seven o'clock?"

"Yes," he said, "but why would I want to?"

"Because it's in your best interests for the real killer to be put away," Charlene said. "And because Officer Carmichael will make you."

"I thought Officer Carmichael was off the case," Frank said.

"I am," he said. "But what I do on my own time is my own business. And there's no bad time for pie."

I wanted to kiss him. Gordon totally got me.

The detective laid his broad hands on my shoulders. "And Val? We need to talk."

He waited until Frank and Doran had walked into the gabled hotel.

"All right, copper," Charlene said. "Spill. There's no way you'd let Val have a gathering of the suspects unless you're working an angle."

He quirked a dark brow.

"Why *did* you go along with our plans?" I asked him.

"Because the only thing Luther's ever killed is liver cells. That arson you mentioned involved a drunken attempt to set a damp pile of leaves on fire. It was in his ex's yard, and too close to the house for comfort. She soaked him and the leaves with the garden hose. She thought the incident was, and I quote, funny, and didn't press charges. But with a confession in hand, no one's going to look any further."

"You mean Shaw won't," Charlene said.

One corner of his mouth lifted in a slow, lopsided smile. "I mean," he said, "your get together might be just what the detective ordered."

I flipped on the overhead lights. It was twilight, and long shadows stretched across Pie Town's booths and tables and checkerboard floor.

Charlene, her white cat draped over one shoulder, lounged at Pie Town's counter and sipped a cup of coffee from the urn.

Gordon, in his ecru fisherman's sweater and jeans, rapped on the front window, and I let him inside.

He glanced at the clock over the counter. Seven o'clock exactly. "I see I'm not late."

"No, and Frank's promised to bring everyone." I wasn't sure how it would go with Doran, but he and Frank had returned relatively peacefully to the hotel together.

"How are you holding up?" Gordon touched my upper arm, and my heart flipped.

I shook my head. I still couldn't quite wrap my brain around the situation. Not only had my long-lost father returned—he also brought a son he hadn't known about. It seemed churlish to complain about the family drama. I was alive. Ilsa and Regina weren't so lucky. "It's been a weird week."

"That's an understatement. I've done more digging into Frank's background. As far as I can tell, he's exactly what he claims—an odd sort of enforcer. There aren't any hints of violence in his past, though I can't say the same for his colleagues. He's not in good company, Val. You need to be careful."

I scrubbed a hand over my face. "I know. Even if I wanted to—and I'm not sure I do—I can't welcome him back with open arms."

He coiled a muscular arm around my waist. "We'll figure this out."

A warm glow bubbled through my veins. "You mean a girlfriend with mob connections hasn't scared you off?"

"Not by a longshot." His head bent toward mine.

My breath hitched, my heart banging against my ribs.

Charlene wolf whistled. "Get a room."

He pulled me into his arms and kissed me, his mouth strong and firm. My knees turned to jelly, and I half-collapsed against him. He tightened his grip.

We broke apart, breathing hard.

"We don't do that often enough," he said.

"I agree."

"Then what's been stopping you?" Charlene asked.

The glass front door opened, the bell over it jingling.

"Where's the party?" Frank trooped inside with Steve and Nigel, plus a grumpy-looking Doran.

Nigel looked around warily. He'd changed into a Belinda Hotel golf shirt and pressed khaki slacks. "Not to throw a spanner in the works, but I'm not sure I'm in the mood for a party—as kind as your offer may be."

The door jangled open, and Ray huffed inside. "I'm here!"

"We see that." Charlene motioned to the empty barstool beside her. "Park it."

Ray hustled over and sat, swiveling his seat to stare at everyone and rumpling his comic-book tee.

"I could use a drink." Steve rubbed his hand over his face. The cameraman's stubble scritched beneath his palm.

"I don't have an alcohol license," I said. "But a lot's happened, and I thought we should . . ."

"Honor it?" A faint smile played at the corner of Charlene's mouth. She'd spent way too much time with the goddesses.

"Right." I motioned toward a grouping of pink tables in the center of the checkerboard floor. The paper place mats were set with forks, napkins and empty coffee cups. Three of my new sampler pie tins sat in the center of the table—two filled with selections of fruit pies, one with savory.

Doran hesitated, then sat on Charlene's other side at the counter.

What was left of the *Pie Hard* crew sat. The tension between my shoulder blades released.

Gordon took up position beside the door, and I poured coffee for everyone from the urn at the end of the counter.

"What's a cop doing here?" Doran asked. "What am I doing here?"

"Unfortunately," I said, "you're a part of this. When you broke into Pie Town it muddied the waters."

"How'd you know it was me?" Doran asked.

"It couldn't have been Ilsa, Steve or Frank. They were together. And you were way too curious about Pie Town . . ." I'd guessed. It happens.

"Curious?" Steve leaned forward, his photographer's vest scraping against the table. "What's there to be that curious about?"

Doran looked away. "Family stuff."

"By now," I said, "I'm sure you've heard the whole story. Frank is my father. He's Doran's as well, and he works for the—"

"Production company," Frank yelped.

"A collection agency," I said.

Steve stared from Nigel to my father.

"Just how in debt are you?" Gordon asked Nigel.

The consultant's dark skin flushed. "Half a million."

My eyes widened. "Please tell me that's dollars and not pounds."

"Aren't dollars enough?" he asked bitterly.

"I'm surprised they let you get that deep in the hole," Gordon said.

Nigel massaged his temple. "I was hitting it big with *Pie Hard*. And the debt was spread around different bookies. But I wouldn't have killed Regina. Regina and this show were the only things keeping me afloat."

"And Regina was generous," I said. That was what had gotten her killed.

"Too generous." Steve shifted in his chair. "I don't see what the point of this is. Luther's confessed."

"Right," I said, "Luther. Why did Regina really keep him on when he was causing so much trouble with his drinking?"

"She had a soft spot for him." Steve shoved his hands in the pockets of his khaki vest.

"But it was more than that," I said, "wasn't it? She felt a kinship with him. They both were fighting demons—his was alcohol, hers was the betrayal of her body—the ALS."

"So why would Luther kill her if she was bending over backwards for him?" the detective asked Steve.

The cameraman and Nigel shared a look.

"Luther could get pretty wild when he was drinking," Steve said.

"Could he?" Gordon asked mildly. "I didn't notice it, and I pulled him out of three bars in the last week."

"Because he failed her," Nigel muttered.

"What?" Charlene asked, cupping a hand to her ear. "Speak up."

"He felt he failed her," Nigel said. "A part of Regina believed that if she could save Luther, she could save herself. But Luther let her down, and he knew it." He shrugged. "What is it about always hurting the ones you love? I'm sure he didn't mean to shove her over the cliff."

"How does that explain Ilsa's death?" I asked.

"It wouldn't," Nigel said, "unless . . . Ilsa was protective of him, right?" He turned to Steve. "We all noticed it. Maybe she found out he'd accidentally knocked Regina over the cliff and was protecting him. But when he realized she knew, he killed her."

Gordon crossed his arms. "Interesting theory."

"But wrong," I said.

Nigel stood. "This is absurd."

I held my breath. We had no right to keep him here, but if he left, our plan would fail.

"I know what you're doing with your grand gathering of suspects," Nigel said, "and—"

"Sit down," Gordon said sharply.

Nigel wavered. Expression mutinous, he sat.

"Let's go back to the arson that destroyed so much of your equipment," I said. I couldn't figure out why someone would lock me inside. But the killer had splashed gasoline around the room before I got there—gasoline from my van's gas tank."

"The killer splashed gas around the pavement and side of the van to make sure we figured out where it had come from," Gordon said. "I could smell it."

"Using gas from the Pie Town van was a crime of opportunity," I said, "meant to throw suspicion on me. And then, when I actually turned up inside the room, the opportunity to make it look like I'd got caught in my own arson was too good to pass up."

"But why?" Abstracted, Nigel rubbed the collar of his golf shirt.

"To throw suspicion away from the real killer," I said. "That's what it's always been about. I thought the break-in at Pie Town was part of it, but I was wrong." I nodded to Doran at the counter.

"Luther has a history of arson," Gordon said. "He made an unserious attempt to set his ex-wife's house on fire, and there was no damage."

"Ilsa couldn't have killed anyone." Steve folded his arms over his broad stomach. "She's dead. That leaves Luther."

"No," I said, "the fire was a red herring. The initial intention was to make Ilsa or Luther look guilty. Seeing my van in the parking lot was a lucky break, and when I turned up in the room, even luckier."

"Good thing I was around," my father said. "You were nearly killed."

"Yes," Charlene said. "Your arrival was suspiciously timely, and for the first time you got to play the hero for your daughter."

"I don't think I like your implication," Frank said.

"When Ilsa was killed," Gordon said, "it was obvious she wasn't the arsonist."

"Which left Luther," Nigel said. "But it doesn't sound like you think he was responsible."

"Do you?" I asked.

"No," the consultant said, staring at the Formica table. "Luther was a wreck but never violent. At least, I didn't think he was until the detective told us about him trying to burn his wife's house down."

"That's right," I said. "You didn't know much of Luther's history, because you joined the team when you joined *Pie*

Hard. But Luther's history with Regina and Steve went back further."

"What are you saying?" Steve asked.

"I'm saying that only one person knew where all the skeletons were hidden." I was right. I knew I was right—but my heart thumped against my ribs. I drew a deep breath. "The same person who lost—" I put the word in air brackets. "—his waste paper basket."

The others looked bewildered.

"I think you've lost the plot," Nigel said.

"He needed the bin from his hotel room as a container for the gasoline he stole from my van," I explained. "He knew it would be ruined by the gas, so the morning of the fire, he called reception to complain about a maid taking it. I expect he just left it in the outbuilding when he was finished."

"Wait," Ray said. "Are you saying stealing the gas was premeditated?"

"Stealing it from a car in the parking lot was," I said. "Finding my van was just good luck. For the killer."

"And only one person," Gordon said, "could have called the executive producer and gotten him to admit who Frank really was, then leaked it to the press. I called your exec. He admitted he told you everything, Steve."

"What if I did call?" Steve lifted his chin. "I had a right to know who I was working with, especially after my wife and Ilsa were killed."

"Your problem," I said, "is that the husband is always the first suspect. You had to do everything you could to throw suspicion others' way."

The cameraman's jaw slackened. "Why would I kill Regina? She was already dying."

"And burning through all your money in the process," I said. "Between the trips to India for miracle cures and her new live-like-you're-dying lifestyle, how much did you expect to have left when she finally died?"

Steve braced his meaty hands on the table. "It was my money too. I was completely supportive."

"That's rubbish." Nigel tilted his sleek head. "You whinged about her spending constantly."

"Ilsa figured it out," I said. "You and Ilsa once had a romantic relationship. She knew exactly how you felt about Regina's illness, and she knew what kind of person you were. That's why it was so easy for her to break it off. Why did she confront you? Was she blackmailing you?"

Steve pointed at my father. "The guy's a mobster! It's his fault my wife's dead."

"And when you learned the truth from your producer, you decided Frank made an even better patsy." I forced my muscles to slacken. Gordon was here. We could do this. "Which leads us to the car bomb."

"You think I blew up his car?" the cameraman asked. "That was a mob hit! They've had their fingers in everything."

"In one of your old TV shows, *Movie Myths*," I said, "you got a crew to blow up a boat. It made the news, because a stuntman was injured. The explosion happened off the coast, nearby."

"You knew who to go to when you wanted explosives to blow up Frank's car," Gordon said. "And we have his statement."

Well, *Gordon* had his statement, being the police.

I started. Even though I'd guessed at the truth, Gordon hadn't told me he'd found the supplier.

"I'm telling you," Frank said, "it wasn't my car. I borrowed it."

"That's ridiculous," Steve sputtered.

"It wasn't hard to track down the crew you worked with on *Movie Myths*," Gordon said. "And your old buddy decided pretty quick he didn't want to be an accessory to—"

Steve leapt from his chair and threw it at Gordon.

The detective ducked, and the chair ricocheted off his arm.

Steve jumped onto the seat of a booth. He dove through the front window and onto the sidewalk. Glass tinkled to the pavement. The front blinds fell sideways and rattled onto the tabletop.

Swearing, Gordon bolted out the door.

Frederick, blue eyes wide, yowled.

A shot. Shattering glass. A scream. A car alarm.

Charlene and I raced out the front door, bumping shoulders in the entry. Doran and the other crew members flowed onto the sidewalk.

Smoke poured from the gym's window next door. A man in sweats and a t-shirt, his face gray, lay on the sidewalk.

Gordon did CPR, pumping his chest with the heels of his palms. "Val, take over."

"What happened?" Stomach churning, I dropped to the sidewalk on the other side of the fallen man and began chest compressions.

"Steve shot a flare into the gym," Gordon said, watching me. "The man wasn't hit, but he collapsed, I'm guessing a heart attack. I've called an ambulance." He jumped to his feet. Swerving around an iron lamp post, he raced down Main Street.

Doran knelt beside the fallen man's head and applied mouth-to-mouth.

I shot him a grateful look.

Charlene came to stand beside us. "Who'd have dreamed Steve could move that fast?"

"Doesn't matter," I panted, my arms aching from the

chest compressions. *Come on, breathe.* "Gordon will catch him."

"Want to switch?" Doran asked.

A far-off siren wailed.

"What's wrong?" I grinned. "Can't you handle it?"

"You really are my big sister, aren't you?" He blew into the stranger's mouth.

"Would that be such a bad thing?"

He tilted his head between breaths. "No."

CHAPTER 32

The ambulance pulled away from the curb, its blue lights flickering on the darkening street. Firemen removed the flare from the front of the health club. The gym owner shooed her clients away from the broken window and scowled at me.

Woeful, I gazed at the matching broken glass in my own front window. The blinds flapped and rattled in the breeze.

"So," my father said. "I wasn't the bad guy after all."

"No," I said, "but you're *a* bad guy."

His shoulders slumped. "That's not fair."

"Dad, it is," I said sadly. He might not have been able to help what he'd become, but I couldn't pretend he wasn't on the wrong side of the law.

He gazed down Main Street after the departing ambulance. "I guess it is. I never meant for any of this to happen—for you to be hurt, for me to work for . . . you know."

"And me?" Doran's raven's-wing brows slashed downward. "I suppose you never meant for me to happen either."

"Truthfully," my father said, "no. But if I had known, I would have left you and your mother alone, like I did Val and her mother."

I touched the sleeve of his tweed jacket. "Can't you get out of this, um, work?"

"Honestly, I don't know what else I'd do."

"Anything," I said. "Anything has to be better than this."

"It may not look like it," my father said, "but I really do help people. I keep them from coming to harm, and I've been able to turn some people around."

Doran snorted and tossed his head. His hair slipped into his eyes.

"He's not wrong." Nigel joined us. "If it hadn't been for your father, things would have been much worse for me. I'm on a payment plan now." His handsome face fell. "Though I've no idea how I'll continue making payments now that I'm out of a job."

My father clapped him on the shoulder of his golf shirt. "Are you kidding? After the disaster of your final show, everyone will want you. I've got connections. I'll hook you up, never fear."

Nigel brightened. "Brilliant!"

"That's how I managed to swing taking over Regina's job," my father said. "I know people, son. As long as you keep our, er, connection out of the press, my employers will work with the plan. Otherwise, they'll insist on making an example of you."

Nigel paled. "Thanks?"

A blue Prius pulled to the curb.

"I believe that's my ride," Nigel said. "I'll see you." He stepped into the car and zoomed off.

My father rubbed his hands together. "So, all's well that ends well."

"Is it?" Charlene stroked Frederick, sleeping on her shoulder. "What exactly are your intentions?"

"What do you mean?" he asked.

"You have two children," she said, "standing here in front of you. What are you going to do about it?"

He shuffled his feet. "I admit it has been nice spending time with Val." He turned quickly to Doran. "Had I known who you were—"

"Whatever," Doran said.

"I'm glad we had this chance," I said. I still hadn't completely forgiven him, but I was willing to try. "But I don't want to be tangled up with your associates any more than my mother did."

He lowered his head. "I understand. But maybe . . . There's always email."

"I would like to be able to chat," I admitted. "Every now and then."

Doran shook his head. "Are you kidding? Do you have any idea how easy it is to crack into most email systems? You'd need to use encryption—real encryption, not one of those lame programs you download for free online."

My father eyed him. "I suppose you know something about that. Could you, er, help set something up?"

His gaze slid sideways. "I guess it's the least I can do. For Val." Doran lightly touched my hand. "Stay in touch." He turned and strode down Main. The street lamps flickered to life.

"He's so angry," my father said.

"Can you blame him?" Charlene pointed at me. "You're lucky this one still wants to have anything to do with you."

Frederick yawned.

A police car double parked in front of the gym. Chief Shaw and a uniformed officer stepped out.

"I'll call you later." My father hurried down Main Street.

Shaw stared at the gaping hole in the gym's front window, then at my matching broken window. "What's this about another confession?"

"You spoke with G—Detective Carmichael?" I asked eagerly. "Did he catch Steve?"

"Mr. Katz? The cameraman? Not that I know of."

I frowned. Where was Gordon? He'd have reported to the police after he'd collared Steve. But maybe word hadn't reached the chief yet.

"Tell me what happened," Shaw said, "from the beginning."

And so Charlene and I did. Sort of. We didn't confess that we'd gathered the suspects together like something out of an Agatha Christie novel. As Charlene told it, we'd simply invited them to Pie Town for a final thank you and farewell. Discussion had grown heated. Accusations were hurled. And Steve had admitted his guilt and fled.

Ray emerged from Pie Town with a wide piece of plywood. "I found this in the alley by the dumpster. Think we can use it for the window?"

"Were you here when this mess went down?" Shaw asked.

Ray shifted the plywood in his arms. "Um. Yeah."

"Now, you tell me what really happened."

I tensed. *Don't tell him about Gordon. Don't tell him about Gordon.* Gordon was off the case, and he wouldn't want us to admit he'd been investigating.

Ray blinked his brown eyes. "What really happened?"

"Sure," Charlene said, "tell him all about—"

"No," Shaw said. "I want to hear this from Ray."

He gulped. "Well. They were having this party for the *Pie Hard* crew, now that everything was over."

I started breathing again.

Shaw's eyes narrowed. "And why were you invited?"

"Val knows I'm a huge fan."

"Why was Carmichael here?"

Ray blinked. "He and Val are dating. Anyway, we were all talking, and no one could believe Luther had done it. And then it kind of came out that Steve had done it, and he jumped through a window."

The chief lowered his chin. "And exactly how did it come out?"

A bead of sweat trickled down Ray's broad forehead. "Um, they were talking about the past, how they'd known each other for so long, and then we were talking about that old *Movie Myths* show, and how a boat had got blown up, and suddenly we all knew that Steve could have blown up Frank's car. You know?"

Shaw through his hands in the air. "I know that you're all coming to the station with me."

"But, the window!" I pointed.

After some arguing, Shaw let us nail the plywood over the broken window before we were all dragged down to the station.

Two hours later, he released us, so I guess our stories hung together. Or else he'd just stopped caring.

Charlene and Ray piled into her Jeep, and I drove home. I stepped from the van and admired my view.

The waxing moon lit a trail across the ebony Pacific. The goddess gals were gone. So was the yurt. A round, flattening of the grass like an underachieving crop circle was the only sign it had ever existed.

I smiled. Last week, the thought of a crop circle would have sent me into a mild panic. Now it seemed funny.

The sky deepened to a lurid violet and tangerine above the darkening ocean. Seated on the picnic table, I called Gordon.

The call went to voicemail, and my stomach tightened. I hadn't seen or heard from him since he'd gone chasing after Steve. But Shaw would have said something if Gordon had been hurt. Wouldn't he?

Worried, I went inside and poured a glass of root beer and Kahlua, keeping everything on the counter, just in case.

Thirty minutes later, the headlights from Charlene's Jeep

swept the lawn. She parked beside the picnic table and climbed the steps to my door.

I opened it before she could knock.

"Heard anything from Grumpy Cop?" She gently removed Frederick from her shoulder and laid him on the dining nook table.

"No. I tried calling him and had to leave a message. Root beer and Kahlua?" I raised my glass and took a long drink. The alcohol didn't calm my jittery nerves.

"We've earned it. Another killer, caught by the Baker Street Bakers."

"We couldn't have done it without Gordon." Why hadn't I heard from the detective?

I poured the root beer and Kahlua into a tall glass and handed it to her.

We clinked glasses, and Charlene angled her head at the door. "It would be a shame to waste this night."

I held the front door for her, and we walked to the cliff. High above us, stars cut the black-velvet sky. Gratitude surged within me. I'd reconnected with my father, discovered a brother I never knew, and I had true friends here in San Nicholas. The moon hanging above the ocean was just the ice cream on the pie, if you liked that sort of thing.

"What are you grinning about?" Charlene asked.

"I was thinking about how lucky we are."

"Yep. We're above ground, and that's something."

Behind us, a man howled, a primal scream that raised the hair on my neck.

A gray, bearlike shadow lurched from a nearby stand of Eucalyptus trees.

I took an involuntary step back, toward the cliff.

Steve's face contorted with rage. "I'll see you both dead!" Hunched low, he barreled toward me.

Unthinking, I jerked left, grabbing for Charlene and missing.

He brushed between us, knocking me sideways.

Charlene shrieked. Dizzy with fear, I whirled toward her and the cliff.

Charlene and Steve were gone.

CHAPTER 33

My heart stopped. I stared, disbelieving, at the inky horizon. "Charlene!" I screamed.

Wind soughed in the branches of the nearby eucalyptus trees.

No, no, no. Not Charlene! "Charlene!"

"Help!" A thin shadow wriggled on the earth by the cliff's edge. Charlene lay flat on her stomach, her lower half vanishing over the side.

"Charlene!" Heedless of the crumbling earth, I raced forward and grabbed the back of her knit jacket.

She slipped through the jacket. One hand clawed at the ground.

I fell to my knees and grasped beneath her shoulder. Desperately, futilely, I heaved her toward me.

At an odd angle, Charlene slipped farther over the cliff's edge.

"You've ruined everything." Steve's voice floated up from the cliff.

I wormed closer to the cliff and peered over.

Steve dangled, clinging to Charlene's wrist. His feet scrabbled for purchase at the sheer cliff side.

"Let her go!" I threw my weight backward.

Charlene yelped with pain.

My hands were slick with fear. "I can't hold you both!"

She slid backwards. "Save yourself!"

Bits of dirt and rock fell, rattling against the earth below.

I lunged forward and grabbed a fistful of her jacket and I think her bra strap. Leaning over the edge, I tried to pry Steve's grip from her wrist. His fingers curled inside her watch band.

"It was better for Regina." He panted. "She would have died in pain. I was doing her a favor."

"Your wife wanted to live," Charlene said, gasping. "You didn't want her to spend all your money doing it."

I gritted my teeth. "Steve, you need to let go."

"If I have to die, I'm taking you with me."

I clawed at his fingers. It was too much weight. "If you don't let go, you'll both fall."

"Good!"

"You asked for it." I unsnapped Charlene's watch.

His eyes widened with terror.

Freed, Charlene tumbled into my arms. There was a dull grunt, a thud.

We lay panting.

Charlene stared at me, horror scrawled across her face. "Is he . . . ?"

Breath ragged, I crawled to the edge and peered over.

Steve huddled on a narrow ledge eight feet below us. He reached for me, trying to scrabble up the cliff. Bits of dirt and rocks gave way beneath his feet.

"He's alive." I rolled onto my back. "And he's not going anywhere."

"Shame." Charlene staggered to the edge of the cliff. Hands braced on her knees, she looked down. "Jerk."

.He called her a rude word.

"That's no way to talk to a lady!" She kicked dirt over the edge.

"Cut it out!" He wiped dirt from his face.

I patted her shoulder. "Okay. We got him. I'm going to call 9-1-1." I fumbled my cell phone from my pocket.

"It was a mercy killing," he said from the ledge beneath us. "Can't you see that?"

Charlene and I looked at each other.

I scuffed dirt over the edge for good measure.

Blue and red lights from half a dozen police cars strobed across my lawn.

I sat on the picnic table and watched the show. Not even Shaw could blame me for this one.

Gordon raked a hand through his dark hair. "If I'd any idea he was coming after you—"

"How could you?" I asked. "We all thought he was headed for Mexico or Canada." Coming here had been banana-pants crazy. "You don't think anyone will believe this was a mercy killing?" I watched a uniformed officer guide Steve into the backseat of a squad car.

"I doubt that angle will play, not after everything else he's done."

Charlene ambled up to the picnic table and jerked her thumb toward the officer shutting the squad car door. "Steve's singing like a canary. He said he had to kill Ilsa, because she was blackmailing him. According to him, it was her fault she's dead."

"I suppose he was forced to come after you two as well?" Blue light from the police cars flickered across Gordon's chiseled face.

"What's scary is, I think he kind of believes he did," she said.

"It's amazing how people can justify their actions," Gordon said.

I made a face. "People like my father." Was it wrong for me to let him into my life, even if it was only via email? Was I justifying the unjustifiable?

He looped an arm over my shoulder, and I snuggled closer to his warmth. He still wore his fisherman's sweater and smelled of clean sweat and his piney aftershave. Steve may have given him the slip, but Gordon was alive, and I wasn't going to back away from him.

"I tracked down one of the officers who came to your house the night of your kidnapping," he said. "He was retired, but he remembered it well. The officer knew there was more to the story. Later, he found out how deep in debt your father was and to whom. Without your parents' testimony, he was never able to prove or pursue anything. He even returned to your house a week later to check in, but your father had left by then. When he pressed your mother on it, she told him Frank was out of your lives and had handled everything."

"You believe my father's story? That he went to work for the mob to protect us?"

"I'm a trust but verify sort of guy, but Frank's story fits what we know. When did you first start suspecting Steve?"

"From the beginning," Charlene said. "The spouse is always the most likely suspect."

I sighed into his broad chest. The sweater was a little itchy against my cheek, but I didn't care. "It usually is the spouse, but Regina had only a couple years left, and I couldn't imagine him risking killing her when all he had to do was wait. Then we remembered things other people had said, about her search for miracle cures and Steve grumbling about expenses on the set. In the end, it came down to the car explosion. I couldn't see the mob blowing up Frank's car because he wasn't working fast enough. Maybe that was naïve."

"Yes, it was," Charlene said. "Oh! I forgot to tell you in all the excitement. You know that true crime show, *Live and Deadly*?"

"Yeah," Gordon said. "They're pretty good."

"Well, they're produced by the same outfit that makes *Pie Hard*. They want to take the *Pie Hard* footage, interview us, and expand it to a two-hour *Live and Deadly* made-for-TV movie! Isn't that amazing?"

"No." I crossed my arms. "No way. Not after everything we went through with *Pie Hard*."

"Think of the publicity!"

"We were magnets for a killer!"

"I know," she said. "We'll be notorious."

"That's not a good thing. Gordon, tell her."

He grinned, pulling me closer. "I gave up trying to tell either of you anything long ago."

And he kissed me.

Peach-Raspberry Pie

Ingredients

2 pre-made piecrusts at room temperature
3 lbs firm-ripe peaches (about 6 large) cut into 1" slices
2 tsp lemon juice, or to taste
2½ T cornstarch, divided
9 T sugar, divided
½ tsp ground ginger
Pinch salt
8 oz raspberries (about 2 cups)

Directions

Preheat oven to 425 degrees F.

In mixing bowl, toss cut peaches, lemon juice, and ½ C of the sugar. Let rest for 30 minutes, then pour off any excess juice, reserving ½ C. Return the reserve juice to the bowl. Add ginger, salt, and 2 T cornstarch, and toss.

In a separate bowl, toss the raspberries with 1 T sugar and remaining ½ T of cornstarch.

Line the pie tin with one crust and poke it with a fork 4-5 times. Pour half the peach mixture into the crust and layer on top of it half the raspberry mixture, then add the remainder of the peaches, and then what's left of the raspberries.

Cut the second crust into strips and weave it over the pie in a lattice top. Trim the edges so that ½ inch hangs over the pie tin and crimp. Place pie into the freezer for 20 minutes.

Remove pie from freezer and dust crust with a bit of sanding sugar. Put the pie on a cookie sheet and bake approximately 30 minutes, until the crust is slightly brown. Reduce the temperature to 350 degrees and bake another 45-60 minutes, until the crust is deep golden brown.

Cool before slicing!

Lemon-Blueberry Cream Pie

Ingredients
1 pre-made piecrust at room temperature

Blueberry Sauce
3 C blueberries
¾ C cold water
¾ C sugar
3 T cornstarch
1 tsp lemon juice

Lemon Cream
1 C heavy cream
8 ounces cream cheese, softened
⅓ C sugar
1 T lemon zest
2 tsp lemon juice

Directions
Heat oven to 450 degrees F. Line pie tin with crust. Poke it several times with a fork. Layer dried beans inside it (this will keep it from puffing while baking). Bake for 10 minutes. Allow to *cool completely* and remove and discard dried beans.

Combine ingredients for blueberry sauce in a medium saucepan. Bring to a boil over medium heat, stirring constantly, and cook until the mixture has thickened (approximately 5-7 minutes). Allow to *cool completely*.

In a mixing bowl, beat the whipping cream until stiff peaks have formed. Add cream cheese and sugar. Beat mixture until it's smooth, then add lemon zest and lemon juice and beat until that's smooth too.

Pour the cream cheese and lemon filling into the crust and spread it around evenly. Spoon the blueberry sauce on top of it and smooth it around. If you like, garnish with additional lemon zest or lemon curls. Refrigerate for at least 2 hours before serving.

Almond Toffee Pie

1 pre-made piecrust for a 9" pie, room temperature
3 large eggs
1 C light corn syrup
⅓ C sugar
¼ C unsalted butter, melted
2 tsp cornstarch
¼ tsp salt
1 C toffee bits
6 ounces (about 1-2/3 C) sliced almonds

Directions

Heat oven to 425 degrees F.

Whisk eggs, corn syrup, sugar, melted butter, cornstarch, and salt until well combined and mixture is smooth.

Line pie tin with crust and crimp edge. Spread toffee bits along the bottom of the crust. Layer sliced almonds on top of the toffee. (The almonds must go over the toffee, or the almonds won't mix properly with the egg mixture when you pour it in . . . now). Pour the egg mixture over the toffee and almonds. Let sit for 2-3 minutes, until some almond slices float to the top.

Place the pie on a rimmed baking sheet and into the pre-heated oven. Cover the edge of the piecrust with aluminum foil or a piecrust shield. Bake 10 minutes. Lower the temperature to 350 degrees F and bake 50-60 more minutes. The almonds should look toasted and the pie will jiggle slightly in the middle. Remove and allow to cool (and set).

Keep an eye out for more

Pie Town Mysteries

Coming soon from

Kirsten Weiss

And be sure to read

THE QUICHE AND THE DEAD

And

BLEEDING TARTS

Available now from

Kensington Books

Connect with Us

Visit us online at
KensingtonBooks.com
to read more from your favorite authors, see books
by series, view reading group guides, and more.

Join us on social media

for sneak peeks, chances to win books and prize packs,
and to share your thoughts with other readers.

facebook.com/kensingtonpublishing
twitter.com/kensingtonbooks

Tell us what you think!

To share your thoughts, submit a review,
or sign up for our eNewsletters, please visit:
KensingtonBooks.com/TellUs.

Romantic Suspense from
Lisa Jackson

Absolute Fear	0-8217-7936-2	$7.99US/$9.99CAN
Afraid to Die	1-4201-1850-1	$7.99US/$9.99CAN
Almost Dead	0-8217-7579-0	$7.99US/$10.99CAN
Born to Die	1-4201-0278-8	$7.99US/$9.99CAN
Chosen to Die	1-4201-0277-X	$7.99US/$10.99CAN
Cold Blooded	1-4201-2581-8	$7.99US/$8.99CAN
Deep Freeze	0-8217-7296-1	$7.99US/$10.99CAN
Devious	1-4201-0275-3	$7.99US/$9.99CAN
Fatal Burn	0-8217-7577-4	$7.99US/$10.99CAN
Final Scream	0-8217-7712-2	$7.99US/$10.99CAN
Hot Blooded	1-4201-0678-3	$7.99US/$9.49CAN
If She Only Knew	1-4201-3241-5	$7.99US/$9.99CAN
Left to Die	1-4201-0276-1	$7.99US/$10.99CAN
Lost Souls	0-8217-7938-9	$7.99US/$10.99CAN
Malice	0-8217-7940-0	$7.99US/$10.99CAN
The Morning After	1-4201-3370-5	$7.99US/$9.99CAN
The Night Before	1-4201-3371-3	$7.99US/$9.99CAN
Ready to Die	1-4201-1851-X	$7.99US/$9.99CAN
Running Scared	1-4201-0182-X	$7.99US/$10.99CAN
See How She Dies	1-4201-2584-2	$7.99US/$8.99CAN
Shiver	0-8217-7578-2	$7.99US/$10.99CAN
Tell Me	1-4201-1854-4	$7.99US/$9.99CAN
Twice Kissed	0-8217-7944-3	$7.99US/$9.99CAN
Unspoken	1-4201-0093-9	$7.99US/$9.99CAN
Whispers	1-4201-5158-4	$7.99US/$9.99CAN
Wicked Game	1-4201-0338-5	$7.99US/$9.99CAN
Wicked Lies	1-4201-0339-3	$7.99US/$9.99CAN
Without Mercy	1-4201-0274-5	$7.99US/$10.99CAN
You Don't Want to Know	1-4201-1853-6	$7.99US/$9.99CAN

Available Wherever Books Are Sold!
Visit our website at **www.kensingtonbooks.com**